Dedicated to
Ruth and Neil
and Evan and Gayle and James

AS GOOD AS DEAD

At night, Tabaea watched the wizard and his apprentice as they studied one spell. At last it was time for the conclusion of the ceremony in which the apprentice would trap a part of her own soul in the enchanted dagger.

Tabaea settled down on the stone, stretched out on her belly with her chin on her hands, staring down at the figures below. She knew that what she was witnessing was a deep, dark Guild secret; she knew that if anyone found out she was watching, she was as good as dead. Even so, Tabaea crept farther forward, her face pressed right against the iron railings of the banister.

Tabaea watched as the apprentice finished her chant and placed her hands on the dagger's hilt. Then the dagger leaped up, and something flashed. The apprentice rose to her feet, the new-made magic dagger in her right hand. The girl's face was smeared with black and red, her hair was a tangled mess, and her robe was wrinkled, stained, and dusty. She looked up, straight at Tabaea.

"Master," the apprentice said. "Who's that?"

By Lawrence Watt-Evans
Published by Ballantine Books:

THE LORDS OF DÛS
The Lure of the Basilisk
The Seven Altars of Dûsarra
The Sword of Bheleu
The Book of Silence

LEGENDS OF ETHSHAR
The Misenchanted Sword
With a Single Spell
The Unwilling Warlord
The Blood of A Dragon
Taking Flight
The Spell of the Black Dagger

The Cyborg and the Sorcerers
The Wizard and the War Machine

Nightside City

Crosstime Traffic

THE
SPELL
OF THE
BLACK
DAGGER

Lawrence Watt-Evans

A Del Rey Book
BALLANTINE BOOKS • NEW YORK

A Del Rey Book
Published by Ballantine Books

Copyright © 1993 by Lawrence Watt-Evans

Library of Congress Catalog Card Number: 93-90079

ISBN 0-345-37712-5

Manufactured in the United States of America

First Edition: July 1993

PART ONE

Thief

CHAPTER 1

The house was magnificent, its dozen gables high and ornate, the cornerposts elaborately carved and painted, the many panes of the broad windows neatly beveled and arranged in intricate patterns. Some of the window glass was colored, but most was clear and of the highest quality; through the crystalline casements Tabaea could see only tightly drawn curtains and drapes—draperies of velvet and silk and other fine fabrics, no simple cotton shades or wooden shutters here.

The house faced onto both Grand Street and Wizard Street, its front door at the corner, angled to face northeast into the intersection. Small shrines were carved into the stone archway on either side of this door, each shrine equipped with both a fountain and an eternal flame. The substance of the door itself was unidentifiable under its thick coat of glossy black enamel, but it was bound and trimmed with polished brass, with gleaming bolt heads forming a complex spiral pattern.

Despite its prominent location, there were no shop windows, no signboards—it was obviously a residence, rather than a business. Curious, that anyone would build so fine a house here in the Grandgate district, Tabaea thought—and worthy of further investigation. She had walked past it many times, of course, but had never paid much attention before.

She admired the shrines, then wandered on down Grand Street as if she were just another ordinary young citizen out for a late stroll on a summer evening, or perhaps an apprentice returning from an errand. She paused at the rear corner of the house and glanced back, as if trying to remember something; what she was actually doing, however, was studying the street to see whether anyone was watching her.

About a dozen people were scattered along the four long blocks between herself and Grandgate Market, but none of them seemed to be looking in her direction, or paying any attention

3

to her. No one was leaning out any of the windows or shop doors. The market itself was crowded, but at this distance that hardly mattered; even in the bright torchlight, the people there were little more than faceless blobs. None of them would be able to identify her later.

Thus reassured, she turned and ducked into the narrow alley behind the great house.

Grand Street was reasonably well lit, thanks to the torches and lanterns illuminating the various shops and taverns, but there were no torches in the alley, and no light came from either the house on her left or the shuttered tea house on her right.

That meant that the only light in the alley came from the cold and distant gleam of the stars overhead, and the firelight of Grand Street behind her. Such limited illumination was not enough; the alley appeared utterly black.

She hesitated, hoping her eyes would adjust, but the longer she lingered this close to Grand Street, the more likely, even with the tea house closed, that she would be spotted and questioned. She crept forward into the darkness, moving by feel, as if blind.

The wall of the house felt solid and smooth and unbroken, and as she advanced into the darkness she began to worry that she might have made a mistake. There might not be any entrance back here.

She set her jaw. The whole point of an alley, she reminded herself, was to let people in the back of a house. And even if this particular alley wasn't here to let people into the back of the big corner house, there must be windows—houses need ventilation, and the larger the house the more windows it would need.

Of course, her pessimistic side reminded her, those windows needn't be within reach of the ground, especially for a girl her size.

Maybe she should have planned this out more carefully, she thought, taken a look at the house by daylight, maybe found out whose house it was, instead of just yielding to a whim like this.

But she was here now, and it would be cowardly to turn back.

All the same, she thought, if she didn't find an entrance soon she might do best to just head home and try again another day.

Then, finally, her hand struck a doorframe, and a smile crept unseen across her face.

She stood and waited, and at last her vision began to adjust.

Yes, it was a door, though she could just barely make out the outline and could see no details at all. She tried the handle.

It was locked, naturally.

She grinned, drew her belt knife, and fished the lockpick from her hair. The darkness didn't matter for this; picking a lock was all done by feel anyway. This was her chance to put her lessons with old Cluros and all her practice at home to the test.

Five minutes later she had the door open and had slipped carefully inside, moving as quietly as she could. The lock had been a simple one; only inexperience, the weight of the bolt, and Tabaea's natural caution had kept her from springing it within seconds. Whoever owned this house had not wasted money on fancy locks and bars.

That was not necessarily a good thing, of course; sometimes a simple lock meant other precautions had been taken—spells, guards, any number of possibilities existed.

Tabaea saw no sign of any of them. Of course, she wasn't at all sure what to look for to spot protective spells; nobody had taught her any of *that* yet. Still, she didn't see anything unusual.

In truth, she didn't see much of anything at all. The mudroom behind the door was even darker than the alley. She felt her way across the little room, almost tripping over a boot scraper, and found an inner door.

That was unlocked, and the chamber beyond just as dark as the mudroom. Reluctantly, Tabaea decided it was time to risk a little light.

She had tinder and flint and steel in her pouch, but it was dark and she was wary of making too much sound—the house might be deserted, or it might not. It took several tries before she had a good steady light.

When she had the tinder burning, she looked around by its flickering light for something more permanent, and spotted a candle by the alley door. She lit that, then blew out the tinder and tucked it away.

Candle in hand, she looked around the mudroom.

As one might expect, there was nothing of any interest. Half a dozen assorted pairs of boots were ranged against one wall; below there was a line of hooks, about half of which held cloaks or jackets; at the other end of the room three heavy wooden chests took up most of the available space, but a quick glance in each showed that they held only scarves, gloves, and other appurtenances.

She was not disappointed; this was just the mudroom, and there was plenty more house to explore. Besides, there were plenty of people in Ethshar of the Sands who couldn't afford gloves and scarves and coats. In any case, it wasn't as if the winters here were so long or cold, as they were said to be in Sardiron or the other Ethshars, that they were truly necessary. A house so rich in winter wear would surely be rich in more marketable goods, as well.

Cautiously, moving as stealthily as she could, Tabaea opened the interior door and peered through, candle in hand.

A smile spread across her face as she saw what lay beyond. This was more like it.

The next room was a dining salon, and the light of her candle sparkled from brass and gold and crystal and fine polished woods. Catlike and silent, she slipped around the door and into the room.

The table was heavy and dark, gleaming almost black in the candlelight, its edges carved with intertwined serpents and the corners with songbirds, wings spread; above it hung an ornate brass and crystal chandelier. The six surrounding chairs were of the same dark wood, carved with serpents and eagles, seats and backs upholstered in wine velvet.

Cherrywood cabinets stood against every wall, and the image of Tabaea's candle was reflected back at her by a hundred panes of leaded glass set in the cabinet doors. Behind the glass panels glittered cut-crystal goblets and fine bone china.

Something moved in the corner of her vision, and for a moment Tabaea froze. Then she realized that the movement came from *inside* one of the cabinets. Warily, she crept closer, and peered through the glass of the cabinet door.

The cabinet held an elaborate silver tea service, and the teapot was moving, walking about on three long, birdlike legs. Tiny metal toes tapped gently on the shelf as it strolled. Then, as Tabaea watched, it sank down, folding its legs beneath it, and settled into motionlessness.

Tabaea smiled and tugged at the empty sack under her belt, but did not yet remove it from concealment. A magic animated teapot was a very pretty prize indeed; such things cost a fortune. Unfortunately, since they were so rare and expensive, and each was a unique piece, they were almost impossible to fence.

The crystal would be worth plenty—but this was merely the beginning. There was plenty more of the house yet to explore.

Three other doors opened into the dining salon, one on each side. For no particular reason, Tabaea chose the door on the left, heading more or less toward the front of the house—as much as this curiously angled corner house had a front, at any rate.

This brought her into a parlor or drawing room, just as dark and deserted as the dining salon; the fireplace was empty even of ash, the windows at the far end shuttered and heavily curtained. Chairs and settees stood here and there; a potted palm was waving in the breeze.

Except, Tabaea realized, there *was* no breeze. She froze again, watching.

The palm continued to wave, swaying steadily back and forth; Tabaea noticed that it seemed to be fanning a particular armchair.

Well, of course—it *was* fanning the armchair! More magic, clearly—a little something to help stay cool on a hot summer day, that was all. Another wizard- or sorcerer-created domestic amenity, like the teapot.

Whoever owned this house was clearly very, very rich, to own two such animated household objects, both devoted to ordinary tasks. Tabaea lifted her candle and looked around again.

Something on the mantelpiece was staring at her.

She stared back for a second, startled, and then realized it was probably a small idol of some sort. It was vaguely humanoid, vaguely froglike, roughly the size of a small cat, greenish brown, with great big pointed ears. She crept toward it for a closer look—maybe it had jewels or gold on it somewhere.

It squealed, bounded to its feet, sprang to the floor, and ran off, squeaking noises that might have been words.

Tabaea almost yelped in surprise, then caught herself and looked around guiltily.

That was how Telleth the Housebreaker had gotten himself caught, flogged, and exiled from the city last year, she remembered; he had dropped a statuette on his foot and sworn at it, and someone asleep upstairs had heard and awoken and come to investigate, with a sword in hand. She knew better than that.

Well, she *had* caught herself, she hadn't made a sound beyond a sort of strangled gasp. Now, if only that weird little creature didn't raise the alarm . . .

What was that thing, anyway? She frowned.

It must be some sort of magical creature, she decided. Tabaea glanced at the waving palm. Well, this house had more than its share of magic, certainly.

She wouldn't mind having a little magic. Like every child in Ethshar, she'd dreamed sometimes of becoming a wizard or warlock, wearing fancy robes, and having people step out of her way in the streets.

It hadn't happened, of course.

Maybe someday, if she got rich enough, she would buy herself magical things, the way whoever owned this house had.

She decided to take a look at the next room, and stepped through an arch into a broad hallway, paneled in dark rich woods. Stairs led to the upper floors—the house was an ostentatious three stories in all, though she suspected the uppermost might be a mere attic—but she was not yet ready to ascend; if anyone was home, he or she was most likely asleep upstairs, and poking around up there was best left until last.

As she stood at the foot of the stairs, a door to her right caught her eye; it was half-closed, whereas the others were all either wide open or tightly shut. That was intriguing; shading the candle with her other hand, she crept over and peered in.

The dining salon and the parlor and the hallway were spacious and elegant, richly furnished, uncluttered, and, so far as she could see by candlelight, spotlessly clean; the room behind the half-closed door was the utter opposite. It was large enough, but it was jammed to overflowing with books, papers, boxes, jars, bottles, and paraphernalia of every kind. The walls were almost completely hidden by shelves and drawers and pinned-up charts. Spills and stains, old and new, adorned the floor and various other surfaces.

Somebody's workroom, clearly—this would be where the household accounts were kept, and all the little things that go into running whatever business the house's owner was in. Those jars were probably old preserves, spare pins, and other such things.

There was sawdust, or some other powder, on the floor, she noticed, and tiny web-toed footprints making a beeline through it. That was probably where that creature had gone when she startled it. She raised the candle higher, to see if the little beast might be lurking somewhere amid the clutter.

For the first time she noticed what hung from the ceiling and paused to stare at it in wonder.

Why would someone have a dried bat hanging in his work-room?

She looked a bit more closely at the contents of the room, and saw an assortment of bones on one shelf, from tiny little bits that could have been from a mouse or shrew, up to what was surely the jawbone of a good-sized dragon. A large jar nearby, she now realized, held not pickles or preserves, but mummified spiders the size of her hand. The red stuff that she had taken for jellies and jams was an assortment of blood—she could read the labels. The biggest jar was dragon's blood, the next one was virgin's blood . . .

She shuddered in sudden realization. No wonder this place had that magical teapot, and the waving palm, and the little web-toed creature.

She was in a wizard's house.

CHAPTER 2

*T*abaea crept silently toward the door at the far end of the workshop.

The sensible thing to do would be to flee, of course. Messing with magicians was dangerous. Everyone knew that, and Tabaea was no exception. A tempting but slightly riskier alternative would be to snatch a few nonmagical treasures, and *then* flee.

But she was unable to resist. She was not going to be sensible at all. Wizardry had always fascinated her, and here she was in a wizard's house. She *couldn't* leave without exploring further!

She would never have dared enter if she had known it was a wizard's house. Since she had noticed the house on her way to and from Grandgate Market, where she had gone in hopes of picking up a few valuables, she had thought of the house as being on Grand Street, and had forgotten that it was also on another major thoroughfare—Wizard Street. Ordinary people didn't antagonize magicians; that was very probably why there weren't better locks and other safeguards. Shops and houses on Wizard Street didn't need them.

She would never have broken in if she had known—but now that she was inside, she just had to see more.

There was light coming from beneath that door—not very much, just a little—and she wanted to see what was causing it. Very slowly, very carefully, very silently, she knelt and lowered her eye to the crack.

Behind the door were stairs going down, stone stairs between gray stone walls. She blinked and looked again.

Stairs going down?

Most buildings in Ethshar of the Sands did not have cellars; the sands on which the city was built, and for which it was named, made digging difficult. Excavations had a tendency to fall in on themselves. That was also why structures were almost never more than three stories in height: anything taller than that tended to sink or fall over. Some people had cellars dug for cold storage—root cellars, wine cellars, and the like—but such extravagances were generally small, and reached by ladders rather than by stairs.

Tabaea had heard about cellars and basements all her life, in tales of faraway places, but had never been in one, unless you counted crawlspaces or the gaps between pilings. The whole idea of cellars tended to put her in mind of the overlord's dungeons—she had heard about those all her life, too, or at any rate as long as she could remember—and of secrets and exotic places. She stared at the stone step and wished she could see more; from her vantage point at floor level she could see the iron rail, the walls, the sloping roof, but nothing below the topmost stair.

However, she could, she realized abruptly, hear something.

She held her breath and listened intently, trying to ignore her own heartbeat. An older man's voice, speaking quietly and intently—she couldn't make out the words.

Could it be the wizard in whose workshop she was?

Of course; who *else* would it be?

Could he be working a spell? Was that an incantation she heard, the invocation of some spirit, the summoning of some supernatural being? She could only hear the one person, no answering voice, but he seemed to be addressing someone, not just muttering to himself.

A shiver of excitement ran through her.

He had to be doing *something* secret, down there in the cellars. He couldn't just be fetching a bottle; he wouldn't be talking like that, and she'd be able to hear him moving around. His voice was steady, as if he were standing or sitting in one place. And he wouldn't be doing his regular work, or just passing the time, in the cellars—cellars were for secrets and mysteries, for concealment, and protection.

Something rustled, and she leaped away from the door, sprang to her feet, the candle in her hand almost, but not quite, blown out by her sudden motion.

That little greenish creature was watching her from atop a stack of papers. It squeaked and scurried away into the darkness, scattering papers as it went.

She watched it go in the dimness and made no attempt to follow. All around her, the shadows were flaring and wavering crazily as her candle flickered; she feared that if she moved anywhere she might trip over something unseen, or bump into something, in that tangle of black and shifting shapes.

Worse, her candle might go out, and the wizard emerge from the cellars before she could relight it. She stood by the cellar door, shielding the candle with her hand, until the flame was strong and steady once more, and the animal, or imp, or whatever it was, was long gone.

At last she turned back to the door, intending to listen again, and caught her breath.

The line of light across the bottom had become an L. She had bumped the door when she sprang up, and it wasn't latched; it had come open, very slightly.

She knew she shouldn't touch it. She knew she should just go, get out of the house while she could—but a chance to watch a wizard at work was too much to give up.

Who knows, she thought. Maybe if things had gone a little differently for her, she might have *been* a wizard. She might have had the talent for it; who could say?

Well, she supposed a master wizard could say, but she'd never had the chance to ask one.

Or maybe she'd just never had the *nerve* to ask one.

She snorted, very slightly, at that. She was Tabaea the Thief, she'd taken the cognomen for herself just last year, she was a promising young cutpurse, burglar, and housebreaker, and she was here in a wizard's house planning to rob him, but she'd never had the nerve to *talk* to one.

Of course, it was too late now, anyway. She was fifteen, and nobody would take on an apprentice who was past her thirteenth birthday.

If her family had been willing to help out when she was twelve, if her stepfather had offered to talk to someone for her . . .

But he hadn't. And when she'd asked he was always too busy, or too drunk. He promised a dozen times that he'd get around to it later, that he'd do something to set her up, but he never had. And her mother hadn't been any better, always busy with the twins, and on those rare and precious occasions when both the babies had been asleep she'd been too tired to go anywhere or do anything, and it wasn't an emergency, Tabaea was a big girl and could take care of herself. She could help Tabaea's sisters and half-brothers with their reading and numbers, but she couldn't leave the house, what if the twins woke up?

And then Tabaea's thirteenth birthday had come and it was too late, and old Cluros was the only one who'd been interested in her, and maybe it wasn't an official apprenticeship, maybe there wasn't any guild for burglars and lockbreakers, but it was better than *nothing*.

And better than a bed in the brothels in Soldiertown.

Besides, she wasn't sure she even had the looks or personality for a brothel; she was always nervous around other people. She might have wound up walking the streets instead and sleeping in the Wall Street Field when she couldn't find a customer who would keep her for the night. Maybe she should have run away, like her big brother Tand, but she never had.

So now she was a sneak thief. Which suited her just fine; she was good at not being noticed. She'd had plenty of practice, all those years staying out of her mother's way and avoiding her stepfather's temper when he was drinking.

At least she hadn't disappeared completely, like Tand, or their father. And her thieving had kept her fed when her stepfather wouldn't anymore. Thennis had taken to begging in Grandgate Market, and Tessa was spending a suspicious amount of time in Soldiertown, but Tabaea was taking care of herself just fine. Being a wizard or something else respectable and exciting would have been much better, certainly, but Tabaea wasn't going to complain. Her career in burglary had gotten her plenty of nice little things over the past two years.

For one thing, it had gotten her here, with a chance to spy on a wizard at some secret business in his cellar. Carefully, inch by inch, holding the knob so the hinges wouldn't creak, she opened the door.

Yes, there were stone steps going down, between gray stone walls. The glow of a distant lamp spilled in through an archway at the bottom, and threw Tabaea's shadow down the full length of the room behind her.

Cautiously, she descended the stairs, pausing on each step, watching and listening. The man's voice—the *wizard's* voice, she was sure—grew louder with each advance, droning on and on. And with each step she could see a little more of what lay beyond that arch.

There was a small square of stone floor and then steps to either side and a black iron railing straight ahead—the cellar went down even further into the ground!

At the bottom she hesitated. Straight ahead she could see through the archway into an immense chamber, lit by a great three-tiered chandelier. That chandelier was directly ahead of her, beyond the archway and the landing and the iron railing. She couldn't really see much of the space below.

But if she advanced any farther, out onto the landing, she would be terribly exposed.

She paused, listening, and realized she could make out words now.

". . . it's a part of *you*," the wizard was saying. "A part of your soul, your essence. It's not just some random energy, something that anybody could provide, or that you could get from somewhere else."

For the first time Tabaea heard a second voice answering, a higher-pitched voice, a woman or a child. She didn't catch the words.

That was simply too fascinating to miss. She crept forward, crouching lower with each step. By the time she passed through the arch she was on her knees, and by the time she peered through the railing she was lying flat on her belly, hands braced to either side, ready to spring up if she was spotted.

The cellar, or crypt, or whatever it was lay before her, a single huge space. The stone-ribbed ceiling arched a dozen feet above her, and the floor twenty feet below—she realized that that floor must be thirty feet below ground, and marveled that the sea had not flooded it.

But then, the walls were massive stone barriers, sloped and buttressed to hold back the sand and water. Those great braced walls enclosed a square thirty or forty feet on a side—the room was almost a cube, she decided. In the center of the far wall was a broad slate hearth below a fine smooth stone chimney; there were, of course, no windows. Heavy trestle tables were pushed against the walls, four of them in all.

The floor was more stone, and in the center a thick carpet was spread, and seated cross-legged on that carpet, facing each other, were two people—a man perhaps half a century in age, and a girl two or three years younger than Tabaea herself. The man wore a red silk robe and held a silver dagger; another dagger and a leather sheath lay on the carpet by his knee, and several other small objects were in a clutter to one side. The girl wore a simple white robe and sat with her hands empty, listening intently; the man was speaking.

"The edge will never dull, as long as you remain whole and strong," he said. "And the finish will stay bright as long as your spirits do."

The girl nodded.

Tabaea stared. This was a wizard, beyond question—and his apprentice.

"If you can so much as touch it, it will cut any bonds put upon you, even heavy chains," the wizard continued. "*Physical* bonds, at any rate—while it can dispel a minor geas, or ward off many spells, there are many others it will not affect."

Tabaea let the muscles of her arms ease a little. The two were intent on their conversation and would only notice her if she were to somehow draw their attention.

"Those are just side effects, of course," the wizard said. "Incidentals. I'm sure, after these past four months, you understand that."

"Yes," the girl said, in a hushed voice.

"So, if you understand what an athame is, and why a true wizard must have one, it's time you learned how to make yours, is it not?"

The girl looked up at the wizard's face and said again, "Yes."

"It will take several days to teach you, but we can at least make a start tonight."

The apprentice nodded. Tabaea folded her hands beneath her chin and settled down to listen, her heart fluttering in her chest.

She had never heard that word the wizard used, but if it was something every wizard needed—well, she had never heard of such a thing. It must be one of the secrets of the Wizards' Guild, something only wizards were permitted to know—probably one of the most important of their secrets.

Knowing such a secret could be very, very useful. Blackmailing a wizard would be impossibly risky, but it might be possible to sell the information somewhere.

Or just possibly, if she could learn the trick, she could make one of these things for herself.

Perhaps she could even become a wizard herself, without a master, without anyone knowing it. If she could learn how to work magic . . .

She listened intently.

CHAPTER 3

*S*arai, a little nervous, looked around the justice chamber.

She was seated at her father's left hand, just off the dais, a foot or two in front of the red velvet drapery that bore the overlord's seal worked into it in thick gold braid. The chamber was long and narrow, deliberately built with a slight slope to the floor, so that prisoners and petitioners would be looking up at the Minister of Justice as if from a pit, or as if they dared to look up at a god descending from the heavens—but would probably not consciously notice the slope at all.

The overlord's palace was full of tricks like that. The Great Council Chamber, under the overlord's Great Hall, was arranged so that all the doors were partially hidden, to make it easier for people to believe that what they said there was secret, when in fact there were spy-holes in several places; the Great Hall itself was open to the huge central dome to overawe petitioners; there were any number of clever constructs. The justice chamber hadn't been singled out.

What the architects had never considered, however, was that this slope left the minister, her father—and herself, at the moment—looking *down*. Or perhaps they considered it and dismissed it as unimportant, or thought it would enhance the minister's self-confidence.

She couldn't speak for her father, but the effect on *her* was to be constantly worried about falling. She felt as if at any moment she might slip from her chair and tumble down that hard gray marble floor into that motley collection of brigands, thieves, and scoundrels waiting at the far end of the room.

She clutched the gilded arms of her seat a little harder.

This was the first time she had ever been allowed in here when her father was working, and she didn't want to do or say anything that would embarrass him or interfere in any way, and, she told herself, that was why she was nervous. She knew that she was being silly, that the slope was really insignificant, that she was in no danger of falling from her chair. After all, she had been in this room dozens of times when it was empty, starting when she was a very little girl, little more than a toddler, and she had never so much as stumbled on that subtle slope—but still, the nervousness persisted.

Maybe, she thought, if she paid more attention to what was going on in the room, and less to the room itself, she'd forget about such foolishness.

". . . and really, Lord Kalthon, how you can take the word of this . . . this *peasant*, over the word of your own third cousin, is utterly beyond me!" said Bardec, the younger son of Bellren, Lord of the Games, in a fairly good imitation of injured dignity.

"It is not, however, beyond *me*," Lord Kalthon replied dryly, "since I have the word of our theurgist that you did exactly what this good woman accuses you of."

Bardec threw a quick, angry look at old Okko; the magician stared expressionlessly back, his long forefinger tracing a slow circle on the evidence table beside him. His white velvet robe hung loosely on him, his forearm was thin and bony, but Okko somehow looked far more dangerous sitting there at Lord Kalthon's right hand than the young and brawny Bardec did standing before them.

"I take it," Sarai's father said, "that you do not choose to plead any mitigating circumstances? You do not ask for the overlord's mercy?"

"No, Lord Kalthon, I most certainly do not, because I am not guilty!" Bardec persisted. "I am *completely* innocent and can only assume that some enemy of mine has somehow cozened this woman into making this absurd charge and that some sort of malign magic has fooled our esteemed Lord Okko into believing it . . .''

"I am no lord," Okko said, cutting Bardec off with a voice like imminent death.

"I wish I could say the same for our young friend," Lord Kalthon said loudly. "He is, alas, a true noble of the city, born of our overlord's chosen representatives. He is also a fool, compounding his original crime with perjury and false accusations. Stupid ones, at that." He sighed, and glanced at his daughter. She was watching the proceedings closely, saying nothing.

Well, he had wanted her to see how the job was done.

"Very well, then," he said. "Since you show no remorse, or even comprehension, I hereby require, in the overlord's name, that this woman's losses be restored threefold from your own possessions and estates—that would be . . ." He lifted the notes dangling from his left hand to where he could read them, and continued, "Three sound hens, three dozen eggs of the first quality, three oxcarts, and six oxen, or the equivalent value in silver. I further command that you receive ten lashes from a guardsman's whip, as a reminder that the nobility of the city are not, as you seem to think, the rulers of the people but only the servants of our beloved overlord, and that by insisting on bringing this case this far you have wasted the time of everyone in this room. In the name of Ederd the Fourth, Overlord of Ethshar of the Sands, Triumvir of the Hegemony of the Three Ethshars, Commander of the Holy Armies, and Defender of the Gods, let it be done."

Bardec began to protest, but the guardsmen at either side did not let that interfere as they dragged him away, kicking and struggling.

"Young idiot," Lord Kalthon muttered, leaning toward Sarai. "If he'd had the sense to pass it off as a boyish prank, he'd have got off with simple restitution and a small fine."

She glanced up at her father, startled.

"But that isn't fair—that means the woman's benefiting from Bardec's stupidity . . ." Sarai whispered.

"True enough—but that's not what's important. This isn't the place; we'll discuss it later." He sat up straight and called, "Next case."

The next case was a property dispute; such things were generally handled by a local magistrate or a guard captain, but in this case one of the parties *was* a guard captain, so the affair had been kicked up the hierarchy to the Minister of Justice.

Nobody questioned the facts of the case, so no magician had been called in, though old Okko remained in his place at the minister's right; Lord Kalthon was called upon to determine not what was true, but what was just.

Sarai listened to the tedious details, involving an unclear will, a broken business partnership, a drunken surveyor, and a temporarily dry well, with half an ear or so, while thinking about other concerns.

Bardec was suffering for his stupidity, and that was fair and just. If he had the wit to learn from his mistake, to change his attitudes, this might be the lesson he needed. If he had not, then at least this punishment might discourage him from gallivanting off with someone else's cart from Grandgate Market next time he got drunk. The money was nothing to him, or at least to his family, but a flogging would register on anybody.

But the woman with the cart was coming out ahead. Perhaps she deserved some compensation for the inconvenience—but why should it be higher when Bardec behaved stupidly in court than if he had been contrite?

Well, it was undoubtedly more annoying for the victim to have Bardec calling her a liar—and perhaps the greater satisfaction was therefore just.

But just the flogging would have been equally satisfying, Sarai was sure.

She listened as the explanation of the property dispute wound up, and her father began asking questions.

It seemed to her that the basic uncertainty in the case derived from the lost contract between the long-dead partners, but Lord Kalthon was not asking about that, nor was he asking Okko to use his magic to determine the contents of the contract; instead he was looking at the diagram one party had provided and asking, "Your family has used the well these past twenty years, then?"

The guard captain nodded. "Yes, sir," he said, standing stiffly at attention.

"And you never had any doubt of your right to it?"

"No, sir."

"But the new survey—do you doubt its accuracy?"

Unhappily, the soldier said, "No, sir."

The merchant began to smile; Lord Kalthon turned to him

and demanded, ''Did you ever object to Captain Aldran claiming the well before this year?''

The smile vanished. ''No, my lord. But my father's will . . .''

''Yes, I know.'' Lord Kalthon waved that away and looked at the diagram again. ''Okko, lend me a pen, would you?''

Sarai watched as her father drew a line on the diagram and showed it to the two claimants. ''As Minister of Justice to the city's overlord, I hereby claim this parcel here . . .'' He pointed with the borrowed quill. ''. . . as city property, to be compensated for according to law and custom at the value of its last transfer of ownership, which I hereby determine to be five rounds of silver, payable in full from the city's treasury. I also hereby direct that the city shall sell this property to Captain Aldran, in compensation for his years of faithful service to his overlord, at a price of five rounds of silver, to be paid by deduction from his salary. All interest and carrying charges are hereby waived, by order of the Minister of Justice.''

''But that well's worth more than that!'' the merchant objected.

Lord Kalthon asked him wearily, ''And the rest of that land isn't?''

''Uh . . .''

''In the name of Ederd the Fourth, Overlord of Ethshar of the Sands, Triumvir of the Hegemony of the Three Ethshars, Commander of the Holy Armies, and Defender of the Gods,'' Lord Kalthon said, ''let it be done.''

Sarai admired the decision.

If she had been in her father's place, she would have had Okko determine the contents of that original contract; then either the captain or the merchant would presumably have won outright. Either the captain's family would be left without the water source they had relied on for decades, or the merchant would be deprived of the inheritance he had depended upon and had borrowed money against. One man would have had more than he needed, the other nothing.

And making a compromise—well, neither man had been particularly interested in a compromise, surely, or the question wouldn't have reached her father. By invoking his power as the overlord's agent he had removed any possibility of arguing with the results or renegotiating the agreement later. Quite possibly neither man was happy—the merchant had less than he hoped, and the soldier would be paying for what he had thought he already owned—but the matter was settled, and both had come away with what they needed, if not what they wanted.

It wasn't necessarily exactly what the law demanded, but it settled the matter.

And, it occurred to her, Bardec's case had done the same thing. Giving the woman the extra money had helped to settle the matter. It might, perhaps, have been fairer if the overlord's court had taken the additional payment as a fine and kept it, since in fact it was a penalty for perjury and for accusing the court, in the person of Okko, of incompetence—but that might have looked greedy.

The important thing, Sarai saw, was to *settle* the question, one way or another, and without leaving anyone any more angry about it than necessary. If Bardec's money had gone to the city treasury, he could have accused Lord Kalthon of greed, of being more concerned with money than with justice; if the merchant had simply been required to sell the well to the captain, there could have been any number of delays and complications, arguments about price and interest, and so forth. Her father was avoiding all that.

She remembered something that had been said at the dinner table once, when they had had Lord Torrut, commander of the city guard, as their guest. Her father had joked about how Lord Torrut might as well be called the Minister of War, since that's what soldiers do, they make war—but then everyone would want to get rid of him, since there hadn't been a war for two hundred years. Lord Torrut had countered that perhaps Kalthon should be called Minister of Peace, since his job was to make peace—but there hadn't been all that much peace in the past two hundred years, either.

Both men had laughed, and Lord Kalthon had said, "We *both* keep the peace, Torrut, and well you know it."

It was true, Sarai saw—they both kept the peace. The city guard was the whip to threaten the horse, and the city courts the apple to reward it. People had to be reasonably satisfied with the results, when they took their disputes to the overlord's courts; they didn't really care what the laws said, only whether the disputes went away and the results looked fair.

Looked fair.

That was something she really hadn't thought about before.

And she'd completely forgotten about the sloping floor until she looked down at the next pair, defendant and plaintiff.

Her mouth fell open in a way most unbecoming a young noblewoman as the case was described. Kallia of the Broken Hand, a demonologist, accused Heremon the Mage of stealing certain esoteric substances from her workshop; Heremon denied the charge.

A wizard, accused of theft? And no mere apprentice, but a mage?

"Very well, Okko," Lord Kalthon said, turning to his theurgist, "what actually happened here?"

Okko frowned, and his nervous fingers finally stopped moving.

"My lord," he said, "I have no idea."

Lord Kalthon stared at the theurgist.

"I'm sorry, Lord Kalthon," Okko said, "but the differing magical auras surrounding the alleged crime are sufficient to confuse even the gods. I cannot get a plain and trustworthy answer to even the simplest question."

"I hate these cases," Kalthon muttered; Sarai didn't think anyone heard him save herself and perhaps Okko. Then he sat up straighter and announced, "Let the accuser stand forth."

Kallia of the Broken Hand strode up the long room, her long black cloak swirling behind her, her face hidden by a deep hood and her hands concealed in black suede gloves. She stopped, gathered her cloak, and stood before the Minister of Justice.

"Show your face in the overlord's palace, magician," Kalthon said, irritation in his tone.

Kallia flung back the hood; her face was thin and pale, her straight hair was black and worn long and unadorned. The three vivid red scratches that ran down one side of her face, from temple to jaw, stood out in shocking contrast to her colorless features. She glared defiantly at Lord Kalthon.

"Speak," Kalthon told her.

"What would you have me say?" Kallia demanded. "I've told my story and been called a liar. I know what you people all think of demonologists, and it's true we deal with creatures even worse than humans, but that doesn't make us all murderers and thieves."

"Nobody here said it did," Kalthon said mildly. "If the overlords of the Hegemony believed demonology to be inherently evil they would have outlawed it. We accept that your occupation does not condemn you—and at any rate, you're here as the accuser. I've been given a summary of your claim, but I'd like to hear it all from your own mouth.''

"It's simple enough," Kallia said, slightly mollified. "Heremon robbed my shop—I woke up when I heard the noise, and I looked down the stairs and saw him leaving with his arms full. He didn't see me, and I didn't say anything, because I was unarmed and defenseless, and he's a powerful wizard. When I came downstairs I found that several of my belongings were missing.''

"What sort of belongings?''

Kallia hesitated, and Kalthon allowed his expression to grow impatient.

"Blood," Kallia said, "jars of different kinds of blood. And gold, and a few small gems, and some small animals—a ferret, some mice, certain rare insects.''

"These are things you need in your, um, in your business?'' Kalthon asked, stroking his beard.

"Does it matter?" Kallia asked wearily.

"It might.''

Kallia frowned. "Then yes, I need them in my work. Demons often demand payment for their services—blood, or gold, or lives, usually.'' She turned and shouted at the observers at the room's lower end, "Not always *human* lives!''

Sarai, perversely, found herself grinning at the woman's defiance and forced herself to stop.

Kalthon nodded. "And you believe the thief to have been this Heremon the Mage?''

"I *know* it was he, my lord!'' Kallia insisted. "I saw his face plainly and his robe, the same one he wears now! I see him almost every day; there could be no mistake. And who but a wizard would want things like virgin's blood?''

"Anyone who thought to sell them,'' Kalthon said calmly. "Particularly when there's gold, as well. So you know Heremon?''

"Of course! Our shops are across the street from one another, on Wizard Street in Eastside.''

Kalthon stroked his beard again. "And you are rivals, perhaps?''

Kallia looked perplexed. "I had not thought so, Lord Kalthon, but why else would he choose to rob me?''

Sarai watched as the interrogation continued. The question of how the thief had gotten into the shop came up; the door had been broken. Kallia was asked why she had had no magical protections for her gold and gems, and she explained that she *did* have protection: a minor demon, a nameless imp, really, served as her nightwatch. The creature had been found dead—further proof, if any beyond the sight of Kallia's own eyes was needed, that the thief was a magician of some power.

Several of the observers were growing visibly bored; most trials were much briefer, with Okko settling matters of fact in short order, allowing Lord Kalthon to get directly to the matter of setting the penalty. This case, on the heels of the boundary dispute over the soldier's well, was dragging things out unbearably.

The next area of questioning was a little more delicate. Given that Kallia was a demonologist, with many of the resources of Hell at her beck and call, why had she resorted to the courts for justice, instead of simply sending a demon after Heremon?

It took some coaxing before she would admit that she was afraid. Heremon was not some mere apprentice; he was a mage and was reputed to be high in the local hierarchy of the Wizards' Guild, a Guildmaster perhaps—though of course, no outsider could ever know for sure anything that went on in that Guild. Kallia feared that if she took personal vengeance upon Heremon, the Guild would retaliate—if, indeed, whatever demon she sent succeeded in the first place; there was no telling what magical defenses the mage might have, particularly since he would surely be expecting some sort of reaction.

She had not cared to risk the enmity of the Wizards' Guild. People who angered individual wizards might live; people who angered the Wizards' Guild did not. So she had resorted to the overlord's government and appealed to the Lord Magistrate of Eastside, who had passed the whole affair on to the palace.

And here she was, and what was Lord Kalthon going to do about it?

Lord Kalthon sighed, thanked her for her testimony, and dismissed her. Heremon the Mage was called forward.

"My lord," he said, "I am at a loss to explain this. Kallia is my neighbor, and I had thought that we were friends, after a fashion, and there can be no doubt that her shop was robbed, for I saw the broken door and the dead demon myself, but why she should accuse me I cannot guess. I swear, by all the gods and unseen powers, that I have never set foot in her shop without her invitation and that I did not break her door, nor slay the demon, nor take anything from her shop.''

''Yet she says she saw you there,'' Kalthon pointed out.

''She lies,'' Heremon said. ''What else can it be?''

The questioning continued, but nothing else of any use came out. Heremon would not speak of the Wizards' Guild, insisting that he had sworn an oath to reveal nothing about it and that it was not relevant.

Lord Kalthon sighed again, more deeply this time, and waved the wizard away. When the participants were out of earshot he leaned over and asked Okko, ''Who lied?''

The theurgist looked up at him and turned up an empty palm. ''My lord,'' he said, ''I don't know. By my divinations, the wizard spoke nothing but truth—but there are spells that would conceal lies from me, simple spells that even an apprentice might use, and that a mage of Heremon's ability . . .'' He didn't bother finishing the sentence.

''What of the woman?'' the Minister of Justice asked.

Okko shook his head. ''Lord Kalthon, she is so tainted with demon scent that the gods I confer with will not admit she exists at all, and can say nothing about whether she lies.''

''Damn.'' He considered. ''Okko, you know something about the other schools of magic, don't you?''

Okko eyed the minister warily and hesitated before replying, ''A little.''

''Who can tell if a demonologist is lying? Who can't a wizard fool?''

Okko thought that over very carefully, then shrugged. ''I would guess,'' he said, ''that one demonologist could tell if another were engaged in trickery. And I'm sure that one wizard, properly trained, can detect another's spells.''

''Then can you find me a demonologist we can trust? One who has no prior connection with this Kallia? And we'll need a wizard, one who's not in the Wizards' Guild . . .''

Okko held up a hand. ''No, my lord,'' he said. ''*All* wizards are members of the Guild. For anyone not in the Guild, to practice wizardry is to commit suicide.''

''Well . . . do your best, then.''

''As you wish.'' Okko bowed his head.

Lord Kalthon straightened in his chair and announced, ''This case cannot be decided today. All parties hereto will return here tomorrow at this same time. Failure to appear will be accounted an admission of guilt and a crime against the Hegemony, punishable at the overlord's pleasure; if there is anyone who has a problem with that, tell my clerk. Next case.''

Sarai sat, only half listening, as the next case, a local magistrate's son accused of rape, was presented. She was thinking over the two magicians' statements.

If Heremon was lying, then why had he robbed Kallia? A successful wizard didn't need to resort to theft, not for the sort of things taken from Kallia. Even dragon's blood was not so rare or precious as all that. There were supposed to be substances wizards used that would be almost impossible to obtain, but they weren't anything a demonologist would have.

But then, if Heremon had not robbed Kallia, why would she say that he had? What could she hope to gain by making false accusations? Could she perhaps have some use for Heremon? Might she need a wizard's soul to appease some demon?

Sarai shook her head. Nobody knew what demonologists might need except other demonologists. That might be the explanation, but she wasn't going to figure it out; she didn't know enough about the so-called black arts.

Could there perhaps be something else at work?

The case before her father impinged slightly upon her thoughts, and she considered the fact that Kallia, while not young and of no remarkable beauty, was a reasonably attractive woman, while Heremon was a dignified and personable man of late middle age. Could there be some sort of romantic, or at any rate sexual, situation involved here? Nobody had mentioned spouses on either side of the dispute.

But both Kallia and Heremon had plenty of resources at their disposal; why would either of them resort to robbery, or false accusations of robbery?

If Heremon were, in fact, the thief, why did he break in through the front door and generally make such a mess of the job? He might not have any experience at burglary, but he wasn't stupid, to have attained his present status—the title "mage" was only given to a wizard of proven ability, one who had trained apprentices and who had demonstrated mastery of many spells.

And if Heremon was *not* the thief, who was? Had Kallia broken her own door and killed her own demon, to fake the theft? Killing a demon did not seem like a trivial matter, especially not for a demonologist, who would need to deal with other demons on a fairly regular basis.

Sarai mulled the whole thing over carefully.

When court was finally adjourned, she and her father returned to their apartments for a late supper. Kalthon the Younger and his nurse had waited for them, so the meal was hurried, and afterward Lord Kalthon settled at little Kalthon's side to tell him a bedtime story.

Sarai might ordinarily have stayed to listen—she loved a good story, and her father's were sometimes excellent—but tonight she had other plans. Instead, she put on her traveling cloak and headed for the door.

Her father looked up, startled. "Where are you going?"

"I just want to check on something," she said.

Kalthon the Younger coughed; he was a sickly child, always down with one illness or another, while Sarai was a healthy young woman, able to take care of herself. "All right," Lord Kalthon said, "be careful." He turned back to his son and continued, "So Valder the king's son took the enchanted sword . . ."

Sarai closed the door quietly on her way out, and a few minutes later she was riding one of the overlord's horses down Smallgate Street toward Eastside, toward Wizard Street.

CHAPTER 4

*L*ord Kalthon drummed his fingers on the arm of his chair.

"Let's go through it once more," he said angrily. "You, the demonologist—what happened here?"

"Rander of Southbeach, my lord," the demonologist said, with a tight little bow and a twitch of the black-embroidered skirts of his black robes.

"I didn't ask your bloody *name*," Lord Kalthon shouted. "I asked what happened! Did Heremon the Mage rob Kallia of the Broken Hand or not?"

Rander's attempt at an ingratiating smile vanished. He glanced hesitantly at the others, then said, "My lord, my arts show that Kallia has spoken the truth as she knows it."

Lord Kalthon glared at him. "And?" he said.

"And so has Heremon the Mage," the demonologist admitted reluctantly.

"And you can't resolve this contradiction?"

"No."

Lord Kalthon snorted and turned to the plump woman in the green robe. "I know you; you've testified before me before. Mereth of the Golden Door, isn't it?"

"Yes, my lord." She bobbed politely.

"Well?"

"My lord," she said, in a pleasant contralto that Sarai envied, "like the demonologist, my spells have achieved confusing and contradictory results. I, too, find that both Kallia and Heremon speak the truth as they know it. Further, I can detect no distortion of memory in either of them. I used a scrying spell to see the crime with my own eyes, and I saw what Kallia described— Heremon taking the gold and other things; but when I used another divination, I was told that Heremon did not. I fear that some very powerful magic is responsible."

Kalthon turned to Okko and said, "Now what?"

Okko hesitated, and looked very unhappy indeed. "Perhaps a witch . . ." he began.

Sarai cleared her throat.

Kalthon turned an inquisitive eye toward his daughter. "Sarai," he asked, "was there something you wanted to say?"

"My lord," she said, secretly enjoying her father's startled reaction to this formal address from his daughter, "I have undertaken a little study of my own involving this case, and perhaps I can save everyone some time and further aggravation by explaining just what I believe to have happened."

Lord Kalthon stared at her, smiling slightly. "Speak, then," he said.

"Really, it's not as difficult as all that," Sarai said, stalling for time as her nerve suddenly failed her for a moment. What if she was wrong? Her father's smile had vanished, she saw, replaced with a puzzled frown.

She took a deep breath and continued. "Kallia swears that she saw Heremon commit the crime, and every indication is that she speaks the truth, that that's exactly what she saw. Furthermore, Heremon swears that he did *not* commit the crime, and every indication is that this, too, is true. But my lord, we are dealing with magicians here, and while it may be that magic can confound the truth, isn't it more reasonable to accept that both Kallia and Heremon *are* telling the truth, and that there's a simpler sort of magic involved?'' Sarai saw her father's puzzlement abruptly vanish and a smile appear.

She hurried on, saying, ''Isn't it more likely that what Kallia saw was not Heremon, but an illusion of some kind? Magic is very good at creating illusions, as anyone who's attended a few performances at the Arena can attest.''

The smile on her father's face widened, and she saw, farther down the room, Kallia and Heremon suddenly look at each other in startled understanding.

''With that in mind,'' Sarai continued, ''I went down to Wizard Street last night and asked a few questions of neighbors of both Kallia and Heremon, always pretending that I thought one of them to be lying, when actually, I had already decided that a common enemy was probably responsible. Some neighbors sided with Heremon, some with Kallia, and many didn't understand how either could be at fault in the case—and a few mentioned that a common enemy might indeed exist, a Tintallionese demonologist by the name of Katherian of the Coast, whose advances Kallia had reportedly refused, and who apparently felt that Heremon had treated him unfairly in business. Might I suggest, my lord, that this Tintallionese be found and questioned immediately?''

Lord Kalthon nodded, and turned to Okko. ''See to it,'' he said. ''Find this Katherian.''

''If he hasn't already left the city,'' Okko grumbled.

That evening at supper, Lord Kalthon remarked, ''It took a demonologist and two warlocks to bring that Katherian fellow in, and that's without counting that it was Okko's magic that found him for us in the first place.''

Sarai looked up from her plate. Tired of the endless round of quarrels her father was asked to resolve, she had left around midafternoon, before the Tintallionese demonologist had been apprehended. ''Really?'' she asked.

Lord Kalthon nodded. ''He was boarding a ship bound for Ethshar of the Rocks when the guard caught up to him—the ship's captain had hired him to fend off pirates, but I think he was just as interested in getting back to his homeland and away from here as in the wages.''

"What happened?" Sarai asked, putting down her fork.

"Well," her father said, with evident relish, "he conjured up a demon right there, a shapeshifter, so the guards all backed off—we don't pay them enough to fight demons, and we don't *ask* them to fight demons. We'd sent along that Rander of Southbeach, who tried to banish the shapeshifter or conjure up something of his own, but Katherian was fighting his every incantation, and Rander was pretty clearly outmatched right from the start. Katherian couldn't call up anything else, Rander did that much, but he had that first one. Fortunately, one of the guards had the good sense to run to the Inner Towers—this was all in Seagate itself, not out on the moles—and fetch out the magician on watch duty there, who happened to be a warlock by the name of Luralla. She tried to subdue Katherian, and the shapeshifter went after her; she was able to restrain it, but while she was doing that she couldn't hold Katherian, so she sent the guardsman to fetch another warlock, and the three of them finally brought the fool in." Lord Kalthon shook his head in dismay. "Some people," he said, "are more trouble than they're worth."

"So what happened?" Sarai asked. "Did he do it? I mean, did Katherian rob Kallia of the Broken Hand?"

"Oh, yes, of course," Kalthon replied. "Okko couldn't do much with him, since he's a demonologist, but Rander and Mereth and a witch by the name of Theas that we found all swear it was Katherian's shapeshifting demon that robbed Kallia and killed her guardian."

"But he didn't confess?"

"No." Kalthon shook his head. "They rarely do, you know."

"Where is he now, then, in the dungeons?"

"Dead, I'm afraid," Kalthon answered. "With magicians, one can't take too many chances. Especially not demonologists. Witches are mostly harmless, so far as we know, and warlocks have their limits, and a wizard or a sorcerer can't do much of anything if you take away all his equipment, and the gods won't help a theurgist do serious violence, but demonologists—well, sometimes I think the Small Kingdoms that ban demonology outright have the right idea."

"You had him executed?" Sarai asked, startled. "So soon?"

"No, no," her father said, "nothing like that. He was killed trying to escape. When we had him brought in for trial he conjured a minor demon to distract us, right there in the justice chamber, and then ran for it. One of the warlocks burst his heart.'' He glanced at Kalthon the Younger, who was listening intently, and then added, ''I told her to.''

''What happened to the demon?'' little Kalthon asked. ''The one he conjured in the chamber.''

''The guards killed it,'' the Minister of Justice replied. ''Cut it to pieces with their swords, and eventually it stopped struggling.'' He sighed. ''I'm afraid that Irith isn't very happy about it.''

''Who's Irith?'' Sarai asked.

''She's the servant who cleans the justice chamber every night,'' Lord Kalthon explained. ''I told her that if she couldn't get the stain out, not to worry, we'd hire a magician to do it.''

''Will you really?''

''Maybe,'' Kalthon said. ''We've certainly used plenty of magic already on this case.'' He sighed. ''More than I like. There are too damn many magicians in this city.''

Sarai nodded.

''And that reminds me, Sarai,'' her father said, picking up the last drumstick. ''Have *you* been dabbling in magic, perhaps?''

Sarai blinked, astonished. ''No, sir,'' she said. ''Of course not.''

''So you really figured out that it was this Katherian all by yourself, then? Just using your own good sense?''

Sarai nodded. ''Yes, Father,'' she said.

Kalthon bit into the drumstick, chewed thoughtfully, and swallowed. ''That was good thinking, then,'' he said at last. ''Very good.''

''Thank you,'' Sarai said, looking down at her plate.

''You know,'' her father continued, ''we use Okko and the other magicians to solve most of the puzzles we get. I mean, the cases where it's a question of what the facts are, rather than just settling an argument where the facts are known.''

''Yes, sir,'' Sarai said, ''I'd noticed that.''

''Every so often, though, we do get cases like this one, with Kallia and Heremon and Katherian, and sometimes they're real tangles. They usually seem to involve magicians, which doesn't help any—such as the one where a man who'd been turned to stone a hundred years ago was brought back to life, and we had to find out who enchanted him, and then decide who owned his old house, and whether he could prosecute the heirs of the wizard who enchanted him, and for that matter we couldn't be sure the wizard himself was really dead . . ." He shook his head. "Or all the mess after the Night of Madness, before you were born—your grandfather handled most of that, but I helped out." He gestured at Kalthon the Younger. "Your brother will probably be the next Minister of Justice, you know—it's traditional for the heir to be the eldest son, skipping daughters, and I don't think Ederd's going to change that. But I think we could use you—after today, I think it would be a shame *not* to use wits like yours."

"Use me how?" Sarai asked warily.

"As an investigator," her father said. "Someone who goes out and finds out what's going on in the difficult cases. Someone who knows about different kinds of magic, but isn't a magician herself. I'd like to ask the overlord to name you as the first Lord—or rather, the first Lady of Investigation for Ethshar of the Sands. With a salary and an office here in the palace."

Sarai thought it over for a moment, then asked, "But what would I actually *do*?"

"Usually, nothing," the Minister of Justice replied. "Like the Lord Executioner. But if there's ever anything that needs to be studied and explained, something where we can't just ask Okko or some other magician, it would be your job to study it and then explain it to the rest of us."

Sarai frowned. "But I can't know everything," she said.

"Of course not," her father agreed. "But you can learn as much as you can. The overlord doesn't expect his officers to be perfect."

Sarai, remembering what she had heard of Ederd IV, overlord of Ethshar of the Sands, wasn't any too sure of that. "What would I do when I can't . . ."

"You would do the best you can," her father interrupted. "Like any of the city's officials."

"I'd need help sometimes," Sarai said.

"You'd be given the authority to call on the guard for help—I'll ask Lord Torrut to assign you a regular assistant. And you could hire others."

"Father, if we need someone to figure out these things, why hasn't anyone already been given the job?"

Lord Kalthon smiled wryly. "Because we never thought of it. We've always improvised, done it all new every time."

"Have you talked to the overlord yet?"

"No," Lord Kalthon admitted. "I wanted to see whether you wanted the job first."

"I don't know," Sarai admitted.

There they left the matter for a sixnight; then one evening Lord Kalthon mentioned, "I spoke to the overlord today."

"Oh?" Sarai asked, nervously.

Her father nodded. "He wants you to be his investigator, as I suggested. And I think he'd like the job to include more than I originally intended—he was talking about gathering information from other lands, as well, to help him keep up with events. He doesn't like surprises, you know; he wasn't at all happy that he had no warning about the rise of the Empire of Vond, in the Small Kingdoms, two years ago."

"But I don't know anything about . . ." Sarai began.

"You could learn," Kalthon replied.

"I don't know," Sarai said. "I don't like it. I need time to think about it."

"So think about it," her father answered.

In truth, she found the idea of being *paid* to study foreign lands fascinating—but the responsibilities and the fact that she would be reporting to the overlord himself were frightening.

Still, a sixnight later, she agreed to take the job.

CHAPTER 5

"*W*e'll go on to the next step tomorrow," the wizard said, putting the dagger aside. The apprentice nodded, and Tabaea, watching from the landing, got quickly and silently to her feet and padded swiftly up the stairs. Her candle had gone out, and she dared not light another, so she moved by feel and memory. She knew she had to be out of the house before the two came upstairs and found her, so she wasted no time in the thefts she had originally planned. Her sack still hung empty at her belt as she made her way back through the workshop, the hallway, and the parlor.

It was in the parlor that she stumbled over something in the dark and almost fell. Light glinted from the hallway; the wizard and his apprentice were in the workroom. Frightened, Tabaea dropped to her knees and crept on all fours through the dining salon, and finally out to the mudroom. There she got to her feet and escaped into the darkness of the alley beyond.

It was later than she had realized; most of the torches and lanterns over the doors had been allowed to burn out for the night, and Grandgate Market's glow and murmur had faded to almost nothing. Grand Street was empty.

She hesitated. She had come down to Grandgate Market in unfulfilled hopes of filching a few choice items from the buyers and sellers there; the wizard's house had caught her eye as she passed on her way to the square, and she had turned down the alley on her way home. All she should do now was to go on the rest of the way, north and west, back to her family's house in Northangle.

But it was so very dark in that direction, and the streets of Ethshar weren't safe at night. There were robbers and slavers and, she thought with a glance eastward at Wizard Street, quite possibly other, less natural, dangers.

But what choice did she have?

Life didn't give her very many choices, she thought bitterly. It was no more than a mile to her home, and most of it would be along two major avenues, Grand Street and Midway Street; it would only be the last two blocks that would take her into the real depths of the city. One of those blocks was along Wall Street, beside Wall Street Field, where all the thieves and beggars lived. That was not safe at night.

But what choice did she have?

She shuddered and set out on her way, thinking as she walked how pleasant it would be to be a wizard, and to be able to go fearlessly wherever one pleased, always knowing that magic protected one. Or to be rich or powerful and have guards—but that had its drawbacks, of course; the guards would find out your secrets, would always know where you had been, and when.

No, magic was better. If she were a wizard, like the one whose house she had been in . . .

She frowned. Would he know someone had been in the house? She hadn't taken anything, hadn't even broken anything—the lock on the alley door had a few scratches, and a few things might be out of place, but she hadn't taken anything, and really, it had been that weird little green creature that had disturbed the papers and so forth.

Even if the wizard knew she had been there, he probably wouldn't bother to do anything about it.

As long, that is, as he didn't realize she'd been spying on him while he taught his apprentice about the athame thing. That was obviously a deep, dark Wizards' Guild secret; if anyone found out she had heard so much about it she was probably as good as dead.

Which meant that so far, no one had found out. And even with his magic, how *could* the wizard find out? She hadn't left any evidence, and he wouldn't know what questions to ask.

She wished she had heard even more, of course; she had heard a little about what an athame could do and the instructions for preparing to perform the ritual to work the spell to create an athame, but not much more than that. It was obviously a long, complicated procedure to make an athame, and she didn't really know just what one was.

It had to be a magic knife of some kind, obviously a powerful and important one, but beyond that she really wasn't very clear on what it was for. The wizard had described several side effects, little extras, but she'd come in too late to hear the more basic parts.

If she had one with her, though, she was sure she would feel much, much safer on Wall Street. It was a shame she hadn't heard *all* of the instructions for making one. She had only heard the beginning. To get the rest she would have to go back the next night.

She stopped abruptly and stood motionless for a long moment, there in the middle of Grand Street, about four blocks west of Wizard Street. The new-risen lesser moon glowed pink above her, tinting the shadows, while a few late torches and lit windows spilled a brighter light across her path, but nothing moved, and the night was eerily silent.

If she went back the next night, she could hear the rest.

And if she learned the procedure, or ceremony, or spell, or whatever it was, she could make herself an athame.

And why *not* go back?

Oh, certainly there was some risk involved; she might be spotted at any time. But the reward would be worth the risk, wouldn't it?

She threw a glance back over her shoulder, then started running onward, back toward home.

She made it without incident, other than dodging around drunkards and cripples on Wall Street and briefly glimpsing a party of slavers in the distance, their nets held loose and ready.

She got home safely. And all the way, she was planning.

And the next night, when darkness had fallen, she again crept into the alley behind the wizard's house, listening intently, waiting for her eyes to adjust to the darkness. This time, though, she carried a small shuttered lantern that she had appropriated from a neighbor in Northangle. Entering on a whim was all very well, but it was better to be prepared.

If she found any sign at all that her earlier visit had been detected, she promised herself that she would turn and flee.

The lock was just as she remembered; she opened one lantern-shutter enough to get a look at it and saw no scratches or other marks from her previous entry. Unlocking it again took only a moment.

The mudroom beyond was just as she remembered, and, as she glanced around, she realized that she had, in fact, stolen something—the candle she had burned for light. In a household as rich as this, though, she was reasonably confident that the loss of a single candle would go unnoticed.

The dining salon was also undisturbed; when she shined her lantern about, however, the teapot rattled in its cabinet and turned away in annoyance.

The plant in the parlor was still waving; the mantel where the little creature had sat was empty.

A few things had been moved around in the workroom, but she assumed that was just a result of normal use. Nothing seemed to be any more seriously disarrayed than before.

At the entrance to the cellars she encountered her first real obstacle: the door was locked.

She put her ear to it and listened intently and heard the wizard's voice. He was beginning the night's lesson—his voice had that droning, lecturing tone to it.

Frantically, she set to work on the lock, and discovered, to her relief, that it was no better than the one on the alley door. Really, it was disgraceful the way the wizard was so careless about these things! If she ever became a rich and powerful wizard, she would make sure that she had better locks than these. Relying *entirely* on magic couldn't be wise.

And she hadn't even seen any sign of magic; really, the wizard appeared to be relying entirely on his reputation, and that was just plain foolish.

The door swung open, and she slipped through, closing it carefully behind her, making sure it neither latched nor locked. With the lantern shuttered tight she crept down, step by step, to the landing.

And just as the night before, there sat the wizard and his apprentice, facing each other across the center of that rug. The wizard was holding a silver dagger and discussing the qualities important in a knife—not magical qualities, but basics like balance, sharpening, and what metals would hold an edge. Tabaea placed her lantern to one side and settled down, stretched out on her belly with her chin on her hands, to listen.

It was scarcely ten minutes later that the wizard finished his disquisition on blades and began explaining the purification rituals that would prepare a knife for athamezation.

Tabaea watched, fascinated.

Night after night, she crept in and watched.

Until finally, there came the night, after studying this one ritual, this one spell, for over a month, when the apprentice— her name, Tabaea had learned, was Lirrin—at last attempted to perform it herself.

Tabaea returned for the conclusion of the ceremony, the grand finale in which the apprentice would trap a part of her own soul in the enchanted dagger that the wizards called an athame. She settled down, once again, on her belly and lay on the stone landing, staring down at the two figures below.

Lirrin had been at it for more than twenty-three hours, Tabaea knew, without food or rest. Her master, Serem the Wise, had sat by her side, watching and calling what advice he could the entire time.

Tabaea, the uninvited observer, had not done anything of the sort. She had watched the beginning of the spell, then slipped away and gone about her business. Throughout the day she had sometimes paused and thought, "Now she's raising the blade over her head for the long chant," or "It must be time for the third ritual cleaning," but she had not let it distract her from the more urgent matter of finding food and appropriating any money left sufficiently unguarded.

When she at last returned, the silver knife was glittering white, and Tabaea really didn't think it was just a trick of the light. The spell was doing *something*, certainly.

She could hear fatigue in the master's voice as he murmured encouragement; the apprentice was far too busy concentrating on the spell to say anything, but surely she, too, must be exhausted.

Perhaps it was the certainty that the objects of her scrutiny were tired, or fascination with this climax, or just overconfidence acquired in her many undetected visits, but Tabaea had crept further forward than ever before, her face pressed right against the iron railing. The black metal was cool against her cheek as she stared.

Lirrin finished her chant and placed her bloody hands on the shining dagger's hilt; blood was smeared on her face, as well, her own blood mixed with ash and sweat and other things. It seemed to Tabaea that the girl had to force her hands down, as if something were trying to push them back, away from the weapon.

Then Lirrin's hands closed on the leather-wrapped grip, and her entire body spasmed suddenly. She made a thick grunting noise; the dagger leaped up, not as if she were lifting it, but as if it were pulling her hands upward.

Something flashed; Tabaea could not say what it was, or just where, or what color it was. She was not sure it was actually light at all, but "flash" was the only word that seemed to fit. For an instant she couldn't see.

She blinked. Her vision cleared, and she saw Lirrin rising to her feet, the new-made athame in her right hand, any unnatural glow vanished. The dagger looked like an ordinary belt knife— of better quality than most, perhaps, but nothing unreasonable. The girl's face was still smeared with black and red, her hair was a tangled mess, her apprentice's robe was wrinkled, stained, and dusty, but she was no longer transfigured or trembling; she was just a dirty young girl holding a knife.

She looked up, straight at Tabaea.

Tabaea froze.

"Master," Lirrin said, tired and puzzled, "who's that?" She pointed.

Serem turned to look, startled.

When the wizard's eyes met her own, Tabaea unfroze. She leaped to her feet and spun on her heel, then dashed up the short flight of steps. She ran out through the wizard's workroom as fast as she could and careened out into the utter darkness of the hallway. Moving by feel, no longer worrying about making noise or knocking things over, she charged down the hall, through the parlor and dining salon, banging a shin against the animated fanning plant's pot in the parlor, sending one of the ornately carved dining chairs to the floor.

The door to the mudroom was open; she tumbled through it, tripping over somebody's boots, and groped for the door to the alley before she even regained her feet.

Then she was out and stumbling along the hard-packed dirt toward the light of Grand Street. She was breathing too hard to seriously listen for pursuit, but at any rate she heard no shouting, no threats, none of the unnatural sounds that accompanied some spells.

At the corner she hesitated not an instant in turning toward Grandgate Market, even though that meant passing in front of the house. The marketplace crowds were unquestionably the best place to lose herself. She hoped that Serem and Lirrin hadn't gotten a good look at her and that Serem had no magic that could ferret her out once she was lost.

By the time she had gone three blocks she felt she could risk a look back over her shoulder. She saw no sign of Serem or Lirrin and slowed to a walk.

If they spotted her now, she would just plead innocent, claim they had mistaken her for someone else.

Of course, if they insisted on taking her anyway, and if they had some magical means of discovering the truth, or if they had none themselves but took her to the overlord's Minister of Justice, who reportedly kept several magicians around for just such matters . . . well, if anything like that happened, she would just have to throw herself on somebody's mercy and hope that the penalty wasn't too harsh. After all, she hadn't actually stolen anything.

She glanced back again and saw lights in the windows of Serem's house; the shutters had been opened, and light was pouring out into the streets.

Maybe they thought she was still inside somewhere—but that was silly. She hadn't even taken the time to close the alleyway door behind her.

Well, whatever they thought, they weren't coming after her, as far as she could see. She let out a small gasp of relief.

And the market square—which was called that even though it

was six-sided and not square at all—was just ahead. In only seconds she would be safe.

Then the arched door at the corner of Grand and Wizard opened, spilling light, and even from four blocks away Tabaea could see that Serem stood silhouetted against it, peering out. Tabaea shuddered and forced herself not to run, and then she was in Grandgate Market, in the milling crowds.

Even so, even after she had seen Serem march out into the street, glare in all directions, and then go back inside, it was hours before she felt at all safe. It was two days before she dared go home, and two sixnights before she dared pass within a block of Serem's house.

CHAPTER 6

*D*uring the days following Lirrin's athamezation, Tabaea reviewed the ritual repeatedly, both silently and aloud. Tessa and Thennis heard her mumbling the incantations and mocked her when she refused to explain—but that was normal enough.

The whole question of how to use what she had learned was a baffling one. The secret of the athame was clearly one of the most important mysteries of the Wizards' Guild, and therefore tremendously valuable—but how could she cash in on it? There was a word that described people who crossed the Wizards' Guild, by stealing from them, or attempting to blackmail them—the word was "dead."

So she couldn't do anything at all that would bring her to the attention of the Guild. That left two other options: sell the secret elsewhere, or use it herself.

And where else could she sell it?

Wizards and sorcerers were traditional enemies, so one afternoon in Summerheat she strolled over to Magician Street, in Northside, and wandered into a sorcerer's shop. The proprietor didn't notice her for several minutes, which gave her a chance to look around.

The place didn't look very magical; there were no animated plants, no strange skulls or glowing tapestries or peculiar bottles. There were some tools, but they looked as appropriate for a tinker or a jeweler as for a magician—pliers and hammers and so forth. Assorted colored wires hung on one wall, and crystals were displayed on another, but Tabaea, who had a competent thief's working knowledge of precious stones and metals, quickly concluded that none of these were particularly valuable.

The sorcerer finally realized she was there; he took in her youth and ragged appearance in an instant, and said, "I'm not looking for an apprentice just now, young lady."

"I'm fifteen," Tabaea replied, annoyed.

"My apologies, then. What can I do for you?"

Tabaea hesitated; she had thought over a dozen possible openings without definitely choosing one, but now she could put it off no longer.

Might as well be direct, she thought.

"I think I might have something to sell you," she said.

"Oh?" The sorcerer was a black-haired man in his thirties, with thick, bushy eyebrows that looked out of place on his rather pale and narrow face. Those eyebrows now rose questioningly. "What might that be? Have you found an interesting artifact, perhaps? Some relic of the Northern Empire?"

"No," Tabaea said, startled. "There were never any Northerners around here."

"True enough. Then it was around here that you found whatever it is?"

"Yes. It's not an artifact—it's a piece of information."

The sorcerer frowned, his eyebrows descending. "I am not usually in the business of buying information," he said.

"It's about wizards," Tabaea said, a note of desperation creeping into her voice.

The sorcerer blinked. "I am a sorcerer, young lady, not a wizard. You *do* know the difference, don't you?"

"Yes, of course, I do!" Tabaea replied angrily. Then, calming, she corrected herself. "Or at least, I know there *is* a difference. And I know that you people don't like wizards, so I thought maybe . . . well, I found out a secret about wizards."

"And you thought that it might be of interest to sorcerers?"

Tabaea nodded. "That's right," she said.

The sorcerer studied her for a moment, then asked, "And what price were you asking for this secret?"

Tabaea had given that some thought and had decided that a hundred pounds of gold would be about right—a thousand rounds, that would be, equal to eight hundred thousand copper bits. That was most of a million. She would be rich, she wouldn't need to ever steal again. Magicians were all rich—well, the good ones, anyway, most of them; surely, they could afford to pay her even so fabulous a sum as that.

But now she found she couldn't bring herself to speak the numbers aloud. Eight hundred thousand bits—it was just too fantastic.

"I hadn't decided," she lied.

The sorcerer clicked his tongue sympathetically and shook his head in dismay. "Really, child," he said, "you need to learn more about business. Let me ask, then—would this secret help me in my own business? Would it let me take customers away from the wizards?"

Tabaea hadn't thought about that. "I don't know," she admitted. Attempting a recovery, she added, "But the wizards *really* don't want anyone to know about it!"

The sorcerer frowned again. "In that case, isn't this a dangerous bit of knowledge to have? How did you come by it?"

"I can't say," Tabaea said, a trifle desperately.

"Well, all right, then," the sorcerer said. "I'm not usually one to buy a closed casket, but you've caught my interest."

Tabaea caught her breath.

"I'll pay you four bits in silver for your secret," the sorcerer said.

Tabaea blinked.

"Four bits?" she squeaked.

"Half a round of silver," the sorcerer confirmed.

Tabaea stared for a moment, then turned and ran out of the shop without another word.

Later, when she could think about it clearly, she realized that the sorcerer had really been making a generous offer. Tabaea had given him no hint of what her secret was, no reason to think it would be profitable for him to know it—and in fact, she saw now that it would probably *not* be profitable.

Wizards and sorcerers were traditional rivals, but they weren't blood enemies. Sorcerers weren't about to wage a full-scale war against wizards—for one thing, there were far more wizards in the World than sorcerers. And what possible use would knowledge of athamezation be to any magician who was not prepared to use it against wizards?

Selling her information, she saw, simply wasn't going to work. That left using it herself as the only way to exploit it.

And the only way to use it was to make herself an athame.

That certainly had its appeal; she would be a true wizard, then, according to what Serem the Wise had said, even if she didn't know any spells. And if she ever *did* learn any spells, the athame would make them easier to use, if she had understood correctly. The knife would be able to free her from any bonds, if she could touch it. It would mark her as a wizard to other wizards, but not to anyone else—and yet she would not be a member of the Guild.

And she had the impression that there was far more to it than she knew. She hadn't heard all of Serem's teachings to Lirrin. She had learned the entire twenty-four-hour ceremony, but had missed a fair amount of the other discussion about the athame.

So, one bright day early in Summersend, two months after Lirrin completed her own athame, Tabaea slipped out of a shop on Armorer Street with a fine dagger tucked under her tunic, one that she had not paid for.

The next problem, now that she had the knife, was to find a place where she could perform the spell. Her home was out of the question, with her sisters and her mother and her stepfather around—if her stepfather had turned up again, that is.

The people of the Wall Street Field had a reputation for minding their own business, but there were surely limits, and the all-day ritual with its blood and chanting and so forth would draw attention anywhere. And what if it rained? Right now the summer sun was pouring down like hot yellow honey, but the summer rains could come up suddenly.

She needed someplace indoors and private, where she could be sure of an entire day undisturbed, and such places were not easy for a poor young woman to find in the crowded streets and squares of Ethshar of the Sands.

Maybe, she thought, if she left the city . . .

But no, that was crazy. She wasn't going to leave the city. There wasn't anything out there but peasants and barbarians and wilderness, except maybe in the other two Ethshars, and those would be just as unhelpful as Ethshar of the Sands.

There were places that most people never went, such as the

gate towers and the Great Lighthouse and all the towers that guarded the harbor, but those were manned by the overlord's soldiers.

She wandered along Armorer Street, vaguely thinking of the South Beaches, but with no very clear plan in mind; she squinted against the sun and dust as she walked, not really looking where she was going.

She heard a man call something obscene, and a woman giggled. Tabaea looked up.

She was at the corner of Whore Street, and a man in the yellow tunic and red kilt of a soldier was shouting lewd promises to a red-clad woman on a balcony.

Those two would have no trouble finding a few minutes' privacy, she was sure—though of course they'd have to pay for it.

That was a thought—she could pay for it. She could rent a room—not here in Soldiertown, of course, but at a respectable inn somewhere. She was so accustomed to stealing everything she needed that the idea of paying hadn't occurred to her at first.

But she could, if she wanted. She had stashed away a goodly sum of money in her three years of thievery and had never spent more than a few bits. Maybe making herself an athame would be worth the expense.

It took two more days before she worked up the nerve, but at last she found herself in a small attic room at the Inn of the Blue Crab, with the proprietor's promise not to allow anyone near for a day and a half.

She had tried to convince him, without actually stating it, that she was a wizard's apprentice and that her master had assigned her some spell that required privacy; fear of wild magic was about the only thing she could think of that would reliably restrain the man's natural curiosity. She wasn't at all sure it had worked.

She had laid in a good supply of candles for light, and a jug of reasonably pure water—the inn's well, the innkeeper boasted, had a permanent purification spell on it, but Tabaea suspected it was just not particularly polluted. She couldn't have any food, she knew, but she was fairly sure that water was permissible. She had brought a change of clothing, for afterward. She had fire and water and blood, and of course, she had her dagger. She had rested well and was as ready as she knew how to be.

Still, she trembled as she began the first chant, the dagger held out before her.

The incantations, the gestures, the eerie little dance, she re-membered them all. She had no master or teacher in attendance urging her on, nor any other helper to light candles for her, so parts of the spell had to be performed in darkness, but she con-tinued, undaunted.

The attic room was warm and close, and as the candles burned down it grew hotter and stuffier. When the candles died, it was almost a relief—but then the sun came up, and by midmorning the heat was worse than ever. She would have opened the win-dow, but to do so would have meant stepping outside the pattern of the ceremony. The innkeeper would have come up and opened the window for an ordinary customer, if only to help cool the inn as a whole, but she had forbidden him entrance.

If she had thought ahead, she realized, she would have had the window open all along. She hadn't, and she had to make the best of it; she couldn't stop now.

In fact, she was unsure whether it was literally *possible* to stop; she could sense the magical energies working around her, a strange, new, but unmistakable sensation. She was afraid that the magic would turn against her if she stopped, so she ignored her thirst, ignored the heat, ignored her fatigue, and continued with the spell, sweating heavily.

Worst of all, she could see her jug of water, and she had the bowl of water used in purifying the metal of the knife, but this part of the ritual did not allow her a chance to drink so much as a drop.

Her voice gave out by midday; she hoped that didn't matter. By that time exhaustion, dehydration, and heat had driven her into a state of dazed semiconsciousness, and she continued with the spell more out of inertia than anything else.

Around midafternoon she came to a part that she could not do without conscious effort. The spell called for her to draw her own blood, pricking her right hand, her throat, and the skin over her heart with the dagger.

Hands trembling, she drew the necessary blood, and used it to paint the required three symbols on the blade, marking the weapon as eternally hers.

The worst was yet to come, though; for the final section of the spell she would need to slash open her forehead and use the point of the knife to smear the blood across her face, mixing it

with the sweat and ash. That would mark her as belonging to
the knife, just as the three runes marked the knife as belonging
to her. She dreaded that part; she had an irrational fear that in
her weakness, she would lose control and cut her own skull
open.

Still, she struggled on.

The moment came; the blade shook as she raised the dagger
to her brow, which terrified her still more. Even if she didn't cut
too deep, what if she slipped and cut an eye?

She closed her eyes as she drew the blade across the tight
skin.

At first she thought she had somehow missed, and she reached
up with her free hand. It came away red.

Quickly, she continued with the ceremony.

She could feel the magic around her—but somehow, even in
her unthinking state, she began to sense that something had gone
wrong.

Hadn't Lirrin's knife been *glowing* at this point?

Tabaea's wasn't. In fact, though it was hard to be certain in
the deepening twilight, the knife seemed to have gone dark, as
if blackened by smoke. But she hadn't managed to light a candle
or other fire in hours; there was no smoke in the room.

She placed the knife before her, as the spell required, and it
seemed almost to disappear in the gloom.

She had no choice but to continue, though. She had the final
chant to get through, and then she would pick up the knife and
the spell would be over—if she *could* pick up the knife. She
remembered Lirrin forcing her hands down as if against strong
resistance.

She hurried through the chant as quickly as she could in
her weakened, frightened, and voiceless condition, thinking
all the while that this had been an incredibly stupid thing to
try all on her own, that it was fantastically dangerous, that it
couldn't possibly work, that the knife might kill her when she
picked it up—and at the same time, underneath her terror,
she exulted in the knowledge that she was *working magic*,
that if she came through this she would be a wizard, that the
dagger would be her athame, and she would be the World's
only Guildless wizard.

She spoke the final word and pressed her hands down toward
the dagger.

They met no resistance at all.

She closed her eyes against the flash as her fingers closed on the hilt.

There was no flash. The eerie sensation of magic at work faded quickly away, and she was just a girl sitting cross-legged on the floor of a hot, airless attic room, holding an ordinary dagger.

But that couldn't be true, she told herself, it wasn't possible. She blinked in the darkness, trying to see the knife, but the daylight was gone, and the light from the window, compounded of lanterns and torches and the lesser moon's pink glow, wasn't enough.

She dropped the dagger and groped for the candles and her tinderbox. In a moment she had a light going, and looked down at the knife that lay on the bare planks.

It was blackened all over, a smooth, even black; the silver blade still gleamed, but with the dark shimmer of volcanic glass.

Tabaea felt it. It wasn't glass; it was still metal.

But it was black.

Hilt and guard were black, as well.

The entire dagger was utterly, completely black, totally colorless.

That wasn't right. Tabaea didn't know much about wizards, but she had seen them in the streets, she had seen the athame that Serem carried and the athame that Lirrin had made. All those athames were perfectly ordinary and natural in appearance, not this unearthly black.

Something had gone wrong.

She remembered the tests that Serem had described, but which she had not seen Lirrin attempt because of her need to flee. She couldn't try any of the ones that involved other people or other athames, but . . .

She wrapped a leather thong from her belt around one arm, tied it off with a simple knot, then touched the black dagger to it.

Nothing happened.

The cord was supposed to untie and fall away, but nothing happened.

She touched the blade of the dagger to her forehead, gently; it came away bloody, but there was no glow, not so much as a flicker of color. The gash on her brow did not heal.

She held the dagger out by the blade, on the flat of her palm;

it did not tremble, did not turn its hilt to her, did not prepare to defend her.

It did nothing that an athame was supposed to do.

It was not an athame.

It was *nothing*.

Staring at the worthless black dagger, hungry, thirsty, exhausted, Tabaea felt her eyes fill with tears. She fought back the first sob, but then gave in and wept.

PART TWO

Killer

CHAPTER 7

Lady Sarai rubbed her temple wearily and tried to listen to what was being said. It had been four years since she had first sat at her father's left hand and watched him work; now, for the first time, she was in his throne and doing his work herself. She had put it off as long as she could, but *someone* had to do it, and her father no longer had the strength.

And, she feared, she wasn't doing it very well. How had her father ever stood up under this constant stream of venality and stupidity?

". . . she told me it was her father's—what am I supposed to do, call in a soothsayer of some kind every time I buy a trinket? How was I supposed to know it was stolen?"

"A *trinket*?" the gem's rightful owner burst out angrily. "You call that stone a *trinket*? My grandfather went all the way to Tazmor to find a diamond that size for my grandmother! You . . ."

Sarai raised her right hand while the left still massaged her forehead. At the gesture, a guard lowered his spear in the general direction of the victim.

The victim's shouting stopped abruptly.

For a long moment, the three principals stood in uneasy silence, watching Lady Sarai as she sat in her father's throne, trying to think.

"All right," she said, pointing, "you get your diamond back. Right now. Give it to him, somebody. No further compensation, though, because you were stupid to let her near it in the first place. Now, get out of here."

Another guard handed the robbery victim the pendant; he took it, essayed a quick, unhappy bow in Lady Sarai's direction, then fled the room, the jewel clutched tight in his hand.

The jeweler began to protest, and even before Sarai raised her hand, the lowered spear moved slightly in his direction.

The thief grinned; her head was down, but Sarai saw the smile all the same. A hot, rough knot of anger grew in her own chest at the sight.

"Straighten her up," Sarai snapped.

A soldier grabbed the thief's long braid and yanked her head back; the smile vanished, and she glared at Sarai. Sarai could see her arms flexing, as if she were trying to slip free of the ropes around her wrists.

"Sansha of Smallgate, you said your name was?" Sarai demanded.

The thief couldn't nod, with her hair pulled back; she struggled for a moment, then said, "That's right."

"You spent *all* the money?"

"That's right, too."

"It's hard to believe you could use up that much that fast—eight rounds of gold, was it?"

"I had debts," Sansha said, tilting her head in a vain attempt to loosen the guard's grip.

"That's too bad," Sarai said, "because now you've got another one. You owe this man eight rounds of gold." She pointed to the jeweler.

"Eleven," the jeweler protested. "The stone was worth at *least* eleven!"

"You paid her eight," Sarai told him. "The stone never belonged to you, only the money you paid her."

The jeweler subsided unhappily, and Sarai turned her attention back to Sansha.

"You owe him eight rounds," she said.

Sansha didn't answer. Sarai had the impression that she would have shrugged, had her hands been free.

"I'm going to buy that debt from him," Sarai said. "So now you owe *me* eight rounds of gold."

"I can't pay *you*, either," Sansha retorted.

"I know," Sarai said. "So I'll settle for the five or six bits on the piece that I'll get by selling you at auction. Somebody give him his money, and then take her down to the dungeon until we can get a slaver to take a look at her." She waved in dismissal as Sansha's expression shifted abruptly from defiance to shock.

She watched as the jeweler was led out in the direction of the treasury, and the thief was dragged, struggling and crying, toward the stairs leading down. Then she let out a sigh, and leaned over toward Okko.

"How did I do?" she asked.

He considered that for a moment.

"I think," he said, "that your father would have lectured the jeweler briefly on his carelessness and might have only promised him the auction proceeds, rather than the full amount of the debt."

"You're right," Sarai admitted. "That's what I should have done." She glanced at the door. "It's too late now, isn't it? It wouldn't look right."

"I'm afraid so," Okko agreed.

"I wish my father was doing this," Sarai said. "I hate it."

Okko didn't reply, but was clearly thinking that he, too, wished Lord Kalthon were there.

"I hope he'll be better soon," Sarai added.

Again, Okko said nothing; again, Sarai knew quite well what he was thinking. He was thinking that Lord Kalthon wasn't going to get better.

Sarai feared that Okko might be right. She was doing everything she could to prevent it, but still, her father's illness was growing steadily worse.

It really wasn't fair.

And her brother wasn't any help—his sickliness was worse lately, too; he coughed all the time, bringing up thick fluid and sometimes blood. And he was too young to serve as Minister of Justice anyway, even if he were healthy; their father should have been around for another twenty years.

She wasn't supposed to be her father's heir, though; she was Minister of Investigation, not Minister of Justice! It was completely unfair that she should be stuck here, settling all these stupid arguments, instead of finding some way to cure her father's illness. Why couldn't some local magistrate have dealt with Sansha of Smallgate, and all the others like her? So what if the jeweler lived in a different jurisdiction from the gem's owner?

Okko looked steadily back at her, and she realized she was staring quite rudely at him. She straightened up, then slumped back in the big chair.

For four years now, she had been learning the arts of investigation—with very little guidance, since there were no older, more experienced investigation specialists to aid her. Her assistant, Captain Tikri, was useful in a variety of ways, especially in her attempts to recruit spies, but he knew even less than she did about finding criminals or determining the facts of a puzzling case. Her father had taught her his own methods, but they were very limited—mostly a matter of which magicians to talk to.

Because magic could do so much in answering riddles and untangling puzzles, she had spent most of her time studying magic—in theory, never in practice. She knew the names of a hundred spells, but had never worked a one; she knew the names of a score of gods and as many demons, and had never summoned any of them; she knew the nature of a warlock's talents, but had not a trace of them herself.

She had studied the working of the various spells of contagion and clairvoyance and whatever else had been used in the solving of crimes and mysteries. She knew how, with the appropriate spells, the merest traces of blood or hair could be linked to their owners; she knew which questions the gods would answer when summoned, and what the souls of the dead were likely to know— it was really rather surprising how many murder victims had no idea how they had died. She knew how warding spells worked, how locks both magical and mundane operated, and how gems could be appraised and identified.

And with all this knowledge, she couldn't do a thing for her father or brother.

It was, of course, the fault of the Wizards' Guild.

"Shall we bring in the next case, my lady?" Chanden, the bailiff, asked quietly.

Sarai blinked. She hadn't even noticed him approaching the throne. "The next?"

"Yes, my lady. Tenneth Tolnor's son claims he was cheated by the wizard Dagon of Aldagmor."

Cheated by wizards. Her mouth twisted. "No," she said. "I'm sorry. That's all for today."

"My lady?"

Sarai knew the polite question was a protest, that she was shirking her duties—no, shirking her *father's* duties, not her own—but she didn't care. She needed to stop. She set her jaw.

"Perhaps a short recess, my lady?"

"All right," she said, giving in. "Half an hour, at least. I need that long. I *need* it, Chanden."

"Yes, my lady." He straightened and turned to face the little knot of people waiting at the lower end of the room—the crooked room, Sarai realized, and a crooked grin twisted her lip. The justice chamber itself was crooked—why hadn't she realized that years ago?

It all depended on magic, after all. They used magicians to tell who was telling the truth and who was lying, to determine what had actually happened when claims conflicted.

But who could tell them if the magicians were lying?

"Lady Sarai, Acting Minister of Justice for Ederd the Fourth, Overlord of Ethshar of the Sands, hereby declares that further judgments shall be postponed one half hour," Chanden announced loudly. "Clear the room, please."

Sarai ignored the murmurs and did not wait for the room to empty; she slipped out the back door as quickly as she could and headed down the passageway toward the southeast wing, where her family's rooms were.

It was all those wizards, she thought, the Guild and its stupid rules. If her father were a wealthy commoner, they could buy a healing spell—but because he was a member of the nobility, because he held a post in the government, the Wizards' Guild forbade the use of magic to prolong his life.

And it didn't matter whether the spell was a simple disinfectant or perfect immortality—*anything* that prolonged life, in any degree, was forbidden to the nobility, as far as wizards were concerned.

What's more, the Wizards' Guild actively discouraged other magicians from healing the nobility, as well. Sarai had had to argue to get other magicians even to look at her father.

Not that it had done much good.

In fact, it was really quite startling how little worthwhile healing magic was out there. As she reached the first flight of steps up, Sarai began counting off the different schools of magic and how they had failed her.

Demonology was inherently destructive; it was no great surprise that demons couldn't heal. The demonologists had all agreed on that.

The sorcerers swore that with the right artifacts, they could heal diseases, even the sort of slow, lingering weakness that was gradually killing Lord Kalthon, or the illness of the lungs that was crippling his son—but the right artifacts could no longer be found. None existed in Ethshar of the Sands.

Sarai had paid a large fee to have a search begun throughout all the World, from the wastes of Kerroa to the Empire of Vond, but so far nothing had come of it, and she doubted anything ever would.

The warlocks were apologetic, but couldn't work on anything that small. Patching up an opened vein, repairing a ruptured heart, welding a broken bone—those warlockry could at least attempt, though success was not always certain. But whatever was wrong with her father, they said, attacked the individual nerves, operating on a scale they could not perceive, and therefore could not affect.

Witchcraft held out some promise at first; the half-dozen witches Sarai had summoned to the palace had tried, at least. They had fed father and son strength, drawing it from their own bodies—but to no avail. When the spell was broken, the weakness returned within hours. Witchcraft could, at great cost to the witch, put the elder Kalthon back on his feet for a day or two, but could do nothing permanent.

"His own body has given up," the eldest, Shirith of Ethshar, explained. "We can't heal it without its help."

But all of those Sarai had tried only when she became desperate. She had begun with the theurgists—after all, didn't everyone pray to the gods for good health?

She reached the second floor and started up the next flight.

Okko had refused to handle the job—although he acknowledged that he was a top-ranked theurgist, a high priest, in fact; his specialties were truth and information. Healing was not his province. He had instead recommended her to Anna the Elder.

Anna had summoned gods, had spoken with them, and had reported back to Kalthon and Sarai.

"We know of three gods of health and healing," Anna had explained. "There are the siblings Blusheld and Blukros and their father, Mekdor. Blusheld involves herself only with the *maintenance* of health and thus will not concern herself with this case—it's too late to ask her aid. Mekdor concerns himself with great wounds and catastrophes, with plagues and epidemics; anything as slow as this wasting disease, attacking only one or two people, is beneath his notice. Thus, this is clearly the province of Blukros."

At that point Anna had hesitated, and Lord Kalthon had tried to save him the embarrassment of explaining, saying that he understood.

Sarai would have none of it; she had demanded that Anna summon Blukros and beseech him to heal her father.

"No," Kalthon had said, "he can't. Not on my behalf."

"Why *not*?" Sarai had demanded.

"Because seven years ago, after having summoned him to help your mother, I offended the god Blukros," Kalthon had explained. "I refused him a silver coin I had promised, and he forever withdrew his protection from me, and from my family."

Sarai had stared at her father and demanded, "But *why*?"

"Because I was angry—your mother had died."

And so, because of her father's long-ago pique, there was no help to be had from the gods. Anna had tried, and he had promised to attempt to call upon Luzro, god of the dead, to see if, once dead, Kalthon could be restored to life—but nothing had come of it.

So theurgy was no help.

And that left wizardry.

And the wizards had healing spells and youth spells and strength spells; they had transformation spells, and if all else failed they could transform Kalthon to some other, healthier form.

But they wouldn't.

She reached the top of the stairs and stamped down the corridor. They wouldn't, because the Wizards' Guild forbade it, and to oppose the will of the Guild was to die.

And the Guild forbade it because they refused to meddle in politics. It was strictly forbidden for any wizard to be a member of the nobility in his or her own right; a century ago, they had even been forbidden to marry into the nobility, but that rule had been relaxed. They could hold office only if the office was one that required a magician—a post such as Okko's, for example.

No wizard could kill a king in the Small Kingdoms, or a baron in Sardiron, or an overlord or a minister or any other high official of the Hegemony, save in self-defense or to enforce Guild rules; the direct heirs of the nobility were similarly off-limits. Wizards were forbidden to use any magical compulsion on any official above the rank of lieutenant in the city guard without written consent from three Guildmasters. And anyone they could not kill, they were forbidden to heal, as well.

"That's stupid," Sarai had said.

Algarin of Longwall, her father's chief wizardly consultant, had turned up an empty palm. "It's the Guild law," he said.

"Why?"

Algarin had had no answer, and Sarai had demanded to see a

more highly placed wizard, so it was the city's senior Guild-master, Serem the Wise, who finally explained it.

"Magic, Lady Sarai," the old man had said, "is power, but of a different sort than the power you and your father wield."

"I can see that for myself," Sarai had snapped in reply.

"And power," Serem had continued, untroubled by her interruption, "must be kept in balance. If it is not, the World will be plunged into chaos."

"Says who?"

"It's self-evident," Serem had replied, with mild surprise. "Imagine, if you will, that a wizard were to become overlord of Ethshar of the Sands."

Sarai had glowered at him, and Serem had revised his suggestion. "Suppose," he said, "that Lord Ederd the Heir had apprenticed to a wizard in his youth. Suppose that he decided he was tired of waiting for his father to die and cast a spell that slew the overlord."

"Then he'd be guilty of treason, and he would be executed," Sarai had replied. "That's easy enough. My father would see to it."

"But how?" Serem had asked. "Suppose this evil wizard were to use his spells to guard himself, and you could not appeal to the Wizards' Guild, because there are, in our hypothetical case, no Guild rules forbidding his actions, no matter what other laws he may have broken."

"There aren't any Guild rules requiring that you wizards obey the laws?"

Serem had hesitated before answering, his first hesitation, but then admitted that there were no such rules.

Sarai had insisted that a rule requiring wizards to obey the same laws as ordinary people would serve just as well as this stupid rule about keeping out of politics, and Serem had then tried to convince her that allowing kings and ministers to live for centuries, as would inevitably happen if the rules were changed, would be a bad thing.

Sarai had not accepted that.

The argument had dragged on for days—sixnights, in fact. In the end, when Sarai refused to be convinced, Serem had simply turned up a palm and said, "My lady, those are the Guild rules, and I have no power to change them."

They were stupid rules, Sarai thought as she opened the door of her father's bedchamber, and she wanted them changed.

CHAPTER 8

The Drunken Dragon was probably not the most dangerous tavern in the city, Tabaea thought as she gulped down the watery stuff that passed for ale in that establishment, but it was the most dangerous she ever cared to see. Coming here had been a serious mistake.

She had been making a lot of serious mistakes lately.

Oh, not as bad as some, certainly. She hadn't wound up in front of a magistrate, or tied to a post somewhere for a flogging, or in the hands of the Minister of Justice or his crazy daughter, like poor Sansha. Tabaea had watched the auction that morning, had seen Sansha sold to the proprietor of one of the "specialty" brothels—not the ones in Soldiertown, which generally employed free women and treated them reasonably well, but one of the secretive establishments in Nightside that catered to the more debauched members of the nobility.

Tabaea shuddered. She had heard stories about what went on in places like that. They *had* to use slaves—free women wouldn't work there. Tabaea wouldn't have changed places with Sansha for all the gold in Ethshar.

And it was all because Sansha had stolen the wrong jewel, a diamond pendant that the owner thought was worth enough to justify hiring magicians to recover it.

Tabaea had stolen plenty of wrong jewels in the past few years—but all hers had been wrong in the other direction, had turned out to be worthless chunks of glass or paste, or at best some semiprecious bauble. And even with the best of them, she'd been cheated by the fences and pawnbrokers.

Mistakes, nothing but mistakes.

She had been making mistakes *all her life*, it seemed. She hadn't run away as a child, like her brother Tand—and she had heard a rumor that Tand was a pilot on a Small Kingdoms trader now, with a wife and a daughter, successful and respected.

Of course, the rumor might not be true; Tand might be starving somewhere in the Wall Street Field, or he might be a slave in the dredging crews, or he might be long dead in an alley brawl, or he might be almost anywhere.

But if she had run away . . .

Well, she hadn't. She stared into the remaining ale, which was flat and lifeless.

She hadn't found an apprenticeship, either. She hadn't even tried. That seemed so stupid, in retrospect.

She had never taken opportunities when they presented themselves. She hadn't married Wulran of the Gray Eyes when he offered, two years ago, and now he was happily settled down with that silly Lara of Northside and her insipid giggle.

She hadn't signed up for the city guard when she was sixteen—though they might not have taken her anyway; they took very few women, and she wasn't really anywhere near big enough.

She hadn't stolen much of anything from her family, and now her drunken stepfather had spent everything.

She hadn't stolen anything from Serem the Wise, when she broke into his house all those nights four years ago without getting caught—she had just kept spying on him until he spotted her.

All she had come away with there was the secret of athamezation, and she hadn't even done *that* right! Here she had this wonderful secret that the Wizards' Guild had guarded for centuries, and all she had to show for it was a stupid black dagger that didn't do anything an ordinary knife wouldn't do just as well.

She pulled the dagger from her belt and looked at it. It was black, from pommel to point, and it seemed to stay sharp without sharpening, but otherwise, as far as she could tell, it was completely ordinary.

She knew, had known for years, that she must have made a mistake in the athamezation ritual—*another* mistake in the long list. She had no idea what the mistake might have been, but something had gone wrong. And when she had tried again, nothing had happened at all. The magic she had felt the first time wasn't there; she was just going through a bunch of meaningless motions.

Well, Serem had said that a wizard could only perform the spell once. Apparently that applied even when the spell was botched.

She put the knife back in its sheath and gulped down the last of her ale. Then she put the mug down and looked around the taproom again.

The place was definitely unsavory. She had come here because it was cheap, and she was, as usual, down on her luck. She had hoped to find a purse to pick, or a man she wouldn't mind going home with, but neither one had turned up. The men here were mostly drunkards, or disgusting, or both, and none of them seemed to have fat purses—after all, why would anyone with significant amounts of money be in the Drunken Dragon? And what little cash its patrons did have they watched carefully.

She wasn't going to find anything useful here.

And that meant that after years of avoiding it, she was going to yield to the inevitable. She would spend the night in Wall Street Field.

There wasn't anywhere else left. The little stash of stolen money she had accumulated in better days was gone, down to the last iron bit. She couldn't go back to her mother's home, not after that last fight, and she had exhausted her credit at every inn in Ethshar. Sleeping in the streets or courtyards would make her fair game for slavers—and she had just seen what had happened to Sansha, so any notion she might have had that slavery could be an acceptable life was gone.

That left the Field.

She sighed and looked out the narrow front window.

The Drunken Dragon stood on Wall Street, facing the Field; a good many of the customers there looked like permanent inhabitants of the Field, in fact. Tabaea guessed that when they could scrape together enough for a drink or a meal, the beggars and runaways and thieves who lived in the Field would come here just because it was close and cheap. They wouldn't care that the drinks were watered and the food foul, that the floors and walls were filthy, or that the whole place stank; they were used to that.

No one else looked out the window; Tabaea had the view all to herself.

Wall Street itself was about thirty feet wide; the dismal drizzle that had fallen all day had left the hard dirt slick with a thin layer of mud, and a thousand feet had left their marks in that mire, but still, it was mostly clear and unquestionably a street.

On the far side, though, the Field was a maze of ramshackle shelters—huts and lean-tos and tents, most of them brown with mud. Cooking fires and the lights from Wall Street provided patchy illumination, but most of the details were lost in the gloom of night and rain.

The Wall itself provided a black backdrop, about a hundred and fifty feet away at this particular spot. Tabaea knew that when the stone was dry and the sun was high the Wall was a rather pleasant shade of gray, but just now it looked utterly black and featureless and depressing, considerably darker than the night sky above. The sky, after all, was covered in cloud, and the clouds caught some of the city's glow. The Wall did not.

Sleeping in the Wall's shadow was not an appealing prospect, but Tabaea knew she had to sleep *somewhere*. And she didn't have so much as a tattered blanket; those inhabitants of the Field with huts and tents were the lucky ones.

But she had nowhere else to go.

She pulled her last copper bit from her pocket and put it on the table to pay her bill; the serving wench spotted it from two tables away and hurried over to collect it. Tabaea rose, nodded in acknowledgment as the coin was claimed, and started toward the door.

Something caught her attention, she wasn't sure what; had the server gestured, perhaps? She glanced around.

A man was staring at her, a big man in a grubby brown tunic and a kilt that had been red once. The look he was giving her was not one she cared to encourage. As she looked back, he got ponderously to his feet; he was obviously drunk.

Quickly, she turned away and left the tavern.

She didn't pause in the doorway. The rain was little more than mist now, and she had sold her cloak a sixnight ago, in any case; she had no hood or collar to raise. Besides, any hesitation might have been taken as an invitation by the man in the kilt. She walked directly out the door and down the single step.

The mud was more slippery than she had realized; she had to reach out and catch herself against the wall of the inn, turning half around. Above her the signboard creaked; she glanced up at it, at the faded depiction of a green dragon dancing clumsily on its hind feet, long pointed tongue lolling to one side, a goblet that had once been gold but was now almost black clutched in one foreclaw. The torches that lit it from either side flickered and hissed in the drifting mist.

At least it wasn't cold, she thought. Setting each foot carefully, she set out across the street.

"Hai," someone called when she was nearing the far side.

Tabaea turned, not sure whether the voice was addressed to her or to someone else.

"Hai, young lady," the voice continued, slurring the words, "are you headed for the Field?"

"You mean me?" Tabaea asked, still not sure who was speaking.

"Yes, I mean you," the voice said, and now she located the speaker. It was the drunken man in the kilt, speaking from the mouth of the alley beside the inn.

"What business is it of yours?" Tabaea answered.

"Now, come on, don't be . . . don't be like that." His consonants were blurred by liquor, but Tabaea had had long practice in understanding the speech of drunkards. "A pretty thing like you can do better than the Wall Street Field!"

"Oh, really?" she demanded. "How?"

"Come with me, and I'll show you," he said.

She turned away, her muscles tensing, her hand sliding down to the hilt of the black dagger. She took another step toward the Field.

Then she looked where she was going and stopped.

Before her was a hut built out of an old table propped up on piles of bricks, the sides partially boarded over with broken doors and other scrap, leaving an opening where the tattered remains of a sheet hung. Leaning out of this aperture was an old woman, who was listening with interest to the conversation between Tabaea and the kilted man. The woman's hair was a rat's nest of gray; her open mouth displayed no more than half a dozen teeth, and those were black. Her face was as withered and wrinkled as an apple in spring.

Beside the hut was a tent, made of the remnants of a merchant's awning; stripes that had once been red were now a pale pink, where they weren't hidden by greenish black mildew. A one-eyed boy of ten or so was watching Tabaea from the open end of the tent. His black hair was so greasy that it stood up in spikes, and Tabaea imagined she could see things crawling in it.

In the muddy waste beyond, in the flickering and scattered

light, Tabaea could see a dozen other faces, young and old, male and female—and all of them hungry and tired, none of them smiling.

She turned back toward the alley. "What did you have in mind?" she asked.

The man in the kilt smiled. "I have . . . have a room," he said, "but it's a bit lonely, for just me. Care to come take a look?"

Tabaea still hesitated.

There could be little doubt what the man had in mind. If she accepted, she would be whoring, really—and at a terribly low price, at that; she would be exchanging her favors for a room for the night, without even a meal, let alone cash, to accompany it.

But if the alternative was the Wall Street Field—well, she could at least take a look at the room. And maybe she could demand additional payment, or simply take it when the man was asleep. He was bound to sleep heavily after drinking so much.

In fact, he might be too drunk to really bother her, once they got to his room. She marched back across the muddy street, moving as quickly as she could without slipping.

She slowed as she neared the alley and saw the big man's face again. There wasn't anything she could point to that was obviously wrong with it, beyond drunkenness—he wasn't deformed or even particularly ugly, he appeared to still have both eyes and all his teeth—but still, there was something about him that made her very uneasy. His nose was very red, and his eyes very dark.

She brushed at her skirt, as if trying to knock away the mud on the hem, and her hand came away with the black dagger tucked in her sleeve. One advantage of that weapon, she reminded herself, was that it didn't sparkle in the torchlight.

Then, with a false smile pasted across her lips, she stepped up to the man in the alleyway. "Where's this room of yours?" she asked. "I'll be glad to get in out of this mist."

"This way," he said, beckoning her into the alley. She smelled cheap *oushka* on his breath—lots of cheap *oushka*. Warily, she followed him into the shadows.

"How far is it?" she asked.

He turned abruptly and caught her in his arms. "Right here," he said. He drew her to his chest, breathing great clouds of alcohol and decay in her face, and the grease on his tunic stained her own. His hands slid down, trapping her arms against him.

"Let me go!" she demanded.

"Oh, pretty, now, you were . . . you were happy enough to come with me when you thought I could put a roof over your head," he said, in a tone that was probably intended as wheedling. "You'll have just as good a time here in the alley."

"Let *go*!" she shouted.

"Oh, come on," he said. "I live in the Field with the others, and over there we'd have shared . . ."

She didn't wait to hear any more. He was holding her arms down, so that she couldn't reach up far enough to pull anything from her belt, but she didn't need to; she yanked the dagger down out of her sleeve and slashed.

The knife was really amazingly sharp. She wasn't able to put any real strength into the blow, with her arms almost pinned, but the black blade sliced neatly through the red kilt and into the leg beneath, leaving a dark red line, almost as black in the shadows as the blade that had made it, a line no wider than a hair across the outside of her captor's thigh.

Tabaea felt an odd tingling as the knife cut flesh; her head seemed to swim, as if the alcohol on the man's breath were suddenly affecting her, while at the same time she felt a surge of strength and well-being.

The excitement, she told herself. It was the excitement and fear getting to her. She had never been in a serious fight, nor had she ever cut anyone before.

Even as she thought that, the drunk reacted instinctively, flinging his arms wide and stumbling backward the instant he felt the first cut; that allowed her arm more freedom, and with that odd feeling of strength flooding through her, with that strange light-headedness giving her irrational courage, she thrust with the dagger, plunging the blade deep into the meat of her attacker's thigh.

He gasped, and a sensation of power overwhelmed her as he fell back against the bricks of the Drunken Dragon's wall.

Then she realized she was free, and habit took over; she whirled, clutching the knife, and ran out onto Wall Street, her feet sliding in the muck as she turned the corner. She caught herself with one hand and got upright again, then headed for Grandgate Market at full speed.

Behind her, the man in the red kilt looked down at his leg, at his ruined kilt; the thin line of the initial slash was slowly widening as blood oozed out, but he ignored that.

The stab wound was spilling blood as a burst barrel spills beer. He took a few steps, out to where torchlight turned his tunic from black to brown, his skin from gray to orange, and his entire left leg redder than his veteran's kilt. Drunk as he was, the pain cut through the alcohol.

He tried futilely to wipe away the blood and only opened the gash wider; blood spilled out in a thickening sheet, and the dim knowledge that he was badly, perhaps fatally hurt finally penetrated.

He let out a gurgling squawk and fainted, facedown in the mud.

Tabaea saw none of that as she ran, slipping and stumbling, along Wall Street. She rounded the S-curve where the Field wrapped around the north barracks tower, and from there it was a straight three blocks to the market. The torches of the gate watch glowed before her.

With safety in sight, she allowed herself to slow. She caught her breath and tried to compose herself—and to her own surprise, succeeded quite well.

She was, she realized, completely awake and alert—and at the same time, she felt light-headed, as if she were drunk.

But she had only had the one pint of ale. And she had been exhausted—why else would she have ever considered sleeping in Wall Street Field?

She wasn't exhausted now. She felt fine.

She felt better than fine; she felt *strong*.

With wonder in her eyes, she looked down at the bloody knife she held.

CHAPTER 9

In the opinion of his fellow guardsmen, Deran Wuller's son was prone to work too hard. He had been known deliberately to volunteer for various duties; he kept his boots polished even when no inspections were anticipated. And when a citizen asked for help—well, any guardsman was required to provide aid, but Deran would do it cheerfully, without griping or delaying or trying to pass the job on to someone else.

If he hadn't been just as eager and cheerful when losing at three-bone, or when helping one of his mates back to barracks after a brawl or a binge, or when dodging the officer of the watch to illicitly collect a few oranges from the groves north of the city, he would have been insufferable. And he had never been known to betray a trust or let down a comrade.

Thus he got along well enough, but got more than his share of odd and unpleasant duties—such as escorting Lieutenant Senden's sister home after she was found drunk and naked in the Wall Street Field.

She had been safely delivered and had even showed signs of sobering up when Deran had departed and headed back toward the north barracks tower. It was well past midnight, perhaps as much as two hours past, when Deran passed the Drunken Dragon and noticed the footprints in the muddy surface of Wall Street.

He did not ordinarily go about staring at the ground, but the mist had turned back to rain, and he had not bothered with a hat or helmet or cloak, so he was hunched forward a little, and so he noticed with mild interest the patterns of footsteps. There were several lines that ran along the middle of the street; that made sense. There were lines running in and out of the Drunken Dragon—mostly out; that, too, made sense, as the Dragon was still open, despite the hour. There were a few lines in and out of the Wall Street Field, each one alone—the Field never slept, as the saying had it, but most of its inhabitants did, so traffic in and out was light and scattered at this time of night.

And there were steps leading in and out of the alley beside the Drunken Dragon. The line coming out was widely spaced and smeared, as if whoever made those marks had been running and slipping.

That was odd.

Most guardsmen, and virtually all citizens, would have shrugged and kept walking. Deran, though, was Deran. He stopped and peered into the shadows of the alley.

Something was lying on the ground in there, and it didn't look like garbage.

If it was someone sleeping there, then whoever it was was fair game for slavers, and Deran should either wake that person up and shoo him across the street to safety, or he should go fetch a slaver and collect a finder's fee, depending on whether he wanted to be benevolent, or to be paid.

If it was anything else . . .

Well, it bore further investigation, and the light in the alley was terrible. Deran turned back a few steps to the door of the inn and took one of the signboard torches from its bracket.

Being in the city guard did have its little privileges, he thought as he carried the hissing brand over to the mouth of the alley. If an ordinary citizen took down a torch from an open place of business it would be theft and good for a flogging.

Dim as it was in the damp weather, the torch made the scene in the alley much clearer. Deran stared down at the man lying there in a spreading pool of blood, blood that had mixed with the muck so that it was hard to tell where the edge of the pool actually was.

There wasn't as much blood as he had first feared, actually; much of the red was the man's kilt.

A red kilt usually meant a soldier or a veteran; if there had been any question about leaving the man where he was—and for Deran, there really wasn't—that put an end to it. The man in the alley was not anyone Deran recognized, but soldiers looked out for their own.

Whoever the unconscious person was, he was a big man, and Deran was not large for a guardsman, and it was late and he was tired and the mud was slippery. He sighed and headed for the door of the Dragon, torch in hand.

A tavern crowd, Deran knew, generally had a distinctive sound of its own. It chattered, or hummed, or buzzed, or even shouted. The patrons of the Drunken Dragon muttered, a sullen, low-pitched sound that quickly faded when a guardsman in uniform stepped in, holding up a torch.

"I need a hand here," Deran announced. "We've got a wounded man just around the corner."

The half-dozen customers who still lingered stared silently at him. Nobody volunteered anything, by word or motion.

That didn't trouble Deran. "You," he said, pointing at the individual who looked least drunk of those present. "And you," indicating another.

"Oh, now . . ." the second man said, beginning a protest.

"Five minutes, at most," Deran snapped, cutting him off, "and if you don't . . . well, we don't need to worry about what would happen then, do we? Because you're going to cooperate."

Grumbling, the two men got to their feet.

Deran wasn't stupid enough to walk in front of them; he had never been in the Drunken Dragon before, but he knew its reputation. He directed the two "volunteers" out the door and followed them as they slogged around the corner.

The wounded man was so much dead weight; he showed no sign of life at all as the three men—one taking his feet and the others a shoulder apiece—hauled him into the tavern and dumped him on a table.

That done, Deran dismissed his two assistants, paying them for their trouble by telling them, "I owe you a favor—a small one. If you ever get in trouble with the guards—*small* trouble— you tell them Deran Wuller's son will speak for you."

The two men grumbled and drifted away, leaving Deran and his prize alone. Deran turned his attention to the bloody figure before him.

There were only two wounds that he could find, both in the fleshy part of the man's thigh—a long, shallow slash and then a deep stab wound that had missed the artery, Deran judged, by no more than an inch. Most of the blood came from the stab; the slash had already started to scab over.

"Are you going to leave him there dripping all over my floor?" demanded a voice from behind Deran. The guardsman turned and found himself facing an aproned figure a bit shorter than himself.

It was the innkeeper, of course—or rather, Deran corrected himself, the innkeeper's night man; Deran doubted that the broad-shouldered fellow with the ferocious mustache was actually the proprietor.

"Until you find me a bandage, that's exactly what I intend," Deran answered. "And a clean rag to wipe the wound first would be a good idea, too."

Grumbling, the night man retreated, while Deran checked the stabbing victim over.

There were no other recent wounds; his heartbeat was strong and regular, his breath steady and reeking of *oushka*. He was, Deran concluded, unconscious as a result of his drinking, not from the wound. While bloody, the injury just wasn't that serious.

The innkeeper's man returned then with a handful of reasonably clean rags, and Deran set about cleaning the man up a little. As he worked, he questioned the night man and the remaining customers.

Nobody knew the man's name. Nobody knew what had happened to him. He wasn't exactly a regular, but he had been there before. He might have been seen with a girl, a black-haired girl wearing dark clothes.

And that was all anyone would tell him.

When Deran pulled the bandage tight, the drunk opened his eyes.

"Am I dead?" he asked blearily. "Am I going to die?"

"You're fine," Deran said. "You might limp for a while."

The drunk tried to raise his head from the table to look at himself, but couldn't manage it. He moaned.

"What happened?" Deran demanded. "Who stabbed you?"

"Nobody," the wounded man muttered. "Was an accident."

Deran shrugged. "Fine. You owe the Dragon two bits for the bandages and the use of their table. If you change your mind about who stabbed you, tell the magistrate . . ." He hesitated, turning to the night man. "This is Northangle, right?"

"Grandgate. Northangle starts at the corner."

"All right, tell the magistrate for Grandgate, then. And if you need me to testify, I'm Deran Wuller's son, Third Company, North Barracks." He yawned. "And that's where I'm headed—I need to get some sleep." He waved and departed.

By the time Deran was out the door the night man was trying to get his wounded customer off the table and back on his own feet.

At the north tower he almost headed straight for his bed, but his sense of duty stopped him. He checked the lieutenant's room first.

Sure enough, Lieutenant Senden was waiting up for him.

"Is she all right?" the lieutenant asked anxiously.

"She's fine," Deran said. "No problem at all."

"Then what took so long?"

"When I was on my way back I practically tripped over this boozer lying in an alleyway."

The lieutenant grimaced. "You called the slavers?"

Deran shook his head. "No," he said. "It wasn't entirely his fault. He'd been stabbed. So I hauled him into the nearest tavern and got him bandaged up. Wasn't anything serious, just a flesh wound in the leg."

"Did he say who did it?"

"No. Might've been a girl he was bothering."

"All right. Goodnight, then, Deran—and thanks."

"My pleasure, Lieutenant."

Deran judged that he had no more than three hours until dawn when he finally fell into his bunk.

Senden, too, was quickly asleep.

The following day he was somewhat irritable, as a result of a late night largely spent in worrying, and carried out his duties in perfunctory fashion; his monthly report to Captain Tikri, a recently added requirement that Senden did not care for, was brief and sketchy. He did note down, "Guardsman Deran reports tending to stabbing victim in tavern. No accusations or arrests made."

Late that afternoon, at the overlord's palace, Captain Tikri had just finished going through the reports from all the guard lieutenants when Lady Sarai stepped into his office. The captain leapt up and saluted, hand on chest.

Lady Sarai waved an acknowledgment, and Tikri relaxed somewhat. "Is something wrong, my lady?" he asked.

"No, no; I just wanted to get out of that room for a few minutes," Sarai explained, "so I came myself instead of sending a messenger. I'm here in both my official roles today, Captain, as Minister of Investigation and as Acting Minister of Justice. Is there anything I should know about?"

Captain Tikri looked down at the reports he had just read. He turned up a palm.

"Nothing, my lady," he said. "Nothing of any interest at all."

CHAPTER 10

*T*abaea had expected the feeling of strength and power to wear off within a few minutes, like the excitement after a narrow escape.

It didn't.

Instead, the strength stayed with her. The light-headedness

faded fairly quickly, but the added strength stayed. If anything, it increased, at least at first.

She had hidden behind a merchant's stall in Grandgate Market, crouched down between a splintery crate and the brick wall of a granary—not a place for long concealment, by any means, but she was out of sight, able to think and plan, until the merchant arrived for the day's business. For the first several minutes, she had just sat, waiting for the weird feeling to pass.

Eventually, though, she had realized that this was not working. She began thinking about it.

She felt strong. Most especially, her left leg seemed to be almost bursting with vitality. She knew she had stabbed the kilted drunk in his left leg, so the connection was obvious. Was it an illusion, though, or was she really, truly stronger than before?

Measuring strength, especially in a leg, was not something that Tabaea had any easy method for doing; she tried out a few kicks at the crate beside her, and then tried hopping, first on her almost-normal right leg, then on her empowered left for comparison.

It was hard to be sure; she knew, from her work as a thief, how people could fool themselves without meaning to. All the same, she concluded at last that yes, the feeling of strength was genuine; somehow, she had become stronger.

And it was fairly obvious how—when she had stabbed that man in the left leg with her dagger, her left leg had become stronger. The connection could hardly be coincidence.

The black dagger, which she had known for four years to be enchanted, had somehow given her that strength because she had stabbed the drunk.

This was serious magic.

Unfortunately, she didn't yet know the details. Was this added strength permanent? Would the magic work again, or had she used it up? Where had the strength *come* from—the dagger's magic, or the drunk? Had the dagger created it, or only transferred it? And what *else* did the dagger do? How dangerous was it? Had it stolen the man's soul? Would it eat *her* soul?

She could think of three ways to find out more about it.

One was to ask a magician—but that was out. How could she do that without revealing that she had stolen the secret of athamezation? Even if she claimed to have found the dagger, many magicians could tell lies from truth.

No, asking anyone was out of the question.

The second possible method was to stab someone or something else and see what happened.

She supposed she would have to do that sooner or later, but she wasn't about to just go out and stab some stranger chosen at random.

And the third way to learn more would be to find the man she had stabbed and see what had happened to him. Had the dagger killed him? Had it devoured his soul? Had something horrible happened to him?

She didn't know his name, but she knew where she had last seen him. That was, she decided, where she should start—but not until dawn. She sat back, resolved to wait until first light.

The next thing she knew, she was waking up because someone was pulling her to her feet.

"Hai!" she said, "wait a minute!"

"The sleeping blossom awakens, then," someone said.

"You call *her* a blossom? An insult to flowers everywhere."

"Oh, she's not as bad as that," a third voice said. "Clean her up and comb that hair, and she'd be fit company."

Blinking, Tabaea saw blue sky over the shoulder of the man who held her and realized that it was well past first light and that she had fallen asleep behind the crate and been discovered by the merchant and his—or her—family. The man was not alone; a woman stood behind him, and two boys to the side.

"I'm sorry," Tabaea said, a little blearily. "I was hiding."

The man and woman looked at each other, concerned; the older boy, who looked about fourteen, was more direct. "Hiding from what?" he demanded.

Tabaea recognized the boy's voice as the one that had called her an insult to flowers everywhere. "From a drunkard who apparently liked my looks better than you do," she retorted.

The woman glanced uneasily over her shoulder.

Tabaea waved her worry away. "That was hours ago," she said. "I must have dozed off."

"Oh." The woman's relief was palpable.

Tabaea found the woman's behavior unreasonably annoying; what was *she* worrying about, when she had her husband and sons to protect her? But there was no point in arguing with these people. "I'll go now," Tabaea mumbled.

The man released her, and she walked away across the market square. The sun was peering over the wall to the east, its light blazing across the gate towers, while most of the market was still in shadow. Steam curled out from the tower walls where hot sun hit cold, damp stone, but otherwise the clouds and mists of the night had vanished, leaving shrinking puddles and drying mud. Merchants and farmers were setting up for the day, and a few early customers were drifting in, but on a day like this, Tabaea knew, most Ethsharites preferred to wait until the streets had dried before venturing out.

She wished she could have done the same.

She noticed, as she neared the northern edge of the square, that she was limping—but it was a very peculiar limp. She was not favoring an injured leg; instead, the limp came about because her left leg was now noticeably stronger than her sound but less-altered right.

If she tried, she found she could eliminate the limp, but it took an effort.

This strange phenomenon reminded her of what she had temporarily forgotten while she slept; she paused, leaning against a canopy pole at the corner of a display of melons, and considered.

She still felt strong, particularly in the left leg, but less so, she thought, than when she had fallen asleep. It was really very hard to judge, but she *thought* it was less—or maybe she was adjusting to the change.

That feeling of added vitality was far less, and the light-headedness was gone entirely, but she knew she was still stronger than before.

Did that mean the drunkard was dying, so that less of his strength was reaching her? Or that the magic was fading? Or something else entirely?

She wouldn't find out here, she decided. She straightened up and marched on up Wall Street toward the Drunken Dragon, fighting the tendency to limp. By the time she had gone a block, she had promised herself that if this spell could be used again, and she ever got up her nerve to do it, she would make sure that she stabbed whoever she stabbed in the center, or at least symmetrically.

She found the alley easily enough. The morning sun was almost clear of the city wall, but still low in the east, and the narrow passage was still shadowy; even so, Tabaea had no more trouble finding the remains of blood than she had had finding the alley.

The man himself was gone—but what that meant, she couldn't be sure. If he was dead, the corpse might have already been removed by the guard, or by thieves intent on selling the component parts to wizards; if he was alive, he might have left under his own power, or been dragged or carried.

The blood didn't look like enough for him to have bled to death, and Tabaea knew that was the only way anyone would die of a thigh wound in a single night; infections generally took at least a sixnight. So he was probably alive, in which case the most likely place to find him was either right next door, in the Drunken Dragon, or across the street in the Wall Street Field.

She stood nervously in the inn door for several minutes, looking over the breakfast patrons; she didn't dare enter, for fear of being trapped in there if he should show up unexpectedly. Besides, the proprietor probably wouldn't appreciate her presence; she had no money to spend, and was, to at least some people, a known thief.

She didn't see her assailant anywhere among the surly and largely hung-over patrons; she turned away, almost stumbling as she momentarily forgot the strength of her own left leg. Standing on the single step, she looked out at the Wall Street Field.

By daylight it looked less threatening, but even dirtier and less appealing. The table-hut and the awning-tent were still there, but their occupants were not in sight—probably asleep inside, Tabaea judged. A few ragged figures were moving about in the mud, and someone was tending a cooking fire.

The man who had attacked her, the one she had stabbed, was probably out there somewhere, in that mud and filth.

But the city wall was easily five miles long, which meant that Wall Street was just as long, and the Field ran beside it for every inch of that way. And that strip of land, five miles long by at least a hundred feet wide, was all occupied. Not all was as thickly settled as here in Grandgate, of course—the marketplace and the guard barracks gave this district by far the most beggars and thieves of any part of Ethshar of the Sands—but all of it was inhabited.

Finding one man in all that would be a long, slow job—and an extremely dangerous one. Tabaea didn't care to try it.

She turned and headed back toward Grandgate Market, fighting her new limp and hoping to find a fat purse to steal. She would figure the dagger's magic out later; right now, she wanted to insure that she could pay for a room for the night.

Patrolling the top of the city wall was not really a military necessity anymore, if it ever had been; the Hegemony of the Three Ethshars had been at peace since the destruction of the Northern Empire and the end of the Great War, over two centuries earlier, and Ethshar of the Sands was forty leagues from either the nearest Small Kingdoms or the Sardironese border. True, the Pirate Towns were a mere dozen or so leagues to the west, but no army could cross that thirty-some miles without advance warning reaching the city. Besides, the Pirate Towns, or any other enemies, were far more likely to attack by sea than by land.

Furthermore, the watchers atop the towers could see farther than a soldier on the ramparts.

But walking the wall was a tradition, and it did serve a purpose both for discipline and for maintenance—it was an active but not unpleasant duty, useful for keeping bored soldiers busy, and those soldiers had strict orders to report any signs of wear and damage along the route.

Deran hadn't been particularly bored, but he'd been assigned the duty and accepted it without complaint. He strolled along the wall, whistling softly, taking his time on the long walk out to the Beachgate tower and back. He studied the stonework as he walked, peered out over the surrounding countryside, and paused every so often to look down at the city itself, at the ragged inhabitants of the Wall Street Field, the tawdry homes and shops on Wall Street, and the rooftops and streets beyond.

By the time he neared the line between Northangle and Grandgate on his return trip, the sun was well down in the west and the shadows were lengthening dramatically. Deran paused and leaned on a merlon, looking down at the Field.

Since it was still daylight, almost all the huts and tents were unoccupied, and the broad patches of mud where blankets were spread at night were bare. Most of the people who slept in the Field were elsewhere in the city, working or begging or doing whatever they did to sustain themselves.

A few people lingered, though. Four ragged young women were fighting over something; a fifth was standing back and shouting at the others. A line of children was running through the maze of huts and tents, intent on some sort of following game. Half a dozen old people, men and women, were huddled together on a faded red blanket, dickering over a pile of vegetables.

Off by himself, a big man in a brown tunic was sitting on the mud, leaning against the side of a shack, watching the others. A bandage heavily stained with dried blood was wrapped around his left thigh, and Deran realized that was the man he had found in the alley the night before.

That was interesting. A chat with him about just how he had come to be stabbed might be a pleasant diversion, Deran thought. He looked about for the nearest stairway—the city wall was theoretically equipped with a stairway every two hundred feet, either down into the interior of the wall itself or on the inward face, down into the Field, but not all the stairs actually existed. Deran was unsure whether this was a result of neglect, or if some had never been built.

There was a wooden stair down to the Field not far away; Deran used it, putting his foot through the bottom step. He shook his head; the step was rotten right through. He would have to report that.

Which meant he would have to explain why he had come down from the wall. He sighed and headed for the man in the red kilt.

The man looked up as the soldier's shadow fell across him, but said nothing.

"Hai," Deran said, "remember me?"

The man in the brown tunic frowned. "I don't think so," he said.

"I was the one who got you out of that alley last night," Deran explained.

"Oh," the man said. He glanced down at the bandage on his thigh and grudgingly added, "Thank you."

"Are you a veteran?" Deran persisted, pointing a thumb at the man's red kilt.

"What business is it of yours?"

Deran's expression hardened—not because he was actually angry, but because it was a useful trick. It worried people, made them more likely to cooperate. Deran had needed more than a year to really get the hang of it.

"I needed to report why I was late getting back to barracks last night," he said. "The lieutenant gave me a hard time because I didn't know your name or who you were."

This was not true, but that bothered Deran not a whit.

"Oh," the man said again. He hesitated.

Deran glowered.

"My name's Tolthar of Smallgate," the man said. "And yes, I was in the guard, but they kicked me out for being drunk while on duty. About five years back."

That was a year or so before Deran had signed up. "*Were* you drunk?" he asked.

"Oh, I guess I was," Tolthar admitted, "but it wasn't my fault. We were walking the wall, and my buddy had a bottle with him, and that's so boring, what else was there to do but drink?"

Deran nodded. Drunkards always had an excuse; he knew that. And he knew how much weight to give it; just because the bottle was there didn't mean they had to drink it.

And he noticed that Tolthar didn't say that his "buddy" had been kicked out of the guard. From what Deran knew of the guard, he doubted that anyone would be expelled for being drunk on duty *once*.

But there was no point in arguing about it. Other matters were more interesting.

"So, who stabbed you?" he asked. "Pick the wrong girl, did you? Or did you make a grab for someone's purse?"

Tolthar frowned. "I don't want to say," he said. "I'll take care of it myself."

Deran frowned back. "You better not mean that the way it sounds," he warned. "We don't like it when citizens stab each other."

"I won't stab anyone," Tolthar mumbled. "That's not what I meant." His rather feeble wits recovered belatedly, and he added, "At least, I won't stab anyone with a *blade*."

"Oh, it *is* a girl, then?" Deran's frown turned to a wry smile. "Just make sure she says yes first, and means it."

Tolthar mumbled something Deran didn't catch.

They talked a few moments longer, saying nothing of any consequence; then Deran turned back to the stairs.

At the barracks he reported to the lieutenant on duty, and gave a warning about the rotten step. As he had expected, the lieutenant wanted to know why he had used the stairs.

Deran explained, not trying to quote the entire conversation, but simply describing the incident the night before and reporting Tolthar's name and that he refused to say who had stabbed him.

"He wouldn't say?"

"No."

"Why in Hell not?" the lieutenant demanded.

Deran turned up an empty palm.

"You think he's planning to ambush whoever it was?"

Deran shook his head. "No," he said, "Tolthar wasn't going to hurt anyone. He just didn't want to say who it was."

"Do you think there's anything odd going on?"

"No."

The lieutenant frowned, then shrugged. "Well, to Hell with him, then. I'll put it in the report and if anyone higher up cares, *they* can worry about it." He pulled a sheet of parchment from the box and began writing out his report.

CHAPTER 11

*T*abaea watched the man in the red kilt with interest as he downed the ale someone had bought him. She had been sure he would return to the tavern eventually, and here he was, just two days later.

He hadn't seen her, she was sure; she was wearing her working clothes, which is to say she had turned her black tunic and black skirt inside out, so the gold and red embroidery didn't show. Her feet were bare, for better traction.

The man she watched, on the other hand, wore heavy boots—badly worn boots—and the same greasy brown tunic and old red kilt he had worn when he attacked her.

He was walking better now—and so was she. His left leg looked stiff; hers felt loose and limber, more so than usual.

She understood it now, at least partially. As the drunk got his strength back, she lost hers.

At least, that was how it appeared. She was still stronger than normal, but less than she had been, and the decline in her vitality seemed to correlate with the healing process of the man's wounded leg.

So what would have happened if she had *killed* him? The dead *never* got their strength back.

And what if she killed someone *now*? Was the dagger's magic still potent, or had she wasted it on that minor flesh wound?

She was not about to go out and kill someone in cold blood to test out her knife; she had never killed anyone and didn't particularly care to start. But she might kill some*thing*. She thought that over carefully as she peered around the doorframe at the man she had stabbed.

That feeling of increased strength had been pleasant, while it lasted. She wanted it back.

She slipped away from the door of the Drunken Dragon and headed northwest on Wall Street, into Northangle.

Probably the easiest nonhuman creature to find—other than bugs or worms, which she didn't count—would be a rat, and she certainly wouldn't mind killing rats, but for one, they were hard to catch, and two, they were vicious, and three, a rat's strength added to her own wouldn't amount to very much—if that was, in fact, what the dagger's magic did. She might not even be able to tell anything had happened upon killing a rat.

She needed something bigger than that—a pig would do, or a goat, or a dog.

A dog . . .

Dogs were not particularly common in Ethshar, but Tabaea had met a few; watchdogs were an occupational hazard for burglars. Killing somebody's watchdog would be a pleasure.

Of course, she couldn't do it legally, but she even knew which dog she wanted to kill—a big black one that guarded a house in Morningside that she had once tried to rob, one night a year or so back when she had been feeling unusually ambitious. The damnable beast had waited until she was inside, then had *stalked* her through the house and almost cornered her, all in utter silence. It was only when she turned and fled that it had started barking and awakened its master.

This time, she would be ready for it, and it wouldn't get a *chance* to bark. She smiled unpleasantly to herself and stroked the hilt of the black dagger.

However, she was going in the wrong direction to reach Morningside. The district took its name from its location, just east of the overlord's palace, near the center of the city, while Northangle was against the city wall. Tabaea turned left at the next corner and headed south.

When she reached Morningside she found her way into the quiet residential neighborhood she sought, where fine houses lined either side of the street. Lintels and cornerposts were carved and painted; polished brass fittings gleamed on doors, shutters, and windows; walls were brick or stone, not plaster.

But there were still alleyways to the courtyards in the rear. Gates closed off the alleys, but Tabaea could sometimes climb gates, or squeeze between the bars.

This one, she remembered, was one she could climb.

The walk from the Drunken Dragon had taken almost an hour; getting through the gate and onto the roof of the kitchen took five minutes.

Tabaea knew that she had to hurry with this part; she was exposed as long as she was on the roof, and despite her black tunic and skirt, anyone staying up late who came out to the courtyard and glanced in the right direction might see her. She scampered up the slope, her bare toes hooking over the joints between tiles to keep her from slipping.

At the top she worked her way carefully along the wall, checking each of the three windows. All three were shuttered for the night; in the first, faint golden light shone between the slats, while the other two were dark.

Peering through the glass of the third window, she was pleased to discover that she could see cobwebs in the corners—the shutters had not been opened recently.

That was good. This was how she had entered previously, so she knew it to be a little-used storeroom; the cobwebs indicated that the occupants had not rearranged the household, or taken to checking the room. Quite probably, they didn't even know that a burglar had broken in before.

The window was locked, but she had brought her shim; she had the latch open in seconds. The hinges were stiff, and they creaked, but she swung the casement wide, ignoring the sound.

The latch on the shutters was even easier than the one on the casement; she flipped it up effortlessly and slid into the darkness of the house's interior.

The storeroom was just as she remembered it—linens and blankets stacked on painted shelves, a row of closed trunks along the wall on either side. The trunks were locked, but she had picked one when she was here before and found nothing but old clothing, broken toys, and the like.

She hadn't bothered with the others, and she didn't bother

with them now; instead she opened the door slowly and care-fully until she had a crack a few inches wide. She squeezed out through the narrow opening and emerged into the upstairs hall-way, alert for any sign of danger.

Light leaked out from under one of the other doors; she could hear voices, as well. No one was in sight, though, and she heard no footsteps, no clicking latches, no squeaking hinges.

Prowling a house while the residents were still awake was not part of her ordinary routine, but the voices gave her the distinct impression that those residents wouldn't be emerging right away. Besides, she was here, and she wanted to get it over with, before her nerve gave out.

Remember that strength, she told herself, and she crept to the top of the stairs.

Last time, she remembered, the dog had been hiding under the stairs. She had gone down to the dining salon, looking for silver or other valuables, and it had come out behind. Looking down toward the front room now she didn't see it—it was prob-ably lurking under the stairs again. She smiled, drew the black dagger, and started down the stairs, moving step by step, slowly and carefully, her eyes constantly shifting.

When she got to the bottom, the dog still hadn't emerged; she took three steps toward the dining salon—and then whirled, knife raised.

The dog was there, halfway out from its hiding place. It growled menacingly, and bared its teeth.

Tabaea didn't wait for it to attack, or to start barking; she jumped on it, knocking the animal to the floor.

The dog tried to get away, but she flung her left arm around its neck and hauled it closer. Without hesitating, she yanked its head back with her left arm and slashed its throat with her right.

Strength flowed into her like sudden fire; she slashed again, to be sure, and almost removed the dog's head—her arm was already stronger, *much* stronger.

And that wasn't all. The creature's vitality burned through her with a force that made the strongest *oushka* seem like a pale shadow, and when it reached her head the whole world seemed to change around her. For a moment all the color drained away, and then it was back, but washed out, like an old, faded tapestry. Meanwhile, outlines sharpened, and the darkness that filled the room seemed suddenly less. The last twitch of the dog's hind leg caught her attention far more sharply than motion ever had before; she almost started at the intensity of it.

And then the smells hit—the hot red stink of the dog's blood, the pungency of its fur, the oily reek of the polish on the wooden floor, the smoky odor of the lamp that was burning upstairs, a hundred, a thousand, a million other scents were spilling through her nose, so clear and sharp and distinct that they were like a painting of the house. It was like a banquet spread before her, each odor unique.

Her hearing was suddenly sharper, too—at any rate, she could hear the woman's voice upstairs say, "Did you hear something?"

The sound was distorted, though; she was unsure whether that was because of the distance and intervening corners and doors, or because something had changed about her hearing.

Whatever had happened, there could be no question that the Black Dagger's magic was not used up. Moving quickly, she rose and headed for the front door, the quickest way out, leaving the dead dog lying on the floor in its own blood.

She knew blood was all over her hands and tunic, as well, but she couldn't afford the time to do anything about it until she was well away from the house. She fumbled with the latch and bolt, then swung the door wide and stepped out onto the stoop.

The smells of the city washed over her like a great storm-driven wave, and she paused for a moment, drinking them in, sorting them out; then she remembered herself and ran.

As she worked her way north through the city streets, staying out of the better-lit areas where her bloodstained hands and clothes would show, she thought through what had happened.

She had killed a dog, and its strength had flooded into her, as she had hoped—but more than that had happened. She had gained the dog's senses, as well—the sensitivity to motion and strong night vision, the incredible sense of smell, and, she realized as she listened to the city around her, better hearing, but only in high pitches.

This was amazing; she had a whole new way of perceiving the city. She could smell things she had never smelled before—but she couldn't always identify them. She knew the salt was the sea, and the smoke came from the lamps and fires of the city; she knew the scents of men and women; but what was that odor like rust, like . . . she had no words for it.

Would this fade away gradually, she wondered, or was this permanent? The dog was dead, nothing could heal it, nothing could give it back its strength—but could she really keep it forever? She flexed her arms, feeling the power there—not, perhaps, any stronger than a big man, but far stronger than that of the young woman she had been an hour earlier, probably stronger than any woman she had ever known. She could feel it.

She could smell her own excitement, though it took her a moment to recognize it for what it was.

Was *that* permanent? Would she be able to use her nose like this for the rest of her life? She wasn't sure she would be able to sleep, with that flood of sensory impressions pouring in on her.

And all this came just from killing a dog. Think how strong she would be if she killed a man.

And think what she might be able to do if she killed a magician!

CHAPTER 12

The cat's death did little for Tabaea's strength, but it gave her incredibly quick reflexes, even sharper night vision and movement perception than killing the dog had provided, and perhaps some other abilities—she wasn't sure whether or not those were real, or her imagination at work. She had never heard that cats could speed up or slow down their perception of time and suspected it was simply an illusion. The ability to balance was very hard to judge. And the ability to catnap was probably there all along, just not used.

Still, she was satisfied with the results.

Killing a dove, on the other hand, was a serious disappointment; no matter what she did, Tabaea still could not fly, nor see behind herself without turning her head. Nor, it seemed, did birds have any abilities she hadn't known about.

It was perfectly clear *why* she couldn't fly, of course—she had no wings. Whatever magic the Black Dagger performed, it did not alter her physical appearance. Her eyes were still on the front of her head, rather than the sides; they had not become slitted like a cat's, either.

Only belatedly did she realize that this was a good thing—otherwise she might have grown fur or feathers or claws and become a freak unable to live a normal life among normal people.

Not, she admitted to herself, that her life was exactly normal. With her improved sense of smell, she could now locate gold by scent alone, and with her cat skills she could now prowl silently in near-total darkness, so her thievery had become markedly more successful—but she still had no permanent home, living instead in a succession of cheap inns; she had no real friends; she saw nothing of her family.

Her new abilities showed no signs of fading, and they gave her the money for a more comfortable existence, but as she sat at a table in yet another inn, staring at yet another six-bit dinner of chicken stew and fried noodles, she found herself profoundly dissatisfied.

She was becoming successful as a thief. But so what?

She had originally taken up a career in theft in order to survive and to put food in her belly without her mother's and stepfather's reluctant help. She had wanted to strike back at the family and the city that had ignored and neglected her. She had wanted to become rich, to have all the things she had been denied. She had wanted everyone to know who she was and to admire her skill and courage and determination.

She had discovered years ago that it didn't work that way. Thieves did not become rich or famous—at least, burglars and cutpurses didn't; there were those who accused various lords and magicians of robbery, but that was an entirely different sort of theft.

In fact, a thief couldn't *afford* to become rich or famous. Too great a success put one in front of the Minister of Justice, and then on the gallows or in a slaver's cells. Even the limited notoriety of being well known among other thieves was dangerous; Tabaea had, over the past few years, seen virtually every well-known thief arrested or beaten or killed. The world of thieves was not closed; word could always leak out into the larger world of victims and avengers. The less-successful criminals were always ready, willing, and even eager, from jealousy or simple hunger, to sell news of their more prosperous brethren.

So she dared not try for more than a reasonably comfortable existence—and even that was risky.

As for paying back her family and the rest of Ethshar, that didn't work, either. Her family had ignored her before, and they ignored her now. The city had always had thieves and paid no mind to another.

Theft was nothing but a means of survival, a career with no room for advancement. Now that she had the Black Dagger and knew how to use it, Tabaea was not satisfied with that. She wanted more.

But what?

She chewed idly on a noodle and thought about it.

She still wanted to be rich and famous and respected, to have everyone know who she was, and to pay attention to her every wish. She couldn't get that as a thief, but now she had the Black Dagger, so she could be more than a thief.

The question was, what could she be?

She still had never served an apprenticeship, and at nineteen she wasn't ever going to. She was even past normal recruiting age for the city guard.

She was strong and fast enough to be a soldier now, she realized, and she gave that possibility some serious thought. She was still small, but she knew she could prove herself if she had to.

And then what? Speed and strength were useful in war, but Ethshar was not at war, nor likely to be. Tabaea did not even have a very clear idea what war *was*. In peacetime the city guard served mostly to guard the people of Ethshar from each other, rather than from outside enemies; they guarded the gates, guarded the palace, patrolled the wall and the marketplace, ran errands for the nobility, escorted prisoners . . .

None of that sounded very exciting. And much of doing it well depended, she realized, not on actual strength, but on the *appearance* of strength, on being big and fearsome enough that people didn't start trouble in the first place.

She looked at the slender fingers holding her fork and grimaced. She didn't look big and fearsome.

Did soldiering pay well? The guard spent freely enough in the brothels and gambling dens of Soldiertown, but on the other hand they lived in the barracks towers, not in big houses, and they owned no fancy clothes, only uniforms and weapons.

And as far as fame went, Tabaea knew the names of half a dozen guardsmen, none of them officers, and those few only because she had encountered them personally. What sort of fame was that?

Soldiers carried swords, which was appealing, and they could rely on a warm bed and filling meals and a modicum of respect—but it did not seem like a really wonderful career, especially for a woman.

She scooped a greasy lump of chicken to her mouth and chewed.

She had food and a bed as a thief; those things were no incentive. And the guard would have no special use that she could see for her animal-derived talents.

Not the guard, then. What else?

Well, who *was* rich and famous?

The overlord was, of course, and the other nobles. But they had all been born into the nobility, a path that was not open to her.

There were rich and famous merchants, but they had had money to start out with, to buy their first cargos or finance their caravans, and most, if not all, had served apprenticeships in their trades.

There were the performers in the Arena, the jugglers and acrobats and singers and magicians.

There were the magicians, even those who did *not* perform—magicians of any sort could be assured of respect.

Performers . . . could she use her feline reflexes to become a juggler or acrobat? She knew that most learned their arts during apprenticeships, but if she could learn the skills on her own, they could not stop her from performing.

And as for magic—well, she was a magician already, wasn't she?

But she was not *openly* a magician.

She swallowed the chicken and started on a chunk of carrot, thinking.

She didn't know all that very much about magic, beyond the secret of athamezation—and of course, she had gotten that spell wrong when she tried to use it. Still, it seemed to her that magic had real possibilities. There were all those different kinds of magicians, for one thing—wizards and warlocks and witches, theurgists and demonologists and sorcerers, illusionists and herbalists and scientists, and all the others.

And with The Black Dagger, she could kill one of each and steal *all* their abilities!

Or could she? She frowned and swallowed the carrot.

At least part of magic was *knowledge*, rather than anything physical, and she didn't know whether the Black Dagger stole knowledge. She certainly hadn't learned anything from the minds of the dog or the cat or the dove—but perhaps beasts were too different.

She hadn't learned anything from the kilted drunk, either—but she hadn't killed him, she had only stabbed him in the leg. She had only acquired the strength he had lost, and even that had returned to him and departed from her as he healed. Stabbing him hadn't robbed him of any of his memories or wits.

Killing a person *would* steal those memories away, wouldn't it?

But would the Black Dagger transfer them to her, or would they simply be lost?

Or was knowledge part of the soul, of the part of a person that did not die? If the victim became a ghost, the ghost would still have its knowledge and memories—the dagger couldn't give them to Tabaea, then. If the victim's soul escaped into another realm, wouldn't it take the knowledge with it?

But then, it was said that certain magicks could even trap or destroy a person's soul—what if the Black Dagger was one of them?

Tabaea had to admit that she had no idea whether her magic knife could steal souls, or transfer knowledge. The only way to find out would be to kill a person, preferably a magician.

She pushed a lump of potato around the plate with her fork as she thought about that.

It would mean murder, cold-blooded murder. She had never killed a person. Killing dogs and cats was one thing, killing a person was quite another.

But then, how else would she ever know what the Black Dagger could do? How else would she ever become a magician, or anything more than a common thief?

She might make it as a performer just with the skills of animals—but then she would never know. And performing might not work.

And magic—she wanted more magic.

And she could have it, if memories transferred, and maybe even if they didn't. All she had to do was kill magicians with the Black Dagger.

Somewhere in the back of her mind it occurred to her that she had never seriously thought about murdering people before; she had never killed anyone in the course of her career as a thief. Cats, of course, were natural hunters and killers; dogs, too, were predators. She had absorbed abilities from a dog and a cat; might some of the predator's blood-lust come along?

She dismissed the idea.

So if she was going to kill magicians to steal their abilities, which magicians should she kill?

Sorcerers and wizards seemed to depend on their tools and formulae—sorcerers, in particular, seemed to need the talismans and artifacts. And wizardry might bring her in contact with the Wizards' Guild, and besides, she already knew that she could never make a proper athame—she had the Black Dagger *instead*.

So those were out.

That left demonologists and theurgists and witches and warlocks and herbalists and scientists and illusionists and plenty of others, of course.

Demonology looked risky—Tabaea thought it was significant that she had never seen an old demonologist.

Theurgists had to learn prayers and invocations and so forth to work their magic; if knowledge didn't convey, then that wouldn't work; she wouldn't know the rituals she needed.

Herbalists were so limited, with their plants, and like wizards and sorcerers, they were powerless without their supplies.

Illusionists just did tricks—there was some doubt as to whether it was real magic at all.

Scientists—Tabaea didn't understand scientists, and most of the scientific magic she had seen wasn't very useful, just stunts like using a glass to break sunlight into rainbows, or making those little chimes that spun around and rang when you burned candles under them. And there were so few scientists around, maybe a dozen in the entire city, that killing one seemed wasteful.

The various sorts of seers and soothsayers were a possibility, but telling the real ones from the frauds wasn't easy. Tabaea considered carefully as she finished her noodles, and decided in the end that prophecy could wait.

Ignoring the more obscure sorts of magician, that left witches and warlocks. They didn't seem to need equipment or incantations or anything, and they indisputably did real magic. One of them would do just fine.

How to find one, then?

She couldn't go entirely by appearance; while most varieties of magicians had traditional costumes, there were no hard and fast rules about it. Telling whether a black-robed figure was a demonologist or a warlock or a necromancer or something else entirely was not easy. She had been mistaken for a warlock once or twice herself, when wearing black—warlocks favored all-black clothes even more than demonologists did.

She knew a couple of magicians, of course, and knew *of* several others. She thought over all of them, trying to decide if there was one she wanted to kill.

No, there wasn't, not really . . .

She stopped, fork raised.

There was that snotty little Inza of Northangle, Inza the Apprentice she called herself now. She was two or three years younger than Tabaea, but she and Tabaea had played together when they were young. Then Inza had gotten herself apprenticed to a warlock, old Luris the Black, down on Wizard Street in Eastside, and after that she never had time to so much as say hello to her old friends. Inza claimed her master kept her too busy, but Tabaea knew it was because she didn't want to associate with a bunch of thieves and street people now that she was going to be a big important magician.

And Inza would be nearing the end of her apprenticeship now, she would be changing her name to Inza the Warlock soon.

If she lived that long.

Tabaea smiled, and her hand dropped from the table to the hilt of the Black Dagger.

CHAPTER 13

*L*ady Sarai leaned in the doorway and asked, "Anything interesting today?"

Captain Tikri looked up, startled; before he could do more than drop the report he was reading, Sarai added, "Don't bother to get up."

"Yes, my lady." He settled back and looked up at her uneasily.

"So, is there anything interesting in your reports today?" Sarai insisted.

"Oh." Tikri looked down at the paper. "As a matter of fact, there is one odd case. It's probably just a revenge killing, but . . . well, it's odd."

"Tell me about it." Sarai stepped into the office and found a chair, one with a dragon carved on the back and the seat upholstered in brown velvet.

"A girl named Inza, an apprentice warlock," Tikri said. "Her throat was cut last night while she slept, and then she was stabbed through the heart—to make sure she was dead, I suppose."

Sarai grimaced. "Sounds nasty," she said.

Tikri nodded. "I would say so, yes. I didn't go myself, but the reports . . . well, I'd say it was nasty."

Sarai frowned and leaned forward. "You said it was probably revenge? Who did it?"

Tikri shrugged. "We don't know who did it—not yet, anyway. Whoever it was came in through a window—pried open the latch, very professional job, looked like an experienced burglar—but then, nothing was stolen or disturbed, so it wasn't a burglary at all."

"Unless the thief panicked," Sarai suggested.

Tikri shook his head. "Panicked? Cutting the throat *and* a thrust through the heart doesn't look like anyone who would panic."

"So it was revenge—but you don't know who did it?"

"No." Tikri frowned. "Not yet, anyway. The girl's master swears she doesn't know of any enemies, anyone who hated Inza or had a grudge against her. Warlocks don't do divinations, of course, so she couldn't identify the killer herself; we have a wizard checking on it instead."

"You don't think it was the master herself?"

Tikri turned up an empty palm. "Who knows? But we don't have any reason to think it was her. And Luris is a skilled warlock; why cut the girl's throat when she could have simply stopped her heart? Or if a warlock wanted to be less obvious, she could have staged any number of plausible accidents."

"That's true." Sarai considered and tapped the arm of her chair as her feet stretched out in front of her—signs that she was thinking. "It's *very* odd, you know, that anyone would kill an apprentice warlock—isn't this Luris now duty-bound to avenge the girl's death?"

Tikri nodded. "Just so. Whoever did this isn't afraid of warlocks, obviously."

"And how could an apprentice have an enemy who hated her enough to kill her? Apprentices don't have time or freedom to make that sort of enemies, do they?"

"Not usually," Tikri agreed.

"How old was she?"

Tikri glanced at the report. "Seventeen," he said. "She would have made journeyman next month."

"Seventeen." Sarai bit her lip. She had been worried about her father, but he was almost sixty, he had had a long and full life. She had been worried about her brother, but he probably wouldn't die of his illness. If he did, if either of them died, it wouldn't be a shock. But a healthy seventeen-year-old girl, five years younger than Sarai herself, had been killed, without warning, apparently without any good reason.

"Has anyone talked to her family?" she asked.

Tikri shrugged. "I think someone sent a message," he said.

"I was also thinking of asking if anyone in her family knew if she had any enemies," Sarai remarked.

Tikri blinked. "Why bother?" he asked. "The magicians will tell us who did it."

Sarai nodded.

"Let me know what they find out," she said. She rose and turned away.

She had intended to stay and talk to Captain Tikri for a while. She didn't have any specific questions or assignments for him; she just thought it was a good idea to know what her subordinates were doing. She wanted to know everything about how the city guard worked, how crimes were investigated, how reports were written, what got included and what got left out— the *real* story, not what she would be told if she asked. She wanted Tikri to talk to her easily and not treat her as some lordly creature who couldn't be bothered with everyday details. Chatting with him had seemed like the best way to work toward that.

The news of the murder bothered her, though, and she no longer felt any interest in light conversation.

There were murders fairly often in Ethshar, of course—with hundreds of thousands of people packed inside the city walls, killings were inevitable. The annual total was often close to a hundred, even without counting the deaths that might have been either natural or magical.

Most of them, however, involved open arguments, drunken brawls, attempted robbery, or marital disputes. Someone breaking into a warlock's house to butcher a sleeping apprentice was definitely not typical.

But there really didn't seem to be much she could do about it just now.

Then a thought struck her, and she turned back. "You said a wizard is doing the divination for this one?"

"That's right." Tikri nodded.

"Who is it?"

"Mereth of the Golden Door. Do you . . ."

"Oh, her! Yes, I know her. Is she working at her home?"

"I think so, yes . . ."

Before Tikri could finish whatever he was going to say, Sarai cut him off. "Thanks," she said. Then she turned away and strode down the hallway.

She did not care to wait for an official report; she wanted to talk to Mereth and find out just what had happened, why this poor Inza had been killed. Mereth's home and shop were on Wizard Street, of course—at least three-fourths of all the magicians for hire in Ethshar of the Sands located their businesses on Wizard Street.

Wizard Street, however, was several miles long, winding its way across the entire city, from Westbeach to Northangle; simply saying a house was on Wizard Street didn't tell anyone much.

In Mereth's particular case, her shop was just three blocks from the palace in the district of Nightside, where Wizard Street made its closest approach; that was probably, Sarai knew, why Mereth got so much investigative work.

Or perhaps Mereth had chosen her home in order to be close to her preferred customers; Sarai really didn't know which was the ox and which was the wagon.

The weather was cool, but not unpleasant, and Sarai didn't bother with a wrap. She marched quickly across the bright stone pavement of the plaza surrounding the palace, across Circle Street, and out North Street—which, with the usual Ethsharitic disregard for unimportant details, ran west by northwest through Nightside, and not north through Shadyside.

Like all the neighborhoods close around the palace, Nightside was largely occupied by the mansions of successful merchants and the city's nobility; this portion of North Street ran between tall iron fences that guarded gardens and fountains. Sarai paid them no attention.

Harbor Street, being a major thoroughfare between the waterfront and Grandgate, was crowded and bustling where North Street intersected it, and was also far less aristocratic than its surroundings. As she crossed the avenue Sarai was jostled by a heavy man who reeked of fish; her hand fell automatically to her purse, but it was still there and seemed intact. If the man had been a cutpurse or pickpocket he had missed his grab.

At the corner of North and Wizard she turned left, and there was Mereth's shop, two doors down on the far side. The draperies were drawn and the windows closed, but the trademark gilded door was ajar.

Sarai hesitated on the threshold, listening; she could hear voices somewhere within, but could not make out the words. She knocked, and waited.

A moment later young Thar, Mereth's apprentice, appeared in the crack, peering out at her. He swung the door wide, but held a finger to his lips for silence.

Sarai nodded.

"She's working, Lady Sarai," Thar whispered. "Do you want to wait?"

"That depends," Sarai replied. "What's she working on?"

"A *murder*," Thar answered, his voice low but intense.

"Then it's probably the very thing I came to ask her about," Sarai said.

Thar blinked. "Inza the Apprentice?" he asked.

Sarai nodded.

"Do you want to come in and wait, then?"

"How much longer do you think it will be?"

Thar frowned. "I don't really know," he said. "To tell the truth, I thought she'd be done by now. I guess I misjudged, or maybe she's using a different spell from the usual—I don't know that much about it. I haven't started learning divinations yet myself. She says that if I keep on as well as I have been, though, I'll start on them after Festival."

Sarai nodded again. "So you don't know how long?"

"No."

The young noblewoman considered for a moment, then said, "I'll wait."

Thar nodded. He stepped aside and admitted her to the consulting room, small but cozy, where Sarai settled into a blue brocade armchair.

Thar hovered for a moment, making sure the important guest was comfortable, then vanished through the archway that led to the rest of the building.

Sarai waited, looking over the room. She had seen it before, of course, but she had little else to do.

There were three armchairs, blue, green, and gold, arranged around three sides of a small square table, a table of carved wood inlaid with golden curlicues. Eight little boxes stood on the table—gold, silver, brass, abalone, crystal, and three kinds of wood, all intricately carved and finely polished. Ink paintings hung on the walls, depicting rocky seashores, lonely towers, and other fanciful locations unlike anything in Ethshar of the Sands; Mereth had said once that these had been painted by her grandmother. An ornate wool rug in gold and red covered most of the floor; the rest was oiled wood. A shelf over the door held half a dozen mismatched statuettes, and a cork sculpture of a dragon wrapping itself around a peasant's farmhouse stood on the windowsill.

It was really a rather pretentious and fussy little room, Sarai thought. For lack of anything better to do, she turned her attention to a study of the ink paintings.

She had just about exhausted all possible interest in that when Mereth finally emerged, breathlessly hurrying through the archway, tunic awry and feet bare.

"Lady Sarai!" she said. "I didn't know you were coming! Sit down, sit down!"

"I've been sitting, thank you," Sarai said, as Thar stumbled after his mistress into the room.

"Oh, yes, of course you have," Mereth agreed, flustered. "Well, whatever you please, then. What can I do for you?"

"You were investigating the death of Inza, the apprentice warlock, I believe."

"Trying to, anyway," Mereth said.

Sarai waited.

Mereth sighed. "I can't see anything," she said. "Nothing works. Not the Spell of Omniscient Vision, not Fendel's Divination—*none* of my spells worked."

Those two spells, Sarai knew, were among the most powerful and useful information-gathering spells of all those known to wizardry; she suspected that between the two of them they provided more than half Mereth's income. "Is it because she was a warlock?" she asked. "I know different kinds of magic . . ."

"No, that's not it, or at least . . ." Mereth paused, collecting her thoughts, then explained, "The warlockry doesn't help, Lady Sarai, but I could get around that, I'm sure, if that was all there were. It isn't. She was killed by magic, *strong* magic—I can't tell what kind."

Sarai blinked. "She was killed with a knife, I thought—her throat was cut and she was stabbed."

"It might have been a knife," Mereth said, "or something else, I can't even tell that much. But I *do* know that whatever killed her was magical." Her tone was definite. "There's no possible doubt."

"But why would a magician kill anyone that way?" Lady Sarai asked. "I mean, aren't there spells . . . spells that leave no traces, or make it look like an accident?"

The wizard looked decidedly uncomfortable and did not answer.

Lady Sarai frowned at her silence. "Mereth," Sarai said, "I'm no fool; I've been the overlord's Minister of Investigation for four years now. I know that people who seriously offend wizards or warlocks or demonologists tend to turn up dead in fairly short order, even if, most of the time, we can never prove anything. People who bother warlocks have heart attacks, or fall from heights, or trip over their own feet and break their necks. People who fatally annoy wizards, I mean more than just enough to wind up with a curse like the Dismal Itch or Lugwiler's Haunting Phantasm, can have any number of strange accidents, but they seem especially prone to mysterious fires and smothering in their own blankets. People who are stupid enough to get demonologists angry usually just disappear completely. Witches don't seem to kill people; either that, or they're too subtle for us. Their enemies have plenty of bad luck, though, even if it isn't fatal. I'm not sure about sorcerers or theurgists or the others. But everyone knows it's bad business to anger magicians, *any* kind of magicians. *I* know that, my father knows that, the overlord himself knows that." She swallowed, remembering that her father had not angered any magicians, but had instead annoyed a god and was now dying as a result. Then she forged on. "Every man in the city guard knows that you don't anger magicians and expect to live. It's not our job to protect people when they cut their own throats. We know magicians kill people sometimes—it's so easy for you, after all. When the victims go asking for it, and the killers don't make a show of it, we don't worry too much. But in this case . . . Mereth, the girl was seventeen years old, never hurt anybody that we can see, and she got her throat cut. We *can't* let this one pass."

"I know, Lady Sarai," Mereth said unhappily. "But honestly, I swear, on my oath as a member of the Wizards' Guild, that I don't know what happened. I don't know why anyone would do it this way; you're right, there are other, easier, less-obvious spells. I don't know who did this, or why, or how; I only know that it was magic."

Sarai studied the wizard for a moment, then sighed.

"A rogue magician," she said. "Wonderful."

CHAPTER 14

*T*abaea stared at the mug and concentrated.

This would, she was sure, be easier if she had an older, more experienced warlock who could help her, could tell her what to do, but of course she could hardly tell any warlocks what she had done. She had to guess what she was supposed to do.

She had seen warlocks, in the taverns, in their shops, and in the Arena, and they had all been able to move things without touching them. That seemed to be the most basic ability that warlocks had. Inza had surely had it.

But how did it work?

Tabaea had no idea how to make it happen; despite her optimistic expectations, none of Inza's memories had transferred, none of what the apprentice had learned in her five years of training. If there were tricks or secrets to the warlock's arts, Tabaea didn't know them.

But Inza's raw magical ability should have transferred, the Black Dagger should have stolen it away and given it to Tabaea, and the only way Tabaea knew to test that was by *trying*. She *hoped* that warlockry worked just by thinking, by concentrating hard enough.

She stared at the empty mug. She stared so hard that her head began to hurt. Somewhere she thought she heard whispering, a muttering in some foreign language; she tried to ignore it.

She shouldn't be able to hear any whispers, she thought, annoyed—not here in this empty house in the middle of the night. She certainly couldn't have heard anything if she were still an ordinary person; this whisper was somehow alien. She supposed it was some trick of her newly enhanced senses, something that a dog could hear when a person wouldn't, but she couldn't think what it might be. Who would be speaking a strange tongue near here? She hadn't seen anyone around the place who didn't look Ethsharitic. And this was a *very* strange tongue, nothing she had ever heard before, she was sure.

Maybe it wasn't human at all. Still staring at the mug, she tried to make out the words and where it was coming from.

There were no words, she realized, and the whisper wasn't coming from *anywhere*. It seemed to be inside her own head.

Then, abruptly, as she focused on the whispering that wasn't really a sound at all, she felt as if something had touched her, or perhaps she had touched something, in a place that she could not locate, a part of her that didn't correspond to anywhere on or in her body. The whispering ran through her, and she could suddenly *feel* the mug, as well as see it, even though it was six feet away.

She could feel it with the whisper.

That made no sense, but that was how it felt; she could touch the whisper, and with it she could touch the mug.

She gripped it tentatively with her . . . her whatever-it-was. She took a deep breath, tightened her hold, and lifted.

The mug shot upward; startled, she threw her head back, eyes following its trajectory. Her mouth fell open and her eyes widened with surprise.

The mug whacked against the ceiling, and at the impact she lost her intangible hold on it. It tumbled down and smashed against the table, shattering spectacularly.

Tabaea stared at the spot on the ceiling where the mug had struck, and her openmouthed astonishment slowly transformed itself into a broad grin.

So *that* was warlockry!

It had worked. And she had liked it; it had felt *good*, had made her feel strong and awake, even stronger than she already was—and since killing Inza, she had roughly twice her former strength, she was no longer just a weak woman, but as strong as most grown men.

This was *great*! She only wished it hadn't taken four years to find out what the Black Dagger could do. She had a lot of lost time to make up for.

The dagger wouldn't teach her anything, apparently, wouldn't steal knowledge or memories, but it would take *power*. Strength, talent, skill—she could take any of those she wanted.

All she had to do was kill the people who had them.

Her grin dimmed.

She had to kill them, if she wanted to keep what she stole. That was the nasty part. She didn't like killing people, not really. It was true that Inza was a stuck-up little beast who had thought Tabaea was just gutter trash, but even so, *killing* her had probably been more than she deserved.

It had been a necessary experiment, of course, to prove the Black Dagger's power, and it had gotten Tabaea her wonderful new talent for warlockry, but still, it was nasty.

Well, Tabaea told herself, sometimes life was nasty. At least, from now on, she would be on the dispensing end of the nastiness, rather than the receiving.

She would pick and choose her victims carefully, though. There was no reason to kill large numbers of people. In fact, for raw strength, there was no reason to kill *people* at all—dogs and cats and other animals would serve just as well, perhaps better, for that.

But skills—agility and dexterity, and of course all the different schools of magic—those would come from people. Dogs and cats had no fingers and couldn't do anything much with their toes, they couldn't transfer anything involving tools, or that called for standing upright.

Scent and vision and hearing, yes—without those, she could hardly have located this empty house and been certain it was deserted. She knew that she would spot the owner's return before he suspected anything was wrong, or would hear or smell him before he got near her, and with her faster reflexes and increased speed she could be gone before he noticed her, and that was all due to the animals.

But for human skills, she needed to kill humans.

She looked down at the dagger on her belt and shrugged.

Well, she told herself, people died every day in Ethshar. Men bragged in the taverns about how many people they had slain. Magicians killed each other and any other enemies they might have. Demonologists sacrificed children or troublesome neighbors to their diabolic servants, and necromancers traded souls for the wisdom of the dead. Everyone knew all that. Surely, no one would notice a few more deaths.

It did occur to Tabaea, somewhere in the back of her mind, that while she always heard about all these horrible deaths, she had never *seen* one, and very few of the people she knew personally had died of anything other than natural causes.

If they *were* natural causes and not vindictive magic.

Well, it was a big city, and even if she had been lucky, everyone knew that people were murdered every day in Ethshar, stabbed or beaten in the Wall Street Field, poisoned or smothered in the lounges and bedrooms of the palace, roasted or petrified by wizards, or carried off to nameless dooms by demons and other supernatural creatures. No one would notice anything out of the ordinary if there were a few more deaths than usual.

That settled, the only questions remaining were who and when.

She had killed a warlock—she reached out and picked up the biggest chunk of the broken mug and sent it sailing in broad circles around the room, all without touching it; now that she knew how, it seemed to grow easier with every passing second. The next step would be either some other form of magic, or some vital, nonmagical skill—archery, perhaps, or swordsmanship. A soldier, then?

Yes, a soldier, but one who knew his trade, not just one of the fat, lazy bullies who guarded Grandgate by day and caroused in Soldiertown by night. An officer, perhaps—one who trained the new enlistees.

And then some more magicians—a demonologist, perhaps, and a theurgist. Even if they needed incantations, maybe she could learn those somewhere, listen to someone at work; it couldn't be that hard, once you had the gift, the skill, whatever it was that made them magicians instead of mere mortals. And then maybe a wizard, despite the Guild and her inability to make an athame, maybe two, they didn't all use the same spells, maybe she could learn something useful. A sorcerer, a witch . . .

She drew the dagger and looked at it.

"We're going to be busy," she said. She smiled. "And it'll be worth it."

CHAPTER 15

"*There's wizardry here,*" the witch said, kneeling by the body.

"You're sure it's wizardry and not some other magic?" Sarai asked from the doorway.

The witch frowned. "Well, my lady," he said, "it's either wizardry or something entirely new, and if it's something entirely new, it's something that's more like wizardry than it's like anything else we've ever known."

"So it could be something entirely new?"

The witch sighed as he got stiffly to his feet. He ran a bony hand through thinning hair.

"I don't know, Lady Sarai," he said. "I know that when warlockry first came along, when I was just finishing my apprenticeship, we had a hard time telling it from witchcraft at first, because there are similarities, and we didn't know the differences yet. I know that theurgy and demonology are opposite sides of the same coin, so that in some ways they look alike and in others they couldn't be more different. Whatever happened here feels like wizardry to me, but it might be that it's something new, and I just don't know the differences yet. But it *feels* like wizardry."

Sarai nodded.

"All right," she said. "Wizardry, then, or something like it. Can you tell me anything about the person who did it?"

The witch shook his head. "No," he said, "I'm afraid not. The magic fouls up everything else."

"Can you tell me anything more about the magic, then?" Sarai asked. "Would you know it if you met the murderer on the street?"

The witch tilted his head and considered that carefully. "I doubt it," he said at last. "What I sense here is the flavor of the single spell that killed him. It doesn't seem likely that the killer would be walking around with that spell still active. I'm not a wizard, but as I understand it, their spells are usually temporary things—they make them fresh each time, as it were."

Sarai nodded again. "But it's the same spell here as the others?"

The witch shrugged. "I think so," he said, "but I can't be absolutely certain. The others were not so recent when I saw them."

For a moment the two of them stood silently, staring at the bloody corpse on the floor. The body, in turn, was staring sightlessly at the ceiling.

"There's one thing," Sarai said. "You and the others all keep saying that a spell killed these people, but it's plain to see that a *knife* killed them. Do you mean that it was an enchanted dagger? That an ordinary knife was wielded by magic? That the dagger was conjured out of thin air?"

The witch hesitated. "I mean," he said, very carefully, "that whatever made the wounds was magical and that the life was drawn out by that magic. If it was a dagger, the dagger was enchanted; whether it was wielded by magic or by someone's hand I have no way of knowing."

"Very well, then," Sarai said, "suppose it's an enchanted dagger, and you happen to bump into someone on the street who's wearing that dagger on his belt. Would you know it?"

The witch hesitated even longer this time. "I doubt it," he

said at last. "But I think—I *think*—that if I saw someone use that dagger to cut someone, I would know it."

"Well, that's better than nothing," Sarai muttered.

"I would, of course, immediately inform you, my lady, if I saw anything of the sort."

"Of course," she said. "Or the nearest guardsman, or whoever."

"Of course."

Sarai turned and headed for the stairs.

This one was the worst yet, and for a very simple reason—she had known the victim. Serem the Wise was one of the best-known enchanters in Ethshar of the Sands—or rather, he had been; now he was nothing but a wandering ghost and a throat-slashed cadaver.

His apprentice—what was her name? Oh, yes, Lirrin. Lirrin was waiting at the foot of the stairs, looking pale and ill. Behind her, in the front parlor, Sarai could see Serem's famous fan-tree, waving away as if nothing had happened; trust old Serem to use solid, permanent enchantments, not the feeble sort that would have died with their creator.

Lirrin would be doing all right for herself, probably—as far as Sarai knew, there were no relatives with a stronger claim to any part of the estate than that of a new apprentice. If Serem had any children or siblings, they were long since grown, and any wives were dead, divorced, or disappeared. Under Ethsharitic custom, a child's welfare came before that of any adult other than a spouse, and Lirrin, at seventeen, was still officially a child. She would inherit the wizard's house and goods, including his Book of Spells and the contents of his workshop.

That might be a sufficient motive for murder, and despite Lirrin's display of grief Sarai might have suspected her, were it not for all the other deaths.

Inza the Apprentice Warlock had been the first, slain in her own bed, her throat slashed, a stab wound in her chest; then there had been Captain Deru, waylaid in an alley off Archer Street, stabbed in the back, and his throat slashed. Athaniel the Theurgist was jumped in his shop, his throat slashed, and a single thrust through his heart to finish him off. Karitha of East End, a demonologist, had been beaten into unconsciousness in her own parlor, her throat cut as she lay insensible.

Strangest of all, even as these murders had been taking place, a dozen animals, mostly stray cats or runaway dogs, had been found dead at various places in the Wall Street Field, with their throats cut open. Had they all been killed before Inza, then Sarai might have guessed the killer was working up his nerve, practicing before he dared risk tackling a human being, but they were not; instead, a dog and a cat had been killed shortly after Inza, the rest one by one in the days that followed, interspersed with the other victims.

And now old Serem was dead, on the floor of his bedchamber, stabbed in the belly, and—like all the rest—his throat had been cut.

And on all of them, men, women, and beasts, the magicians found lingering traces of a strange magic, probably wizardry, that blocked any divination or scrying spell.

Mereth swore she couldn't identify the killer. Okko could tell nothing of what had happened. Luris the Black had offered to help, to avenge her dead apprentice, but she was as useless as any warlock when it came to knowledge, rather than raw power.

And now this witch, Kelder of Quarter Street, had failed, as well.

"He hasn't killed any witches yet," Sarai remarked as she marched down the stairs. "One of you will probably be next; he seems to be trying for one of every sort of magician."

"There are still sorcerers, Lady Sarai," Kelder replied, "and the various lesser disciplines, the herbalists and scientists and illusionists."

"True," Sarai conceded. "Still, I'd lock my door, if I were you, and maybe invest in a few warding spells. Besides your own, I mean." Witches did not have any true warding spells of their own, she knew, but she also knew that witches didn't want outsiders to know it.

"Perhaps you're right, my lady," the witch agreed. "I would like to say that I don't fit the pattern in these killings, but in truth, I don't *see* a clear pattern."

"Neither do I," Sarai admitted.

That bothered her. There *ought* to be more of a pattern in who was killed, and how; criminals were usually abysmally unimaginative. This one, though . . .

They had no idea of any motive. The killer had slain the apprentice warlock, leaving Luris untouched, but here he or she had killed Serem, the master, and had left the apprentice, Lirrin, untouched. Athaniel had had no apprentice, nor, of course, had Deru, since the city guard did not operate on an apprenticeship system. Karitha's apprentice was a boy of fourteen who had been visiting his parents on their farm somewhere outside the city. Serem's apprentice inherited everything; Karitha's, due to the existence of the demonologist's husband and nine-year-old daughter, inherited nothing but a few papers and the right to stay on until Festival.

There was no pattern, no connecting motive, no common factor among the victims that Sarai had yet discovered.

Lirrin was inheriting a large and valuable house and a great deal of wealth, which would make an excellent motive, and she was a wizard of sorts, as well—could she have arranged the entire thing, staging the other killings in order to throw off suspicion? It was hard to believe that anyone could be so cold-blooded; besides, if that was it, she had been foolish to kill Inza and not Luris, thereby missing the chance to create a false pattern and divert suspicion onto Inza.

And why kill the dogs?

Besides, Karitha was killed by a very strong person—she had been picked up and flung against a wall at one point. And the killer had not been gentle with Deru or Athaniel, either. Lirrin scarcely looked strong enough to do anything like that. She wasn't as scrawny and underfed as some apprentices, but she still had more bone showing than muscle.

Of course, with magic, anything is possible . . .

Sarai realized that she had reached the bottom of the stairs and was now staring into Lirrin's face from a distance of only four or five feet.

"I'm sorry," Sarai said, trying to sound sincere.

She *was* sorry that Serem was dead, genuinely sorry, but right now she was thinking too hard about who might have killed him to get real emotion into her voice.

Lirrin grimaced. "I guess you see things like this all the time, Lady Sarai," she said, her voice unsteady.

"No," Sarai said. "No, I don't. Usually the guard takes care of . . . of deaths without calling me in. They're usually simple—someone lost his temper and is sitting there crying and confessing, or there are a dozen witnesses. If it's not that obvious, then we call in the magicians, and generally we have the perpetrator in the dungeons the next day." She sighed. "But this time," she said, "we seem to be dealing with a lunatic of some sort, one who uses magic that hides all his traces. So they called me in, because I'm supposed to be good at figuring these things out.

And I'm trying, Lirrin, I really am, but I just don't know how to catch this one."

"Oh," the apprentice—the *former* apprentice, Sarai reminded herself, since the apprenticeship was over and done, and Lirrin would have to prove herself worthy of journeyman status before the representatives of the Wizards' Guild, despite missing the final year of her studies—said, in a tiny voice.

Sarai hesitated before saying any more, but finally spoke. "Lirrin," she said, "you're Serem's heir, and that means you're responsible for his funeral rites. But before you build a pyre, I have a favor to ask, a big one."

"What?" Lirrin was clearly on the verge of tears.

"Could you summon a necromancer to see if someone can speak to Serem's ghost? His soul won't be free to flee to Heaven until his body is destroyed; if we can question him, ask who stabbed him—he must have seen who it was. He might not know a name, he might not remember everything—ghosts often don't—but anything he could tell us might help."

Lirrin blinked, and a tear spilled down one cheek. "You said there were others . . ."

Sarai sighed again.

"There were," she admitted, "but with the first few we didn't know it would be necessary until it was too late, until after the funeral. We did finally try with the demonologist; her soul was gone without a trace, probably taken by some demon she owed a debt to. We hope to do better with Serem. With your permission."

"Of course," Lirrin said weakly. "Of course."

The smoke from the pyre drifted lazily upward; the weather was starting to turn cooler again, and the air was clear, the sky a dazzling turquoise blue.

"Damn it," Sarai muttered.

Captain Tikri glanced sideways at her, then across at Lirrin. The apprentice seemed oblivious to everything but the burning remains of her master. The handful of friends and family in attendance were lost in their own thoughts or talking to one another.

"Troubled, Lady Sarai?" Tikri murmured.

"Of course I am!" she said in reply. "It's all so wasteful and stupid! Even this funeral—it's just empty ritual. His soul isn't even in there; there's nothing to be freed!"

"You're sure?"

"The necromancer was sure, anyway, or at least he said he was."

Tikri didn't reply for a moment; when he did, it was to ask, "Which sort of necromancer was it?"

"A wizard," Sarai answered. "Does it matter, though?"

Tikri shrugged, showing her an empty palm. "I don't know," he said. "It might. My Aunt Thithenna always used a theurgist to talk to Uncle Gar, after he died—at least, until the priest said she should leave him alone and let him enjoy the afterlife. Worked fine."

Sarai sighed. "Your Aunt Thithenna was lucky," she said. "Half the time theurgical necromancers can't find the one you want, even when there *isn't* any question of other magic. And demonological necromancers are worse—unless the ghost you want is a dead demonologist; they're lucky to contact one out of ten. Sorcerers and warlocks don't do necromancy at all— they're probably smart. It's a messy business. And as often as not the ghost doesn't remember anything useful."

"What about a witch, then?"

It was Sarai's turn to shrug.

"It's a little late now," she said. "I know theurgists and de-monologists don't need the body, but witches do, even more than wizards. I did have a witch look at him, though—Kelder of Quarter Street. You know him, don't you?"

Tikri thought for a moment, then nodded.

"Well, he's not a real necromancer," Sarai said. "But he couldn't see anything."

"Too bad." Tikri hesitated, and said, "There's news, though. I was going to wait until after the funeral to tell you, but maybe I should mention it now."

"Oh? What is it?"

"It's not good news."

Sarai sighed again. "In this case, I wasn't *expecting* good news. What is it, another body?"

"No, no," Tikri hastily assured her. "Not *that* bad."

"Not even a dog?"

Tikri shook his head.

"Well, then?" Sarai demanded.

"Well, it looks like we have more than one killer. Mereth and her apprentice were studying the traces in Athaniel's shop—the actual break-in was done by warlockry."

Sarai frowned. "But it wasn't warlockry that killed him. Mereth was sure of that."

Tikri nodded. "So if our killer is a wizard, he has a warlock working with him," he said.

"Maybe it's a warlock who's gotten hold of an enchanted dagger somewhere," Sarai suggested.

"Maybe," Tikri conceded. "But why would a warlock be doing any of this? A warlock can stop a man's heart without touching him; why cut throats?"

"Why would *anybody* do all this?" Sarai retorted.

"A demonologist making a sacrifice, maybe? Or a wizard collecting the ingredients for a spell?"

"And how would a demonologist or a wizard do warlockry?" Sarai started to take a deep breath to say more and accidentally caught a lungful of smoke from the pyre; she lost whatever she had intended to say in an extended coughing fit. Tikri stood silently by, waiting.

When she regained control of herself, Sarai was no longer thinking entirely about warlocks or motives; the coughing had reminded her of her father's failing health and poor Kalthon the Younger with his fits. Her family was not exactly robust or numerous anymore. She had to face the possibility that any day, she could find herself the new Minister of Justice permanently, not just filling in—and she would still be Minister of Investigation, as well.

As a girl, she had never expected to have this sort of responsibility; her father and brother were supposed to handle the Ministry of Justice, and back then there had been no Minister of Investigation yet. By rights, she shouldn't have had a government job at all; she should have been married off years ago to a wealthy merchant, or to some noble not too closely related to her. She should be raising chickens and sewing clothes and tending children, not standing here watching a murdered friend burn and worrying about who killed him instead of remembering his life.

The idea of being the overlord's investigator had sounded intriguing four years ago, but the idea of spending the rest of her life at it, at hunting down demented criminals and sadistic thugs, or worse, *failing* to hunt them down . . .

It was beginning to wear on her. She wondered how her father could stand going on being Minister of Justice, year after year.

But of course, maybe he couldn't stand it, maybe that was why he was dying.

And here before her was the body of a man who could have saved her father, and had refused. Maybe, Sarai thought bitterly, she should be applauding, instead of mourning.

Then she blinked, startled.

Could *that* be the killer's motive?

It wasn't at all likely that all the victims had wronged any one person by their actions, but might they have done so by inaction? Was there something the killer wanted that all of them, the warlock, the soldier, the theurgist, the demonologist, the wizard, had failed to provide?

It seemed like a reasonable possibility. It didn't explain the almost ritualistic throat-slashing, or the use of both warlockry and wizardry, though.

Sarai remembered that Tikri thought there was more than one killer involved. That made sense—the man who threw Athaniel and Karitha around had clearly been immensely strong and must have been large and muscular, while Inza's killer appeared to have slipped in through a window open only a few inches. Deru's killer had been big enough to kill him while he was awake, without leaving signs of a struggle, but had done so from the back—and an experienced old brawler like Deru would not have turned his back on anyone he considered a threat. That called for someone strong, but not big and burly.

But if there was more than one killer, why? Why would a group want to commit these murders? It seemed even less likely than an individual—unless it was some sort of conspiracy or cult at work.

Was there, perhaps, a secret conspiracy of magicians? Had Inza and Serem and the others been offered a chance to join, and been killed to insure their silence when they refused?

But why kill them all the same way, then? Was that a warning to others, perhaps? Or was it in fact a ritual? Was this a cult of some sort, perhaps followers of a demon that had somehow escaped from the Nether Void without coming under a demonologist's control? Or people enthralled by some wizardry, perhaps? There were wizards who could command elemental spirits or animals or ghosts—why not people? Or might the killers be ensorceled? Sarai had heard rumors, dating all the way back to the Great War, of sorcerers who could control the thoughts of others.

Cults and conspiracies—what was she up against? Could there be a cult of killers? She seemed to remember stories of such a thing.

"Tikri," she asked, "have you ever heard of an organization of assassins?"

"Do you mean the cult of Demerchan?" the soldier asked, startled.

Demerchan—that was the name. All she knew about it was vague legends and unfinished tales. "Do I? Could they be responsible for these killings?"

Tikri hesitated, then admitted, "I don't know."

"I don't either," Sarai muttered.

She didn't know—so she would just have to find out. And not just about Demerchan. There were magicians involved. She intended to check out the organizations of magicians that might be involved—the Wizards' Guild, the Council of Warlocks, the Brotherhood, the Sisterhood, the Hierarchy of Priests, and any others she could uncover.

"Tikri," she whispered, "I'm going to need several men. And women, too, probably."

Captain Tikri shot her a glance, then nodded.

CHAPTER 16

Four days later, a dozen blocks away, Tabaea lay back on the bed and stared up at the painted ceiling. This inn was a far cry from the dingy, malodorous places on Wall Street where she had spent most of her nights just a few months before. The sheets were clean, cool linen; the blanket was of fine wool, dyed a rich blue and embroidered with red and gold silk; the mattress was thick and soft, filled with the finest eiderdown.

No more burlap and straw for Tabaea the Thief, she told herself. *Three* fluffy pillows. A bottle of wine and a cut-glass goblet at her bedside, a fire on the hearth, and a bellpull in easy reach. Even the beams overhead were decorated, a design of red flowers and gold stars against a midnight blue background. The plaster between beams continued the blue, sprinkled with white stars and wisps of cloud.

She ought, she supposed, to be happy. She had more money than ever before in her life, she was stronger and healthier and more powerful than she had ever imagined she could be. She could take almost anything she wanted.

But she was not happy, and that "almost" was the reason why. There were things she wanted that she couldn't have. True, she had gotten away with half a dozen murders, but they had not all yielded the results she sought.

She had killed Inza, and now she could work warlockry—but only at an apprentice level, at least so far. And sometimes it felt so good doing it that it scared her; she knew nothing about it and was afraid she was doing something wrong, something that, even if it didn't harm her directly, would draw the attention—and the wrath—of the *real* warlocks, or, worse, of whatever it was that was responsible for the whispering she drew her power from.

She had killed Captain Deru, and with his strength added to the rest she was stronger than any man in Ethshar; she could wield a sword with the best of them and could put an arrow in a dog's eye at sixty paces; but she still *looked* like a half-starved, plain-faced girl, and no one stepped aside at her approach, and no one was intimidated by her bellow.

She had killed Athaniel, and that had done her no good at all; the gods still didn't listen when she prayed and still didn't come at her call. She didn't know the right formulae, the invocations, or the secret names; none of that had transferred.

She had killed Karitha and had discovered that demons were just as picky as gods in how they were summoned.

She had killed Serem, and she really wasn't even sure why, because by then she had known what would happen. She didn't know the incantations, the ingredients, or the mystic gestures. She didn't even know the names of any of the spells. And of course, she had no athame and could not make one; she had only the Black Dagger, instead.

Maybe the dagger was her reason for killing him, she thought, in frustration over his part in saddling her with it. True, it had given her power and strength, and it had saved her from that awful drunk, but it was so *maddening*, having this magic right there in her hands and not understanding any of it.

She hadn't really thought the dagger had influenced her at the time, but yes, she admitted to herself, it probably had something to do with it.

Whatever the reason, she had killed him, and it hadn't done any good.

And finally, just a few days before, she had killed a witch by the name of Kelder of Quarter Street. She had seen him at Serem's funeral and had followed him home. That had *some* result, anyway—she seemed to have acquired at least one new ability; she could feel odd, sometimes incomprehensible bits of sensation fairly often, especially when near other people.

She could not, however, make very much sense of them. She was no apprentice; she had no one to tell her what anything *meant*. When she sensed a wet heat from a man's thoughts, or an image of red velvet, or a tension like the air before a thunderstorm, what did that represent? The cool blackness from the potted daisies here in her room at the inn—was that normal? Did it mean they were thriving, or dying?

The truth was that she could gain more useful information about the world and its creatures through her canine sense of smell than through any of her supernatural abilities.

And her warlockry seemed to be getting worse. Not by itself; at first, she had thought she was just being distracted, or forgetting what she had managed to learn, but now, looking back on it, she was fairly certain that every time she had killed another magician, her warlockry had weakened. The effect was most noticeable when she added witchcraft to her collection of skills. Now she had to listen intently to find that whisper; it wasn't intruding uninvited as it had at first.

Did the different magicks interfere with each other, like kittens stumbling over their litter-mates?

If she had killed a witch *first*, could she have made sense of what she saw and felt? Would she be able to do more, even without training?

It was all rather discouraging. There was so much she didn't know. Here she had, at least in theory, the ability to perform five different kinds of magic, and she didn't know how to use *any* of them properly!

And no matter what she did, no matter how powerful, how fast, how perceptive she became, she still *looked* like a ragged half-grown thief, and those around her still treated her accordingly. She had had to pay cash in advance for this room, and the innkeeper had clearly been astonished when Tabaea had pulled out a handful of silver.

And she couldn't tell anyone about any of it; there was no one she could trust, no one she could talk to. If she ever admitted anything, they would all know that she was a murderer, and she'd be hanged.

It just wasn't working out the way she had thought it would.

There had to be something she could do to *make* it work, though. Maybe if she knew more about all the different kinds of magic, she thought, she would be able to get some use out of them. She couldn't just steal the knowledge, of course—the Black Dagger didn't work that way; she now knew that beyond any doubt, she would never *learn* anything from it.

And of course, she was too old to be an apprentice. She was nineteen, almost twenty.

But maybe, if she listened—she had superhuman hearing now, at least in the upper registers, thanks to a dozen dead animals. She could get in anywhere, with her lockpicking and house-breaking skills, her animal stealth, her stolen strength, and her warlockry.

If she crept into a magician's home and watched and listened, if she found a new apprentice just beginning his training . . .

It was certainly worth a try.

Moving like a cat—not figuratively, but literally—she leaped from the bed and crept to the door, then down the hall, down the stair, through the common room, and out into the gathering night.

CHAPTER 17

The legendary assassins' cult of Demerchan, Captain Tikri assured Lady Sarai, was quite real and headquartered somewhere in the Small Kingdoms; beyond that he knew nothing definite. At Lady Sarai's insistence, Tikri sent a well-funded agent to attempt to learn more.

Until the agent returned there was nothing else to be done about Demerchan, so Sarai turned her attention to other organizations, ones that happened to be closer at hand—the organizations that represented the different schools of magic. She knew of five—the Wizards' Guild, the Council of Warlocks, the Brotherhood, the Sisterhood, and the Hierarchy of Priests. Neither sorcerers nor demonologists nor any of the lesser sorts of magicians, such as herbalists or scientists, seemed to have any unifying body—at least, four years of research into magic had failed to find any sign of one operating in Ethshar.

Lady Sarai didn't think it was worth worrying about herbalists or the like, and she couldn't do much about the sorcerers or demonologists, but the five known groups definitely wanted attention—especially the wizards and warlocks, since the killers had left indications of wizardry and warlockry.

The Wizards' Guild was by far the most powerful of the organizations—*every* wizard was a member, bound by Guild rules, as well she knew. *Every* wizard in the World was responsible to his or her local Guildmaster.

Most people thought that the Guildmasters ran everything, but Sarai knew better. She had learned a year before that the Guildmasters, popularly believed to all be equals in the government of the Wizards' Guild, in fact answered to a select few called the Inner Circle—*that* secret, she was given to understand, could cost her her life if she were too free in its dissemination.

If she wanted to speak to someone with real power in the Wizards' Guild, she knew she should speak to a member of the Inner Circle—but if the very existence of the Inner Circle was secret, she could hardly expect anyone to tell her who was a member.

Serem the Wise might or might not have been a member; her informant thought that he had been. This particular rumor had come up in a discussion of Serem's apparent successor as the senior Guildmaster in Ethshar of the Sands—Telurinon of the Black Robe was definitely *not* a member of the Inner Circle and was said to have hopes of changing that.

But if Telurinon was not in the Inner Circle, was he *really* the city's senior member of the Guild?

Well, whether he was or not, he was her best possible contact with the Guild; she sent him a message asking if a private meeting could be arranged for her to speak to the Guild's representatives in Ethshar of the Sands.

While she waited for a reply, she considered the other organizations.

The Council of Warlocks was a much looser body than the Guild; while every warlock she spoke to seemed more or less to acknowledge its authority, at least within the city walls, no one mentioned rules or discipline or death threats when discussing the Council. The membership of the actual Council seemed to change fairly often—since it was nominally composed of the twenty most powerful warlocks in the city, its members were also the warlocks most likely to hear the Calling and vanish without notice.

She wasn't sure just who the current chairman was; Sarai was fairly certain that Mavis of Beachgate had left the city, either Called or fleeing southward by ship, hoping to get farther from Aldagmor before the Calling could claim her.

Luralla would know, though; she had the warlock called in and asked her to take a message to the chairman of the Council.

Those groups were the important two, but for the sake of thoroughness, Lady Sarai considered the others.

Only a minority of theurgists had any connection with the Hierarchy of Priests; Sarai wasn't sure whether that would have made them more or less suspicious under other circumstances. As it was, though, Okko happened to be the high priest, and Sarai simply couldn't take seriously the idea that he might be behind some fiendish conspiracy.

Still, she did go so far as to question him briefly while a witch by the name of Shala of the Green Eyes sat concealed in an adjoining room, watching for lies or any sign of guilt. Shala had been hired almost at random, after a walk down the western portion of Wizard Street—Sarai wanted to avoid using anyone Okko might recognize or might have had any chance to subvert.

Shala found no evidence that Okko was concealing anything and assured Sarai that the old theurgist was telling the truth when he swore he knew nothing about the murders he hadn't told Lady Sarai.

Of course, there might be another organization of theurgists— but really, theurgists committing murder? The gods didn't approve of that sort of thing.

That brought Sarai to the witches.

Witches had two organizations, segregated by sex—which

made no sense that Sarai could see, since she hadn't come across any differences between how witchcraft worked for men and how it worked for women. Neither of them was very structured—the Sisterhood generally chose their leaders by lot at erratic intervals, while the Brotherhood elected them annually, and there was no permanent hierarchy in either group. Between them, they included perhaps a third of the thousand or so witches in the city. The Sisterhood was somewhat larger than the Brotherhood—but then, Sarai had the impression that there were more female witches than male.

Of the witches she had dealt with, Sarai knew at least one was a member of the Sisterhood—Shirith of Ethshar, who had tried unsuccessfully to heal Lord Kalthon. There were no annoying delays while meetings were arranged; Shirith and her apprentice came when invited and met with Lady Sarai in the Great Council Chamber that same evening.

Sarai had chosen the council chamber, rather than one of the innumerable smaller rooms in the palace, to impress upon the witches just how important this was—and also because the chamber gave an impression of great privacy, even while Okko would be listening from a concealed room adjoining, and Mereth of the Golden Door would be watching by means of a scrying spell.

She dressed for the meeting in a nondescript tunic and skirt. She not only didn't wear the impressive robes of the Minister of Justice—she had had a set altered to fit her when first she found herself forced to act in her father's place—but she dressed far more simply than was her wont, to add to the air of secrecy.

The thought struck her as she straightened her skirt that she was probably entitled to some sort of formal costume as Minister of Investigation; she had never worried about it before, since it was not in the nature of the job to make public appearances.

Perhaps this plain black skirt and dark blue tunic would serve. Her mouth twisted in a semblance of a smile at the thought.

She could hear her father's labored breathing as she crossed to the door; Kalthon the Younger was asleep in his chamber, but their father was awake, lying on the couch—or at any rate, as awake as he ever was anymore.

She took a moment to kiss his brow, then left the apartments and hurried down the corridor.

She found the two witches waiting in the council chamber,

looking very small and alone in the two chairs they occupied of the hundred or so that the room held. Three red-kilted guards were standing watch, one at each door; Sarai dismissed them.

"Shirith," she said, when the doors had closed behind the guards, "I'm so glad you could come."

The elder witch rose and curtsied. When she stood again she smiled wryly, and said, "Perhaps, Lady Sarai, you have not yet realized just how unlikely any citizen of Ethshar is to ignore a summons to the Palace from the Acting Minister of Justice, especially one delivered by a member of the city guard in full uniform, including sword."

Sarai had not thought of it in those terms. She had sent a soldier because he was handy—most of the officials of the overlord's government used the city guard for their errands outside the palace.

To an ordinary citizen, though . . .

Well, she saw Shirith's point. And perhaps it was just as well; she had wanted to impress the witches with the severity of the situation, after all.

"Do you know why you're here?" Sarai asked. She knew the more skilled and powerful witches could hear the thoughts in people's heads, if they tried, and Shirith was undoubtedly skilled.

"Do you want me to?" Shirith countered. "Ah, I see you do, if only to save time. I'm sorry, Lady Sarai, but I'm afraid that . . . oh."

She paused, then said, "The killings. Poor Kelder."

Sarai nodded.

"If you could tell me more, Lady Sarai . . ." Shirith began.

Lady Sarai explained quickly, well aware that Shirith was filling in missing details with her witchcraft.

"I'm afraid," Shirith said at last, "that I can't help you. We in the Sisterhood are naturally concerned, even though Kelder was obviously not one of our members. I can attest that I am in no way involved in these killings, nor is any member of the Sisterhood with whom I have spoken in the past month. Your theurgist will confirm that I speak the truth; I don't know what the wizard's spell will show, but if it tests veracity, then that, too, should support me."

So much, Sarai thought, for secrecy.

"Well," Shirith said apologetically, "once I start listening to what lies behind your words, I can't always help hearing more than you might want."

Sarai waved that away. "It doesn't matter," she said, "and I didn't really suppose that the Sisterhood was behind the murders. Can you vouch for the Brotherhood, as well?"

"Not as definitely," Shirith admitted, "but I can send their leaders to you for questioning."

Sarai nodded. "That would be useful. Do you have any other suggestions? Anything you would advise me to do to track down these killers who use both wizardry and warlockry?"

Shirith shook her head. "No," she said, then added, "it's odd, that combination; wizards and warlocks have distrusted each other since the Night of Madness, and from what I've heard, warlockry fits better elsewhere."

"What do you mean?" Sarai asked. Then she remembered something Kelder had said, when the two of them were studying Serem's corpse.

"Well," Shirith said, "it appears, from all I've heard, that witchcraft and warlockry are much more closely related to each other than either one is to wizardry."

"I've heard that, too," Sarai admitted.

"Do you know who you might want to talk to?" Shirith suggested. "Teneria of Fishertown, from Ethshar of the Spices. The word in the Sisterhood is that she's made some remarkable discoveries about connections between witchcraft and warlockry—especially remarkable, since she's still only a journeyman."

"Thank you," Sarai said, making a mental note of the name. "I'll do that."

In the three days that followed Sarai spoke to a four-man delegation from the Brotherhood and removed that group from suspicion, as well. She sent a messenger by sea to Ethshar of the Spices, to fetch this Teneria of Fishertown. She had notices circulated to demonologists, sorcerers, and other magicians of various kinds that she sought any information they could provide about whoever was responsible for the recent murders.

But she received no reply from either the Council of Warlocks or the Wizards' Guild, nor did she learn who had killed those men, women, and dogs.

CHAPTER 18

There had been no killings for three sixnights, but Sarai did not believe anyone was safe. The conspirators, whoever they were, might just be lying low, or perhaps the phase of the greater moon might be related, in which case the next murder could occur at any moment.

And during this lull there had been some very curious break-ins. No one was harmed, nothing stolen, but several magicians of different sorts, alerted by Sarai's far-flung inquiries, had reported signs that they had been spied upon, their workshops entered, their books read. What's more, the signs left by these strange invasions had included traces of wizardry, warlockry, and even witchcraft. This last had prompted further questioning of Shirith and several other witches, but again, all swore to their innocence, and other magicians said those oaths were truthful.

Sarai was convinced that these break-ins were the work of the murderous conspiracy, but she still had no idea what the conspirators were up to. Furthermore, she still had not met with the Council of Warlocks or the representatives of the Wizards' Guild.

With all this going on, she really did not much care that Lord Tollern, Minister of the Treasury, was not happy with her. Finding the killers and unmasking the conspiracy was more important than money. Money was only worth what it could buy, and when she hired magicians and sent ships to Ethshar of the Spices and so forth, Sarai was buying information.

"That's all very well," Lord Tollern told her, "but you can't spend the city's entire treasury on this."

"Why not?" Sarai demanded.

"Because we need it for other things, as well. Oh, I don't deny that this conspiracy is dangerous, Lady Sarai, I don't deny it at all, not for a moment. But it isn't the *only* danger that old Ederd has to worry about. What good will it do to stop these

119

mysterious magical murderers, if it allows common thieves to run amok, or we let the walls fall into ruin, or the harbor silt up so that no ships can dock?''

"I'm not spending *that* much!'' Sarai protested.

"No,'' Tollern admitted, "but this isn't anything we've budgeted for, you see. My dear, can't you find some way to settle this whole matter quickly?''

"How?'' Sarai asked. "I'm doing the best I can, but I can't even get the Wizards' Guild to talk to me.''

"My dear Lady Sarai, you're Minister of Investigation and Acting Minister of Justice; surely you can *order* them to talk to you, in the name of our beloved Ederd the Fourth. Even the Wizards' Guild would not be quick to refuse a command from the overlord himself. Defy one of the triumvirs of the Hegemony? That's a risky business, even for a magician.''

Sarai hesitated. She knew the treasurer was technically correct, but she hadn't dared to directly invoke the overlord's name before. Any power used too often was power wasted, and she knew that Ederd did not take kindly to those who called upon his authority too freely. Up until now, people had cooperated willingly—or had been intimidated much more easily; as Shirith had pointed out, most citizens did not care to argue with soldiers sent by one of the government ministers.

"I'll think about it,'' she replied.

The following day she sent not a lone messenger, but a squad commanded by a lieutenant, to *order* the Council of Warlocks, in the name of Ederd, Overlord of Ethshar, to wait upon the Minister of Investigation in the Great Council Chamber, at a time to be mutually agreed upon.

The reply arrived that same evening; the meeting was held the following day.

She prepared for the meeting in her family's apartments, gathering her wits and her notes, trying not to look at her father as he lay unconscious in his bed. This time, acting in the overlord's name, there would be no pretense of privacy or informality; she wore the attire of a Minister of Justice.

It occurred to her, as she made the turn into the broad marble passage that led from the outer apartments into the central mass of the palace, that she should have arranged for attendants to accompany her—when she entered the justice chamber in her father's place she was always preceded by Chanden the bailiff and Okko the theurgist and a couple of guardsmen and followed by the door guards. The overlord himself, when entering a room on official business, might have a retinue of anywhere from a handful of bodyguards to a parade of a hundred soldiers and officials. As Minister of Investigation, Sarai realized, she was surely entitled to bring a couple of guards and her chief of staff, Captain Tikri.

She couldn't very well bring Okko, since as before, he and Mereth were to spy on the meeting, but some guards would have been a good idea.

Well, she wouldn't worry about it. She had put Tikri in charge of arranging seating and keeping an eye on the warlocks, so he wouldn't be available in any case.

When she reached the council chamber there were guards posted outside the door—Tikri's work, of course. One stood on either side of the gilded archway; each was a big man, in his best uniform of mustard yellow tunic and bright red kilt, and each carried a gold-shod spear with a very nasty, practical-looking barbed head. At the sight of Lady Sarai they snapped to attention and thumped their heavy spears on the stone floor.

They did not, however, open the door; Sarai hesitated.

As she did, a small door in the side of the passage opened, and a servant in the overlord's livery stepped out.

"Lady Sarai," he said, bowing low. "Just a moment, and we'll have your way prepared."

Sarai blinked. Tikri had apparently been more thorough than she had expected. "Is everyone here?" she asked.

The servant said, "We have twenty people here who have identified themselves as the Council of Warlocks. That's all I know, my lady."

"Thank you," Sarai said. "What needs to be prepared, then?"

"You'll have to ask Captain Tikri, my lady."

Before she could ask another question she heard footsteps and turned to find a party approaching. Captain Tikri was in the lead, with half a dozen soldiers in gleaming breastplates marching at his heels, while two minor palace officials hurried alongside.

It appeared that even if *she* hadn't thought of providing an entourage, Tikri had.

"Are you ready, my lady?" Tikri asked.

Sarai, smiling, nodded.

Two soldiers stepped forward and flung open the doors; one

of the officials stepped in and proclaimed loudly, "Stand and obey! Behold the Lady Sarai, Minister of Investigation and Acting Minister of Justice to Ederd the Fourth, Overlord of Ethshar of the Sands, Triumvir of the Hegemony of the Three Ethshars, Commander of the Holy Armies and Defender of the Gods! Bow to the overlord's chosen representative!"

He stepped aside, and two other soldiers marched in and up to the low dais at the far end. Lady Sarai, picking up her cue, followed them; behind her came the other official, Tikri, and the two remaining guards.

The two who had opened the doors now closed them, from the inside, and took up positions as guards, while the official who had announced her hurried around the side of the room.

Sarai walked slowly up the aisle, keeping her eyes straight ahead, but she still got a good look at her audience.

All of them wore the monochromatic robes and peculiar hats that had somehow become the accepted occupational garb for magicians of every sort; for most of them, the single color was black, but she saw one in red velvet, one in dark green, and two in shades of blue. There were old men and youths, ancient crones and handsome young women. She saw a few familiar faces, but mostly strange ones.

And all of them bowed, as ordered. Lord Tollern had been right; they were cowed.

At least, for the moment.

She reached the dais and made her way to the center; there she turned and faced the crowd, waiting while her entourage took up positions around her.

The official who had announced her had now made his way around the room to one of the front corners; he bellowed, "By courtesy of the Lady Sarai, you may be seated!"

It wasn't really very different from presiding over her father's court, once she got started—right down to listening to feeble excuses.

"I swear, my lady, we had every intention of meeting with you," the chairman insisted—Vengar the Warlock, he called himself, and Sarai did not recall ever meeting him or hearing his name before this. "It was simply a matter of logistics; there are twenty of us, after all, each with his or her own schedule, each with his or her own concerns, and coordinating such a meeting . . ." He didn't finish the sentence; instead, he said, "We had not realized the importance you attached to it. We have nothing to tell you as a group that we have not told your agents separately; none of us are involved in these killings; and at any rate, the deaths have stopped, have they not?" He glanced uneasily at the door guards, and asked, "Or have there been others we were not informed of?"

"There have been none of these killings reported for three sixnights," Sarai confirmed. "However, there could be more at any time, and the overlord's government cannot tolerate such things."

"Of course," Vengar agreed. "But what has this to do with us? We are no part of Lord Ederd's government."

"No," Sarai agreed, "but at least one of your people, a warlock, is involved in the killings."

"Who says so?" a younger warlock demanded—Sirinita of somewhere, Sarai thought her name was.

"Kelder of Quarter Street," Sarai replied. "A first-rate witch who was aiding me in my investigations. He assured me that both wizardry and warlockry were involved."

"Why doesn't he speak for himself?" Sirinita called angrily.

"Because he's dead," Sarai answered, just as angrily. "He was the last victim—that we know of."

"How convenient!" Sirinita replied, her voice dripping sarcasm.

This disrespect was too much for some of the other warlocks, provoking a shocked murmur from several of them. "My apologies, Lady Sarai," Vengar said, throwing a furious glance at Sirinita. "You are sure of this? A warlock was involved in the killings?"

"Quite sure," Sarai replied.

Vengar frowned. "I regret to say," he said, "that we are still unable to help you. Ours is purely a physical magic; we have no way to read the thoughts or memories of other warlocks, and we do not spy on each other. It may well be that one or more warlocks participated in these crimes; it may even be that those participants were among the warlocks of Ethshar of the Sands, and as such nominally subject to this council. Still, we have no knowledge of them, nor any means of obtaining such knowledge."

"You're certain of that?" Sarai asked.

"I swear it," Vengar answered.

"You all say so? You all swear it?"

There was a general mutter of agreement, but Sarai was not

satisfied; she went through the entire score, one by one. All gave their oaths that they knew nothing about the murders that Sarai did not.

Finally, the vows complete, Sarai announced, "I accept your word. Still, you claim to represent the warlocks of this city, and that means that you are partially responsible for them, as well. I therefore charge you all to tell me at once if you learn anything more, and further, I hereby require, in the overlord's name, that if at any point in this investigation I call upon the services of the Council of Warlocks, that those services will be forthcoming. It doesn't have to be any of *you* who does what I ask—send your journeymen, your apprentices, whoever you please, but when I call, I expect cooperation." This speech was composed on the spur of the moment; she was up against a magically gifted multiple murderer, who might reasonably be expected to be very dangerous. Knowing that she could call on several powerful warlocks would be reassuring. "Is that clear?" she asked.

Sirinita spoke up again. "Who are *you*," she demanded, "to give orders to the Council of Warlocks?"

"I," Sarah answered, "am Minister of Investigation and Acting Minister of Justice to Ederd the Fourth, Overlord of Ethshar of the Sands, Triumvir of the Hegemony of the Three Ethshars, Commander of the Holy Armies—which means that I have those holy armies, which is to say the city guard, at my disposal."

"You seek to frighten us with mere soldiers?" Sirinita sneered.

"Not exactly," Sarai said. "I hope to frighten you with the knowledge that if you defy me, you'll be forced to use your warlockry over and over to defend yourselves for as long as you stay in this city—and we all know what happens when a warlock uses a little too much of his magic, don't we? The twenty of you are the most powerful warlocks in the city—but you and I realize what most people do not, that that also makes you the twenty most vulnerable to the Calling. True, you'll easily be able to defeat a dozen guardsmen apiece, but I have several thousand soldiers I can send and send and send, until the Calling does my work for me. And there's nothing south of here but ocean; if you try to flee farther from Aldagmor, that means the Small Kingdoms far to the east, or the Pirate Towns to the west—is that really what you want?"

She stared questioningly at them; no one answered.

After a moment of silence, Sarai said, "I don't like making

threats, you know; I'm not trying to make enemies of you, any of you. I'm just explaining that I *do* know who and what you are, and that I *will* have your cooperation, one way or another. This investigation is very, very important to me.''

There was a reluctant mutter of acknowledgment.

With that, Sarai dismissed eighteen of the warlocks, but asked Vengar and Sirinita to stay for a moment.

"Sirinita," she said in a low voice, when the others had gone, "I don't know why you seem so displeased that the overlord's government should require the cooperation of the Council of Warlocks. Is there some personal issue at stake here?''

Sirinita, a magnificent creature who looked scarcely older than Sarai but far more powerful, and who stood several inches taller, peered down her nose at the noblewoman. "I became a warlock," she said, "because I was tired of being told what I could and couldn't do. I worked my way up to the Council at an earlier age than anyone else for the same reason. And I *still* don't like it.''

Sarai sighed. "I will keep that in mind, then.'' She dismissed them both; she had only wanted Vengar as a witness and restraint on Sirinita, should she prove dangerous.

Then, for several minutes, she sat on the edge of the dais, thinking.

She had completely forgotten her entourage until Captain Tikri cleared his throat. She looked up.

"Yes?'' she asked.

"My lady,'' Tikri said, "one of my men reports that a stranger wishes to speak with you.''

Sarai blinked up at him. "What sort of a stranger?''

Tikri shrugged. "He's dressed as a magician,'' he said. "That's all we know. That, and that he knew where to find you.''

"Send him in,'' Sarai said, puzzled.

The moment she spoke, the door at the back of the council chamber opened, and a figure in white appeared. Sarai watched silently as he approached.

He was a man of medium height, heavily built, wearing a robe of fine white linen; a hood hid any hair, and his weathered face was clean-shaven—Sarai could not remember ever before seeing a man so obviously mature without so much as a mustache.

He stopped a few feet away, looking down at her. He did not bow.

"I am Abran of Demerchan," he announced.

Sarai stared silently up at him.

"It has come to the attention of our organization, Lady Sarai," Abran said, speaking slowly and clearly, as if he were reciting a prepared speech in a language not his own, "that you suspect we are responsible for a series of unnatural deaths that have taken place in this city. I am here on behalf of Demerchan to address this suspicion."

"Go on," Sarai told him.

Abran nodded, and said, "You know of Demerchan as a cult of assassins; that description is inadequate, at best, but it is true that at times we have slain outsiders. However, we have not struck down any of those whose slayer you seek. I swear, by my name and by all the gods, that Demerchan had no part in the deaths of Inza the Apprentice, Captain Deru of the Guard, Athaniel the Theurgist, Karitha of the East End, Serem the Wise, or Kelder of Quarter Street. If you doubt me, consider that Demerchan has existed for centuries—why, then, should we suddenly kill these, and in this new and noticeable way?"

"Any number of possible reasons," Sarai answered, a little surprised by her own courage in answering this intimidating figure. "Someone could have hired you, for example."

"But none did," the spokesman for Demerchan replied. "You have your concealed magicians who can tell truth from falsehood; they will tell you I speak the truth."

Sarai was rather annoyed by this; what was the point of putting Okko in another room if everyone knew he was there? "There are spells that can fool any magician," she remarked.

"I need no such spells," Abran insisted. "I promise you, if we of Demerchan had sought to remove these people, none of you would ever know that their deaths had not been mere happenstance and coincidence. We are not so obvious as this new power that stalks your city; our ways are subtle and various."

"That's what you *claim*," Sarai said.

For the first time, Abran allowed himself to appear visibly annoyed.

"Yes," he said, "that is what we claim, and we make this claim because we know it to be true. Why would we want to slay these people? None of them had troubled us; indeed, we do not trouble ourselves with Ethshar of the Sands at all, in the normal course of events. Our interests lie farther east.''

"Maybe you're extending those interests," Tikri suggested from behind him. "Things have been pretty stirred up in the Small Kingdoms lately—that's where you people operate, isn't it? But the Empire of Vond has been changing things . . .''

"Even if we were troubled by Vond, which we are not, why would Demerchan want anything to do with Ethshar of the Sands?" Abran asked.

"I don't know," Sarai admitted.

"Lady Sarai," Tikri said, "regardless of whether he's responsible for these mysterious deaths, hasn't this man just admitted that he's part of a conspiracy of murderers?"

Sarai, somewhat startled, realized that Abran had, indeed, done just that. She nodded to Tikri, who started forward.

Before the captain could touch the white-robed figure, however, Abran raised his hands, spoke a single strange word, and vanished.

"Damn," Tikri said, stopping short.

Sarai bit her lip. This was magic, of course.

Well, she had some of that available herself, just now. "Okko! Mereth!" she called. "Did you see where Abran went? Is he still here, invisible?"

"Keep the doors closed!" Tikri called.

Okko's voice sounded from his hiding place. "I find no trace of him."

And no trace was ever found—a search of the room turned up nothing, a hastily summoned witch could detect no sign that anyone fitting Abran's description had ever been in the Great Council Chamber. A canvass of the inns failed to locate any such visiting foreigner.

Okko and Mereth agreed that he had been there, however, and Okko said that there had been no sign at any time in the conversation that Abran was lying.

When Sarai finally retired, late that night, she was unsure just what she had seen and spoken to, unsure whether to believe what he had told her—but all in all, she thought that he was most likely just what he said he was, that he had spoken the simple truth, and departed by means of a prepared spell of some sort.

If so, then Demerchan was not responsible, nor, she believed, were any of the other magicians' groups—except, perhaps, the Wizards' Guild.

CHAPTER 19

Teneria of Fishertown arrived the next day, a thin, solemn young woman Sarai judged to be not yet twenty.

Sarai had intended to arrange a meeting with representatives of the Wizards' Guild, rather as she had with the Council of Warlocks, but the witch's arrival distracted her from that; instead, she settled down in Captain Tikri's office and chatted with Teneria about the connections and differences between witchcraft and warlockry—or tried to.

"I understand you're a witch, but that you're supposed to be expert on the other sorts of magicians," Sarai said.

Teneria shook her head. "Not *all* magicians, my lady. It just happens that a little over a year ago I found myself in the company of a warlock for a time, and the two of us discovered some interesting things about our two varieties of magic. Where most magicks conflict one with another, we found that we could make ours work together, and thereby become more than the sum of their parts. So since then I've tried to study the interactions between witchcraft and the other magicks—but I haven't learned much, yet. I've been too busy earning a living and living my life."

Sarai nodded. "What became of the warlock, then?"

Teneria hesitated. "He went to Aldagmor," she said at last.

Sarai blinked.

"Went to Aldagmor?" Captain Tikri asked. "How do you mean . . . ?"

Teneria shrugged, and Sarai waved Tikri to silence. "Went to Aldagmor" surely meant that he was drawn by the Calling, and was gone forever; no warlock ever returned from Aldagmor. If Teneria's interest in him had been personal, as well as professional, the subject was probably a painful one, and it didn't seem relevant to the matter at hand.

The conversation continued, and the two were just getting

comfortable with one another when a knock sounded on the office door.

Tikri answered it, as Sarai and Teneria watched. They heard a woman's voice say, "Hello, Captain; I wasn't sure you were in, your door isn't usually closed."

Sarai recognized the voice. "That's Mereth of the Golden Door," she told Teneria. "She's a wizard specializing in divinations."

"What can I do for you, wizard?" Tikri asked.

"I just wanted to be sure that Lady Sarai wouldn't be needing me today," Mereth replied. "I have a meeting to go to . . ."

Tikri glanced at Lady Sarai, who frowned. What sort of a meeting was Mereth talking about? "Bring her in," she told the captain.

Tikri opened the door and motioned for Mereth to enter; she stepped in, looked around the cluttered little room, and spotted Sarai and Teneria. Teneria rose from her chair.

"Oh, hello, Lady Sarai," she said cheerfully.

"Good morning, Mereth," Sarai answered. "I'd like you to meet Teneria of Fishertown; she's a witch who will be helping us investigate the murders. From Ethshar of the Spices."

"Oh," Mereth said, startled. "You're bringing in foreign advisers, too?"

"Yes, I thought . . ." Sarai stopped in midsentence. Something about the way Mereth had phrased her question had belatedly caught her attention. "What do you mean, 'too'?" she asked.

Mereth looked flustered. "Well, I mean the Wizards' Guild has been sending for experts as part of *their* investigations—there's a wizard from the Small Kingdoms called Tobas of Telven who's due to arrive any day now, and a witch who works with him named Karanissa of the Mountains."

"A witch?" Sarai asked. A witch working with a wizard? She glanced at Teneria.

Mereth shrugged. "That's what I heard. And they're trying to find Fendel the Great: they hope they can convince him to come out of retirement . . ."

Sarai started; even before she became Minister of Investigation and began seriously studying magic, she had heard of Fendel the Great. She had thought he was long dead. "Wait a minute," Sarai said. "What do they want with these people? What do you mean, '*their* investigations'?"

"Well, I mean their investigation of the murders, of course, Lady Sarai. After all, it involves wizards—someone murdered a Guildmaster, and that means that everyone responsible must die as quickly and horribly as possible, and then there's the fact that whoever did it used wizardry, and the Guild doesn't allow anyone to use wizardry except real wizards, and besides, the magic involved might be an entirely new spell, and the Guild . . ."

"*And they didn't* tell *me*?" Sarai shouted.

Mereth, cowed, blinking at her silently.

"What's this meeting you were going to?" Sarai demanded. "Is it connected with this?"

Mereth nodded. "I'm supposed to meet the Guildmasters at the Cap and Dagger and tell them what I know from helping you," she explained timidly. "Ordinarily I suppose they'd use the Guildhouse, but they . . ."

"When?" Sarai demanded.

"Noon."

"Where is this Cap and Dagger? That's an inn?"

Mereth nodded. "On Gate Street, between Wizard and Arena," she said.

"Good," Sarai said, rising from her chair. "Captain Tikri, I want as many guardsmen as you can find to accompany me; Teneria, I would appreciate it if you would join us. Mereth, I am going with you to this meeting."

"I don't . . ." Mereth began uncertainly.

"I didn't ask," Sarai snapped.

An hour later, as noon approached, Mereth walked up Gate Street with a burly soldier on either side; immediately behind her came Sarai and Teneria, and following the two of them came Captain Tikri at the head of three dozen uniformed men. The normal midday traffic stepped aside as this formidable party approached, and they arrived unhindered at the door of a large and elegant inn, where a signboard above the door displayed a silver dagger across a red-and-gold wizard's cap.

At Sarai's order, soldiers flung open the door of the inn and marched in with swords drawn.

Close behind them, Sarai marched into the common room and found a dozen astonished men and women in magician's robes looking up at this unexpected intrusion. She saw Algarin of Longwall, Heremon the Mage, and a few other familiar faces among them.

"What is the meaning of this?" demanded an elderly man

Sarai recognized as Telurinon, the senior Guildmaster. "You're interrupting a private gathering, young woman."

Sarai announced, "Guildmaster Telurinon, you will address me properly. I am Lady Sarai, Acting Minister of Justice, and you are all under suspicion of treason."

That created a stir, during which Sarai stepped into the room and allowed Mereth, Teneria, Tikri, and the other soldiers to enter, crowding the good-sized room.

"What are you talking about?" Telurinon demanded. A soldier thrust the point of his sword toward the wizard's throat, and Telurinon belatedly and begrudgingly added, "My lady."

"I am talking about what appears to be deliberate subversion of the criminal-justice system of this city," Sarai explained. "You wizards have been withholding information from the Minister of Investigation, refusing to speak with her, while using undue influence on her employees to obtain the results of her own efforts."

"Aren't *you* the Minister of Investigation?" someone asked.

Sarai nodded. "That's right," she said, "but right now I'm here as Minister of Justice—since you all chose to ignore my invitations as Minister of Investigation."

"What's going on?" a white-haired wizard asked. "I thought we were all here because some rogue was using wizardry without our leave; I want no part of treason."

"You are all here," Sarai said, "because someone, or some group, is responsible for killing half a dozen innocent citizens of Ethshar, most of them magicians. It's my belief that this is the work of some sort of cult or conspiracy, one that is based on magic, and because of that I formally requested the assistance of the Wizards' Guild to help me find those guilty of these crimes, so that they may be stopped. My requests were ignored."

"Why don't you find them yourself?" Algarin shouted. "You claim to be the overlord's investigator—investigate it yourself, then!"

"I have," Sarai replied angrily.

"From what I've heard so far, you've hired a bunch of magicians to investigate, you haven't done anything yourself!"

"And just what would you suggest I do?" Sarai demanded.

"*I* don't know," Algarin replied. "I'm a wizard, and while I may have worked for your father a few times, I don't pretend to be an investigator!"

"Then don't tell me how to do my job," Sarai retorted. "I've investigated this. We've questioned everyone connected with the victims, everyone who was involved; we've looked at all the evidence we can find."

"Ha! You're just taking credit for work that was done by magicians—wizards, mostly!"

"I'm not taking credit for anything," Sarai answered. "There's no credit to take—we haven't caught the people behind these killings. And that's why I'm asking everyone here to help, to tell me anything you can that might help."

"Why should we?"

"Why *shouldn't* you?" Sarai put her hands to her hips and shouted angrily, "This conspiracy, if that's what it is, killed one of your own Guildmasters! Don't you want Serem the Wise avenged? Aren't you worried that you might be next? Or with all this talk about credit, are you worried that wizards might get the *blame* for these killings? It's wizardry that's at the heart of them, as far as we can determine—is the Guild covering something up?"

"*You're* the one who's covering up!" the wizard shouted back. "*You're* the one who isn't getting her job done! And it's *because* it's magicians getting killed, *because* you want the Wizards' Guild to take the blame!"

"What the hell are you talking about?" another wizard asked, before Sarai could reply.

"It's true!" Algarin insisted. "She's jealous of us all, jealous of our magic! We solve far more crimes with our spells than she does with her so-called investigations, and she's jealous!"

Telurinon, who had stood silently during this argument, spoke again. "I believe I see the reason for this baseless charge of treason. She's Lord Kalthon's daughter; he's ill, probably dying, and we've refused to heal him—the Guild does not heal aristocrats, as you all know, and perhaps Lady Sarai resents that. I've heard these nobles claim we're all playing at being gods and getting above ourselves when we make such rules; maybe the lady would like to put us back in our place."

Captain Tikri's fingers were closed on the hilt of his sword, but Sarai put out a hand and stopped him before he could draw it. "No violence," she whispered, "not with so much magic here."

With Lady Sarai thus distracted for a moment, Mereth tried to speak in her defense; other voices rose in protest against

Telurinon's words as well, and in seconds the entire room was a chaos of shouting and arguing voices. Fists waved in the air; none, so far, had been aimed at anyone.

"You have no right to blame us because you can't find the people responsible!" someone shouted at Sarai.

"I'm *not* blaming you!" Sarai shouted back. "I'm just asking you to help me find them!"

She let the bickering continue for a moment longer, but when it showed no sign of reaching any conclusion, Sarai shouted over the hubbub, "Guildmaster Telurinon! Whatever my reasons, the charge stands and requires an answer—why did you refuse my request for a meeting and the Guild's assistance in this?"

Telurinon turned back to face her, abandoning his argument with other Guildmasters.

"Because, my lady," he said, "this is a matter that the Wizards' Guild wishes to handle on its own. Someone has killed a Guildmaster; we cannot allow that person to be brought before the overlord's courts, or thrown in the overlord's dungeon—whoever it is must die, as horribly and publicly as possible, as a direct result of our Guild's actions."

"Well, damn it," Lady Sarai shouted, "why didn't you meet with me and *say* so?"

The argument died away, as the wizards turned to listen.

"I have no problem with recognizing the Guild's claim to vengeance," Sarai said. "The overlord's government makes no claims to priority in these matters. I would be delighted to arrange terms whereby, in exchange for the Guild's *full cooperation*, I would, as Acting Minister of Justice, turn the guilty parties over to the Guild for execution."

Telurinon blinked stupidly at her.

"Well, there, Telurinon," Heremon called. "I *told* you you were being hasty." Several other voices murmured agreement.

"You barged in here, accused us of treason . . ." Telurinon began.

"I had to get your attention," Sarai retorted. "You were ignoring me."

"You brought all these soldiers . . ."

"I can send them away. If you'll agree that we'll all sit down together and pool our information, and that henceforth I am to be kept informed of everything the Guild learns about this matter and every action it takes concerning it, then I'll send the soldiers away.'' She smiled at Telurinon. ''What do you say, Guildmaster?''

Telurinon turned helplessly to the other wizards; a moment later, with Telurinon abstaining and only Algarin dissenting, they had agreed to do as Sarai suggested.

Swords were sheathed and the soldiers dismissed, all save Captain Tikri and two others who remained as Sarai's assistant and bodyguards. Mereth, Sarai, Teneria, and Tikri found seats, and the meeting began.

The discussion started well enough; Sarai gave an account of the known crimes to date and let Mereth report on what her spells had shown her. Then Sarai spoke again, mentioning that both wizardry and warlockry had been involved.

''We were aware of that, my lady,'' Telurinon said chidingly.

Sarai ignored him and recounted the other meetings she had held with Okko and the witches and warlocks; Mereth confirmed what she said. The wizards seemed to be especially interested in the evidence that the Council of Warlocks knew nothing about the killings and had no magic that could help.

For their part, the wizards reported that they knew little about the actual killings beyond the fact that the murders had involved magic. A necromancer by the name of Thengor reported that his own studies indicated no theurgical or demonological involvement and that the souls of the victims were nowhere in the World, while some of the others expressed doubts about the accuracy of any necromantic reports.

''We did discover,'' Heremon said, when Thengor had finished, ''that whatever magic was involved is a sort of *negative* wizardry—it appeared to counteract any wizardry used in its presence. Guildmaster Serem did not come by his cognomen 'the Wise' entirely without earning it; while he was notoriously careless about the usual wards and warning spells, he had cast several personal protective spells upon himself. The murderer's weapon seems to have instantaneously nullified all of them when it struck.''

That was interesting, and something Sarai had not known; she leaned forward attentively.

''That's why we sent for Tobas,'' Algarin said.

Sarai looked at him questioningly, but it was Heremon who explained, ''Tobas of Telven is a young wizard who has made a specialty of the study of counterwizardries, of spells that prevent other spells from functioning. He lives in the Small Kingdoms, but Guildmaster Telurinon has invited him to join us here in Ethshar, to see if he can tell us anything about the magic this killer uses."

Sarai nodded.

That seemed to conclude the exchange of information; the Guild had gotten no further in actually determining the identity of the killers than Sarai had. Accordingly, Sarai and Telurinon threw the meeting open to speculation.

"Lady Sarai, you said it might be a cult," a woman asked. "I know what Thengor told us, but do you think it might be demonologists after all? Maybe it's the demons themselves using the other magicks—they can do that, can't they?"

"What kind of a cult?" another voice demanded.

"I don't know," Sarai replied. "A cult of assassins, maybe . . ."

"Demerchan!" The name was repeated by half a dozen voices.

"No," Sarai said, "I don't think so." She described her unexpected visit from Abran of Demerchan. Mereth confirmed her account.

"Maybe it's the Empire of Vond that's behind the killings," a woman suggested. "Wasn't Vond himself supposed to be some sort of superwarlock?"

"Call in the Vondish ambassador, Lady Sarai! Demand an explanation!"

"No, it's Demerchan!"

Several voices chimed in with their opinions, and for a moment, chaos reigned.

"What could Vond hope to gain by killing those six people?"

"Fear!"

"Magic!"

"They knew too much!"

"It's a sacrifice to a demon!"

"Not Demerchan, Vond! Vond is doing it to disrupt and weaken the Hegemony!"

"Demerchan is killing them to prepare the way to take over the city!"

"It's a conspiracy that's trying to overthrow the overlord!"

The discussion deteriorated into several small arguments, and Sarai prepared to take her leave; she had made her point and learned about as much as she could reasonably expect to learn.

And while the wizards argued and Lady Sarai straightened

her skirt, Tabaea the Thief crouched in the shadows a few yards away at the top of the staircase, safely out of sight, listening.

Learning about this meeting had been easy; two different wizards had mentioned it in her hearing as she spied on them. Getting in to eavesdrop, however, had been more difficult. She had thought about trying to slip in under some false identity, perhaps as one of the inn's maids, but had lost her nerve, and instead settled for breaking in through an attic window and hiding at the top of the stairs.

She had been late in arriving and had fled temporarily when all the soldiers marched in, but even when she abandoned her post in the shadows, Tabaea had the ears of a cat—or rather, several cats, and a bird, and several dogs. She had missed some of the discussion and couldn't see what going on from her chosen place of concealment, but she heard most of it.

They were blaming the Empire of Vond for the killings, which was crazy—that was way off at the other end of the World, wasn't it? And they were blaming the cult of Demerchan, whatever that was. They were blaming demonologists, and the Council of Warlocks, and even each other. They were blaming Lady Sarai for not catching the killer. They were blaming demons and monsters and just about everything except the Northern Empire. Someone even suggested that spriggans, those squeaky little green creatures like the one that had startled her in Serem's house so long ago, were not the harmless little nuisances they appeared to be, but diabolical killers working under the direction of some renegade archimage.

Tabaea smiled broadly at that. Spriggans, killing people? The idea of spriggans as deliberate murderers was completely absurd.

Lady Sarai was leaving, and someone named Teneria of Fishertown was going with her. Teneria had not said much of anything, but Tabaea had heard someone explain that she was a witch who knew about ways witchcraft and warlockry were related.

Tabaea wished Teneria had spoken up more. After all, Tabaea had both the warlock talent and some witch's skills and would have liked learning more about them.

Not that she was still as ignorant as she had been when she began. She had listened to warlocks and witches as they talked among themselves and as they lectured their apprentices. She knew that warlockry came down to two abilities, the ability to move things without touching them and the ability to create or remove heat and that everything else was just applications of those. She knew that warlocks had infinite power available and that they drew on a mysterious source somewhere in the wilderness of southern Aldagmor, far to the northeast. She knew about the Calling—she didn't know what it was, nobody did, but she knew that any warlock who used too much power was irresistibly drawn to the mysterious source of that power and never seen again. She knew that the first warning of the Call would be nightmares, and she had sworn that if she ever again had a nightmare she would give up warlockry.

As for witchcraft, that drew its power from the witch's heart and belly, which was why witches were so limited in what they could do. A witch could die of exhaustion doing tasks a warlock or wizard would find easy. Witches, therefore, had learned subtlety, had learned to use knowledge more than power—but Tabaea had only the power and not the knowledge, and she wasn't sure she had the patience to learn.

It did occur to her that thanks to the Black Dagger, she surely had more raw strength in her heart and gut than any other witch who had ever lived; still, she was not sure of how to use it. She wasn't really sure how to use *any* of her stolen skills and strengths, though she was learning.

Tabaea found it very amusing that the magicians all thought she was a conspiracy, rather than an individual; she giggled quietly into the palm of her hand. Little Tabaea the Thief, a World-spanning conspiracy of evil?

Besides, she wasn't evil, not really; she just wanted her share of the good things in life. She wanted to be on top, instead of on the bottom.

One of the wizards had suggested that the conspirators intended to overthrow the overlord and take over the city. Tabaea hadn't thought of that.

Overthrow the overlord? Rule Ethshar of the Sands?

She liked that idea. She liked it very much indeed. The entire city at her beck and call? Servants to fulfill her every whim? Her choice of the baubles and pretties on Luxury Street, or of the handsome men of Morningside? What a lovely thought—Tabaea the First, Overlord of Ethshar!

No, not overlord—that wasn't enough. The overlord ruled as part of the triumvirate and as first among the lords; she wanted to rule on her own, like the monarchs in the Small Kingdoms. Rather than overlord, she would be queen! Queen of Ethshar!

And why stop with the city? Why not conquer the entire World and be empress? She was not giggling anymore; she was starting to take the idea seriously. Why not?

Well, because she was just one woman, that was why. She had her magical powers, of course—she was stronger, more powerful than anyone. She knew, from her eavesdropping and some careful experimentation, that most magic could not work against her: The Black Dagger seemed to nullify any wizardry; she had warlockry of her own, and the one thing a warlock's power couldn't seem to touch was another warlock; witchcraft could not directly defeat her because she was stronger than any other witch; theurgy was inherently nonviolent and therefore could not harm her.

Sorcery was still an unknown, though; demonology and some of the minor arts were mysteries, too. And she was not at all sure what would happen if someone managed to get at her with an ordinary weapon. It was not likely that anyone ever could, given her stolen senses and strength and speed—but on the other hand, she still had to sleep sometimes.

But who had to know any of that?

Conquer the city . . .

She would, she decided, have to think this over very carefully indeed.

Moving as silently as a cat, she hurried away, back to the window she had left open, and then out to the open air.

CHAPTER 20

*S*arai sat dejectedly in Captain Tikri's office. She had spent the day taking Teneria the witch and Luralla the warlock to the scenes of the various murders, hoping that Teneria might be able to learn something useful with her unique understanding of how witchcraft and warlockry were related; Luralla had been along more as a power source for Teneria than anything else.

The net result was nothing; Teneria could do no more than

confirm what other witches had already learned. Wizardry and warlockry had been used, and the murderer had left no psychic traces.

Sarai gathered from Teneria that this last was unusual, but just what it meant was not clear. Some witches could choose not to leave traces; warlocks often left no traces, but did not appear to have any voluntary control over it; some spells that wizards used could hide or erase traces. Which of those applied here, Teneria could not say.

The witch was off to her room in the palace now, to refresh herself a little, and Luralla had gone home, leaving Sarai and Tikri in the office. A spriggan had followed them back to the palace; Sarai shooed it away with a shove of her toe, and the little creature backed away, but did not leave the room.

"I hate this," she muttered to herself. "I should be tending my father, or listening to his cases for him. There must be a sixnight's backlog by now."

"Then why don't you go handle some of them?" Captain Tikri asked from behind her. She turned, startled. "I couldn't help hearing," he said, not very apologetically at all.

"That's all right," she said. "I *should* go—but I couldn't concentrate on it."

"You might want to try, though—a distraction might help clear your thoughts on this whole mess."

Sarai stared at Tikri for a moment, then nodded. "Maybe you're right," she said. "I should . . ."

"Excuse me," an unfamiliar voice said.

Startled, Sarai turned around and found a small man in a nondescript brown tunic and breeches standing in the doorway.

"Yes?" she asked.

"I'm Kelder of Tazmor," the man said, speaking with a curious accent. "I got your message."

Sarai paused to gather her wits somewhat before she asked, "What message?" The accent, she realized, was Sardironese.

"Ah . . . you *are* Lady Sarai, aren't you?" Kelder asked.

"Yes, I am," Sarai admitted. "But I still . . ."

"You sent messengers to Sardiron," the little man said, "asking for help in solving a series of murders—didn't you?"

"Oh, yes, that message," Sarai said. "Of course. And you . . . ?"

"I'm a sorcerer," Kelder explained. "A forensic sorcerer. When I got your message I came south as quickly as I could."

"Oh, I see; and you've just arrived? Do you need a place to stay? I'm sure a room . . ."

"No, no," Kelder assured her. "I have a very comfortable room at an inn out by Grandgate; I arrived in the city several days ago."

"Oh. And you've been seeing the city?" Sarai asked.

Kelder nodded. "You might say that, Lady Sarai. You see, I've been investigating these murders independently—I didn't want to allow myself to be influenced by any preconceived notions you might have. This is the sort of study where my specialty can really shine, Lady Sarai. I think that the use of forensic sorcery has been shamefully neglected in Ethshar, not just in this city, but throughout the entire Hegemony. To the best of my knowledge, you haven't consulted any sorcerers on this case."

"Forensic sorcery?" She glanced at Tikri, who shrugged. "I didn't know there was such a thing."

"It's rather a neglected field," Kelder admitted.

"I *did* talk to sorcerers, you know," Sarai said. "None of them were able to help."

Kelder shrugged. "Ethsharitic sorcerers," he said scornfully. "Amateurs."

"And you're a professional?" Tikri demanded.

"I like to think so," Kelder said, a trifle smugly. "I've been studying forensic sorcery ever since I was an apprentice. In general, Sardironese sorcery is considerably more advanced than anything you have here."

"The Northern taint," Tikri remarked.

"Yes, exactly," Kelder agreed, ignoring the captain's insulting tone. "The Baronies of Sardiron, and especially my homeland of Tazmor, were part of the Northern Empire throughout the Great War. Thanks to the relics of the Empire, we have far more to work with than you Southerners."

"So you've come south to show us how it's done?" Tikri suggested sarcastically.

"No," Kelder said, still unoffended. "I was at Sardiron of the Waters when Lady Sarai's messengers arrived, looking for information about cults or conspiracies, maybe involving surviving Northerners, and I thought I might be able to help."

Tikri glanced at Sarai. "You thought we might be dealing

with Northerners? My lady, they've all been dead for two hundred years!''

Sarai shrugged. "We *think* they've all been dead for two hundred years," she said. "The World is a big place."

"Oh, I think they have," Kelder said.

"So, sorcerer," Tikri said, "you know something about cults and conspiracies?"

"No," Kelder said, "but I know forensic sorcery. So I came here and studied the places where the killings occurred—I confess, it wasn't until I followed you and those other two women today that I was sure I had located them all. And of course, I was too late to study the bodies, unfortunately."

Sarai looked at him with renewed interest. The funny little man with the northern accent was full of surprises. "You followed us?" she asked.

The sorcerer nodded.

"Do you think you learned something?" she asked.

"Yes, my lady," he said.

"And what might that be?" Tikri asked. "Was sorcery involved in these crimes?"

"Not that I know of," Kelder said, "but that doesn't mean very much. Sorcery doesn't always leave traces. But I did learn that there were four people who had, prior to today, been in each room where a person was murdered."

"Four?" Sarai stared. "So it *was* a conspiracy . . ."

"Yes, four, my lady, two men and two women, but it was not necessarily a conspiracy. I could not determine the exact *times* that these people were there, only that they had been. And I have identified one of the four as the final victim, the witch Kelder of Quarter Street—I assume that he visited the rooms in the course of investigating the crimes. One or more of the others might have been legitimate visitors as well, perhaps even among the other investigators. Should all three prove to have been there for other reasons, then perhaps *that* will prove that there was more than one murderer. Have your investigations found anyone who visited all those places?"

Sarai blinked. "Well, *I* did, after the killings."

"Yes, of course," Kelder agreed, "I should have expected that. Then I assume one of the two women was yourself—might I test that hypothesis, please?"

"How?"

"With this talisman." He drew a flat silver object from inside his tunic and held it out. A circle of milky crystal was set into the center of a metal oblong roughly the size of Captain Tikri's hand. "If you would be so kind as to touch your fingertip to the white disk . . ."

Sarai glanced at Captain Tikri, who shrugged. Then she reached out and touched the crystal.

"Thank you. And do you perhaps . . ."

"I was in all of them," Tikri interrupted.

"Ah. Then could you . . . ?" Kelder held out the talisman again.

Tikri glanced at Sarai.

"Do it," she said.

Tikri obeyed, tapping one forefinger lightly on the white crystal.

"Thank you, sir." Kelder pulled the talisman away and closed both his hands around it, holding it near his chest, not quite touching the fabric of his tunic. He stared down at it for a moment, stroking the metal with his thumbs, clearly concentrating hard.

Sarai watched with interest; she had rarely seen sorcery in action before, and nothing at all like this.

After roughly a minute and a half, the little Sardironese looked up at Sarai again.

"It's definite," he said. "You, Lady Sarai, were one of the women, and the captain here was the other man. There is evidence that the two of you, and my late namesake, all visited the sites *after* the other woman. I therefore suspect that this other woman is connected with the crimes. Unless there was another . . ."

Sarai shook her head. "I can't think of any other woman who visited all the rooms before I took Teneria and Luralla around this morning," she said. "Mereth saw some of them, but she didn't go to every room. Can you tell us anything more about this woman?"

Kelder glanced down at his talisman. "She has black hair and brown eyes," he said. "And is not tall, certainly not as tall as you, though I cannot specify her height any more exactly than that. She is thin and light on her feet, with a rather square face, a wide nose, and pale skin. She usually wore black clothing and may have gone barefoot. Beyond that . . ." He turned up an empty palm. "Beyond that, I'm afraid I know no more."

"That isn't Mereth," Sarai said. "The height's right, but not the rest of it. Are you sure of this?"

"Oh, absolutely. A woman fitting that description visited each murder site within a sixnight or so of the killings."

Sarai looked up at Tikri. "That description doesn't bring anyone immediately to mind," she said. "Does it for you?"

"No." Tikri frowned. "I'm not sure how much we should trust this information."

The sorcerer tucked his talisman back in his tunic. "That's entirely up to you, of course," he said, "but I give you my word that it's reliable information. I don't know that this woman killed anyone, but she was very definitely there. If I had been able to see the bodies, I could have told you whether the same knife was used in every case . . ."

Sarai waved that aside. "We already know that," she said. "The wizards tested that for us. It was the same knife every time."

"Oh." Kelder essayed a quick little bow of acknowledgment.

Sarai smiled at him. "I'm not disparaging your information, Kelder of Tazmor," she said. "Thank you for bringing it to us. If you learn anything more, please come and tell us."

"Of course." Kelder bowed again, and stepped away.

Sarai looked up at Tikri. "Do you think this woman is the killer?"

Tikri shook his head. "No woman smaller than you could be strong enough to have committed these murders single-handed. Perhaps she's the high priestess of a cult that's responsible for this—if she exists at all."

"I think she exists," Sarai said. "Why would the sorcerer lie?"

"To throw us off the track," Tikri suggested. "Perhaps he's part of the conspiracy."

"I hadn't thought of that," Sarai admitted, staring at Kelder's back and chewing thoughtfully on her lower lip. "We could check his story, though."

"How?"

"Witchcraft. Where's Teneria?" Sarai turned, peering out the door as if she expected to find the young witch standing in the hallway.

Thin, black hair, light on her feet, usually wore black—that described Teneria, Sarai realized. The height was probably wrong, though; the journeyman witch stood very close to Sarai's own height. And her long, narrow face, with its pointed jaw, hardly looked square, and while her nose was noticeable, that was because it was long, with a bump in it, not because it was wide. Her complexion wasn't particularly pale. And weren't her eyes green?

She wasn't there to check.

Sarai snorted with sudden annoyance. Was she going to be matching every female she met against the sorcerer's description, from now until the murderers were caught?

She debated sending Tikri to fetch Teneria, but before she could decide, Teneria actually *did* appear in the doorway.

"Just the person I was looking for!" Sarai called.

Teneria entered and bowed before Lady Sarai, then asked, "How may I be of service?"

"You don't already know?" Sarai asked wryly.

The ghost of a smile flickered across the witch's rather somber face. "No, my lady," she said. "Not at the moment."

"I need to know what's true and what isn't," Sarai said. "You witches are good at that."

Teneria cocked her head to one side and replied, "In a way. We can generally tell when people believe what they say— whether that's actually the truth is sometimes an entirely different matter. And it works better with some people than others."

Sarai nodded, and asked, "Suppose you spoke to a woman I thought had been connected with the murders; could you tell me whether she had, in fact, been connected?"

Teneria frowned. "That would depend. Probably. If she spoke at all, almost certainly. If she spoke freely, with no magical constraints, absolutely. But I would not necessarily be able to ascertain the *nature* of the connection."

"Could you tell if a person had actually committed one of the murders?"

"Oh, yes, I would think so. Unless there was a very great deal of magic hiding the fact."

"Suppose you were to walk down the street, or through the market; could you pick a murderer out of the crowd?"

Teneria shook her head. "Only if I was incredibly lucky. The murderer would have to be thinking about the actual killing and feeling a strong emotional reaction to those thoughts, with absolutely no magical protection of any kind. Even then, I couldn't be sure without stopping to investigate. What might look like a murderer's thoughts at first glance could just be a housewife worried about killing a chicken for dinner.''

''I thought it was probably too much to ask,'' Sarai admitted. ''If you could do that, we'd have just had witches working for my father for years, instead of relying on Okko and the others for most of it.''

Teneria shrugged.

''But if we brought you a person and asked, 'Is this the murderer,' you could tell us?'' Sarai asked.

''Ordinarily, yes.''

Sarai nodded. ''Good enough,'' she said. She pointed. ''That man in the brown tunic there is a sorcerer by the name of Kelder of Tazmor; he claims to have magically established that a particular woman was present in each room where a murder was committed—though not necessarily at the time of the killing. I want you to find out how reliable his information is.''

Teneria followed the gesture, but said nothing at first.

''Does sorcery interfere with your witchcraft?'' Sarai inquired.

''Not usually,'' Teneria replied. ''Sometimes.''

''Will it this time?''

Teneria turned and walked away from the dais, toward Kelder. ''I'll let you know,'' she said, over her shoulder.

Ten minutes later, she let them know. Kelder believed absolutely in what he had told Sarai and Tikri. Sarai thanked the young witch, and stared down at the spriggan that was clutching at her ankle.

Who *was* that woman Kelder had described?

CHAPTER 21

*C*aptain Tikri's files were a mess. Lady Sarai had thought her own records, up in her bedroom, were not as organized as they ought to be, and had always been embarrassed when she thought of the tidy shelves and drawers that her father and his clerks maintained. By comparison with Tikri's random heap of reports and letters, her records were a model of order and logic.

"What are you looking for, anyway?" Tikri asked, as Sarai dumped another armful on his desk.

"I don't know," Sarai said, picking a paper off the stack. "But I hope I'll know it when I see it."

"How will you know it if you don't know what it is? I'd offer to help, but how can I?"

Sarai sighed.

"What I'm after," she said, "is some record of a crime that the conspirators might have committed *before* the murders. Once they killed Inza, we were looking for them, and I'm sure they've been careful, and certainly *we've* been careful, checking out everything that we thought might be connected. Right?"

"Right," Tikri said, a trifle uncertainly.

"Well, this conspiracy probably didn't burst out of nowhere, full-grown and completely ready, the night poor Inza died," Sarai explained. "They must have been preparing before that. They may have killed more dogs, for example, before working their way up to people. They may have injured people without killing them. They may have stolen things they needed for their magic. And maybe, since they weren't so experienced yet, they left traces and clues. *Now* do you see what I'm after?"

"Oh," Tikri said. He hesitated. "How far back do you want to go?"

"I don't know," Sarai admitted.

"You may not find anything."

"I *know* that," Sarai said, flinging down a thick report and glaring angrily at Tikri. "Don't you think I know that? But I don't have much of anything *else* left to try. The Wizards' Guild wants to catch whoever it is for themselves, because it won't look as good for them if I do it, so they won't help me any more than they have to." Tikri started to protest, and Sarai cut him off. "Oh, they'll put up a pretense of cooperation, I'm sure," she said, "but half of them probably still think I'm trying to blame them for all this, or steal the credit. I won't know if they're covering up something or not; I can't be sure, and they aren't about to tell me. The Council of Warlocks is no help; they're all afraid that if they do anything to help me they'll draw down the Calling on themselves. The Brotherhood is less organized than a children's street game; they don't even know who's in charge, or who their members are. The Sisterhood isn't much better—

they don't know how many witches there are in Ethshar, let alone what any of them are doing. And none of them seem to be getting anywhere with their magic, anyway. So what *else* would you suggest I do?''

"The magicians can't help at all?''

"They can't help any *more*. Okko says the gods can't see anything through the haze of wizardry; Kallia says the demons won't tell her anything, and she doesn't know whether they know anything to tell. The warlocks all swear their magic doesn't handle information. Kelder's told me all he can, and that's more than I could get from any Ethsharitic sorcerer. Wizards and witches tell me what magic was used, what went where, but they can't give me names or faces. So I'm reading these papers. Don't you *ever* sort them?''

"No," Tikri admitted.

Sarai let out a wordless noise of exasperation and turned back to the reports.

Tikri, hoping to be of help, began picking up papers and glancing through them, as well. The two sat, reading silently, for several minutes.

"Here's a report of a missing dog," Tikri ventured.

Sarai glanced up. "Let me see it."

Tikri obeyed; Sarai skimmed through the report quickly, then put it to one side. "It might be worth another look," she said.

A moment later she found one herself.

"What ever happened in this case?" she said, handing two pages to Tikri.

Tikri read enough to remind himself what had happened. "Oh, this," he said. "Nothing happened. We never found out who it was."

Sarai took the two sheets back. " 'Guardsman Deran reports tending to stabbing victim in tavern,' '' she read. " 'No accusations or arrests made.' '' She looked up. "That's in your handwriting."

Tikri nodded. "That's right," he said.

"The other one isn't," Sarai pointed out.

"No, that's the lieutenant who was in charge, Lieutenant Senden," Tikri agreed. "He sent it in the next day."

"And you actually managed to keep the two together? It *is* the same stabbing?"

Tikri shrugged. "Sometimes I get lucky," he said. "It's the same one."

" 'Guardsman Deran Wuller's son tended to two knife wounds, a slash and a stab, on the upper left thigh of a man who gave his name as Tolthar of Smallgate, who claimed to have been discharged from the city guard five years previously for being drunk while on duty,' " Sarai read aloud. " 'It was Guardsman Deran's conclusion that the stabbing was a result of a disagreement with a young woman; witnesses at the scene reported that the so-called Tolthar had been seen talking with a woman shortly before the stabbing. Those elements of their descriptions of the woman that are in general agreement were as follows: Thin, black hair, below average height, wearing dark clothing.' " She put down the report. "Short, thin, black hair, dressed in black," she said. "A stab and a slash. Sound familiar?"

"But it wasn't his throat," Tikri protested.

"She probably couldn't get *at* his throat," Sarai pointed out. "He was awake."

"But drunk."

Sarai glowered at Tikri. "Are you seriously claiming you don't see any possible connection?"

"No," Tikri admitted. "I'm just not *sure* there's a connection."

"Neither am I," Sarai said, "but it's worth investigating, isn't it?"

"Oh, I suppose so," Tikri said.

"Then send for this Lieutenant Senden and this man Deran Wuller's son and have them find Tolthar of Smallgate and bring him to me for questioning."

"Now?"

"Do you know of a better time? Yes, now!"

Tikri put down his own stack of reports and headed for the door, in pursuit of a messenger. In so doing he almost collided with a messenger who had been about to knock at the open door.

"Yes?" Sarai asked, as Tikri apologized and slipped past.

"I'm looking for Mereth of the Golden Door," the messenger said warily, eyeing Tikri's departing back. "She has a visitor, and someone told me she might be here."

"Mereth isn't here right now," Sarai replied. "What visitor is this?"

The messenger finally looked into the room. "Oh, is that you,

Lady Sarai? It's three visitors, really—the man gives his name as Tobas of Telven and the women as Karanissa of the Mountains and Alorria of Dwomor."

Sarai recognized two of the names. These were the foreign experts the Wizards' Guild had sent for. "Show them in," she said.

The messenger hesitated. "Well, they aren't . . ." she began.

"Bring them here!" Sarai commanded, fed up with delays and explanations.

"Yes, my lady," the messenger said, bowing; she turned and hurried away.

For the next few minutes Sarai sat looking through old reports; then the messenger knocked again.

A spriggan scurried into the room, and Sarai took a moment to chase it to the corner and warn it, "If you tear a single piece of paper, or chew on one, or spill anything on one, I'm going to rip your slimy green guts out and wear them as a necklace; is that clear, you little nuisance?"

"Yes, yes," the spriggan said, bobbing its head and staring wide-eyed up at her. "Not hurt paper. *Nice* paper. Nice spriggan not hurt paper."

"Good," Lady Sarai said, turning away and finding a young man standing in the doorway. He looked just about her own age; she had expected this famous expert on certain wizardries to be a good deal older.

Well, maybe he had some way of disguising his age—an illusion of some sort, or a youth spell. But then, he looked rather sheepish just now, and Sarai had trouble imagining a wise old wizard, one capable of a youth spell or other transformation, looking so embarrassed when he had done nothing to cause it. Maybe this wasn't Tobas of Telven at all.

"I'm sorry about the spriggan," the young man said.

"Oh, it's not *your* fault," Sarai said, waving a hand airily. "The little pests are turning up everywhere lately."

"Well, actually, I'm afraid it *is* my fault," the man insisted. "I created the spriggans. By accident. A spell went wrong on me about six years ago, and they've been popping up ever since. And they still tend to follow me around even more than they do other wizards, which is why that one came running in just now."

"Oh," Sarai said, unsure whether she should believe this story. It was true that spriggans had only been around for a few years, but had they really come from a single botched spell?

"I'm Tobas, by the way. You're Lady Sarai? Or . . ." He paused, confused.

"I'm Lady Sarai," Sarai confirmed.

"Ah." Tobas bowed politely in acknowledgment, then stepped aside and ushered a black-haired young beauty into the room—one whose green velvet gown failed to hide a well-advanced pregnancy. "This is my wife, Alorria of Dwomor," Tobas said proudly.

Alorria did not bow, Sarai noticed, and a silver coronet held her hair back from her face—she was presumably a noblewoman of some sort from one of the Small Kingdoms.

Or maybe the coronet was just an affectation, and bowing was uncomfortable because of her belly; Sarai had no firsthand experience to compare.

A second woman, taller, thinner, older, and not visibly pregnant, but also black-haired and beautiful, appeared in the door. Where Alorria wore green velvet, this other wore red.

"And this," Tobas said, "is my other wife, Karanissa of the Mountains."

"She's a witch," Alorria volunteered.

Tobas nodded agreement. Karanissa bowed.

Sarai didn't comment, but her lips tightened. Over the years she had met a few men who had two wives, and even one eccentric old fellow with three, and she hadn't liked the men, their wives, or the whole idea very much; it had always seemed a bit excessive and in doubtful taste. This wizard not only had two wives, he had brought both of them along, despite Alorria's pregnancy.

The black silk tunic that Tobas wore was hardly extravagant, and his manners seemed acceptable, but still, bringing not just one wife but two, and claiming to be responsible for an entire species, in addition to his supposed expertise in magic—Sarai thought that despite his show of diffidence, this wizard appeared a little too pleased with himself for her liking. She was not favorably impressed.

"I understand you're an expert on the magic we're dealing with," Sarai said, without further preamble. She was not disposed toward idle pleasantries with this man.

"Well, not really," Tobas said, with a wry half smile. "I don't know what you're dealing with. I understand it's an enchanted blade that appears to have a neutralizing effect on wizardry, and I know a little something about *that*, though—about things that neutralize wizardry. I don't honestly know a great deal, but probably I know a little more than anyone else.''

''*Do* you,'' Sarai said. The fellow spoke well enough and wasn't really an obvious braggart, but she still didn't like him. ''Why is that?'' she asked.

''Oh, well, I have rather a personal interest in it,'' Tobas explained. ''I happen to have inherited a castle . . .''

''No, you didn't,'' Alorria protested, ''you found it abandoned.''

''Oh, be quiet, Ali,'' Karanissa said. ''That's close enough to inheriting.''

''It isn't the same thing at all!''

''Shut up, both of you,'' Tobas said—not angrily, but simply making a request. To Lady Sarai's surprise, it was obeyed, and the wizard continued.

''Let us say, then, that I have *acquired* a castle that happens to be under a spell cast during the Great War that renders wizardry ineffective,'' Tobas explained. ''And for reasons I prefer not to explain, I can't just sell it or abandon it; I pass through its neighborhood fairly often, and being a wizard, I find the spell very inconvenient—I can't use my magic there. So I've taken to studying what little is known about neutralizing wizardry, in hopes of someday reversing the spell.''

''Ah, I see,'' Sarai said. ''And are you close? Have you learned much about this sort of negative magic?''

''No.'' Tobas shook his head. ''Hardly a thing. But I'm still trying. This thing you've got here—I spoke to Telurinon about it and some of the others, before Heremon insisted I come find Mereth and talk to you. They tell me that someone has an enchanted weapon that appears to absorb wizardry, that they've been studying it, but they weren't getting anywhere, because this thing is completely immune to wizardry, so much so that they only know there's magic there because wizardry *isn't*, you see.''

Sarai looked blank.

''Well, ordinarily,'' Tobas explained, ''wizardry is sort of everywhere at once, in the light and the air and the earth, but wherever this thing has been used, this enchanted dagger or whatever it is, wizardry doesn't work right anymore.''

''So it's an entirely new kind of magic?'' Sarai said.

''Maybe,'' Tobas said, ''or maybe it's just a special sort of wizardry. I don't really know a thing about it. But I thought it wouldn't hurt to come and take a look.''

"Besides, we felt so sorry for all those poor people who were killed," Karanissa said. "We felt we had to try to do *something*.''

"If we can," Alorria added.

"Tobas is a wizard, Karanissa's a witch," Lady Sarai said. "Are you a magician, too, Alorria?"

The woman in the coronet shook her head quickly. "Oh, no, nothing like that," she said hastily. "I just wanted to come along . . . I mean, Tobas is my husband.''

Lady Sarai nodded. She wondered, though; was it comfortable to go traveling about when one was, by the look of her, six or seven months pregnant? Sarai had the feeling there was a story here she didn't know, but it wasn't really any of her business, so she didn't pursue it. "And do any of you know anything about the conspiracy that's behind the killings?" she asked. "Or is it just the murder weapon you're interested in?"

"Is it a conspiracy?" Tobas asked, interested. "I hadn't heard that. Please, Lady Sarai, you must understand, we only arrived in the city a few hours ago, and all we've heard about these terrible crimes came from the other members of the Wizards' Guild. Naturally, they've paid most of their attention to the magic involved. I'd be very glad if you could tell us more. Do you have any idea who's behind it?"

Lady Sarai eyed the wizard suspiciously. He wasn't entirely living up to her first impression of him as a self-assured and superior boor.

"We have a description of a woman," she admitted. "There are guards out now looking for someone who may know who she is. We know she's involved somehow.''

"And you think this man will tell you where to find her?''

"We certainly hope so. If not, once we have a name, won't a fairly simple spell lead us to her?''

"If it's a true name," Tobas admitted. "The first name she knew herself by.''

"Well, if it's *not* her true name," Sarai said, "we'll send the city guard to look for her, too.''

"Lady Sarai," Alorria asked, "what will you do with her when you find her?''

"We'll arrest her, of course! On suspicion of murder. And bring her to the Palace for questioning.'' Only after she had spoken did Sarai remember that she was addressing a member of the Wizard's Guild, and the Guild wanted Serem's murderer turned over to them.

Well, this woman would need to be questioned to be sure she *was* Serem's murderer. Anyone intelligent would see that.

"Of course," Tobas said. Then he remarked, "It may not be that easy, arresting someone who was able to kill several different magicians."

Sarai glanced at him, startled. "That's a good point," she said. "If she *is* the killer. I'll have to see that whoever is sent after her takes special precautions."

"But you think this woman you seek is part of a conspiracy?" Tobas had moved around to the front of the desk; now he leaned back comfortably against it. Karanissa settled against a wall. To Lady Sarai's distress, Alorria began looking around for a clear patch of floor to sit on—the chairs were stacked with reports. The spriggan in the corner rustled papers and peered out curiously; Lady Sarai turned and kicked at it, sending it squealing out the door.

"Maybe we should go somewhere more comfortable," Lady Sarai suggested. "And I'll tell you all about it."

CHAPTER 22

*T*olthar of Smallgate stared into the empty mug, wishing he had the price of another pint. The Drunken Dragon never gave credit, especially not to him, so there was no point in asking for it, and he didn't have so much as an iron bit left in his purse.

He didn't feel well enough to rob anyone, either, though he thought he might once he sobered up a little. It was too late in the day to find honest work, or to expect much from begging— not that he really wanted to try either one. That meant that dinner, if he got any at all, would probably come out of Mama Kilina's stewpot, over in the Wall Street Field.

Maybe that little hellion, Tabaea the Thief, would turn up there tonight. After all, her lucky streak couldn't last forever.

That assumed, of course, that it was a lucky streak that had kept her out of the Drunken Dragon and out of the local portion of the Wall Street Field for the last few sixnights. He thought that if she had gotten herself killed someone would know about it; that meant she was still somewhere in the city. Tolthar couldn't imagine that she would ever leave Ethshar of the Sands; the people he knew, the people he thought of as his own kind, simply didn't do that. The outside world was for rich merchants and stupid farmers, not the people who lived on the fringes, who spent an occasional night in the Field.

The idea that Tabaea might have found a permanent job somewhere never occurred to him. Thieves and beggars simply didn't do that, in Tolthar's view of the World, and Tabaea, as her very name proclaimed, was a thief.

He supposed she might have wound up in a brothel somewhere, but that wasn't usually permanent. Slavery was permanent, but he thought he would have heard if she had been auctioned off. He had friends—or rather, he had people who were willing to talk to him—who had promised to tell him if they saw Tabaea anywhere.

So he assumed that she'd committed a few successful burglaries.

But the money would run out; it always did. Sooner or later, he would find her again, in the Dragon or at Kilina's stewpot, or somewhere else among his familiar haunts.

And when he did, she would pay for the wounds in his leg. They were healed now; the leg was as good as new, but she owed him for the pain, the blood, and the time he had spent limping. She owed him for the embarrassment of having to talk to that young snot of a guardsman, Deran Wuller's son.

And he had a wonderful idea of how she could repay him for his troubles. She might even enjoy it; he wouldn't mind if she did. Sometimes it was even better that way.

He shoved the mug aside and got to his feet. He was not entirely sure where he was going, whether he would head directly for Mama Kilina or make a stop or two along the way, but he knew he would have to stand up, so he went ahead with that part of the job. Once he was upright he didn't have to worry about the proprietor of the Dragon harassing him to buy another ale or get out.

His head swam slightly. Maybe, he thought, he should have spent some of his last coppers on food, rather than ale.

Well, it was too late now. He turned toward the door.

Then he sat heavily back down. There was a guardsman standing in the doorway, and Tolthar recognized him. It was Deran Wuller's son. Deran might be there for something entirely unrelated to Tolthar, but Tolthar did not care to try walking out past him.

Then Deran stepped in and marched straight toward Tolthar. He pointed, and Tolthar realized there were two other soldiers behind Deran. One of them had a lieutenant's band on his arm.

"Oh, gods," Tolthar muttered. "Now what?"

"Tolthar of Smallgate?" Deran asked loudly, stopping a step away.

Tolthar winced at the volume. "Yes," he said, "you know I am. What is it this time?"

"We are ordered to bring you to the palace immediately," Deran said.

Tolthar's eyes widened, and the shock of Deran's words seemed to cook away a good part of the alcohol in his body.

"Why?" he asked. "What did I do?"

"You're wanted for questioning," Deran said, a bit more kindly. He didn't like seeing anyone, even a worthless drunkard like Tolthar, needlessly frightened. "They didn't tell us, but I think they want you as a witness, not for anything you've done yourself."

"I haven't seen anything," Tolthar protested. "I haven't heard anything, either. I don't *know* anything."

"Well, you can tell the folks at the palace that," Deran said, reaching for him. "Come on."

Tolthar pressed back against his chair, but the guardsman's hand clamped around his arm like a noose drawn tight. Reluctantly, he yielded to the inevitable and allowed himself to be led out.

As he and the three soldiers marched down Wall Street in a tight little group, one at each side and the third behind, Tolthar remembered all the other people he had seen escorted away over the years. He had even escorted a few himself, before he was kicked out of the guard—but to a district magistrate, not the palace.

A good many of them never came back; they were executed, or sold into slavery, or exiled. Others took a beating, or paid a fine, and then, presumably chastened, went on with their lives. A few returned untouched and continued as if nothing had happened.

Tolthar hoped very much that he would be one of those few.

At the gate, the party turned right; Tolthar was escorted across one side of Grandgate Market and into Gate Street. He could see the dome of the palace ahead already, even though it was still over a mile away—the dome was the highest structure in the city, even taller than the Great Lighthouse, and it towered over the surrounding buildings, above the rooftops, a great dark semicircle against the scarlet sunset. In the mornings Tolthar had seen it gleaming golden-white, like a huge pale moon rising in the west, but now it was shadowed and ominous. The sun was sinking just to the left of the dome, almost behind it, and for a moment Tolthar fancied that the dome was some sort of shadow-sun trying to blot the true sun out of the sky.

The foursome marched down seven blocks to the fork and bore right onto Harbor Street; now the sun was a tiny red sliver nestled at the base of the looming dome of the palace, and the sky was darkening overhead.

Tolthar glanced at Deran, then up at the dome.

"Can you tell me where you're taking me, and why it's the Palace instead of the magistrate's office?" he said. "Am I going to see the Minister of Justice?"

"We're taking you to Captain Tikri's office," Deran said, "to talk to Lady Sarai, the Minister of Investigation. She's also Lord Kalthon's daughter, and Acting Minister of Justice."

"But you aren't taking me to the justice chamber?"

"The captain's office."

"Why?"

Deran shrugged apologetically. "They didn't tell us," he said.

That brought them to the second fork, where they bore left onto Quarter Street. The dome of the palace had blocked out the sun entirely, or perhaps the sun had set; Tolthar couldn't be sure. The sky overhead had darkened to a deep sapphire blue, and the lesser moon shone pink in the east.

They came to Circle Street, then to the colorful pavement forming a ring around the palace; they marched directly across, past the final line of stalls owned by elite and fortunate merchants. The palace itself stood before them now, the dome hidden by the wall and the eaves.

Tolthar had never been here before; even during his days in

the guard, he had never drawn duty in the palace. He had never been closer than Circle Street.

Somewhere behind that wall lived old Ederd IV himself, overlord of Ethshar of the Sands, master of the fates of over a million men, women, and children—one of the three most powerful mortals in the World. And Lord Kalthon, Ederd's Minister of Justice, would be there, who could have a man flogged, hanged, beheaded, exiled, or sold on a moment's notice. Lord Torrut, commander of the guard, was in there, as well—and his slightest word could send ten thousand men out to fight, kill, and die.

Tolthar did not particularly care to join them.

He had no choice, though; when he hesitated on the threshold of the little side door the soldiers heaved him through without even slowing.

The floors inside were stone—not rough slate or flagstone, like an inn's hearth, but polished granite and marble. Tolthar had never seen such floors.

The walls, too, were stone—some of them, anyway; others were paneled in wood, or hidden by drapes or tapestries. He could see them through the archways and open doors as he was hurried through what seemed like an endless maze of antechambers and corridors.

At last his escort stopped at the door of a small chamber with bare walls of pale gray stone; in the center of the room stood a large desk, with wood-and-brown-velvet chairs behind and before. Papers, scrolls, and ledgers were spread across the desk and stacked on the floor.

Two people were in the room: a tall young woman with thick brown hair and a large man in the uniform of a guard captain. They were standing by the desk, arguing. At the sound of arriving footsteps they stopped and turned toward the doorway.

"Captain Tikri," one of the guardsmen said, "this is Tolthar of Smallgate."

"Thank you, Lieutenant," the man in the captain's uniform said. "Bring him in."

Deran and the lieutenant brought Tolthar into the little office, while the third man returned to the corridor.

The woman was wearing clothes of fine gold linen, and Tolthar might have guessed that she was a noblewoman of some sort, but he was still startled when Tikri addressed her as Lady Sarai.

"Which magician shall I send for, Lady Sarai?" he asked.

"More than one," the young woman replied. "I don't want any doubt about this. Teneria, certainly, and Mereth, if you can find her, and Okko, and I suppose you should get that Tobas and his witch wife back here, and anyone else you think we might want." As an afterthought, she added, "Not the pregnant wife, though—she's not a magician."

"This may not have anything to do with the case, remember," Tikri reminded her. "And we have half a dozen other chances, if this one doesn't work out."

"I know that," Lady Sarai snapped. "But this man is here, now, and he's one of the more promising possibilities." She turned to the guards. "Sit him down," she ordered.

Abruptly, Tolthar found himself seated, on the chair in front of the desk. He stared up silently at the woman.

"Do you know who I am?" Lady Sarai demanded.

Tolthar blinked and didn't answer.

"He's drunk," Deran remarked. "We dragged him out of a tavern in Northangle."

Lady Sarai nodded. Tolthar didn't bother to argue, although he didn't feel very drunk anymore.

A messenger appeared in the doorway. "You wanted me, Captain?" she asked.

"Yes," Tikri said. He crossed the room quickly. "You go ahead, Lady Sarai." He stepped out into the corridor to give the messenger her instructions.

"Close the door, Lieutenant," Lady Sarai directed. "Let's have some privacy."

Senden obeyed. Lady Sarai stepped up close to the seated Tolthar and stared down at him.

"You're drunk?" she asked.

"A little," he admitted. He was beginning to recover his nerve.

"That might be just as well. Do you know who I am?"

"They call you Lady Sarai," Tolthar said. "I can still hear."

"That's my name; you know who I am?"

"Lord Kalthon's daughter," Tolthar answered.

Lady Sarai's face hardened. "I am Lady Sarai, Minister of Investigation and Acting Minister of Justice to Ederd the Fourth, Overlord of Ethshar of the Sands, Triumvir of the Hegemony of the Three Ethshars, Commander of the Holy Armies and Defender of the Gods, and I am speaking to you now in the performance of my duties and with the full authority of the overlord. Do you understand that?''

"Uh . . ." Tolthar hesitated, then said, "I'm not sure."

"That means that I can have you flogged, or tortured, or killed, right here and now, without having to worry about appeals or consequences. And I'll do it if you don't cooperate."

Tolthar stared up at her. He did not see Deran and Senden exchange doubtful glances behind him.

"Now," Lady Sarai said, "I understand that on or about the fourth day of the month of Summerheat, you received two knife wounds in your left leg. Is that correct?"

"Yes, my lady," Tolthar replied softly, thoroughly cowed.

"These were both inflicted with the same knife, at approximately the same time?"

"Yes."

"And that knife was used by a woman?"

"That's right," Tolthar admitted.

"How tall was she?"

"Uh . . . if you want . . ." Did they think he didn't know who had stabbed him?

"How tall was she?" Sarai shouted, leaning closer.

"She's short," he said quickly. "I mean, not tiny, but she's . . . she's pretty short."

"What was she wearing? What color?"

"Black," Tolthar said, "she usually wears black."

"What's the shape of her face like?"

Baffled, Tolthar wondered why Lady Sarai didn't just ask for Tabea's name. He said, "I don't know . . ."

"Did you *see* her face?"

"Well, yes . . ."

"What shape is it?"

"Let me think for a minute!"

Sarai backed away from him slightly, giving him room to breathe. "Take your time," she said.

"Thank you, my lady," Tolthar said, resentfully. He tried to picture Tabea's face. "Sort of straight," he said, "and wide. She has a square chin, almost."

"A long nose?"

"No, it's more wide."

"Brown hair?"

"I think it's black . . ."

"Green eyes?"

"I didn't notice, I thought they were brown . . ."

"Dark skin?"

"No, she's pale . . ."

"Full-bodied?"

"Skinny as a steer in Srigmor."

"Clumsy?"

"If she were clumsy, do you think I'd have let her get me with the knife?" Tolthar protested angrily. "I wasn't *that* drunk!"

The door opened, and Lady Sarai paused in her questioning. She looked up as a thin, black-haired girl entered.

For a moment, Tolthar thought it was Tabaea herself, and he began to imagine elaborate schemes to blame him for some crime he had not committed, to punish him for making false accusations; then he saw that this person wasn't Tabaea, that she was taller and generally thinner, though perhaps fuller in the chest. And the new arrival had a long, narrow face that was not like Tabaea's at all.

"Teneria," Lady Sarai said, "we think this man may have survived an attack by the killer. We want you to check his wounds, if you can, to see if the same knife was used."

"I'll try," the woman Lady Sarai had called Teneria said quietly.

"They're healed," Tolthar protested. "My wounds are healed!"

"I'll try, anyway," Teneria replied.

"Thank you," Lady Sarai said. "But first," she added, turning back to Tolthar, "I believe that this man was about to tell us the name of the woman who stabbed him."

The long-awaited question came as a great relief.

"Tabaea," Tolthar said. "Tabaea the Thief."

CHAPTER 23

*T*abaea was coming down the stairs of her current residence, a pleasant little inn called the Blue Dancer, and thinking out her plans for the evening, when she heard the sound of soldiers walking. There was the distinctive slapping of scabbard against kilt, the heavy tread of the boots—definitely soldiers, on the street out front, drawing nearer. She sniffed the air, but with the inn's door closed she could make out nothing unusual. Dinner had been beef stewed in red wine, and she could still smell the lingering aroma of every ingredient, and of the half-dozen different vintages that had been served to the Dancer's customers. The chimney was drawing well, so the scent of the hearthfire itself was relatively faint, but its heat was making Beren, the serving wench, sweat as she swept the floor; Tabaea could smell that, too. She could distinguish the moist odors of Beren's cotton tunic and wool skirt.

Dogs were amazing creatures, Tabaea thought. She had never realized how amazing until she had started killing them. They could *all* smell all these details.

The booted steps were coming directly up to the door of the inn; Tabaea wondered why. Soldiers were a common enough sight in the taverns and inns of Wall Street, but the Blue Dancer was a quiet and rather expensive place several blocks down Grand Street from the market, and the city guard was not generally found here unless someone had sent for them.

There were other footsteps as well—she hadn't heard them at first, with the door and the windows closed and the various sounds of the city drowning them out, but someone in slippers was walking with the soldiers, someone wearing a long, rustling garment.

Suddenly nervous, Tabaea hurried down the last few steps. The guards couldn't have anything to do with *her*, of course—nobody except the innkeeper and a few strangers knew she was here, no one would have any reason to connect her with any recent disturbances—but still, she didn't care to be caught in her room upstairs if there was trouble.

Now the soldiers were at the door, five of them, in addition to the person in slippers, and one soldier was lifting the latch. Now even Beren heard them; she straightened and leaned her broom in the chimney corner as Tabaea slipped back into the little alcove under the stairs. The table there was usually occupied at meals by young lovers, as it was the most private spot in the dining room; there was nothing suspicious about it if Tabaea should happen to sit there on a quiet evening, just minding her own business.

And it would scarcely be her fault that she could hear everything that went on in the main room.

"Can I help you?" Beren asked.

"We're looking for a woman named Tabaea," an unfamiliar man's voice said. "We don't know what she's calling herself. A little below average height, thin, black hair—probably alone."

Tabaea could almost hear Beren frowning.

"Let me get my master," the serving wench said.

"Is she here?" a different voice asked.

"I don't know," Beren replied, "I'll ask." Tabaea watched through the archway as Beren vanished into the kitchen.

Tabaea bit her lip, worrying and wondering. Why were these men—these *soldiers*—looking for her? How did they know her name, or what she looked like?

And what should she do about it?

It registered that the alcove was a dead end, that she could be trapped in it. True, she could hold off a small army, as they wouldn't be able to get at her more than two or perhaps three at a time, and she could use the table as a shield, but they could besiege her there and wait her out.

That would not do. Better to get out *now*, while she could!

But the soldiers were in the front door, while Beren and the innkeeper might be emerging from the kitchen at any moment, blocking that route. That left the window.

Tavern windows varied greatly in Ethshar, in number, size, placement, and nature. The Blue Dancer gloried in a single great bow window, a long, graceful curve made up of several hundred small panes, framed not in lead, but in imported hardwood, an exotic touch that added to the inn's expensive atmosphere. Three small casements were built into this structure, for ventilation; none of them looked large enough for even a person of Tabaea's size to fit through.

Tabaea knew that appearances could be deceiving, though. Moving as quietly as she could—which was very quietly indeed—she rose and crept to the edge of the sheltering arch.

There, she reached out with her poorly developed and ill-understood abilities, the witch-sight and warlock sense, and dimly perceived the intruders.

She could distinguish their scents, as well, but identity was not what interested her now. She wanted to know where they were looking, to be sure that she was somewhere else.

One was watching up the stairs, very carefully. Another was

guarding the door. The one in slippers . . . that one was a woman, and she smelled of magic. That was bad. She was looking about the room with interest, not focusing on anything in particular.

One of the soldiers was watching the magician; he was no threat to anyone just now.

That left two soldiers and a magician who were looking out into the dining room; one soldier was watching the kitchen door, the other was peering into the dimly lit farther recesses—including the one where Tabaea stood.

She nudged the one in the door, ever so slightly, with a little warlock push; he started, and made a surprised noise.

The others turned to look at him, and Tabaea made her run, fast and smooth and silent, across the room and up onto the broad sill. She was almost there when she was spotted; her distraction had only held for a fraction of a second.

She swung open the nearest casement and thrust her head through; her ears scraped the frame on either side, her hair snagged on the latch.

"Damn," she whispered. She wouldn't fit out that way.

"Hey!" a guardsman called, and Tabaea, desperate, pushed at the wooden frame with the heel of her hand.

She had never really tried her accumulated strength; she had never had any reason to. Most of her killings had been for skill, more than strength. She knew she was strong—she had flung that demonologist, Karitha, around like a doll. But she had not realized until this very moment just *how* strong she had become.

Her hand punched through the polished window frame as if it were paper, spraying splinters of wood and glass into the street beyond.

"Stop her!" someone shouted, and the guards started for her. Frightened, Tabaea kicked at the window.

Debris burst out into Grand Street like spray from a wave-struck rock; the casement itself hung for an instant by one corner, then tumbled onto the street with a shattering of glass.

Tabaea dove through the hole and landed, catlike, on her feet; she leaped up and ran, eastward, without thinking.

Behind her, men were shouting.

Run, hide, run, hide—her years as a thief had drummed that into her. When anything goes wrong, you run; when you have run the pursuit out of sight, you hide. If they find you, run again. No need to think or plan; just run and hide.

And the best places to hide weren't empty attics or dark alleys; the best places were in crowds and busy streets, where there was always another escape route, were always other faces to distract the pursuers.

And the very best place of all was the Wall Street Field, where the clutter of destitute humanity lay down an obstacle course of ramshackle shelters and stolen stewpots, where most of the people would be on her side, where the soldiers felt outnumbered.

She ran east on Grand Street, straight toward Grandgate Market and access to Wall Street.

Behind her, the soldiers poured out the door of the Blue Dancer; a raised sword whacked the signboard and set it swinging, and even through the shouting Tabaea could hear the metal links creaking. Booted feet ran after her.

The woman, the magician, did not run; Tabaea could vaguely sense her presence, far back and growing farther with every step. She was working a spell, Tabaea was certain, some kind of spell that would flatten her, steal her powers, turn her to a statue or a mouse. She ran, expecting to be felled at any instant, by spell or sword.

She was not felled; she ran headlong into Grandgate Market, not even panting, and spun to her left, turning north toward the part of the Wall Street Field she knew best. Late-night shoppers on their way home, the last merchants in the midst of packing up for the night, and a few strolling lovers, turned to stare after her.

The guards were shouting, but they were farther behind than ever; she was outrunning them. Other soldiers were emerging from the towers by the gate, but not in time to cut her off. She was into the Field, into the strip that ran alongside the barracks towers, and no one had touched her yet.

Then a man, his red kilt and yellow tunic visible in the light of a nearby torch but his face in shadow, stepped out in front of her, reaching out to grab her; she thrust out an arm and knocked him aside without slowing.

She rounded the corner of the North Tower into the wider part of the Field and promptly tripped over a sleeping figure.

She stumbled, but caught herself, arms outflung, balanced like a cat, then was up and running again.

There were no torches here, no lanterns; yellow light leaked from the distant windows of Wall Street; the orange glow of the greater moon limned the top of the city wall above her, and the scattered remnants of the evening's cookfires made pools of lesser shadow here and there, but most of the Field was in darkness. Its inhabitants, asleep or awake, were but shadowy lumps in the gloom; her cat-eyes, still not yet fully adjusted from the cozy light of the Blue Dancer's dining room, let her see movement, but not colors or details. She danced through the dark, avoiding bodies and shelters at the final fraction of a second.

Then, abruptly, fire bloomed *above* her, orange light a thousand times brighter than any moon. She stumbled, stopped, and looked up.

A warlock hung in the air, glowing impossibly bright, like an off-color piece of the sun itself. She knew he was a warlock, but she couldn't have said how she knew; the light simply *felt* like warlockry.

Without thinking, she reached her own warlockry up to counter him, to extinguish the glow, but his power was greater than hers; it was like fighting the tide. She could stop anything he did from reaching her, but she couldn't put out the light or drive him away.

Around her, she realized as she pressed her power upward, were people, dozens of people, the people of Wall Street Field—the poor and dispossessed, the downtrodden, the homeless, the outlawed.

"Help me!" she called.

No one answered, and she could hear soldiers coming, she could smell leather and steel and sweat. Someone tossed a rock in the general direction of the flying figure, but it never even came close.

It gave her an idea, though.

She could not fight him with warlockry, she was outmatched that way, but warlockry was not all she had. She knelt and snatched up a chunk of brick, still warm from a cookfire, and flung it upward—not with magic, but with the strength of her arm, the strength she had stolen from Inza and Deru and the rest.

The warlock shied away, and the light dimmed somewhat.

The soldiers were coming; Tabaea snatched out her belt knife, intent on giving them a fight.

The knife was like a sliver of darkness in the warlock's glow; Tabaea held the Black Dagger ready in her hand.

Above her, the warlock still hovered, glowing, but she had his measure now; he could hold himself up, suppress her own warlockry, and provide light, but that left him no magic to spare for anything else.

Someone else shied a stone at the warlock; he turned it away, but Tabaea could sense that it distracted him slightly.

Further, he was beginning to worry, she knew—probably about the Calling. How close was he to the threshold, to the first nightmares? He could draw upon all the power he wanted, and because he had started with more than she Tabaea could never match him, but if he drew too much . . .

She decided the warlock was not really the major threat.

The first soldier paused a few feet away, watching the knife.

"Tabaea the Thief," he called, "in the name of Ederd the Fourth, Overlord of Ethshar of the Sands, I order you to surrender!"

"Go to Hell, bloody-skirt!" she shouted back.

Other soldiers were surrounding her, forming a fifteen-foot circle with her at the center; the Field's usual inhabitants had fallen back into the darkness. Tabaea tried to pick up something with warlockry, but the magician in the air above her wouldn't allow it.

There were a dozen guardsmen encircling her; at a cautious signal from the one in front of her, they all began closing in slowly.

"Oh, no, you don't," Tabaea said. She lunged forward, with inhuman speed, and thrust the Black Dagger's blade under the ribs of the man before her.

His eyes widened, and he slashed belatedly with his sword, cutting her arm. Blood spilled, black in the orange light, black across her black sleeve.

It really didn't hurt very much at all, to Tabaea's surprise, and what pain there was was lost in the hot surge of strength she was receiving from the man she had stabbed. Then one of the other soldiers, one of the men behind her, struck.

That hurt, and the wave of strength she had just felt vanished; the blow to her back was a shock, a burst of pain, and her head jerked backward. Then it snapped forward again, involuntarily, and she found herself looking down at her own chest.

Something projected from her tunic, something dark that had cut its way out through the fabric, stretching it out and then cutting through, something dark and hard and smeared with thick liquid.

Then she realized what it was. She was looking at the point

of a sword that had been thrust right through her, a sword covered with her heart's blood.

She was dead. She had to be.

But she didn't *feel* dead. Shouldn't she already be losing consciousness, be falling lifeless to the ground?

She pulled her own blade from the soldier's body; dark blood spilled down his pale tunic, and he crumpled to the earth. *He* was dead, no doubt about that.

But she wasn't. She reached down, grabbed the blade that protruded from her chest, and shoved it back, hard. She felt it slide through her, back out, and she whirled swiftly, before whoever held it could strike again.

She could feel a prickling, a tingling, and she suddenly realized that she probably had a gaping wound in her, that she might yet bleed to death. She felt no blood, though.

Tabaea looked quickly down at her chest, and sensed that the wound was closing of its own accord. That was magic—it had to be. It wasn't anything she was doing consciously, though, and she didn't think it was witchcraft or warlockry. It didn't feel like those.

It felt like the sensation she got when the Black Dagger cut flesh. Whatever was happening, she was sure it was the Black Dagger's spell at work. Whether it would truly heal her, or at least keep her going until she could do it by other means, she didn't know. It had to be the dagger that was keeping her alive, and she didn't understand how or why, but she had no time to worry about that now. She looked up.

The soldiers were staring at her, eyes wide; no one was moving against her. One man held a bloody sword, its tip just an inch or two from her chin.

Tabaea realized, with astonishment, that they were afraid of her.

And then she further realized, with a deep sense of surprised satisfaction, that they had very good reasons to be afraid.

She knocked the sword aside, held up the Black Dagger, and smiled a very unpleasant smile.

"It's not going to be that easy," she announced, grinning. "If I were you, I would throw down my weapons and run."

"Elner, call the magicians," a guardsman said. Tabaea turned and smiled at him.

"I *am* a magician," she said. Then, moving faster than any human being could without magical assistance, she slashed the soldier across the chest—not fatally, just a nasty gash that would weaken him, and in so doing would strengthen her. He gasped, and stepped back, his hands flying up to stop the blood, his sword falling to the dirt at his feet.

She thought she understood, now, what had happened. That sword thrust should have killed her, obviously, but it hadn't—or rather, not completely. She was fairly sure she had lost one life.

But the Black Dagger had stolen a dozen for her—including dogs, cats, magicians, and the life of the man who had led this party to capture her.

She didn't know whether dogs and cats carried as much life as people, and she did not particularly want to find out; she wasn't going to throw her lives away recklessly. Still, she was stronger and faster than anyone else in the World, and as long as she took a life for every one she lost, she could not die.

She liked that idea very much.

"I am *the* magician," she said. "Not just a witch or a warlock or a wizard, but all of them!" She suddenly remembered what she had heard, listening to the Guildmasters at the Cap and Dagger; she laughed, and said, "Bow, you fools! Bow before Tabaea the First, Empress of Ethshar!"

"She's crazy," someone said.

The Black Dagger moved again, faster than any other human hand could move it, fast as a striking cat, and the guardsman who had impaled her fell back, bleeding. The bloody sword fell from his grasp.

"You think I'm crazy?" she shouted. "Then just try to stop me! Didn't you *see*? He put a sword right through me, and it didn't hurt me!"

"Call the magicians, Elner," someone called mockingly from the crowd of civilians.

More guardsmen were arriving, pushing through the crowd; behind them came the robed figures of magicians.

"Magicians?" Tabaea stooped and snatched up the sword, left-handed, and flung it upward with all the speed and strength and skill of her dozen stolen lives.

The warlock shrieked, and the light went out; the orange glow vanished like the flame of a snuffed candle, plunging the Field into darkness.

When the shriek ended, silence as sudden as the darkness fell. Cloth rustled as the warlock fell out of the sky, and then he landed with a sodden thud, off to one side, upon a mixed group of soldiers and bystanders.

"You think I'm afraid of *magicians*?" Tabaea screamed over the sudden tumult.

In fact, magicians were about the only thing she *was* still afraid of—she had no idea whether she could defend herself against all the different kinds of magic. Warlockry, yes—she could hold off another warlock indefinitely. Witchcraft, absolutely—she had greater vitality, and therefore more power, than any other witch that had ever lived.

Gods and demons and wizards, though—who knew? Sorcery, any of the subtler arts, she could not be sure of. She was bluffing—but she didn't think anyone would dare to test her. She stood, dagger ready.

Something came sweeping toward her out of the darkness, something Tabaea could not describe, with a shape and a color she couldn't name; reflexively, she raised her knife, and the black blade flared blue for an instant.

Then whatever it was was gone.

Magic—it had been magic, certainly. Wizardry, probably. And the knife had stopped it. She *was* safe from magic other than witchcraft and warlockry—at least some of it.

She could do anything—and she knew what she wanted. She had already said it.

Tabaea the First, Empress of Ethshar!

"Listen, you people!" Tabaea shouted, "you people who live here in the Wall Street Field, listen to me! *Why are you here?*"

She paused dramatically and sensed half a hundred faces turned attentively toward her—soldiers and magicians and beggars and thieves.

"You're here because the fat old overlord of this stinking city, the man who claims to protect you, has sent you here!" Tabaea proclaimed. "He's taken your homes with his taxes, stolen your food to feed his soldiers, and given you nothing in return but dungeons and slavery!" She pushed aside a soldier and stepped up atop a makeshift wooden shelter. "Haven't you had enough of this? Haven't you had enough of seeing the rich get richer, seeing them buy your friends, your neighbors, your sons and daughters from the slavers, when they've stolen a few coins in order to eat? Haven't you heard enough of girls and boys tortured in the Nightside brothels to please the perverted tastes of some wealthy degenerate?" The words seemed to be coming from somewhere deep within her, of their own accord; one of her victims, she realized, someone she had killed, must have been skilled in oratory. And she could augment that, now that she had seen how; she warmed the air about her, then let a faint orange glow seep out.

A warlock and an orator both; she suppressed a smile. Self-delight would win no converts; only anger would do that. "Haven't you had *enough*?" she screamed at the people of the Field.

Some of the soldiers were backing away; some of the civilians were muttering.

"*I* say that Ederd has had his chance!" Tabaea shouted. "*I* say his time is over! Let the old man step aside, and let a woman of the people see justice done in this city! Not the justice of slaver and swordsman, but *true* justice! Not Lord Kalthon's justice, but *my* justice! The justice of one who has no need to fear nor favor, because I cannot be harmed! Beholden to no one save those who aid me now, I *am* the Empress of Ethshar! Who's with me?"

A dozen voices shouted.

"I said, *who's with me*?"

This time, a hundred chorused in reply.

"Then let's show old Ederd who's in charge here! Come with me to the palace! We'll throw Ederd and his lackeys out in the Wall Street Field and take the palace for our own! Come on!" She turned and stepped off the shelter, but not down to the ground; instead she caught herself in the air, warlock fashion, and propelled herself forward, above the crowd.

Using too much warlockry wasn't safe, of course; she doubted she was any more immune to the Calling than anyone else was. But warlockry was showy, and that was what she needed right now.

The soldiers had mostly faded away, falling back into the darkness, out of sight of the angry crowd; Tabaea and her followers marched unimpeded out of the Field onto Wall Street and down Wall Street to Grandgate Market. Many of the people behind her had torches or makeshift clubs, she saw with pleasure; one had picked up a soldier's fallen sword. She was at the head of an army.

The Empress Tabaea, at the head of her army. She smiled broadly.

"Come on!" she called. "Come on!"

CHAPTER 24

*I*t was Alorria of Dwomor who rousted Lord Torrut out of his
bed; the soldier who had guarded the bedchamber door stood
nervously beside her, holding a lamp.

"She said it was an emergency, sir . . ."

"It *is* an emergency," Alorria said, tugging at the bedclothes.
"There's an uprising!"

Lord Torrut was not a young man anymore and did not wake
as quickly as he once had; he looked up blearily at the unfamiliar
but unmistakably attractive face and smiled. "Ah, young
lady . . ." he began. Then his head sank a little, and he
saw the rest of her. His eyes widened. "Is it the baby?" he
said. "Soldier, go fetch a midwife!"

"No, it's not the baby," Alorria snapped. "The baby's fine
and not due for sixnights. There's an uprising! They're marching
on the palace!"

Torrut sat up and shook his head to clear it; then, speaking as
he reached for his tunic, he asked, "Who's marching? What's
going on?"

"There's a woman named Tabaea who has just declared herself
Empress of Ethshar, and she's raised an army of the poor
and discontented from the Wall Street Field. They're marching
here to take the palace and kill the overlord." Alorria stepped
back, to give the commander of the city guard room to stand.

"From the *Field*?" Lord Torrut said, astonished; he stopped
with one arm in its sleeve and the other bare. "You don't need
me for that! A hundred men and a magician or two should be
able to handle it."

Alorria shook her head. "*Tabaea's* a magician—a very powerful
one, the one that Lady Sarai's been looking for for months,
the one who's been murdering other magicians."

"Well, but surely . . ."

"The magicians are trying to stop her, and Captain Tikri's

171

getting the palace guard ready to defend against her, but so far nothing's working. She's already walked right through a squadron of guards, out on Wall Street; she crippled a warlock and brushed aside the wizards' spells as if they were mere illusions.''

Torrut stared at her for a moment, then turned to his door guard. "Is this true?" he demanded.

The guard turned up an empty palm. "I don't know, my lord," he said. "This woman was sent by Lady Sarai and Captain Tikri, but that's all I know."

"Damn." Torrut slid his arm into the empty sleeve and then reached for his kilt. "Who are you, young woman? Why wasn't one of the regular messengers sent?"

"My husband's a wizard," Alorria explained. "Everyone else was busy, and I wanted to help, so they sent me to fetch you."

Torrut nodded. "Good of you. Listen, I want you to take this soldier to vouch for you and go wake the overlord. I don't know what's going on here, or how much danger there really is, but I'm not about to let anyone say I didn't do my best to protect Ederd. While you do that, I'll go down and see what's happening for myself."

"Wake the *overlord*?" Alorria squeaked. Even though she was the daughter of a king herself, she lived in awe of the three Ethsharitic overlords. Beside her the guardsman looked very unhappy indeed.

"That's right," Torrut said, standing up and pulling his kilt into position. "*Somebody* better." He smiled. "Don't worry, Ederd's a gentle old man; he won't have your heads lopped off for disturbing him. For that matter, despite his age, he doesn't mind looking at a lovely young woman any more than I do. All this fuss may be nothing, but I think Ederd would want to know." He reached for his sword belt. "Now, go on, both of you!"

They went.

When Alorria had come up to the level where most of the higher nobility had their apartments, the stairways and passages had been quiet and dim; now, though, she could hear voices and running footsteps and could see lights behind a dozen doors. "Which way?" she asked.

The guard pointed.

Officials were hurrying about; Alorria knew that the magicians were gathering two flights below, to prepare a defense against Tabaea's advance, and to find a way to kill the mysterious self-proclaimed "empress."

And out in the streets, Tabaea was marching steadily closer.

Once Tabaea was out of the Wall Street Field, she got as far as the intersection of Gate Street and Wizard Street before she encountered any further organized resistance. There, though, she found herself facing a living barricade of soldiers, swords drawn, formed up in a line three deep that stretched from one side of the avenue to the other.

"Are you trying to keep me from the palace? From *my* palace?" she shouted.

The lieutenant in charge of the formation called back, "Drop your weapons, all of you! I call on you in the name of Ederd the Fourth, Overlord of Ethshar, to surrender!"

Tabaea laughed. "I could just go around the block," she called, "but I think I'll teach you all a lesson." With the Black Dagger ready in her hand, she marched forward.

The line of soldiery braced to meet her.

When she came within striking distance, the soldier directly in front of her called out, "Stop, or I'll kill you!" He raised his sword high.

"Go ahead and try!" Tabaea called back, without stopping.

The man stabbed at her; catlike, she dodged the thrust. Her hand flicked out, like a cat's paw at a mouse, and closed around the sword's blade.

Startled, the soldier tried to snatch it back, but Tabaea tore the weapon out of his hand and flung it aside.

The soldiers to either side were striking at her, as well, now; she ducked and wove, dodging their blows. She snatched the swords away from two more soldiers. The line formation had broken, now; they were all coming to get at her, forming a tight little knot around her.

She smacked away swords, dodged their thrusts, grabbed one in her fist, and bent it until it broke; behind her she could hear her ragtag army muttering, brushing up against the soldiers, but not really fighting.

It didn't matter. She didn't need them.

A sword hit her squarely in the side, and she felt an instant of incredible pain, but then it was gone; she had lost another life. Angry, she lashed out with the Black Dagger and sliced open a soldier's throat. As he started to fall back she finished him with a thrust to the heart; she wanted a life to replace the one she had lost.

She picked up another guardsman and threw him against his companions; then another, and another. She used her hands and her warlockry both.

"You can't stop me!" she shrieked. "*No one* can stop me!"

The Black Dagger flared blue, and something crackled like dead leaves in a hot fire. Someone was trying to use magic against her.

"No one!" she repeated, "not even wizards!"

The dagger flared again, greenish this time. Tabaea jabbed it into a soldier's belly.

A moment later the guard broke; several men fell back under the lieutenant's orders, but others ran off down side streets, either Wizard Street or Arena Street, and a few ducked into the Cap and Dagger.

And of course, half a dozen or so lay unmoving on the ground.

"All right, men," the lieutenant shouted. "She won't make it easy, we'll leave this one to the wizards!"

"Run away!" Tabaea called. "Look at them, you people, look at them run! Send your wizards, I don't care! They can't stop me!" She waved the dagger in the air, and a cheer went up from her "army." "Come on!" she called, and again she marched toward the palace.

At the palace, the more ordinary officials and workers listened closely as the magicians reported on the encounter.

"Bad," Karanissa said, "very bad. Three dead, at least. All on our side."

"She's still coming?" Lady Sarai asked.

"Oh, yes; the fight hardly even slowed her down."

"What if we let her pass, but stopped her army?" The question was directed at the entire room, rather than at Karanissa.

"We could," Okko agreed, "but what would that accomplish, if we can't stop *her*?"

"Well, she couldn't very well rule the city all by herself, could she?"

"No," Okko agreed, "but I think she could kill everyone here, one by one, starting with the overlord himself, until the survivors started obeying her."

"Would she *do* that?" one of the overlord's scriveners asked, horrified.

"Yes," Teneria said flatly. "She would."

Sarai turned to the wizards. "What spells have you tried against her?"

"Several," Tobas said. "From simple curses to the White Death. Whatever is protecting her blocks them all instantly."

"Is there *any* way to stop her?" Lady Sarai asked.

"Probably," Tobas replied, "and we'll keep trying spells. But most of them would take more time than we have to prepare. And some of them would take out large parts of the city with her."

"And we don't really know which to use," Karanissa pointed out. "Since we haven't yet figured out what keeps her alive, we can't be sure of how to kill her."

Lord Torrut stepped into the room at that point and demanded loudly, "What's happening?"

Several people rushed to tell him; he quickly chose one to serve as his spokesman and began quietly absorbing information.

"I wonder where the other conspirators are?" Tobas asked.

Karanissa shook her head, but before she could say anything, Kelder of Tazmor answered quietly, "I don't think there is any conspiracy. I think there's just Tabaea."

"You never found traces of anyone else, did you?" Lady Sarai asked, startled. "She's small enough, and strong enough, and seems to have several different magicks available—how can she *do* that?"

"There's just Tabaea," Karanissa agreed. "At least, there's just Tabaea and the rabble from the Field."

"It's all just her . . ." Lady Sarai's voice trailed off; then she asked, "What happens if we *can't* stop her?"

No one had an answer for that, until Karanissa suggested, "We die, probably."

"There's no need for that," Lord Torrut said, startling the others. "We don't die; we retreat, we regroup, we reconsider our situation, and when we're ready, we retaliate."

"But how . . ." Sarai began.

"Listen, little Sarai," Torrut said, cutting her off, "you and your father have made fun of me for years for being a warrior with no wars to fight. Well, now I have a war—and by the gods I swear that I'm going to fight it, and I'm going to win it. It's not who wins the first battle that matters, it's who wins the *last* battle. This Tabaea is going to win the first one, but I intend to make sure it's not the last."

The whispered side conversations had died away as Lord Torrut spoke; now everyone was listening to him.

"This Tabaea doesn't like the overlord—that means we need to get him out of the palace before she gets here, and while we're at it, I think we had better get his entire family out, with him: Ederd the Heir and Zarrea and Edarth and Kinthera and Annara, all of them. If she's lived in the Wall Street Field then she probably doesn't like the guard, and she doesn't like me, and Sarai, she probably doesn't like your father, Lord Kalthon—you'd better get him and your brother out of here, too. And magicians—she doesn't like magicians."

"But where do we *go*?" Lady Sarai asked, dismayed.

"She's coming from Grandgate, is she? Then we go to Seagate. We put the overlord and his family and anyone who's too old or too sick to fight on a ship, and we sail it out of here, out of her reach."

"How do you *know* when it's out of her reach?" Tobas asked.

That stopped Lord Torrut for a moment; then he smiled, showing well-kept teeth. "I don't," he said. "I'm guessing. But if she could stop a ship at sea . . . well, has she shown any sign of being able to affect what she can't see?"

"No," Karanissa said, "not yet."

"How can we fight back from a ship, though?" Lady Sarai protested.

"Until we know *how* to fight back," Lord Torrut pointed out, "what does it matter where we are?"

Lady Sarai was not entirely satisfied with this, but she could think of no good answer. "I would never have thought a murder case could turn into something like this," she muttered to herself.

No one heard her, as Lord Torrut continued, "I sent that woman Alorria to rouse the overlord. And I'll leave it to this group here to get old Ederd and anyone else who Tabaea might want to kill out of the palace and down to Seagate before she gets here; and while you're doing that, I'll be doing what I can to slow her arrival."

"Then you're not going to flee yourself, Lord Torrut?" someone asked.

"Of course not!" Lord Torrut grinned outright. "At long last, I have a war to fight!"

PART THREE

Empress

CHAPTER 25

Lady Sarai could hear distant shouting as she tucked the blanket around her father; Tabaea and her army must have gotten as far as Quarter Street, at the very least. Kalthon the Younger sat upright at the back of the wagon, looking slightly dazed; Lady Sarai could see his expression clearly in the light of the torch the wagon's driver held.

"Sarai, I don't understand," her brother said again.

"You don't have to," Sarai said. "You just do what I told you."

"But aren't you coming?"

Sarai hesitated. She looked down at her father. He had appeared to be more or less awake when they left the palace, and had moved partly under his own power, but now he gave no sign of consciousness; he probably couldn't hear anything, might well have no idea what was going on around him. "No," she said, "I'm not."

"But why *not*?" young Kalthon protested. "If this crazy magician would kill us all, won't she kill you, too?"

"Oh, I suppose she will if she catches me and finds out who I am, yes." Sarai attempted a mocking smile, but it didn't work very well—or perhaps her brother couldn't see it in the dark; her face was probably in shadow from where he sat.

"Then shouldn't you come with us?"

"No." She gave the blanket a final tug, then let herself slide back over the side of the wagon.

"Why *not*?" Kalthon's wail was heartbreaking. "How am I going to manage Daddy without you?"

"You won't be alone; there will be people to help. The overlord's going, too, and all his family. His granddaughter Annara will help. And Ederd the Heir." She hoped Ederd the Heir would, at any rate; he was a healthy man, not yet fifty, but prone to turn morose and useless at times. His daughter Annara was

179

just a year older than Sarai, though, and still cheerful and energetic.

"But what will *you* do? Are you staying in the palace? Is this horrible woman going to kill you?"

"No," Sarai said. "No, she won't kill me. I won't stay in the palace. I'll hide somewhere in the city."

"But if you're hiding, why can't you come with us?"

Sarai sighed. "Kallie," she said, "I'm sending you and Dad and the others away so you'll be safe, but someone has to stay here to fight Tabaea, and I'm going to be the one from our family who does that."

"What about Ederd the Heir, then? Shouldn't he be staying?"

"No, because he's too valuable. He's the overlord's heir."

Kalthon couldn't argue with that, but he still didn't like it.

"I think you should come with us," he said.

"No, Kallie," Sarai said gently. Then she stepped away and told the waiting driver, "Go, quickly!"

He obeyed wordlessly, setting the torch in its bracket and cracking the reins over the horses.

Lady Sarai watched them go, the horses trotting, the wagon bumping its way down Palace Street, toward the docks at Seagate. The torchlight wavered madly with the wagon's motion, sending light and shadow dancing insanely across the darkened housefronts on either side.

Sarai hoped that using horses wouldn't be too conspicuous, especially at this hour of the night; the palace stables had held no oxen, and besides, oxen would be dangerously slow. A few of the richest merchants were using horses to draw their wagons now, weren't they?

She hoped so. Or if not, then she hoped Tabaea wouldn't know any better; it was entirely possible the little thief wouldn't even recognize a horse, or wouldn't know that they were traditionally the exclusive property of the nobility.

The royal family was all safe now, or as safe as she could make them—Ederd IV, his wife Zarrea, his sour old bachelor brother Edarth, the aging son who would one day be Ederd V, *his* wife Kinthera, and their daughter Annara, all rousted from their beds and sent hurrying on their way to a hastily chartered ship. And now Lady Sarai's own family, her father and brother, were following. Okko, too old to fight—if theurgists *could* fight, which they generally couldn't—had gone as well.

Lord Torrut hadn't fled, of course; he was out there somewhere, trying every sort of trap, ambush, and delaying tactic he could improvise. Sarai was fairly sure that Captain Tikri was with him. And most of the magicians she had collected in the palace were taking shelter at various places in the city, on Wizard Street or elsewhere.

And of course, she was staying, herself—but where?

There was a temptation to remain in the palace after all, but to pretend to be someone else—borrow a maid's apron, perhaps, or join the assistant cooks in the kitchens. After all, as far as she knew, Tabaea had never seen her and wouldn't recognize her face.

That was too risky, though. Tabaea might have spies, or her unknown magic might expose the deception, or some innocent servant might slip up and reveal Sarai's rank.

No, Sarai knew she would have to find somewhere else—but where?

She realized she was still staring down the black and empty length of Palace Street, though the wagon was out of sight; she turned away with a wry smile.

Maybe, she thought, she should go to the Wall Street Field. After all, wasn't that where anyone in Ethshar went who had lost her home and been thrown out into a hostile world? And wouldn't it be appropriate, now that Tabaea's ragtag followers would be taking their places in the palace?

But it wasn't everyone from the Field who was marching with the self-proclaimed empress, and Sarai realized, with a bitter little laugh, that the Field was probably the place in all the city outside the palace where she was most likely to be recognized as Lord Kalthon's daughter.

The barracks towers in Grandgate would be almost as bad—and besides, a woman alone there would hardly be safe. Besides, Grandgate, or any part of Wall Street, was a long way from the palace. She wanted somewhere closer at hand, somewhere she could keep an eye on things, the way the magicians did.

The magicians were mostly on Wizard Street, of course—and not necessarily the closer sections, since for many their spells could serve them even at a distance.

She frowned. She was no magician, and she hardly belonged on Wizard Street. She had a little money with her—not much, but a little. Why not just take a room at an inn?

No, she told herself, that would be too exposed, would involve too much dealing with strangers, and at this hour, would be far too noticeable. Ordinary travelers didn't take rooms hours after midnight, did they?

A high, thin scream sounded somewhere to the northeast, on the other side of the palace. The shouting was much closer, and she could hear other noises, noises she couldn't identify. Tabaea must be almost to the palace, and here she was, still standing on the plaza across from Palace Street.

She stepped off the stone pavement onto the bare earth of Circle Street, and choosing her direction at random, she turned right—she didn't want to follow Palace Street, or even the fork for North Palace Street. She wanted to put distance between herself and the fleeing nobles.

The next turn off the circle was Nightside Street, and she passed that by, as well, and the next. Here her choice was largely pragmatic; both streets were utterly black and unlit, while closer at hand the glow from the windows of the palace spilled out over the outer walls and made Circle Street relatively navigable.

She could hear the hissing of fountains left running, out there in the darkened gardens and forecourts; the sound, normally pleasant, was turned sinister and menacing by the circumstances. Sarai wondered whether the wealthy inhabitants of the mansions of Nightside were aware of what was happening just a few blocks away. When they awoke in the morning, how long would it take them to realize that the World had gone mad, that their overlord had been deposed, and that a thieving young magician was ruling the city? Would Tabaea leave them alone, or would she pillage those mansions behind their iron fences?

Well, if Sarai had her way, Tabaea wouldn't have *time* to disrupt the city's life that much. And right now, Lady Sarai did not care to try finding her way through Nightside's unlit streets.

Sooner or later, despite the dark, Sarai knew she would have to move farther out into the city, away from the palace; she wished there was more natural light to help her. The greater moon was rising in the east, casting orange light on the rooftops, but not yet penetrating to the streets below, while the lesser moon was far down in the west, its pale pink glow of no use at all.

By the time she reached North Street the roar of battle was overpowering, and farther ahead, farther around the circle, she could see reflected torchlight and the shadowed backs of soldiers. North Street was no more brightly illuminated than the others she had passed, but she could scarcely go any farther around the circle if she meant to escape; she turned left onto North Street, despite the darkness.

And then, suddenly, she knew where she was going. She *would* go to Wizard Street, just three blocks away. She would go to Mereth's shop, Mereth of the Golden Door. Even if Mereth wouldn't take her in, surely the wizard would know of someone who would.

Now that she had a destination in mind, Sarai began to hurry.

Behind her, a man's dying scream sounded above the fighting. Sarai winced. It seemed so pointless, fighting Tabaea every step of the way like this; didn't Lord Torrut see that? He was letting his men die for nothing.

But there was nothing Sarai could do about it, not anymore. She fled down North Street.

The stub of a lone torch still burned unnoticed above a shuttered shop on Harbor Street; Lady Sarai glanced at it, grateful for the slight relief from the surrounding night. To see Harbor Street utterly empty and almost dark seemed very odd indeed; she had never before been out so late and never seen the streets so deserted.

Behind her, the shouting seemed to be fading away. By the time she turned left onto Wizard Street, she was no longer entirely sure whether she heard shouting, or the distant roar of the sea.

Here there were no torches, only whatever light moons and stars might provide, but Sarai could see that the door of Mereth's shop was shut, her signboard unlit. The shop windows were tightly closed, draperies drawn, but a thin line of light showed around the edges; it would scarcely have been visible were the street brighter, either with daylight or the glow of the evening's torches and lanterns.

Sarai hurried to the door and rapped gently on the gilded panels.

For a long moment, nothing happened; then, abruptly, the door was flung open. "Get in!" someone ordered.

Sarai obeyed, and the door slammed shut behind her, leaving Wizard Street once more dark and empty.

CHAPTER 26

The palace door was locked and barred, but Tabaea didn't mind; she braced herself against the paving stones of the plaza, put her shoulder to the brass-covered panels, and shoved with all her supernatural strength. The latch shattered, the brackets holding the bar snapped, and the twisted, ruined door swung open. Tabaea laughed and shouted, "Come on!" She waved to her followers; some of them surged forward, close on her heels, but others hung back, intimidated by the idea of intruding on the palace itself.

Tabaea stepped through the broken portal into a broad and shadowy marble corridor; somewhere far ahead light spilled through an archway, and the contrast of the distant glow with the surrounding darkness seemed to exaggerate the length of the passage.

Or did it? Tabaea was unsure; the palace was far larger than any other building she had ever been in. Perhaps the corridor really *was* that long.

The euphoria of her triumphant march from Grandgate faded quickly at the sight of the polished stone floor, the countless doors on either side, and a gleaming staircase barely visible in the dim distance. This hardly seemed to her like a part of her own familiar city, or like anything human at all. She had thought old Serem's house was almost offensively magnificent, yet this palace hall dwarfed anything in the wizard's home.

But it was *hers* now, she reminded herself. She sniffed the air, but that told her little; people had been through here recently, but were not here now. The faint familiar odors of furniture, of lamps and candles, and of polishing oil reached her, mingled both with the smells of her followers and the street outside, and with scents she could not identify. No longer feeling particularly bold, she nonetheless put on a bold front and marched forward. Her footsteps tapped loudly on the shining marble, and echoed eerily from the stone walls.

Behind her came a score of the vagabonds and scoundrels who had followed her from the Wall Street Field; their feet, bare or slippered or wrapped in rags, did not make the sharp tapping her good new boots did, but slapped or scraped or shuffled. Like her, they were awed by what they saw; their shouting dropped to whispers that echoed from the stone, chasing each other back and forth along the passage.

"Where is everybody?" someone asked.

"Who do you mean?" Tabaea demanded, turning. "Who did you expect here? We fought the city guard in the streets!"

"I mean the people who live here," the beggar said. "The overlord and his family, and all the others."

"Fled, probably," someone said. "Or cowering in their beds."

"Did you think they'd be waiting by the door to welcome us?" Someone laughed.

"Come on," Tabaea said. She had intended to shout it, but somehow couldn't bring herself to do it; instead she merely spoke loudly. She turned forward and marched on down the corridor.

The doors on either side were mostly closed; a few stood ajar, but the rooms beyond were dark, and Tabaea did not bother to explore them. They passed arches opening into large dark rooms, and those, too, Tabaea hurried quickly by without further investigation. Three of her followers carried torches; they waved them in the open rooms to be sure no soldiers lurked in ambush there, but then hurried on after their leader.

Ahead, that lone light spilled its golden glow across gray marble floor, walls of white marble veined with gray, and Tabaea hurried forward to see where it came from.

The answer was a disappointment; a perfectly ordinary oil lamp, apparently forgotten by whoever had extinguished the others, burned atop a black iron bracket on the side of a pillar, lighting another passageway that ran crosswise to the one they were in. This other corridor, Tabaea saw, was not so inhumanly, perfectly straight, but instead curved away in the distance.

And it gave her a choice, and therefore a problem; which way should she go?

The left-hand passage curved to the right; the right-hand passage curved to the left. Whichever of the three she took, she

would be proceeding deeper in toward the center of the palace—
in which case, there was no reason to prefer one over the other.
She marched on straight ahead.

Now that the light was all behind her, shining over her shoulders, she could see more clearly what lay ahead. The corridor
continued another forty feet or so, then ended in a dark open
space—she could not judge its extent, only that its walls and
ceiling were out of sight. All she could see, beyond the corridor's end, was a set of broad steps leading up into the darkness,
steps of polished yellow marble.

Where had the builders of this place *gotten* all this stone,
Tabaea wondered; she hadn't known there was so much marble
in all the World.

She marched on to the end of the passage; there she paused
and looked around. She sniffed the air, but caught no suspicious
odors.

To either side, walls began at right angles to the corridor, then
curved away into darkness; ahead, under the great staircase,
were walls and, she thought, doors. There were carvings in
niches and statues standing on pedestals here and there—one
stood on either side of the bottommost step. Everything was of
stone, in white and gold and maroon.

She let her gaze drift up the staircase; she had expected the
top to be utterly black, like the unlit hallway of an inn late at
night, but instead there was a faint glow, and she thought she
could make out vague shapes. There was a certain airiness about
it, somehow, and a hint of the pastel colors of moonslight.

She considered a warlock light, but decided against trying it;
she hadn't really learned how to do one properly yet, and she
was very wary about overusing warlockry. Instead she waved
the torchbearers back and let her eyes adjust. After all, she reminded herself, she could see as well as any cat.

She blinked and drew in her breath.

"Come on," she said, waving her little band forward and
marching up the marble steps.

At the top she paused. The sensible thing to do would be to
use the torches, but she couldn't resist the more dramatic gesture; she waved, and her warlock fire-lighting skill struck a hundred candlewicks. Golden light flickered, then blazed forth, and
Tabaea stepped forward into the Great Hall of the Overlord of
Ethshar of the Sands.

She stood on a broad floor paved in tesselated stone, a square floor a hundred feet across. Far above, the palace's immense dome curved gracefully through shadowed distance, too far up for the light of candles to illuminate it well; a hundred-foot ring of sixteen hexagonal skylights set into the dome gave a view of the stars.

Three of the four walls were broken at the center by a broad stair; Tabaea and company had just mounted one of these, the others lying to their left and directly across. To the right, the fourth wall had no stair, but instead an elaborate display of carvings, gilt, and scarlet draperies, all centered around an ornate golden chair on a wide dais. Magnificent golden candelabra, wrought in a variety of shapes, lined the walls to either side of this display, and it was these that now provided the light.

"The throne room," someone murmured, as Tabaea's followers emerged into this splendor.

"And the overlord's throne," someone else added, pointing at the golden chair.

Tabaea grinned, her enthusiasm suddenly returning.

"Wrong," she said, bounding gaily to the throne. She leaped up and stood for a moment on its scarlet velvet cushion, watching as the last few stragglers trickled into the room.

"This is *not* the overlord's throne," she proclaimed, "not anymore!" She paused dramatically, then slid down and seated herself properly. "This is *my* throne now," she said. "Mine! Tabaea the First, Empress of Ethshar!" She smiled—not at all a pleasant smile.

After a second's hesitation, the little crowd burst into wild applause.

As they cheered, Tabaea ran her hands along the arms of the throne, enjoying the feel of it; the arms were of solid gold, she thought, worn smooth by centuries of use.

Under one arm she found a loop; curious, she tugged at it. It yielded an inch or so, then stopped. She could have forced it, but decided not to; there was no point in breaking something before she even knew what it was.

It occurred to her belatedly that the loop might have been a trap, something intended to dispose of usurpers like herself, but if so, it obviously wasn't working.

She sat and looked out at the room, at the people cheering for her, at the dim soaring dome above, the shining stone floor, the gold ornaments and silken tapestries, and an immense satisfaction settled over her.

It was hers. All of it, hers.

At least for the moment.

She sniffed the air, sorting out the scents in the room. Nothing was very fresh; no one had been in here for at least an hour before her arrival. The throne smelled of an old man—Ederd IV, of course; wasn't he seventy or eighty years old? Tabaea had never paid much attention to politics.

However old he might be, he was still the only one who had sat in this throne—until herself, of course.

Others had come and gone, men and women of all ages. She could smell the cold stone, the dust on the tapestries, and the lingering scents of the overlord's courtiers. They had stood and knelt on that vast expanse of unfurnished floor. They had been there just that day, Tabaea was sure—but now it might as well have been a century ago, because they were gone, their overlord overthrown. It was all hers now.

She heard footsteps on the stairs, and leaped down from the throne, snatching the Black Dagger from her belt.

A woman was on the stairs; Tabaea could smell her. A woman was approaching, and she was frightened.

Tabaea's followers, the twenty or so that had made it this far, had heard nothing, sensed nothing, until they saw their leader jump from her throne and crouch, knife ready. Their babbling euphoria vanished; a few began to retreat toward the stairs by which they had entered, while the others stared nervously in every direction.

"What is it?" someone asked.

Then the woman's head came into sight as she ascended the staircase to the right, as seen from the throne—the side opposite where Tabaea had entered. By her expression, she was utterly terrified; she hesitated at her first glimpse of the new masters of the palace, then continued up the steps.

She wore a gold tunic and a skirt of dark red, almost maroon, with a white apron protecting the front; her long brown hair was pulled back into a ponytail. She was not particularly young, nor particularly attractive. She looked harmless; what's more, she smelled harmless. Tabaea relaxed somewhat, rising up from her fighting stance, but keeping the dagger ready in her hand.

At the top step the woman in the apron hesitated again, one hand on the rail. She looked over the ragged crew before her, then turned toward the empty throne and spotted Tabaea, in her fine embroidered tunic that was smeared with blood and pierced by holes and tears left by sword thrusts, and her long black skirt stained with mud from the Field.

The newcomer curtsied, catching her apron and skirt up and bobbing quickly.

Tabaea blinked; she had hardly ever seen anyone curtsy before, and certainly never to her. That was reserved for the nobility.

"Um . . . Your Majesty?" the woman said. "My lady? I'm sorry, I don't know how to address you."

Tabaea smiled. " 'Your Majesty' will suit me quite well," she said.

"Very good, Your Majesty. You rang for me?"

"I did?" Tabaea remembered the loop on the throne. "Ah, yes, so I did."

"How may I serve you?"

Tabaea sheathed her knife and stood as tall as she could on the dais. "You may begin," she said, "by explaining how you know who I am, and by telling me who *you* are."

The woman in the apron curtsied again. "My name is Ista, Your Majesty; I'm just a servant. I was on duty downstairs when you rang. As for knowing who you are, I don't know for certain, but we were told that the old overlord was fleeing because a great magician had declared herself empress, and he could not stop her. I assume you are she."

"That's right," Tabaea said. "Tabaea the First, Empress of Ethshar of the Sands!" She waved toward the others. "And these are my court!" She laughed, and stepped back to the throne. "So old Ederd's fled?"

"Yes, Your Majesty."

Tabaea settled onto the scarlet cushion, grinning broadly. "But you're still here?"

"Oh, yes, of course, Your Majesty; the palace is my home. Where else would I go?"

"And you'll serve me, as you served Ederd?"

Ista bobbed her head. "If you'll permit me, Your Majesty."

"I will," Tabaea said, gesturing magnanimously. "What about the other servants?"

"I can't speak for them all, Your Majesty, but most of them are still here and ready to obey you."

"Oh, excellent! And what about the others? Ederd had a family, didn't he? And there are all the others, the so-called Minister of Justice and the rest—what of them?"

"Fled, Your Majesty. Lord Ederd the Heir, Lady Zarrea of the Spices, Lord Edarth of Ethshar, Lord Kalthon, all of them fled.''

"Well, let them flee, then—maybe they can take shelter in the Wall Street Field!'' She laughed. "So this palace is all mine, then?''

"Yes, Your Majesty.''

"Then show me my new domain, Ista—give us all the grand tour!'' She stood again and made a shooing gesture.

Ista hesitated, then curtsied once more. "What would you like to see first, Your Majesty?'' she asked.

CHAPTER 27

The three brocade armchairs were already occupied when Lady Sarai stepped into Mereth's front room—Alorria sat in the green, sound asleep; Kelder of Tazmor was in the gold, awake but visibly weary; and an old man Sarai didn't recognize dozed in the blue. Two soldiers leaned against the wall, one of them brushing his elbow against an ink painting; young Thar, who had admitted Sarai, eyed that nervously but said nothing. A few salvaged belongings were in battered knapsacks, stacked in odd corners, looking rather grubby and out of place. The little decorative boxes had all been shoved to one side of the table, making room for a plate covered with crumbs—whatever food had been provided, Sarai had clearly missed it.

"Is Mereth here?'' Sarai asked. "Or Tobas?''

Thar shook his head. "No,'' he said, "they're over at the Guildhouse.''

Lady Sarai blinked. "*What* Guildhouse?'' she asked.

"Guildmaster Serem's house, on Grand Street,'' Thar explained. "Lirrin turned it over to the Wizards' Guild until Serem's murderer is caught.'' He shrugged. "She doesn't need all that space, anyway.''

Sarai nodded. That explained why there had been several other wizards there, as well as Lirrin, when she took Teneria and Luralla to see the murder scene. Naturally, the wizards hadn't said anything about it to her. "Are they . . . what's happening there?" she asked.

"*I* don't know," Thar said. "I'm just an apprentice."

"Are they looking for a way to stop Tabaea?"

"I don't know—honestly, Lady Sarai, I don't know."

"I'm going there," Sarai said. She turned back toward the door.

"No, Lady Sarai," Thar protested, "not at *this* hour! In the morning we'll all go, but right now everyone needs to rest. That's what Guildmaster Telurinon said. I'll be taking Princess Alorria myself."

"We don't have time to rest," Sarai objected. "*Tabaea* isn't sleeping, is she?"

"I don't know, maybe she is, but whatever she's doing, *we* should rest. Or at least, you should—I have to stay up in case anyone else comes."

Lady Sarai hesitated.

"Tabaea isn't going to come after us tonight, my lady. Honestly, she won't."

Sarai studied Thar's face and saw a child trying hard to be grown up, a child on the very edge of complete exhaustion. She thought if she argued he would probably start crying.

She didn't want that, and besides, he was right; she was incredibly tired herself. It had been an abominably long day. Hard as it was to remember, when she had gotten up the morning before, about twenty hours ago, she had not yet heard the name "Tabaea the Thief," and she had never met Tolthar of Smallgate.

"The chairs are all taken," she said.

Thar smiled with relief. "The guest beds are all taken, too," he said, "but you can use mine. I have to stay up and watch the door, anyway."

Sarai nodded.

The apprentice's bed was lumpy and narrow, and she didn't sleep well; it seemed as if she had only just managed to get comfortable, at long last, when a guard's polite cough awakened her.

"They're getting ready to go to the Guildhouse, my lady," he said. Then he ducked back beyond the curtain that separated

Thar's niche from Mereth's kitchen, leaving her to her own devices.

Lady Sarai rose and brushed herself off, then straightened her clothes as best she could; there was no need to get dressed, since she had brought none of her clothing out of the palace with her except the outfit she was wearing. She had packed a few things for her father and brother, but had not worried about her own needs.

She made a quick trip to the privy in the courtyard behind the shop, then rinsed her face with water from the kitchen pump—Mereth was lucky, having a pump right there; or perhaps, since she had surely paid a good bit of money for it, "lucky" was not exactly the right word.

Feeling a little more alert and socially acceptable, Sarai hurried back down the corridor to the consultation room.

A crowd of people was gathered there—everyone who had been present the night before, and others as well. Sarai recognized some of them, but by no means all; there were magicians of various sorts, minor officials in the overlord's government, and people who could have come from anywhere.

And they were all arguing about something, but Sarai could make out nothing of what they were debating. She looked around for help.

The two guards were both there, but this time, instead of standing to one side, they were among those arguing most intently. Thar, however, was leaning silently against the archway, looking distressed.

"What's happening?" Sarai asked him.

The apprentice looked up at her unhappily. "They're arguing about how to go to the Guildhouse."

Sarai blinked. "I had assumed we would walk," she said.

"Well, yes," Thar agreed. He paused, considering, then added, "Except maybe some of the wizards and warlocks—I suppose they might fly."

"Wouldn't that attract attention?"

"Probably."

"So if we're walking," Lady Sarai asked, trying not to let her exasperation show, "what are they arguing about?"

"Whether we should all go at once, or go separately. Some of them think we should go together, in one big group, but the others think that would be too noticeable."

"That's stupid," Sarai said. "Of course we'd be too noticeable.'' She raised her voice and announced, ''I'm going to the Guildhouse now; I'd be glad to travel with one or two others.''

''But Lady Sarai . . .'' one of the guards began.

Lady Sarai did not stay to hear what he might have to say; she marched out the door onto Wizard Street.

The morning was a bright and cheerful one; she could hear children laughing as they chased each other through the alleys, and somewhere a block or two away a hawker was shouting out praises of his wares. There was no outward sign at all that a dangerous lunatic had overthrown the government the night before, that the overlord and half his court had fled.

In fact, Lady Sarai suspected that most of the city was unaware of Tabaea's accession to the throne. It would probably be a few days before the average citizen became aware of any change.

Or perhaps not—one of the shops across the way was shuttered and barred. Had the proprietor fled?

Or maybe the proprietor was in bed with a fever, or just taking a day off to go down to the beach. Lady Sarai snorted at her own eagerness to see some difference in the city. Just because her own life was all awry, that didn't mean that the entire city's was.

She did expect that Tabaea's usurpation of power would have its effect eventually, since she doubted very much that Tabaea and her cohorts could rule the city as well as the old overlord had, but it would be a slow, subtle thing. A city the size of Ethshar mostly ran by itself. Lady Sarai thought of it as a great spinning top, and it was the government's job to keep it balanced—a touch here, a touch there. Tabaea would be bound to miss a wobble here, push too hard there, and before long the whole thing would careen wildly out of control, maybe come smashing to a halt.

But for now, it looked just as it always had. She paused a few steps from Mereth's gilded door, looking about.

''Lady Sarai!'' someone called. Sarai turned, a finger to her lips.

It was Alorria who had spoken; she stood in the doorway, leaning forward, her feet still safely within the threshold in case she had to slip quickly back inside. Behind her stood Kelder of Tazmor on one side, Thar on the other.

''Don't use the title,'' Sarai said mildly. ''It might be unhealthy just now.''

"Oh," Alorria said. She looked uneasily out at the street.

"What is it?" Sarai asked.

"I'd like to come with you," Alorria said. "I think they're going to argue all day, and I want to see my husband. And I don't know the way to this Guildhouse they talk about. And I don't like traveling alone."

"I would be glad to provide an escort," Kelder said, in his odd Sardironese accent, "but I fear I don't know the house's location, either."

"Well, come on then, both of you." Sarai waited while the two of them hurried out. Kelder, she noted, carried a large knapsack; a floppy, broad-brimmed hat shaded his face, and his feet were ensconced in large, well-worn boots. As for Alorria, while she was not dressed for serious travel, she wore three assorted pouches on her belt; both were probably better equipped than she was herself, Sarai thought wryly.

Together, the three of them strolled northeastward on Wizard Street, moving at a leisurely pace so as not to tax the pregnant Alorria. The sun was bright, and Sarai quickly regretted not having a hat like Kelder's. When she had left the palace in the middle of the night she hadn't worried about sunlight.

They crossed North Street and a block or so later moved on from Nightside into Shadyside—but it was hardly shady today; the shadow of the palace dome could never have reached this far out; the name was more symbolic than descriptive.

"Warm," Alorria remarked. She pulled a gauzy red kerchief from one pouch and draped it over her head, then secured it in place with her coronet. Sarai admired the effect—barbaric, but not unattractive.

She glanced enviously at Kelder's hat—that wasn't exactly barbaric, but it was rather outlandish. There was nothing unreasonable about that, since he was an outlander.

The two foreigners made rather a striking contrast—Kelder in his rough and practical attire, Alorria in her barbarian Small Kingdom splendor of silks and gold. The coronet and kerchief might be pretty, but on the whole, Sarai thought she would prefer Kelder's hat.

And thinking about Kelder, something struck her.

"You said you don't know where the house is," she said accusingly, "but of course you do."

"I do?" Kelder asked, startled.

"Certainly! You've been there."

"I have? No, La . . . no, I haven't."

"You *said* you had been there. Did you lie to me?"

"No! How did I lie? I haven't been to the wizards' Guild-house, and I never claimed I had."

"Yes, you have, if you really did the investigating you told me about. It's the old wizard's house. Serem's."

"Ah," Kelder said, nodding. "I see. Then it stands at the corner of Wizard Street and Grand Street, and we are now on Wizard Street, are we not? Need we just follow this right to the door, then?"

"If we want to take all day, we could do that," Sarai agreed, "but Wizard Street turns south and makes a long detour, through Morningside and Eastside, before it comes back north through Midway to Grandgate. We'll be turning and following Harbor Street from Shadyside to Midway, then Gate Street from Midway to Grandgate, and then we'll meet Wizard Street again for the last few blocks."

"Ah," Kelder said. "I see. The streets of Sardiron are not so complex."

"Sardiron isn't as big."

Just then a pair of spriggans ran across the street in front of the threesome, shrieking. Someone shouted imprecations after the creatures. Alorria sighed.

"I wish Tobas had never invented those things," she said.

"Did he really?" Sarai asked.

"Not on purpose," Alorria explained. "A spell went wrong. But yes, it was really his doing."

Sarai looked at her, then around at the shops, at the sign-boards promising miracles of every sort, at the window displays of strange apparatuses or stuffed monsters, at the posted testimonials from satisfied customers.

Magic really could do amazing things. If anyone could ever get it all *organized*, all working toward the same end, who knew what might be accomplished?

And of course, who knew what might go wrong?

"Harbor Street," Alorria said. "Isn't that where most of the fighting was last night?"

"I think the worst was on Quarter Street," Sarai said, "but yes, there was fighting there. We'll be reversing the route of Tabaea's march for about half our journey—the entire time we aren't on Wizard Street, we'll be on the streets she used." She had not really thought about that before; it would be interesting to see if there was more obvious evidence of Tabaea's accession than there was on Wizard Street.

Alorria shuddered. "I've never been on a battlefield before," she said.

"A battlefield?" Sarai had never thought of any part of Ethshar of the Sands as a battlefield. Battlefields were far-off places, in the Small Kingdoms or on the borders of Sardiron, not here in the heart of civilization. But what else was Tabaea's route from Grandgate to the palace, but a battlefield?

"We'll see it soon enough," Sarai said. "We turn at the next corner."

CHAPTER 28

At first, when Tabaea awoke, she didn't remember where she was. She looked up at the ornate canopy, the incredibly high, elaborately painted ceiling with its gilded coffering, and wondered what sort of an inn she had found this time.

The bed was broad and long and soft, the coverings rich and luxurious—a bed fit for the overlord, she thought.

And then memory came back. It *was* a bed fit for the overlord—or for the empress who had deposed him.

But it couldn't be real, she thought, sitting up. It must have been a dream. Even with all her magic, she couldn't have overthrown the overlord in a single night . . .

Could she?

A bellpull hung by the bed; she jerked at it, then slid out from under the coverlet and onto her feet.

She was wearing a red silk gown that she had never seen before—no, she corrected herself, she remembered changing into it last night. The chambermaid had tried to take away her old clothes, and Tabaea had refused.

Sure enough, draped across a chair was her skirt, still muddy; hung on the back was her embroidered tunic.

A dozen holes had been punched through it, it had been

slashed several places, and dried blood had stiffened it horribly. It looked like ancient scraps of untanned black leather.

Tabaea shuddered. Those holes and slashes had been made by swords and spears and arrows, and they had gone right through *her*, as well. That was her own blood that stained the fabric. She looked down at the robe she wore, then tore it open.

Faint scars traced across her breast. No one would ever have believed they were the remains of wounds less than a day old.

Tabaea blinked. *Were* they less than a day old? How long had she slept?

A door opened, and a young woman leaned in. "Yes, Your Majesty?" she asked.

"What time is it?" Tabaea demanded. "And what *day* is it?"

"It's midday, Your Majesty, or close to it, on the sixteenth of Harvest, in the Year of Speech 5227."

Tabaea relaxed slightly. She had marched to the palace on the night of the fifteenth, she was fairly sure. "Who are you?" she asked.

"Lethe of Longwall, Your Majesty. Your morning maid." She curtsied, still half-hidden by the door. Tabaea noticed that she was wearing the same gold tunic, red skirt, and white apron as the woman last night, Ista, who had given Tabaea a tour of her new home.

But this was definitely not Ista. Lethe was younger, shorter, and plumper. Ista worked at night. Lethe, it seemed, worked mornings.

"My morning maid." Tabaea grinned. "Fine. Excellent." She glanced around the room, and then down at the robe she had just torn.

"Fetch me some clothes, Lethe," Tabaea said. "Clothes fit for an empress. And rouse my court—the ones I brought with me and anyone who didn't flee with old Ederd. I intend to hold audience in half an hour, and I want them all there."

"Yes, Your Majesty." Lethe vanished, closing the door behind her.

Tabaea hopped back onto the edge of the bed and sat for a moment, swinging her feet and looking around the room, at the carved and polished woodwork, the ornate ceiling, the fine tapestries.

Then a tap sounded on the door.

"Come in," Tabaea called.

The door opened, and Lethe reappeared, but still did not fully enter the room. "Your Majesty," she said, "I've passed on your orders, and the mistress of the wardrobe is bringing selections from the closets of Annara the Graceful and others, but she asked me to tell you that there's been no time to make new dresses or alter what was here, so that she cannot promise any will fit properly at first."

"Who's Annara the Graceful?" Tabaea asked.

Lethe blinked, startled. "Why, that's the overlord's . . . I mean, the former overlord's granddaughter."

"Oh," Tabaea said. She had never taken much of an interest in politics. "He has grandchildren?"

"Only the one."

"Too bad. Is she pretty?"

Lethe hesitated. "I couldn't say," she answered at last.

Tabaea hopped off the bed again. "I take it she dressed well, at any rate."

"Yes, Your Majesty."

"I don't expect miracles about the fit . . ." Tabaea began. Then she stopped.

"But on the other hand," she said, "why *shouldn't* I expect miracles? Lethe, go fetch me the court magicians!"

Lethe's face turned white.

"Your Maj . . . Majesty," she stammered, "I can't."

"Why not?" Tabaea demanded, more curious than angry. "Are they so terrifying as all that?"

"No, Your Majesty; they're gone. They fled last night, for fear you would slay them all. They said that you had already killed many magicians."

"Oh." Tabaea considered that. Even after spying on several magicians as they discussed the murders, it had never occurred to her that killing half a dozen people could terrorize *all* the other magicians so thoroughly. It wasn't quite the effect she had in mind. She had just wanted one of each, to absorb their powers and abilities.

Well, what was done was done. "It doesn't matter," she said. "We'll make do with ordinary tailors and seamstresses to adapt my new clothes, then, rather than magic."

"Yes, Your Majesty."

A thought struck Tabaea. "What do they pay you, Lethe?" she asked.

"I have a room here in the palace that I share with three other maids, Your Majesty, and I get my meals, and six bits a day, as well." She lifted a corner of her apron. "And my clothes," she added.

"Is that all?"

Lethe nodded.

"From now on, Lethe, you'll be paid a round and a half—with none of those expensive magicians around, I'm sure the treasury can pay *all* you servants twice as much!"

"Yes, Your Majesty. Thank you." Lethe curtsied.

"And the dungeons—last night Ista showed me the stair to the dungeons, but we didn't go down. Are there prisoners down there?"

"Yes, Your Majesty."

"I want them freed. Right now. All of them."

"Yes, Your Majesty." Lethe started to turn to go, then stopped and stepped out of the way as two men marched in, hauling a large wooden trunk. Behind this came a tall woman in a green and gold gown, perhaps the most extravagant garment Tabaea had ever seen.

"Your Majesty," this new arrival said, as the men set the trunk on the floor, "it's such an honor to meet you! I'm Jandin, mistress of the wardrobe."

"I'll go tell the guards," Lethe called, ducking out. Almost out of earshot, she added, "If I can find any." The two men departed close on her heels, and the door closed behind them.

Jandin flung open the trunk, revealing a glittering array of expensive fabric, fine embroidery, and bright jewelry. Tabaea gasped, and her eyes went wide.

"Now, if Your Majesty could give me just the tiniest clue as to how you wish to appear today," Jandin said, "I'm sure I can find something here that will suit us . . ."

An hour later, as the nervous courtiers milled about the Great Hall in two distinct groups, the old and the new, their desultory conversations were cut short by the sound of trumpets. All eyes turned toward the rear staircase, and a few unfortunates quickly scurried to one side or the other to get out of their ruler's path.

As Tabaea rose into sight someone stifled a giggle.

The empress was wearing the most incredibly gaudy dress that anyone present had ever seen. The basic colors were red and green, in alternating panels divided by gold borders. Jewels in a dozen hues glittered along every golden border and in elaborate patterns on the panels, as well. Gold braid circled the waist, hips, and bust, and edged each cuff; fine gold chains draped across the bodice. Padded crests rose from either shoulder. Gold-edged slashes in the puffed sleeves revealed tight black velvet undersleeves. She also wore dangling earrings of intricately wrought gold, and a headpiece of woven peacock feathers.

Several jaws dropped at the sight.

"I'll be damned," someone muttered as Tabaea made her slow march down the full length of the hall to the throne. He leaned to a companion and whispered, "I know that dress—Annara had it made for a show in the Arena. It was supposed to represent greed and tastelessness."

"Do you think Tabaea knows?"

"She couldn't—she wouldn't wear it if she knew."

"Maybe someone's played a trick on her?"

"That's one very risky trick to play on a known murderer and self-proclaimed empress!"

The speakers had no way of knowing that Tabaea, with her stolen abilities, could hear every word they said. She flushed angrily, but continued her procession, up onto the dais. With each step she considered what, if anything, she should do to Jandin; the wardrobe mistress had not suggested the dress, but she had not said anything against it when Tabaea had pulled it out, either. And she had put it in the trunk in the first place, hadn't she?

But on the other hand, Tabaea realized that this incident might well determine the whole tenor of her reign, whether she was seen as a ruthless tyrant or a merciful and generous benefactor. She had heard those courtiers call her a "known murderer," and she didn't like it. That was not the image she wanted.

Therefore, when she reached the dais, she turned and announced, "Welcome, my people!"

No one answered; no one knew what reply was expected.

"The brutal reign of the heirs of Anaran is ended!" Tabaea announced. "Today we begin a new era of justice and mercy! I hereby decree an end to slavery in this city; all slaves in Ethshar of the Sands are to be freed immediately! I decree forgiveness for those who have been driven to crime by the cruelty of my predecessors; all prisoners in the dungeons are likewise to be freed immediately! I decree that the brutal oppression of innocents by the city guard is to cease immediately; all guardsmen are to surrender their swords and are hereby charged with finding food and lodging for all those who have been forced to take shelter in the Wall Street Field! I decree that those who serve me shall be paid according to their true worth, and that for the present, that shall be assumed to be twice whatever my foul predecessor, the so-called overlord, saw fit to pay them!''

"She's mad," a courtier muttered, "completely mad!"

''*No!*'' Tabaea shouted. "I am *not* mad!'' She leaped from the dais and marched across the room, a pointing finger thrust out before her.

The courtiers parted, and she confronted the man who had dared to speak.

"Who are you?" she demanded.

The man bowed. "Lord Sancha, Minister of the Port," he said. "At Your Majesty's service."

"Minister of the Port?" Tabaea asked.

"I have that honor, Your Majesty."

"Not anymore," Tabaea said. She laughed. "Sancha is no name for a portmaster, in any case. You're now Sancha the Fool, and your job is to entertain me with your foolishness." She had heard of such things in old tales about the Small Kingdoms; she had no idea whether Ethshar had ever had a court jester before, and she didn't much care. It had one now.

"As Your Majesty wills," Sancha said, bowing more deeply— *much* more deeply, an exaggerated, absurd bow.

Tabaea smiled. He was taking to his new post already. She reached out and grabbed his nose, then turned and led him to the dais. Those watching assumed that Lord Sancha was playing along as he followed, struggling wildly to keep his nose from injury; they had no idea just how strong Tabaea actually was. She was, in fact, hauling Sancha against his will, and the process was quite painful. She pushed him to the floor beside the throne, then sat down.

"It seems we need a new Minister of the Port," she said, "and undoubtedly there are other posts to be filled, as well, as I understand many of the officials of the city chose to depart with old Ederd. Fortunately, I brought some people to fill these vacated positions." She waved at the motley group that had followed her from Grandgate; some were still in their own ragged clothing, while others had plundered the palace and put on newer, cleaner, and better clothes. Some were dressed splendidly, others ineptly; the result was a far more mixed group than the original rags had produced, and a far more mixed group than the more uniform and sedate crowd left from the overlord's court.

"Now, if you'll come forward, one at a time, and tell me who you are," Tabaea said, "we'll see if we can't put together a better government than this city has ever seen before!"

CHAPTER 29

At first glance, Harbor Street appeared unchanged—but upon a closer look, Sarai noticed differences. Windows were broken, buildings blackened by smoke, and walls chipped by blades and flying debris. Dark stains could still be seen in the dirt. And several businesses, perhaps the majority, were closed, although it was full daylight.

At least there weren't any bodies or other remains; someone had cleaned up after the fighting, clearing away the dead and wounded, dropped weapons, broken glass, and the rest.

Even so, the journey impressed upon Sarai that Tabaea had done real damage to Ethshar of the Sands. She arrived at the Guildhouse in a very somber and thoughtful mood indeed.

Someone she didn't know opened the door to her knock, and showed the three of them, Sarai and Kelder and Alorria, into the parlor. Alorria inquired after Tobas, and was promptly led away; Kelder and Sarai waited in uncomfortable silence for a second or two before Mereth, rumpled and worried, came to welcome them.

"How many died?" Sarai asked Mereth, after only the most perfunctory greetings.

"I don't know," Mereth said. "I don't think anyone's counted. At least, no one here; I suppose Lord Torrut knows."

"Where is Lord Torrut, then?"

Mereth shrugged. "I don't know, Lady Sarai. In hiding somewhere, probably—or perhaps he's holed up in the barracks towers; so far, almost all of the city guard has remained loyal to him."

Lady Sarai looked around at the parlor, which had continued undisturbed by Serem's murder, by the house's usurpation by the Wizards' Guild, by the overthrow of the city government. The animated plant still fanned the air endlessly.

She shooed away a spriggan and then settled slowly onto a divan embroidered with pink and green flowers.

"Is that wise?" she asked.

Mereth blinked, puzzled. "Is what wise?"

"I take it that Lord Torrut is still resisting," Sarai said, "even though Tabaea's in the palace and the overlord has fled."

"Well, he isn't actually fighting anymore," Mereth said, seating herself in a nearby armchair, "but I'm sure he isn't taking orders from her."

"And I wonder if that's wise," Sarai said. "Maybe we should just let her govern and not damage the city further."

"But she's a murderer!" Mereth protested, "and a thief, a burglar! And she's . . . wizards aren't allowed in government."

"Is she a wizard?" Sarai asked. "She's not a member of the Guild."

"She's a magician, and she's something *like* a wizard, and the Guild doesn't want *any* magicians interfering in politics. It's dangerous. It's a bad precedent."

"Then perhaps it's the job of the Wizards' Guild to remove her," Lady Sarai said. "I don't see any reason to throw away more lives trying to depose her. And whether we like it or not, at the moment she *is* the ruler of Ethshar of the Sands, and she can't rule without the city guard—the guard is what gives the government authority, and no one can run the city without it. I think perhaps Lord Torrut should reconsider."

"*I* don't," Mereth said. "Maybe if she finds out that she can't run the city she'll pack up and leave."

"Somehow, I doubt she'll do that," Sarai replied. "And who's to say that she can't be a good ruler? It's not as if Ederd was chosen by the gods, or worked his way up to be overlord; he just happened to be born right."

"Isn't that enough?" Mereth asked, shocked. "He's Anaran's heir!"

"Anaran was a fine general, but does that mean all his descendants are going to be natural rulers?" Sarai said. "They've ruled Ethshar of the Sands for seven generations now; doesn't that mean that less than one part in a hundred of Ederd's blood comes from Anaran?"

"Oh, but they've intermarried with the families of the other overlords, and bred back in . . ."

"So what?"

"Lady Sarai," Kelder interrupted, "at least Anaran's descendants did not take their thrones by force, or murder innocents in their beds."

"That's true," Sarai admitted. "But I still don't like it. I don't want anyone else to be killed."

"None of us do," Mereth said. "Or at least, we don't want anyone other than Tabaea to be killed."

"Mereth?" The voice came from the archway opening into the central hall; Sarai and Kelder turned to find Lirrin, Serem's former apprentice, standing there.

"You're needed downstairs," Lirrin said.

"What's happening downstairs?" Sarai asked. She blinked; *was* there a downstairs? She hadn't noticed that when she visited the house in the course of her investigation.

"Guild business," Lirrin said apologetically. Mereth rose, gathering her skirts, then looked back at Sarai.

"Oh." Sarai glanced at Kelder, who shrugged.

"I'm no more a wizard than you," he said. "We can wait here together and pass the time."

"I'm sorry, Lady Sarai," Mereth said. "I'll be back as soon as I can." She and Lirrin vanished down the hallway.

That left Kelder and Sarai alone in the parlor; for a moment they sat in awkward silence.

"Do you still have all those talismans and trinkets of yours?" Sarai asked at last.

"Of course," he said, gesturing at his pack.

"Do you think they could tell you anything more about Tabaea that might be useful in deposing her? She was in this house once, after all."

"Oh, I doubt it," Kelder said. "There will be traces, but what they can tell us will be limited. If you like, I can see what there is to see."

"I'd be very interested."

Kelder bobbed his head in a semblance of a bow. "Then I'll try," he said. He opened his pack and began rummaging through it.

A moment later he emerged holding a thin silver box set with square-cut gems. "A *denekin allasir*," he explained, tapping an uneven rhythm upon it.

"What's that mean?" Lady Sarai asked.

"I haven't any idea," Kelder admitted. "It's just what it's called."

"What does it do?"

Kelder proudly explained, "It reads traces a person has left—flakes of skin, bits of hair, even the air he or she breathed—and then displays for me a pattern of lights, in this row of jewels here, that I can interpret to tell me about that person. What I can see will vary; sometimes it's a great deal, sometimes it's nothing at all."

Lady Sarai looked at the row of jewels Kelder pointed to. She could see odd little curls of light, glowing deep within the stones, but they made no pattern that she could see. "And what does it tell you about Tabaea?" she asked.

"Well, this is the device that gave me the description I gave you," Kelder said. "I don't suppose it will find any trace of her in here, though; the murder was upstairs, and I assume Tabaea came in through the bedroom window."

"Did she?"

Kelder hesitated. "I don't know," he said. "Shall we find out?"

Sarai nodded.

"If she used the stairs, we'll probably find . . ." Kelder began, as he tapped at a dark blue gem on the side of his little box. Then he stopped in midsentence and stared. He began tapping other jewels and various places on the surface of the *allasir*.

"What is it?" Lady Sarai asked.

"She was here," Kelder said.

"That's not so very surprising," Sarai began.

"No, no, Lady Sarai," Kelder said, cutting her off. "She was here *four years ago*. Several times."

"Perhaps she knew Serem, then," Sarai suggested. "Perhaps she bought a potion from him, or sold him something he needed for one of his spells. It's hardly as shocking as all that."

Kelder blinked.

"I suppose you're right," he said. "Yes, of course you're right." He sighed. "And here I thought I'd found something important."

"Well, perhaps you did," Lady Sarai said comfortingly. "There *might* be a connection. Why don't we go discuss it with the others, the wizards?"

"Do you think that's a good idea?" Kelder asked.

"Yes, I do," Sarai said, getting to her feet. "I'm tired of being shut out by them, anyway. Maybe we can trade this discovery of yours for some of *their* information." She pushed aside the plant that was waving determinedly at her and headed for the hallway. Kelder followed.

In the central corridor Sarai stopped, suddenly aware that she didn't know where the wizards were.

"That way," Kelder said, holding out his silver box.

Following his directions, Sarai soon found herself on the stairs to the old wizard's great underground chamber, which she had not known existed; surprised into caution and silence, she crept down the steps slowly and carefully.

Before her, she saw a score of wizards—Mereth, Tobas, Lirrin, the Guildmasters Telurinon, Heremon, and Algarin, and others she knew only slightly or not at all. No one else could be seen; despite Tobas's presence, Alorria was not there.

Voices rose from below.

". . . the dagger," an unfamiliar voice said, "it must be that dagger she carries that's stopping all our spells."

"I don't think there's much doubt of that," replied Telurinon. "Which leaves us with the question of where the dagger came from, and what it is, and how this thief obtained it."

"We've been using the Spell of Omniscient Vision," Mereth's voice said. "We've managed to follow her back for a few months, though it's very difficult, the way she's constantly moved around and never lived in the same place for more than a few sixnights. She's always had that dagger, as far back as we've gone. She always had that embroidered tunic and black skirt, and a few other things, as well—I've made a list—are you sure it's the dagger?"

A chorus of voices replied, all in the affirmative.

Lady Sarai cleared her throat.

No one heard her, as Telurinon said, "I'm sure you've all seen the significance of the fact that this woman's magic appears to reside in a dagger . . ."

"Ahem," Lady Sarai said loudly. She really did not want to be accused of spying on wizards.

Several eyes turned toward her, and someone shrieked.

"Excuse me," Lady Sarai said, trying very hard to stay calm, "but Kelder and I have just learned something that we thought might be of use."

Guildmaster Telurinon stepped forward from the corner where he had been standing, and glared up at the new arrivals.

"*Lady* Sarai," he said, "what is the meaning of this intrusion? Surely, despite your display the other day at the Cap and Dagger, you know better than to enter uninvited into the private councils of the Wizards' Guild!"

Lady Sarai glared back. "And surely *you*, sir, know better than to leave the doors unlocked and unwarded when conducting private councils! Therefore, this could hardly have been such a council, or else neither of us would have made such a foolish mistake!"

Mereth giggled nervously; Tobas threw her a warning glance.

"The doors of this house *are* locked and warded, my lady, and you are here only because the door was opened for you," Telurinon replied. "Still, I see your point and concede that you have not forfeited your life."

"How gracious of you," Lady Sarai said. "Now, as I started to explain, the forensic sorcerer, Kelder of Tazmor, has learned something that might be of use in your investigations."

"And what might that be?" Telurinon asked, in the unconvinced tone of one merely being polite about a waste of his time.

Sarai moved aside and beckoned Kelder forward; the sorcerer stepped up to the railing and announced, "I have found traces of Tabaea the Thief's presence in this very house—in fact, on this very stairway—dating back some four years, to the summer of 5223."

"You mean she *lived* here?" Algarin asked.

"No," Kelder answered. "The only traces of her presence upstairs were those left when she murdered Serem the Wise. But on several occasions in 5223 she passed through the front parlor, down the hallway and onto this staircase where I now stand."

"Only that year?" Tobas asked. "Not since then?"

"Not since then," Kelder confirmed.

"Why did she come down here?" Mereth asked. "Why would Serem allow it?"

"She didn't go down there," Kelder said. "The trail stops right here, at this railing."

The wizards looked at one another.

"She *spied* on him," someone said.

"She spied on *us*," Lirrin answered. "That was when . . . I mean . . . I began my apprenticeship on the eighth of Rains, 5223."

"These visits," Telurinon asked. "Can you date them precisely?"

Kelder shook his head. "Not to the day, certainly. I doubt any were as early as Rains, though—I would judge them to fall mostly in the later part of Greengrowth, and perhaps into the first half of Longdays."

The wizards exchanged looks again.

"Leave us," Telurinon said.

Lady Sarai said, "But . . ."

"Go!" Telurinon bellowed. "We thank you for this information, but we must speak *in private* now—Tobas, see that the door is locked and warded."

"Yes, Guildmaster," Tobas said. He headed for the stairs.

Sarai and Kelder did not wait for him; they turned and retreated, back up the steps and out through Serem's cluttered little workroom. They were in the hallway when Sarai heard the door slam shut.

"Lady Sarai?" a woman's voice called.

Sarai turned and saw Karanissa on the stairs. Teneria and Alorria were behind her, watching over her shoulders.

"We sensed some upset," she said.

"We intruded on Guildmaster Telurinon's meeting," Sarai explained.

"Oh." The witch glanced at the door to the workroom. "That's unfortunate," she said. "Telurinon can be very difficult." She hesitated, then asked, "Have you had breakfast, either of you?"

"No," Lady Sarai admitted. "At least, I haven't. Have all of you?"

"Yes, but don't let that trouble you." Karanissa trotted quickly down the stairs and led the way to the kitchens, where she found biscuits, jam, and a variety of fruit for Sarai and Kelder.

Teneria and Alorria joined them there, and the five sat comfortably chatting for some time.

They were still there, though the food was long gone, when Telurinon marched in and informed them all that they were no longer welcome in the Guildhouse.

"It's nothing personal," he said, after the initial shock had passed. "The incident this morning demonstrated, however, that it's a serious mistake to allow anyone not a member of the Guild to be in the building when we have such important and secret matters to discuss as we do at present."

"Wait a minute," Sarai protested. "We had an . . ."

"Lady Sarai," Telurinon retorted, cutting her short, "or rather, Sarai of Ethshar, we had an agreement to share information relevant to your investigation of a series of murders. Well, that investigation is over now—the identity of the killer is known, her whereabouts are known, and the question is not who is responsible, but how to punish her, which is purely a Guild matter and none of the concern of the city government. And furthermore, *you*, along with your overlord, have been removed from office. We have no more information to share with you."

"But . . ."

"And even if that were not the case," Telurinon continued, "we never invited you to wander into our councils whenever you chose. There are times when we wish to discuss matters that we never agreed to share with you or anyone else outside the Guild, matters that it is absolutely forbidden for anyone outside the Guild to know." He turned to the others. "I expect that your husband will find a comfortable inn for you all, Alorria and Karanissa—the Cap and Dagger, perhaps. Or if you prefer, I'm sure some other member of the Guild will be glad to accommodate you."

For a moment no one spoke; then Telurinon turned to go. Alorria stuck her tongue out at his departing figure, and Sarai, despite herself, giggled.

When the mage had gone, the giggle vanished.

"Now what will I do?" she asked.

CHAPTER 30

"*I*s this all of them?" the Empress Tabaea said, looking over the immense crowd that was jammed into her throne room and spilling down the three grand staircases.

"All who would come," her newly appointed chancellor replied.

Tabaea turned to him, startled. "Some wouldn't come?"

"Yes, Your Majesty. Some people refused your invitation."

"Why? Did they say why?"

"Some of them did."

"Why, then?"

The chancellor hesitated, scuffed a foot on the marble, and then said, "Various reasons, Your Majesty."

Tabaea could smell his nervousness, but was not in a mood to let him avoid explanations. "Name a few, Arl. Just for our enlightenment."

"Well, some . . ." He glanced warily at her, and seeing more curiosity than anger, he continued, "some didn't trust you. They suspected a trick of some kind, that you were going to enslave them all, or kill them."

"Why would I want to do *that*?" Tabaea was honestly baffled. She could smell that Arl was telling the truth; his tension had decreased as he spoke, rather than increasing, and liars didn't do that.

Chancellor Arl shrugged. "I couldn't say, Your Majesty."

"What other reasons did they give?"

"Well, some said they were happy where they were, that they enjoyed living in the open—there are a few people who are like that, Your Majesty . . ."

"I know." She cut him off with a wave of her hand. "I never understood why they stay in the city, instead of out in the wilderness somewhere, if that's what they want, but I've met them. What else?"

"A few said they wouldn't bother moving because they didn't think . . . uh . . . they said that it wouldn't last, they'd just have to go back in a few days . . ."

He was getting nervous again. "Why?" the Empress demanded. "Do they think I'm going to change my mind and throw everyone out again?"

"That, or that you . . . um . . . won't remain in power."

"Oh." Tabaea frowned. "Well, they're wrong about *that*, anyway. The overlord's run for his life and isn't coming back, and I'm going to stay right here."

"Yes, Your Majesty."

Tabaea turned back to the crowd, then asked her chancellor one final question. "How many are there, here?"

"I have no idea, Your Majesty," Arl admitted unhappily. "I didn't think to count them."

Tabaea nodded, then addressed the crowd. "People of Ethshar!" she said, "welcome to my palace!"

A halfhearted cheer rose, then died.

"I am Tabaea the First, Empress of Ethshar, your new ruler!" Tabaea continued. "The days of oppression are at an end, and the cruel descendants of Anaran driven from us! All the people of Ethshar of the Sands are now free and equal—there shall be no more nobility to lord it over us, no more slaves to suffer unjustly!"

She paused for more applause, and after an uncertain beginning, she received a satisfactory ovation.

"No citizen of my city need cower in the Wall Street Field for fear of the overlord's guards and tax collectors," Tabaea said. "Those who have no homes of their own will now have a home *here*, with me, in the palace built by the sweat of slaves . . ."

The chancellor cleared his throat and looked up at the dome— the dome which every educated person in Ethshar knew had been built mostly by magic, not by muscle. Tabaea carried on, ignoring him.

". . . a palace far larger than any conceivable government might need, built entirely for the ostentatious display of power and wealth! You may all stay here as long as you wish, and in exchange I ask only that you help clean and maintain the palace, that you run those errands I and my aides might ask of you, and that you stand with me against any misguided fools who might try to restore the foul Ederd to my throne. What do you say?"

The applause was not all that Tabaea had hoped for—several of her listeners were unenthusiastic about those unspecified errands and the call to help defend the palace—but she decided it would do.

When the crowd had quieted—which really, Tabaea thought, happened a little too quickly—the empress raised her arms for silence, and continued.

"As some of you probably know," she said, "much of the former overlord's city guard has not yet accepted my authority. I ordered them to turn in their swords, as a sign that they would no longer rule through fear, and many have refused to do so." In fact, fewer than a hundred had handed in swords, and she knew that there were supposed to be ten thousand men in the city guard. "Some of these renegades have scattered among the people, abandoning their posts; others have gone into hiding,

where they seem to have maintained a semblance of organization, in defiance of my orders. While I, since I am no oppressing
tyrant, have no need for the large numbers of thugs and parasites
my predecessor retained, still, there are some tasks appropriate
to soldiers that yet need doing—searching the city for slave-
owners who ignore my order to free their prisoners, for one. If
any of you would like to volunteer to help with this glorious
liberation, report to my new and loyal general, Derneth, for-
merly Derneth the Fence, at the northeast door of the palace
today at midday. And all of you are free to come and go as you
please—this palace is home to *all* my people, from this day
forward!''

The applause was a little better this time, Tabaea thought. She
smiled and waved, then stepped back and sat down on her throne.

The crowd dissipated slowly as Tabaea sat and watched, her
smile gradually growing rigid and fixed. She had expected it all
to vanish rather quickly, as her guests went about their business,
but it didn't; some stubbornly refused to vanish at all, quickly
or otherwise. Some of the people simply stood, watching her
nervously, and gave no sign of leaving; a few approached the
dais cautiously, then stopped, or changed their minds and retreated.

''You haven't told them what to do,'' Arl whispered.

''They can do what they like,'' Tabaea snapped, the pretense
of a smile disappearing instantly.

''But some of them don't know what that *is*, Your Majesty,''
her chancellor explained. ''Not everyone in the Wall Street Field
was there through simple misfortune, you know; some were
there because they didn't fit anywhere else—they're mad, or
simpleminded, or blind, or deaf, or crippled, or deranged in
various other ways.''

''So what?'' Tabaea demanded. ''They're still people!''

''Yes, of course, Your Majesty,'' Arl agreed hastily. ''But
some of them aren't entirely capable of thinking for themselves;
they don't know what to do unless someone tells them.'' He
looked out at the few dozen people who still lingered. ''And I
think some of these people have favors to ask of you, but don't
know how to go about it.''

Tabaea glared up at Arl, then at the waiting citizens. A handful, noting her expression, headed for the stairs, but the others
remained; at least one smiled tentatively at her.

''All right, Arl,'' Tabaea said, ''have them form a line, and

I'll hear them. I suppose an empress has to do some work to earn her keep, like any other honest citizen.''

"Yes, Your Majesty." Arl bowed hesitantly; he had never been in the palace before Tabaea's conquest the night before last, had never formally learned anything of court etiquette, and in any case Tabaea's rules might well differ from what had gone before—if Tabaea *had* any rules—but he had seen a few plays, had seen the overlord's visits to the Arena and how he was treated there, and thought that a bow was appropriate at this point.

Then he stepped to the front of the dais, where he paused for a moment to think how to word what he wanted to say. When he thought he had it worked out, he took a deep breath and announced, "Her Imperial Majesty, Tabaea the First, Empress of Ethshar of the Sands, will now hold audience. Those who wish to address the emp . . . address Her Majesty may form a line." He pointed to a spot just before his own feet.

He had the feeling that a true chancellor, or chamberlain—wasn't this something a chamberlain would do?—would have made that sound better, somehow. Until two days ago, Arl had been a beggar and swindler, not a courtier; he had used fancy words, all right, but for persuasion, not formal announcements. It was a different sort of skill.

Of course, it was his old skill, carefully applied to his "old friend" Tabaea, that had gotten him his impressive title and powerful position in the first place.

People were lining up, just the way they were supposed to; Arl was pleased with himself. Without waiting for everyone to settle into place, he took the first one, an old woman, by the hand and led her up onto the dais. After a moment's hesitation, he turned and sent her on her way to the throne, but did not accompany her.

Uncertainly, the woman took a few tottering steps, then stood before the throne, looking down at Tabaea.

The empress looked back.

The old woman was supposed to kneel, Tabaea thought, and she showed no sign of doing it. Her scent didn't provide any useful information about what she was feeling or planning—she wasn't scared or excited. Her movements gave no clues.

Well, she was supposed to kneel, and Tabaea decided that she *would* kneel. Her warlock's touch reached out and gripped the woman's knees, forcing them to bend.

The old woman almost tumbled forward; she was far slower catching herself than Tabaea had expected. At last, though, she steadied, and knelt before the throne.

Tabaea addressed her.

"What is it you want, woman?"

"I want a turn in the pretty chair," the woman mumbled.

Tabaea stared at her.

"I want a turn," the woman repeated, pointing at the throne.

For a moment, the empress couldn't believe she had heard correctly. When she did believe it, her first reaction was fury.

Then she remembered what Arl had said about some of the people from the Field; the old woman was obviously demented.

"No," Tabaea said gently. "It's *my* throne. I'm the empress."

"You said we could share," the woman protested.

"The *palace*," Tabaea said. "Not the throne."

"We don't share the pretty chair?"

"No," Tabaea said. "We don't."

"Oh." The old woman looked down at her knees, and announced, "I fell down."

"You knelt," Tabaea explained. "When you speak to an empress, you must kneel."

"Oh." She showed no sign of rising, of leaving; the line of other petitioners was growing restless, Tabaea could see it and smell it and hear it.

"Is there anyone taking care of you?" Tabaea asked.

"No."

"That's too bad," Tabaea said. "I think you could use some help. But you'll have to go now."

"Will you take care of me?"

"No, I'm too busy. I'm the empress."

"I like you."

"That's nice. Go away, now, and let someone else have a turn."

"But I didn't get to sit in the pretty chair."

Tabaea stared at the old woman, frustration beginning to overwhelm her determination to be patient and understanding. She wished someone else would come and drag the old fool away, that there was someone she could signal, but Arl was much too busy keeping order among the others, and she had no one else there to help her. Her other new appointees had been sent off about their various businesses, and what with desertions and confusion she didn't have all the guards and servants that the overlord had kept close at hand.

To get rid of this nuisance she would either have to call for help or use her own two hands, either of which seemed beneath her dignity as empress.

Tabaea began to see that there was a contradiction here, between her desire to be an absolute ruler, honored and respected, and her desire to avoid oppressing her people. She might want to be a fair and reasonable empress, but obviously, there were people in the city who wouldn't be fair and reasonable subjects.

And with people like that, soldiers would be very useful.

Even if she *had* had a thousand soldiers in the palace, Tabaea realized, in her determination to be a good and kind and fair and accessible ruler she would have sent them away while she was holding court. She now saw that this would not have been a good idea. She resolved that when things were more organized, when she had a proper city guard of her own, she would keep a couple of soldiers nearby.

For now, she had to improvise. The warlock power reached out and pinched the old woman's nostrils shut.

"Go away," Tabaea told her, as the woman gasped for breath.

The invisible grip vanished, and the woman got to her feet.

She did not leave, however; instead she reached out and slapped Tabaea across the face. "You nasty!" she shrieked. "You squeezed my nose!"

Tabaea, with her animal responses, had seen the blow coming and ducked aside; what should have been a resounding blow was just a gentle brush across one cheek.

Still, it could not be tolerated; in an instant, Tabaea was on her feet, picking the old woman up by the throat, one-handed.

She looked up at the astonishment on the ancient face and said, "You should die for that. The person of your empress is not to be touched. Because of your age, because my reign is new and you understand little, you won't die this time, but don't ever let me see or smell you again."

Then she flung the woman out onto the marble floor of the audience hall. Brittle old bones snapped, and the woman lay in a heap, moaning softly.

"Get her out of here," Tabaea said.

No one moved.

"*Get her out of here!*" Tabaea shouted, pointing at the line of waiting petitioners.

Two men from the back ran to obey; a few of the others abruptly decided that whatever requests they might have had could wait until a more propitious time, and scurried away down the side stairs.

Tabaea settled back on the throne, touched her unmarked cheek, then turned to Arl and snapped, "Next!"

CHAPTER 31

*I*t had been Lady Sarai's own suggestion that she not stay at the same inn as Tobas and his wives; she had been worried that such a group would be too distinctive. Instead, she had gratefully accepted a loan of a dozen copper rounds and had found herself lodgings at the Fatted Calf, an inn on Soldiertown Street, a block south of Grandgate Market. The rather inept painting on the inn's signboard had given it the nickname the Bloated Beef, and that had seemed to imply a cheerful good humor.

That was not, Sarai discovered, reflected in the inn's rather tense atmosphere. Her night there was an uneasy one; whenever she had set foot outside her own room she had been in constant fear that someone would recognize and denounce her.

The conversation in the common room had been strained for almost everyone; two burly men had announced that they were friends of the new empress, members of the new court, and as such entitled to the best *oushka* in the house, at no charge. The innkeeper had been inclined to refuse, and a former guardsman—at least, he wore no sword, though he was still in the traditional red and yellow and had spoken of fighting Tabaea's mob on Harbor Street—had supported that refusal, whereupon the two thugs had beaten the guardsman soundly and thrown him out into the street.

Those others among the guests who might have been inclined to help found themselves badly outnumbered by those who were cheering the thugs on and had declined to intervene, thereby avoiding an all-out brawl.

The thugs got their *oushka*. They also got the company of a frightened young woman. One of them eyed Sarai herself, but when Sarai bared her teeth, in as threatening a snarl as she could manage, he turned away and didn't pursue the matter.

And Sarai stayed the night, as she had planned, since it was too late to go elsewhere and she had nowhere else to go, but the next morning she left quickly, taking a pastry with her for her breakfast.

Like anyone strolling in that part of the city with no particular destination in mind, she found herself wandering into Grandgate Market. For a while she strolled about, nibbling her pastry while looking over the merchants' goods and the farmers' produce; superficially, it all appeared quite normal, unchanged by Tabaea's accession.

On a closer look, though, anyone reasonably observant—and Sarai knew herself to be at least reasonably observant—would notice that there were no guards at the gate.

There were subtler differences as well. The great gates themselves stood open, but the doors that led into the towers did not; they were instead locked and barred. The familiar yellow tunics and red kilts of soldiers were not only not to be seen at the gate, they were nowhere in sight, not in the gate or the market or the streets.

The rather sparse crowd in the marketplace did not seem particularly troubled by the guards' absence; in fact, if anything, Sarai thought the buyers and sellers looked somewhat more prosperous than usual.

That didn't seem right; she looked again.

There was a real difference, she realized, but it was not that the merchants or farmers or their customers were attired any better than their usual wont. Rather, the difference was that there were no beggars. In all of Grandgate Market, no one wore rags, any more than anyone wore the red kilt of the overlord's service.

Sarai wondered at that. Tabaea might well have promised to eliminate poverty, but how could she have possibly made any significant change so *quickly*?

And for that matter, where did all the soldiers actually *go*? Ten thousand people—well, seven or eight thousand, anyway; she knew that the guard had not been up to its full authorized strength for decades—could not simply vanish.

Or could they? It was a big city, after all. There were hundreds of miles of streets and alleyways out there, and all a soldier needed to do to hide was to get out of uniform.

And there were plenty of little-used military and government installations, as well—the towers at Beachgate and Northgate and Smallgate, the Island Tower out past the South Channel, the Great Lighthouse, the four towers guarding the harbor, all the dozens of watch-stations along the wall, the tunnels and passages under the wall, even the Arena's maze of storerooms and corridors, all of those were under Lord Torrut's jurisdiction before Tabaea's arrival. Companies of guardsmen could be gathered in any of them.

The soldiers could even still be in the two immense barracks towers here at Grandgate itself, or in the six towers that guarded the city's main landward entrance; just because the doors were closed and no soldiers were in sight, that didn't mean there were no soldiers inside. Sarai wandered northward across the square, toward the gate, the towers, and the barracks.

The tower doors were unmistakably closed and barred; the windows were shuttered, those that had shutters. From her vantage point in the market she could see no signs of life anywhere in the entire elaborate complex that guarded the entrance to Ethshar of the Sands.

Idly, she wandered on northward, out of the market and into the Wall Street Field.

And in the Field she finally found a place that did not appear normal in the least.

Most of the shacks and hovels were still there, though some had been knocked down or had simply collapsed; the stones that some of those who dwelt there had used as boundary markers or weights to keep blankets in place were still scattered about, indicating rough paths between bedsites. The charred remnants of cookfires could still be seen here and there.

The hundreds of Ethsharites who had lived there, though, were gone.

Normally, Lady Sarai would not have dared to enter the Field without an escort of well-armed guardsmen. Normally, the place would be constantly abuzz with conversation, shouts, arguments, the cries of children, and the rattle of crockery. Babies would be wailing, youngsters would be laughing and chasing one another through the chaos.

The only sounds now were the flapping of unfastened doorcloths, the snuffling of dogs and other animals scavenging in the ruins, and the distant hum of Grandgate Market and the rest of the city going about its business.

The effect was eerie and utterly unsettling; despite the growing heat of the day, Sarai shivered and pulled her loose tunic a little more closely about her. Even that didn't help much, as it reminded her that this was the third day that she had been wearing this same tunic, this same skirt.

Her uneasiness was such that she almost screamed when a spriggan giggled nearby, leaped down from atop a ramshackle lean-to, and ran shrieking past her feet. Cursing, she watched the little nuisance scurry away.

When she had regained her composure, she forced herself to think.

Where had everyone gone?

She knew that some of the people here had followed Tabaea in her march to the palace, but surely, not *all* of them had! The mob that the magicians had reported had hardly been large enough to account for the entire population of the Field!

Where were the rest of them, then? Had Tabaea done something terrible to those who had refused to follow her? Old tales Sarai had heard from her mother as a child came back to her, stories about how Northern demonologists, during the Great War, would sacrifice entire villages to appease their patron demons, or to pay for horrible services those demons might perform. Sarai had long since decided that those tales were just leftover lies, wartime propaganda, but now she wondered whether there might be some truth to the legends, and whether Tabaea might have made some ghastly bargain with creatures no sane demonologist would dare approach.

Of course, she told herself, she might be jumping to conclusions. She didn't even know for certain how much of the Wall Street Field really was abandoned; it could just be a block or two here by the barracks. Perhaps the city guard, before disbanding or fleeing or whatever they had done, had cleared this area for some obscure reason.

She walked on, past huts constructed of broken furniture and collapsed tents made of scavenged draperies, and sure enough, as she rounded the corner from Grandgate into Northangle, she saw the smoke of a small fire sliding up the summer sky.

"Hello!" she called. "Who's there?"

No one answered; cautiously, almost timidly, Sarai inched

closer, until she could see the little cookfire and the old woman sitting beside it.

"Hello!" she called again.

The woman turned, this time, and spotted Sarai.

"Hello yourself," she said.

"May I talk to you?" Sarai asked nervously.

"Don't see how I can very well stop you," the old woman replied. "I'm not planning to go anywhere if I can help it, and I doubt I have the strength to chase you away if you don't care to go." She poked at her fire with what looked to Sarai like an old curtain rod.

Sarai could hardly argue with this. She crept forward, then squatted beside the fire, at right angles to the old woman. To remain standing seemed rude, but she could not quite bring herself to sit on the dirt here, and there were no chairs, no blankets within easy reach.

"My name's Sarai," she said.

"Pretty," the old woman remarked. She poked the fire again, then added, "I don't usually give my name out to strangers. Most of the folks who used to live here called me Mama Kilina, though, and you can call me that if you need a name."

"Thank you," Sarai said, a little uncertainly.

For a moment the two sat silently; Sarai was unsure how to phrase her question, whether there was anything she should say to lead up to it, and Mama Kilina clearly had nothing that she particularly cared to say.

Finally, however, Sarai asked, "Where did everybody go?"

Mama Kilina glanced at her, a look that was not hostile, exactly, but which made it clear that the old woman didn't think much of the question. "Most folks," she said, "didn't go anywhere special. I'd suppose that everyone in the Small Kingdoms or the mountains of Sardiron must be going about all the usual business in the usual way, without paying any mind to what we've been doing here in Ethshar. And for that, I doubt the fifth part of the city knows anything's out of the ordinary, even here."

"I mean . . ." Sarai began.

Mama Kilina did not let her say any more; she raised a hand and said, "I know what you meant. I'm no dotard. You mean, where did most of the folks that ordinarily stay here in the Field for lack of anywhere better to go, go? And if you think, Sarai, as you name yourself, you might see that that question's got half its own answer in it, when it's asked right, just like most questions.''

Sarai blinked. ''I'm not sure I . . . oh. You mean they had somewhere better to go?''

''Well, they thought so, anyway. I didn't agree, and that's why I'm still here.''

''Where did they go, then? What's this better place?''

''What's the best place in Ethshar, to most ways of thinking?''

''I don't know, I . . . oh.'' Sarai finally saw the connection. ''The palace, you mean. They've all gone to the palace.''

''You have a little wit to you, I see.'' Mama Kilina's tone was one of mild satisfaction.

''But they can't all live there!'' Sarai said. ''It's not big enough! I mean, the palace is . . . well, it's huge, but . . .''

Mama Kilina nodded. ''Now, you think that's a better place?'' she asked. ''*I* don't, not with all that riffraff bedding down in the corridors, as I suppose they'll be doing.''

''Oh, but that's . . . I mean . . .'' Sarai groped for words, and finally asked, ''Is this Tabaea's idea?''

Mama Kilina nodded. ''That young woman's got no sense at all, if you ask me,'' she said. ''What she wants to be empress for in the first place I don't know, and how she can call herself an empress when all she rules is one city, and everyone knows an empress rules more than one people . . .'' She shook her head. ''I suppose she heard about that Vond calling himself an emperor, out in the Small Kingdoms, and she liked the sound of it, but Vond conquered half a dozen kingdoms before he called it an empire.''

''What exactly did she say? Did she come out here herself to invite everybody?''

''She sent messengers,'' Mama Kilina explained. ''A bunch of prissy fools got up in clothes that wouldn't look decent even on someone who knew how to wear them came out here and told us all that from now on, the palace belonged to all the people of Ethshar of the Sands, and we were all free to come and go as we pleased, and to live there if we wanted to until we could find homes of our own. And all those eager young idiots went galloping off down Wall Street to take her up on it and get a roof over their empty heads.'' She shook her head and spat in disgust, into the fire, where the gob of expectorate sizzled loudly.

''That whole mob living in the palace . . .'' Sarai said. The idea was horrifying—all those stone corridors jammed with people, with ragged beggars and belligerent thieves, strangers crowding into the rooms, into her office, into the family apartment—somehow the idea of Tabaea invading was nowhere near as upsetting as the notion of that entire indiscriminate mob. She wanted to get up and run back down there to save her family's possessions, to chase the squatters out of her old room, but of course she couldn't, she didn't dare show her face in the palace . . .

Or did she?

With all those strangers wandering in and out, who would recognize her? Who would stop her? She could just walk right in and see what Tabaea was up to, she could search out Tabaea's weaknesses—if she had any.

Of course, *some* people might recognize her, people who had seen her at her father's side. If she wore a disguise of some sort, though, no one would ask her who she was or what business she had in the palace.

This was just too good an opportunity to miss. She had been wondering where she could live, and here, it seemed, was the answer.

She could live in the palace, just as she always had!

CHAPTER 32

*T*obas had been idly turning a cat's skull over in his hands; now he flung it down on the table in disgust, cracking the jaw and loosening a fang.

"You're mad," he said.

Telurinon drew himself up, obviously seriously affronted. "I do not think," he began, "that there is any call for insults . . ."

"And that's just more evidence that you're mad," Tobas said, a little surprised at his own daring even as he said it. He had never before spoken to any other wizard, let alone a Guildmaster, so bluntly.

"Might I remind you . . ." Telurinon began.

Tobas interrupted again. "Might I remind *you*," he said, "that this Black Dagger is the cause of all the trouble we've seen in this city, trouble enough to bring me here all the way from Dwomor and to drag all of the rest of you away from your own affairs to attend these meetings. It's prevented us from killing someone that Guild law says *must* die. And you want to make *another* one?"

"I think we should at least consider the possibility," Teluri-non said. "After all, this artifact is, by its very nature, utterly immune to all other wizardry, and protects its wielder from wizardry as well. Our spells, as we have demonstrated repeatedly over these past few days, cannot touch its bearer. That being so, how *else* are we to defeat this Tabaea and destroy her utterly, as we must, except by creating another Black Dagger to counter the first?"

"If the esteemed Guildmaster will permit me," Tobas said, with thinly veiled sarcasm, "how are we to defeat whoever wields this *second* Black Dagger you propose to create?"

"Why, we'll have no need to defeat him," Telurinon said, honestly startled. "That's the entire point. We'll choose someone we can trust."

"*Will* we," Tobas replied. "Need I point out to the esteemed Guildmaster that whoever creates this dagger cannot be a wizard? The Spell of the Black Dagger is a perversion of the Spell of Athamezation and cannot be performed by anyone who has ever owned an athame—and therefore, since the athame is the mark of the true wizard and the sole token of membership in our Guild, whoever creates the new dagger must be an outsider. Has the Wizards' Guild *ever* trusted an outsider in *anything*, let alone something as important as this? How are we to explain to this outsider why *he* must perform this spell, rather than one of us? How are we to explain how this spell was ever discovered in the first place, if no wizard can perform it? And how can we trust anyone with a weapon like this, when by creating it in the first place we're admitting that we can't defeat it? Even if our hypothetical hero doesn't decide to make himself emperor in Tabaea's stead and doesn't go about murdering magicians, do we really want someone wandering the World with such a weapon? Even supposing we find some noble and innocent soul to serve as our warrior, and this trusting fellow builds himself up to be Tabaea's equal or superior and slays her, leaving himself in possession of *two* Black Daggers *and* the knowledge of how to make more, yet is *so* good and pure and wholesome that he never even *thinks* of turning those daggers against his sponsors in the Guild—even supposing all that, what happens when our original recruit dies, and passes the daggers on to his heirs, who might not be quite so cooperative?''

''We won't allow that,'' Telurinon said, rather huffily. ''When Tabaea is defeated, both daggers will become the property of the Guild.''

''Says who?''

''*We* say it, damn your insolence!'' Telurinon shouted.

''And who are we, that the bearer of a Black Dagger need listen to us?''

Telurinon glared at Tobas, mustache thrust out angrily. Before he could argue further, Mereth spoke up.

''And how would we build up our man?'' she asked. ''Tabaea killed people, half a dozen of them. She killed a warlock and a witch. For our dagger-wielder to match her, *he* would have to kill a warlock and a witch. I don't think that's a good idea at all.''

''Of course not!'' Telurinon yelled. Then he repeated, more quietly, ''Of course not.'' He frowned. Reluctantly, he admitted, ''I see that there are difficulties with the scheme. While I am not convinced that these difficulties are insuperable, they are, I fear, undeniable. In which case I must ask if, bluntly, anyone has a better idea.''

It was at that moment that Lirrin, who was acting as doorkeeper, appeared at the railing above the chamber and made the sign of requesting recognition.

''What is it?'' Telurinon demanded.

''It's Lady Sarai,'' Lirrin replied. ''She's at the front door and says she wants to talk to Mereth, or whoever's available.''

''Tell her to come back later,'' Telurinon answered.

Lirrin bowed and ascended the stairs, out of sight.

''There must be *something* better than another Black Dagger,'' Mereth said, when Lirrin was gone.

''There are any number of incredibly powerful magicks we could use,'' Tobas remarked. ''Can that dagger really stop *all* of them?''

''Apparently so,'' Telurinon said. ''We've been throwing death spells at her ever since we first heard her name, after all, and what the dagger doesn't stop, Tabaea can probably handle by herself. Remember, she has the speed and eyesight of a cat, a dog's sense of smell, the strength of a dozen men, and multiple lives—she must be killed repeatedly, not just once, to be destroyed. Even if we got the dagger away from her, she would be a threat.''

"If we got the dagger away from her, we could dispose of her in any number of ways," Heremon the Mage pointed out. "She wouldn't be protected against wizardry anymore."

"She would still have *some* protection," Mereth replied. "She would still be both witch and warlock, and wizardry is unreliable against either one. We would want to use something really drastic, to be sure."

"We have plenty of drastic magic at our disposal," Tobas pointed out. "We have spells all the way up to the Seething Death—it's hard to imagine anything much more drastic than that."

"I don't know if we need to be so drastic as all that," Telurinon muttered.

"What's the Seething Death?" Mereth asked.

"Never mind," Tobas said, "we don't want to use it."

"You're supposed to be an expert on countermagicks, aren't you, Tobas?" Heremon asked.

"Well, not exactly," Tobas said. "I happen to have a castle in a place where wizardry doesn't work, that's all."

"You do?" Mereth eyed him curiously. "A place where magic doesn't work?"

"Wizardry, anyway; witchcraft still works there, and I don't know about the others," Tobas explained. "I'm not inclined to invite a bunch of theurgists and sorcerers out there to experiment."

"But it's really a place that wizardry doesn't work? I thought those were just legends." Mereth said.

"Oh, no," Tobas said. "It's real. And it appears to have been created on purpose, by a wizard—apparently there's a spell that will do that, will make a place permanently dead to wizardry."

"Do you know it?"

"By the gods, no," Tobas said, "and I wouldn't want to use it if I did. Think about it, Mereth—it makes a place *permanently* dead to wizardry. The one I know about has been there for centuries, and it covers half a mountain and part of a valley. We're powerless there, just ordinary people. We don't want any *more* places like that around, and certainly not in a city like Ethshar!"

"I suppose not," Mereth agreed.

"If we could get *Tabaea* into a place like that, though," Heremon suggested, "then wouldn't *her* magic stop working? Wouldn't she be just another vicious young woman?"

"I don't know," Tobas said. "It's very hard to say just what magical effects are permanent and which are only maintained by magic. I mean, if you had cast a perpetual youth spell on yourself a hundred years ago, you wouldn't instantly age a century in the no-wizardry area—but you *would* start aging at a normal rate. So perhaps Tabaea would lose all her acquired abilities, and perhaps she wouldn't."

"Besides, how would we get her there?" Mereth asked.

"A Transporting Tapestry, perhaps?" Heremon suggested. "One of those that a person can step into and emerge wherever the picture showed? I believe you've said you own such a thing, Tobas?"

"Two of them," Tobas admitted. "A set. One of them goes into the dead area, all right, but I *need* it—I mean, it's absolutely essential." He paused, and then added, "Besides, I can't get it here."

"*Can't?*" Telurinon snorted. "Tobas, are you sure you aren't putting your own convenience before the welfare of an entire city, perhaps the entire World? Where in the World is this tapestry, that you cannot bring it hither?"

"Well, that's the thing, Guildmaster," Tobas said. "It isn't *in* the World—it's somewhere else, somewhere that can only be reached with the other tapestry. And I can't bring the tapestry out because the tapestry itself *is* the only way out."

"Oh," Telurinon said. He frowned and stroked his beard.

"Is that possible?" Heremon asked. "I never heard of such a thing!"

"Oh, I don't doubt it," Telurinon said. "Tobas would scarcely lie about that, and the Transporting Tapestries have always been quirky and untrustworthy things. That's why we don't use them more."

"I thought it was the cost," Mereth muttered.

"Oh, that, too," Telurinon agreed. "But during the Great War cost and reliability weren't as important as we consider them now, and they made a great many of those damnable tapestries, and a good many of them went wrong. About half of them would only deliver people at certain times of day, or when the weather was right—if you stepped in at the wrong time, you just wouldn't be *anywhere* until the light or whatever it was matched the picture. There was one fool who got the *stars* wrong, outside a window; it took the astrologers months to figure out what had gone wrong with that one, and meanwhile the people who stepped into it have been gone for three hundred years and they still aren't going to step out again for decades yet—and *that's* assuming that the room in the tapestry is still there when the stars are right!''

"I've had some experience with that sort of thing," Tobas remarked. "They're tricky devices, all right."

"Yet you trust one to get you safely out of this nowhere of yours?" Heremon asked.

Tobas shrugged.

"What if," Mereth suggested, "we gave Tobas *another* Transporting Tapestry that he could take into this wherever-it-is, and then he could hang it there and bring the one that shows the no-magic place out through it?"

"Where would we get another one?" Heremon asked. "Doesn't it take a year or more to make one?"

"Telurinon said there were many of them made during the Great War," Mereth said. "What happened to them all?"

Telurinon blinked. "Um," he said.

A sudden smile spread across Tobas's face. "You know, I've wondered sometimes about how some of the elder Guildmasters seem to be able to travel so quickly, yet I never see them flying."

"Well, there might still be a few old tapestries in use," Telurinon admitted. "But not so many as all that; some of the old ones show places that aren't *there* anymore, and therefore they don't work."

"You don't appear somewhere in the past, when the place *did* exist?" Heremon asked.

"Oh, no," Telurinon said. "Transporting Tapestries can never move anyone back in time. They aren't *that* powerful or eccentric. If the place did exist, but doesn't anymore, they just don't work."

"But you have some that still work," Mereth said. "Why don't you give one to Tobas, in exchange for his to the no-wizardry place?"

"Well, I suppose we might," Telurinon said uneasily, "but they're all Guild property; I'd have to consult with, um, the others . . ."

"And will the Guild put their own convenience ahead of the welfare of an entire city?" Tobas said, grinning.

"We'll just have to see about that," Telurinon said angrily. "And besides, even if we get this tapestry of yours here to Ethshar, Tobas, how would we get Tabaea to step into it?"

"Will she be *able* to step into it if she's carrying the Black Dagger?" Heremon asked.

"And if we're going to get her to step into a Transporting Tapestry," Tobas asked, "do we need all the rigamarole about the dead area? What happened to that one that had the stars wrong, Guildmaster? If we could get her to step into that, we'd have however many decades you said it would be until she came out again . . ."

"I don't think a tapestry will *work* on the Black Dagger," Heremon said. "You might wind up permanently ruining the tapestry."

"And I don't think Tabaea's likely to step into one in the first place," Mereth said.

"I think we'd better come up with something else," Tobas said.

"Why don't we all take a little time to think about it?" Heremon suggested. "We can meet back here in a few hours, after we've had a chance to come up with more ideas."

"And meanwhile," Mereth said, "I can see what Lady Sarai wants."

With that, the wizards arose and scattered, the meeting adjourned.

CHAPTER 33

*T*o all appearances, Lady Sarai of Ethshar was no more.

In her place, a young woman with a face broader, darker, and less distinctive than Sarai's, wearing as nondescript an outfit as Mereth could provide, had wandered into the palace, where she roamed the wide marble passageways, gaping—or pretending to do so—at the splendors of the place.

No one who encountered this slack-jawed young woman would be likely to connect her with the ousted aristocrats, or to suspect her of spying; and in fact, none of the dozens of vagabonds and scoundrels who did encounter her even noticed her. She was just another refugee from the Wall Street Field, come to live in the corridors of the palace.

Sarai was pleased. The disguise worked very well indeed; she owed Algarin of Longwall a debt for this—or at the very least, she would forgive him his earlier offenses.

She had first asked Mereth to help, but Mereth had been unable to oblige; she simply didn't know a suitable spell. It had been a surprise when Algarin, hearing what Sarai wanted, had volunteered his services.

But then, the alteration of her features was probably not the most valuable thing she had received from the wizards, and it had been Mereth, rather than Algarin, who told Sarai a good deal of what the wizards had discussed after sending Sarai and the others out of the Guildhouse.

She had not revealed any Guild secrets, of course, nor had Sarai asked her to. She had, however, confirmed what Sarai had already suspected from her inadvertant eavesdropping—Tabaea's power derived originally from a single wizardly artifact: a black dagger. She appeared to have no true command of wizardry, as she had not been seen to use any other spells, but she had used the dagger somehow to steal other sorts of magic.

Tabaea might not have really mastered those other magicks, though.

Mereth had also spoken, with some scorn, of the various plans the wizards had suggested for dealing with Tabaea. Sarai knew that they did not have any simple counterspell for the Black Dagger, nor any simple means of killing or disarming Tabaea. The Guild might yet devise something, but as yet, Mereth told her, they had not.

That somehow didn't surprise Sarai much. The Wizards' Guild was very, very good at some things, but in this case they seemed to be completely out of their depth.

But then, so was everybody else, Sarai herself included. As she roamed the sadly transformed halls of the palace, Sarai could see that plainly. Even the conquerors, the city's outcasts, didn't seem comfortable with the new situation. They had not moved into the palace as if they were the new aristocracy, but rather as if it were a temporary shelter, a substitute for the Wall Street Field; it was with a curious mixture of annoyance and amazed relief that Sarai discovered that for the most part, the invaders had not dared to intrude on any of the private apartments or bedrooms. Her own family's rooms were untouched, as were most of the others that had been abandoned, and those courtiers and officials who had remained behind were, for the most part, undisturbed.

Instead the newcomers were camped in the corridors, the stairways, the audience chambers, and the meeting rooms. They had no beds, but slept on carpets, blankets, stolen draperies, or tapestries taken from the walls; they did not take their meals in the dining halls, but wherever they could scrounge food, eating it on the spot. The palace servants sometimes brought trays through the passages, handing out tidbits.

There was no organization at all; the people simply sat wherever they chose and moved when the urge struck them. They chatted with one another, played at dice and finger games, and, Sarai saw with disgust, stole one another's belongings whenever someone's back was turned.

These were the new rulers of the city?

After a tour of the palace that took her slightly more than two hours, however, Sarai found herself in the Great Hall, watching Tabaea at work, and realized that *here* were the real rulers of the city. The people in the corridors below were parasites, hangers-on, like the lesser nobility of old.

Still, she was not particularly impressed with what she saw. Tabaea held court as if she were settling arguments between unruly children—which was often appropriate, Sarai had to admit, but not always. And she didn't have the sense to delegate anything; no one seemed to be screening out the frivolous cases. Tabaea was serving as overlord, and as her own Minister of Justice, and half a dozen other roles as well.

Sarai watched as Tabaea heard a dispute between an old woman and the drunkard she claimed had stolen her blanket; as she received a representative of the Council of Warlocks who wanted to know her intentions, and whether she acknowledged killing Inza the Apprentice, and if so whether she intended to make reparations; and as she listened to a delegation of merchants from Grandgate Market who were upset about the absence of the city guard.

Tabaea gave the drunkard to the count of three to return the blanket; his failure to meet this deadline got him a broken hand as the empress forcibly removed the blanket.

She freely admitting killing Inza, but claimed that it was a matter of state and no reparations or apologies would be forthcoming; furthermore, she saw no need to tell anyone of her plans, especially not a bunch of warlocks. They could wait and see, like everyone else, or consult fortune-telling wizards or theurgists—but no, she wasn't holding any particular grudge, and they were free to stay in Ethshar of the Sands and operate as they always had, so long as they didn't annoy her. The warlocks' representative was not especially pleased by this, but he had little choice; he had to accept it. When she dismissed him, he bowed and departed without further argument.

As for the merchants, she asked if there had been any increase in theft or vandalism in the guards' absence.

"I don't know," the spokesman admitted, as his companions eyed one another uneasily.

"Not yet," one of the others muttered; Tabaea clearly heard him, however.

"You think the thieves will be bolder in the future, perhaps?" Tabaea asked, her tone challenging.

For a moment, no one replied, and a hush fell on the room. The delegates shifted their feet uneasily, looking at one another and stealing glances at the empress. At last, one spoke up, far more courageously than Sarai would ever have expected.

"I think that at the moment, all the thieves in the city are here in the palace," he said. "And when they either finish looting the place, or they realize they aren't going to get a chance to loot it, they'll be back out in the market."

"And what if they find they don't *have* to loot it?" Tabaea shot back. "What if they find that the new government here is more generous than the old, and that anyone can have a decent living without being forced to steal?"

"I don't know anything about that," the brave merchant answered. "I think there'll always be thieves, and I want someone to protect us from them."

"You have *me*," Tabaea said. "That's all you need."

The merchant's expression made it quite plain that he did not consider his new empress, whatever her abilities, to be an adequate replacement for several thousand soldiers, but his nerve had apparently run out; he said nothing more, and the scruffy little man who seemed to be serving as Tabaea's chamberlain herded the group down the stairs.

Next up was a woman who claimed she had been unfairly forced from her home; as she gathered herself together and inched up to the dais, Sarai, standing at the head of the left-hand stairway, considered what she had just heard.

Tabaea was no diplomat; her treatment of the warlock and the merchants had made that plain. The case of the stolen blanket was interesting, though; she had not hesitated in the slightest before ordering the man to give the woman the blanket. Had Tabaea really known who was lying, as quickly as that?

It could be, of course; if Tabaea had acquired the right magical skills, she might be able to instantly tell falsehoods from truth. She hadn't had to consult any magicians other than herself, certainly.

Or maybe she had just guessed. Maybe she assumed that the accused were always guilty. Maybe she would always prefer women to men, or the sober to the intoxicated. From one case, Sarai really couldn't say . . .

She had reached that point in her thoughts when the arrow whistled past. Her eyes widened, and she saw the impact very clearly as the missile struck Tabaea, Empress of Ethshar, in the throat.

Sarai stared as blood dribbled down the pale skin and onto the front of Tabaea's absurdly gaudy dress; the sight of the woman standing there gasping, with the arrow projecting from her neck, was horribly unnatural. Sarai was vaguely aware of clattering footsteps behind her as someone descended the stairs so fast that it was almost as much a fall as a climb, and then the fading sound of running feet as the archer fled down the corridor below. The sound was very loud and distinct in the shocked silence following the shot.

Then Tabaea reached up and ripped the arrow free; blood gushed forth, spattering the dais and drenching her dress. Someone screamed—a single voice at first, then a chorus of shrieks and shouts.

The empress took a single step, staggered—and then straightened up.

As Sarai watched, the gaping red hole in Tabaea's throat closed, the skin smoothed itself out, and the wound was gone as if it had never been.

"Where did that come from?" Tabaea demanded, in a voice as strong as ever.

Several fingers pointed, and Tabaea strode through the room, imposing in her anger despite her small size, with the bloody arrow still clutched in her hand. She headed for the stairs where the assassin had lurked. All present, regardless of who they might be, hastened to get out of her way—Sarai among them.

She had to admit, as she watched Tabaea pass, that was a very impressive bit of magic, the way that wound had healed—if it had all been real, and not some sort of illusion. She turned back to the throne room.

The dais was soaked with blood; if it was an illusion, it was a durable one. And, Sarai saw, a line of bloody drops and smears on the stone floor marked Tabaea's path from the dais to the stairs.

Sarai did not really think it was an illusion at all.

She wondered who the assassin was, and why he had made his attempt. Had Lord Torrut sent him, perhaps? And would he get away, or would Tabaea catch him?

If she caught him, Sarai was sure the man would die. She hoped it wouldn't be too slow or painful a death.

She looked around again, at the remnants of the crowd, at Tabaea's chamberlain standing by the dais looking bewildered, at the rapidly drying blood the empress had lost. She thought of the warlock, and the merchants, and the drunk with the broken hand, of Grandgate Market and the gate itself left unguarded, and of the palace corridors jammed with beggars and thieves. She thought of the empress of Ethshar abandoning everything else to chase her own would-be assassin, because she had no guards to do it for her, no magicians to track down and slay the attacker.

This was no way to run a city.

Quite aside from any question of Tabaea's right to rule, it was clear to Sarai that the murderous young woman didn't know *how* to rule properly.

She would have to be removed—but as the scene with the arrow had demonstrated, as Mereth's report of the Wizards' Guild's repeated failures, removing her wasn't as simple as it might seem, with the Black Dagger protecting her.

Sarai paused, looking after the departed empress. At least, she thought, there was an obvious place to start. If the Black

Dagger protected Tabaea, then the Black Dagger had to be eliminated.

Of course, Tabaea knew that. It wasn't going to be easy to get the enchanted knife away from her.

Easy or not, a way would have to be found. And since no one else seemed to be doing it, Sarai would have to do it herself.

She sighed; it was easy to say she should do it. The hard part, Sarai told herself, was figuring out *how*.

CHAPTER 34

"*L*et me help you with that, Your Majesty," Sarai said, reaching out for Tabaea's blood-soaked robe.

Tabaea looked around, startled. "Thank you," she said, pulling the robe free. Sarai accepted it and folded it into a bundle; half-dried blood smeared her arms and dripped on the carpet.

"You're not one of my usual servants," Tabaea remarked, as she unbuckled her belt and tossed it aside. She tugged at her sticky, bloody tunic and asked, "Where's Lethe? Or Ista?"

"I don't know, Your Majesty," Sarai replied. "I was nearby, and I just thought I'd help." She hoped very much that if Lethe or Ista showed up that neither would see through her disguise, or recognize her voice.

Of course, those two had mostly waited on the overlord and his immediate family, not on Lord Kalthon and his children; while they both knew Lady Sarai by sight, neither had been a close friend.

And both of them were tired of cleaning up Tabaea's blood, so they probably wouldn't be in any hurry to answer the empress' call. This latest attack, an attempt at decapitation, had been even messier than previous unsuccessful assassinations.

Sarai had seen it, of course; she made a habit of unobtrusively following Tabaea about her everyday business, watching any time an assassin might strike. She wanted to know more about Tabaea's capabilities; she wanted to be there if Tabaea *did* die, to help restore order; and she wanted to be there if there was ever a chance to get the Black Dagger away.

She had an idea about that last that she hoped to try. That idea was why she was now playing the role of a palace servant.

She supposed she hadn't really *needed* to watch the actual decapitation, but she had been too fascinated to turn away. For a moment, when the assassin's sword finished its cut through the imperial neck and emerged from the other side, Sarai had thought that this might be too much for even Tabaea's magic—but then she had seen that the wound was already healing where the blade had entered, that the head had never been completely severed from the body, and that Tabaea was already tugging the Black Dagger from its sheath.

Each time someone had openly tried to kill the empress, Tabaea had pursued her attacker, and two times out of three she had caught and killed someone she claimed to be the assassin.

At least, Sarai thought she had; certainly, she had caught the archer the first time, and judging by her remarks to her courtiers and the satisfied expression on her face, she had caught this swordsman, as well.

She hadn't caught anyone when magical attacks had been made, of course, but those attacks hadn't inflicted any deadly wounds, either; the Black Dagger had dissipated any wizard's spell used against her, and Tabaea, using her own powers, had fought off all the others before they got that far.

She hadn't eaten the poisoned meals, either; Sarai didn't know why.

At least, she had turned away meals she *said* were poisoned, but Sarai had no way of knowing whether poison had actually been present, or that Tabaea hadn't cheerfully consumed poisons in other meals without detecting them—and without being harmed.

And for that matter, if magical attacks had reached her undetected, perhaps they had used up some of her store of stolen lives—but Sarai had no reason to think that had happened. As far as Sarai could see, neither magic nor poison had affected Tabaea's vitality.

The more direct assaults, however, surely did.

If Sarai correctly understood how the Black Dagger worked—which she doubted, since her information was third-hand at best, relayed by Mereth or Tobas or one of Tobas's wives from analyses provided by various wizards—then each time Tabaea killed someone, she added another life to her total; each time she received a wound that would have killed an ordinary person, a life was lost from that sum.

So while she had lost three lives to assassins, she had recovered two of them, tracking down her enemies and stabbing them to death before they had a chance to escape. Neither one had even gotten out of the palace.

That must have been a ghastly sight for the would-be killers, Sarai thought, to look back and see Tabaea, covered with her own blood and wielding that horrible dagger, in hot pursuit. And it had presumably been the last thing they ever saw—at least, for two out of three.

The chase was over now, and Tabaea had retreated to her apartments, to change out of her bloody clothes, to wash the blood from her skin and hair, before going on about the business of ruling the city. She had sent her chancellor and her other followers away, so that she could clean up in private.

And this was what Sarai had been waiting for. The instant Tabaea had set out after the assassin, Sarai had hurried to the imperial quarters, where she had filled the marble tub and hung the kettle over the fire.

"The bath is ready, Your Majesty," she said. "I hope the water's warm enough; it's not my usual job."

"I'm sure it'll be fine," Tabaea said wearily, as she handed Sarai her tunic and ambled into the bath chamber. Sarai accepted the garment, bowed, and hurried after.

Tabaea dropped her skirt, stepped out of her girdle, and stepped into the tub.

"It *is* a bit cool," she said. "See to the kettle, whatever your name is."

"Pharea, Your Majesty," Sarai said. She put the bloody clothes aside and fetched the kettle from the fire, then poured steaming hot water into the tub, stirring it in with her other hand.

She wanted Tabaea to be comfortable, to take a nice, long bath—and give her a good head start.

"You're nervous, Pharea," Tabaea said.

Sarai looked up, startled.

"Don't be," the empress said, "I won't hurt you."

Sarai was not reassured, but she tried to hide her discomfort. "Of course not, Your Majesty," she said. "I suppose it's just the blood."

"Your Majesty?" a new voice called.

Sarai turned, as Tabaea said, ''Ah, Lethe! Come in here and help me get this blood out of my hair.''

Sarai bowed, collected Tabaea's remaining garments, and backed out of the bath chamber as Lethe stepped in. The servant gave Sarai a startled glance, then ignored her as she tended to her mistress' needs.

Sarai collected Tabaea's bloody clothes into a bundle, and dumped it in the hallway, to be disposed of or cleaned, whichever was more practical—she really didn't know and didn't much care. Her servant act was almost over. In a few seconds she would have what she wanted. She returned to the bath chamber and leaned in.

''I'll just close this door to keep the steam in, shall I?'' she said.

''Yes, thank you, Pharea,'' Tabaea said with a wave.

Sarai closed the door, quietly but firmly.

Then she hurried to Tabaea's belt, still lying on the floor where the empress had flung it; she snatched the Black Dagger from its sheath, took her own knife from concealment beneath her skirt, and substituted the ordinary belt knife for Tabaea's magical weapon. She tucked the Black Dagger carefully under her skirt, then looked around, checking to see if she had forgotten anything.

As she turned, she caught a glimpse of herself in a mirror; at first, she paid no attention, but then, startled, she stared at the glass.

Her magical disguise was gone; she was no longer Pharea, a moon-faced servant, but herself, Lady Sarai.

The Black Dagger had done that, obviously; it had cut away the illusion spell.

She certainly couldn't afford to stay here, in that case, not that she had intended to. Moving quickly, but not hurrying so much as to attract attention if someone saw her, she stepped out into the passageway and closed the door behind her.

And then, carefully not hurrying, trying very hard to appear as ordinary as possible, she strolled down the hall, down the stairs, and a few minutes later, out of the palace entirely, across the plaza onto Circle Street.

She had done it. She had the Black Dagger.

Now what?

She didn't want to do anything hasty or ill-considered. The obvious thing to do would be to go to the Guildhouse on Grand

Street and tell the wizards that Tabaea had been disarmed—but Sarai did not always trust the obvious.

Would magic work against Tabaea now? She still had the strengths and talents of a dozen or so people, even if she could no longer add more. And there was the question of whether it would be for the best in the long run if wizards removed the usurper empress; however much she might like some of the individual members, Sarai did not like or trust the Wizards' Guild. They had claimed they didn't meddle in politics, yet she was quite sure that if she told them the Black Dagger was gone, they would immediately assassinate Tabaea. Like it or not, Tabaea was the city's ruler. What sort of a precedent would it set if she helped the Wizards' Guild kill a reigning monarch and go unpunished?

Not only would they surely go unpunished, they might expect to be rewarded for such a service. They might well demand a larger role in running the city, or some tangible expression of gratitude. Sarai did not for a minute believe that their strictures against interfering in politics, or their insistence that they wanted to kill Tabaea for themselves rather than the good of the city, would prevent them from expecting payment for such a service to the overlord.

What if they demanded the Black Dagger?

Sarai frowned. She didn't like that idea. The Black Dagger was *dangerous*.

Of course, *wizards* were dangerous—but still, why hand them even more power?

And then again, it might be, for all she knew, that the Black Dagger would only work for Tabaea. It might be that the wizards already knew how to make such daggers.

It might be that Tabaea would be able to make another as soon as she found that this one was gone, in which case Sarai really shouldn't be wasting any time—but still, she hesitated. Wherever the Black Dagger came from, whether more could be made or not, Sarai was sure that the wizards would want it.

Well, the wizards had things she wanted—not for Ethshar, but for herself. What if she were to trade the dagger to them in exchange for a cure for her father and brother?

This all needed more thought, despite any risk that Tabaea would make another dagger. The time was not yet right, Sarai decided, for a quick trip to the Guildhouse.

But then, where *should* she go?

Lord Torrut, she decided. There was no point in letting more assassins die for nothing, not when a single spell might now be enough to handle the problem. She had no doubt at all that the assassins were sent by Lord Torrut; when open battle had failed, he had gone underground, but she was sure he was still fighting.

The question was, where?

The obvious place to start looking was the barracks towers; with that in mind, she headed out Quarter Street toward Grandgate Market.

And as she walked, a thought struck her.

Ordinary swords and knives and arrows could not kill Tabaea, as long as she had extra lives saved up—but what if she were stabbed with the Black Dagger? Wouldn't that steal *all* her lives at once?

Maybe not; it would certainly be a risky thing to try. Most particularly, it would be risky for an ordinary person, with an ordinary person's strength, to attempt to stab Tabaea, with all her stolen power.

But what if someone used the Black Dagger to build herself up to be Tabaea's equal, or her superior, and *then* stabbed Tabaea?

Whoever it was couldn't go about murdering magicians, of course, or even just ordinary people, but perhaps if there were condemned criminals . . .

Did the dagger's magic work on animals? Sarai remembered that dogs, cats, and even a pigeon had been found with their throats cut; Tabaea had, at the very least, experimented with animals. Someone with the strength of a dozen oxen might be a match for her.

Of course, if anyone tried that, then the knife's new wielder would be a threat to the peace of the city—unless it was someone completely trustworthy, someone who would simply never want to disrupt the normal flow of events.

Someone, for example, like Sarai herself.

She glanced briefly toward the Guildhouse as she crossed Wizard Street, but walked on toward the Wall Street Field without even slowing.

In the Guildhouse, Tobas watched uneasily from the landing.

"I know that I sort of suggested some of this," he said, "but I'm not sure it's really a good idea."

Mereth glanced at him uneasily, then turned her attention back to Telurinon. The Guildmaster was seated cross-legged on a small carpet, his athame held out before him, its point directly over a shallow silver bowl supported on a low iron tripod; he was chanting intently. Fluid bubbled and steamed in the silver dish. A sword lay on the floor beneath the bowl, and an old and worn noose encircled the tripod, the sword's blade passing under it on one side and atop it on the other.

"Well," Mereth said, "if *any* kind of wizardry can kill Tabaea, *this* can—can't it?"

"I don't know," Tobas said. "I just hope it doesn't kill *everybody*."

"Oh, it won't do *that*," Mereth said, not anywhere near as certainly as she would have liked.

"It might," Tobas replied. "The original countercharm is lost, has been lost for four or five hundred years now, and in all that time no one's been foolish enough to risk trying it. The spell book I found it in had a note at the bottom in big red runes, saying, 'Don't try it!,' but here we are, trying it."

"But we've got it all figured out," Mereth insisted. "As soon as Tabaea's dead, the warlocks pick it up and push it through that tapestry of yours, to the no-magic place, and it'll be gone!"

"That assumes," Tobas pointed out, "that the warlocks really can pick it up and that the tapestry really will transport it. For the former we have only the warlocks' word that they can lift *anything* that isn't too immense, and for the latter, all we have is assumptions and guesses. What if, instead of the tapestry transporting the Seething Death, the Seething Death destroys the Transporting Tapestry?"

Mereth went pale.

"Oh, gods," she said. "What if it *does* destroy the tapestry? Tobas, why didn't you say anything sooner?"

"I *did*," Tobas replied. "I argued until my throat was sore and my lungs wouldn't hold air, and Telurinon promised to think it all over carefully, and when I came back he'd started the ritual."

"Oh, but . . . but it's so dangerous . . . How *could* he?"

Tobas turned up an empty palm. "He's frustrated," he said. "We've all been throwing spells at Tabaea for a sixnight now, and they've had even less effect than Lord Torrut's archers and booby traps—by the way, did you hear about the tripwire and razor-wheels? The spies said it took Tabaea almost five minutes to heal."

Mereth shuddered.

"Well, anyway," Tobas continued, "all his life Telurinon has had these spells too terrible to use, he's heard about how wizardry is more powerful than *anything*, and now there's someone who just absorbs anything we throw at her—I can see why he'd want to try some of the real World-wrecker spells on her. He'll probably never have another opportunity to use any of them. But I don't think he should use the Seething Death."

"Then why don't you *stop* him?"

"Oh, now, you know better than that," Tobas chided her. "Have you ever interrupted a wizard in the middle of a spell?"

"Um . . . once." Mereth winced at the memory. "When I was an apprentice. Nobody died, but it was close."

"Low-order magic, I assume?"

"Very."

Tobas nodded. "Ever see the Tower of Flame?"

Mereth turned to him, startled. "No, have you? I wasn't even sure it was real!"

"Oh, it's real, all right," Tobas replied. "It's in the mountains southeast of Dwomor. You can see it for a dozen leagues in every direction; it lights up the whole area at night. It just keeps going and going and going, spewing fire upward out of a field of bare rock. The best records say it's been burning for eight hundred years now, and the *story* is—I can't swear it's true—the story is that it was only about a second- or third-order spell that went wrong, some ordinary little spell, meant to sharpen a sword or something."

"Yes, but . . ."

"And for myself," Tobas said, interrupting her protest, "I'm not about to forget that every spriggan in the World, and there must be hundreds of them by now, maybe thousands, but every single one of them is out there running around, causing trouble, because I got a gesture wrong doing Lugwiler's Haunting Phantasm."

"But . . ."

"Not to mention," Tobas added forcefully, "that all our problems with Tabaea and the Black Dagger are the result of a mistake during an athamezation."

"So you aren't going to stop him," Mereth said.

"That's right," Tobas said. "That's got to be tenth-, maybe twelfth-order magic he's doing down there; I can't handle anything like that, hardly anyone can, even among Guildmasters, and I'm not about to risk seeing a spell like that go wrong. It's bad enough if it goes *right*."

"What happens if it doesn't?" Mereth asked. "I mean, Telurinon could make a mistake even if we *don't* disturb him."

Tobas shrugged. "Who knows? Dragon's blood, serpent's venom, a rope that's hanged a man, and a sword that's slain a woman . . . there's some potent stuff in there."

"How is it *supposed* to work?"

Tobas sighed. "Well," he said, "when he's finished, that brew in the silver bowl there is supposed to yield a single drop of fluid that's decanted into a golden thimble. It's almost stable at that point; it won't do anything to the thimble as long as the drop stays entirely within it. But when the drop is tipped over the edge of the thimble, whether it's deliberately poured, or spilled, or whatever, the spell will be activated, and whatever it falls upon will be consumed by the Seething Death, which will then slowly spread, destroying everything it touches, until something stops it."

"And we don't know of anything that will stop it," Mereth said.

"Right. Unless Telurinon's scheme to transport it to the dead area works."

"What if the Black Dagger stops it?"

Tobas shrugged. "Who knows?" he said.

Mereth blinked. "I'm not sure I understand exactly," she said. "The way I understand it, the Seething Death forms a sort of pool of this stuff, right? A pool that gradually spreads?"

"That's right."

"How will that stop Tabaea? Are we planning to push her into the pool?"

Tobas grimaced.

"No," he said. "Telurinon intends to pour the drop directly on her head."

Mereth was a wizard and had been for all her adult life; she regularly worked with bits of corpses and various repulsive organic fluids. What was more, she had worked for the Minister of Justice and his daughter, the Minister of Investigation, studying and spying on all the various things that the citizens of Ethshar did to one another when sufficiently provoked. All the same, she winced slightly at the thought of pouring that stuff on someone's head.

"Ick," she said. Then, after a moment's thought, she asked, "How?"

"The warlocks," Tobas told her. "As soon as it's ready, the warlocks will transport it to the palace and pour it on Tabaea. Then, as soon as she's dead, they'll lift her corpse, so the stuff won't get on anything else, and send Tabaea and the Seething Death through the tapestry. It's all ready to go, rolled up by the front door."

"Couldn't they just send her through the tapestry alive? Then we wouldn't have to use the Seething Death at all!"

Tobas sighed again. "Maybe they could," he said, "but they don't think so. She's a warlock herself, while she's alive, and she can block them. I don't understand that part, I'm not a warlock any more than you are, but that's what they say."

"Have they *tried*?" Mereth demanded.

Tobas turned up an empty palm. "Whether they have or not," he said, pointing at Telurinon, "it's a little late to turn back now, isn't it?"

CHAPTER 35

*S*arai winced, eyes closed, as she slit the dog's throat. The animal thrashed wildly, and hot blood sprayed on Sarai's hands, but she kept her hold.

And as it struggled, Sarai felt a surge of heat, of strength, all through her; without meaning to, she tightened her grip on the dying dog and felt the flesh yielding beneath her fingers. Her heart was pounding, her muscles were tense.

Then the dog went limp, sagging to the ground between her legs, and the world suddenly seemed to flood in on her; her ears rang with strange new sounds, and her vision seemed suddenly sharper and more intense, as if everything was outlined against the background of the Wall Street Field—though for a moment, the colors seemed to fade away, as if drowned out by the clarity of shape and movement.

Most of all, though, scents poured in. She could smell everything, all at once—the dog's blood, her own sweat, her sex, the dirt of the Field, the sun-warmed stone of the city wall, the smokes and stenches of every individual shop or home on Wall Street or the blocks beyond. She could tell at once which of the empty blankets and abandoned tents of the Field were mildewed or decayed and which were still clean and wholesome; she could smell the metal of the Black Dagger itself.

For a moment she stood over the dead dog, just breathing in the city, marveling at it all. She had known that dogs could smell better than mere humans, of course, everyone knew that, but she had never before realized how *much* better, and she had never imagined what it would be like.

Her attempts to find Lord Torrut had, so far, been unsuccessful; she had found no one in the barracks or the gatehouses. Now, though, she wondered if she could locate him by smell, track him down by following his scent. She had heard about dogs doing such things and had always dismissed the stories as exaggerations, but now, she had to reconsider. She could smell *everything*.

She was stronger now, too; she could feel it. The dog had not been particularly strong or healthy, just a half-starved stray scavenging in the almost-empty Field, but she had felt the power in her grip as she held it while it died.

Tabaea had killed a dozen men—Sarai tried to imagine just how strong that made her feel, and couldn't.

And Tabaea had killed several dogs, as well, Sarai remembered—she, too, had experienced this flood of scent and sound and image.

Scents—that explained some of Tabaea's mysterious abilities. It wasn't magic, not in the way Sarai and the others had assumed; she could *smell* people approaching; she could hear them, like a watchdog. People said dogs could smell fear, as well, could tell friend from foe by scent—could Tabaea?

Until now, Sarai had viewed Tabaea as a mysterious and powerful magician, her talents and abilities beyond any ordinary explanation, her mind beyond understanding; now, suddenly, she thought she understood the usurper. Sarai had assumed that Tabaea had created the Black Dagger deliberately, knowing what she was doing; that she had studied magic, had set out to conquer Ethshar. It was the Black Dagger that gave her her physical strength and immunity to harm, the wizards had told Sarai that, but now Sarai began to believe that *all* Tabaea's power came from the dagger.

Without it, did she have *any* magic?

Well, she presumably still had her warlockry, and maybe witchcraft—Teneria and Karanissa had said that Tabaea had the talent, as they called it, but didn't know how to use it properly.

And she had her canine sense of smell and her accumulated strength and stolen lives.

Sarai remembered the dead cats and the dead pigeon; could Tabaea have stolen the bird's ability to fly? What had she gotten from the cats?

Well, Sarai thought, holding up the bloody dagger, there was one way to find out, wasn't there?

The first cat came as a revelation; the addition to her strength was nothing, smell and hearing got no better, but the increase in her speed and the intense sensitivity to movement were as big a surprise as the dog's sense of smell. *That* was how Tabaea could react so quickly when she fought!

The pigeon was a waste of time; that explained why dead birds hadn't littered the city when Tabaea was building herself up.

The next step, Sarai decided, was an ox, for the raw strength it would provide; Tabaea had used people, but Sarai had no intention of committing murder.

Unfortunately, there were no stray oxen wandering in the Wall Street Field. Buying an ox was not difficult—if one had money. Sarai had no money to speak of, just a few borrowed coppers in the purse on her belt. The family treasure had gone to sea with her father and brother, while the family income was gone with Lord Tollern and the overlord.

Perhaps she could borrow more money somewhere, she thought. The obvious place to go would be the Guildhouse, since that was where the richest and most powerful of her nominal allies were, but she still did not care for the idea of walking in there with the Black Dagger on her belt. She thought she could trust Mereth, and Tobas seemed like a reasonable person, but Telurinon and Algarin and the rest . . .

Tobas was not living in the Guildhouse, though; he and his wives were staying at the Cap and Dagger. Lady Sarai sniffed the air, without consciously realizing she was doing it. She stretched, catlike, then flexed her shoulders in a way that would have fluffed a pigeon's feathers out nicely. Then she wiped the

Black Dagger clean, sheathed it, and headed out of the Field, up onto Wall Street, and toward Grandgate.

From the market, she turned down Gate Street; the Cap and Dagger was six blocks down on the right.

As she walked, she soaked in the odors and sights of a city turned strange and rich by her augmented senses. She could, she found, tell what each person she passed had eaten for his or her last meal and how long ago that meal was; she could detect the slightest twitch of a hand or an eye. She spotted rats foraging in an alley and knew that she would never have seen them without the Black Dagger's spell.

She saw someone glance oddly at her and realized that she was moving strangely, her gaze darting back and forth, her nose lifted to catch the air. She forced herself to look straight ahead.

Then she was at the inn; she stood in the door until the innkeeper came to ask what she wanted.

Sarai was sure she had not seen the man before and wondered where he had hidden himself when the wizards held their meeting in his establishment.

"I'm looking for a man named Tobas of Telven," she said. "Or if he's not here, one of his wives."

The innkeeper frowned, then directed her to a room upstairs. Sarai thanked him, and was about to head up, when the man reconsidered. "Maybe I'd better come with you," he said. "I don't know you, and I don't want any trouble."

"There won't be any trouble," Sarai said, but the innkeeper insisted. Together, they ascended the stairs and found the door of the room Tobas, Karanissa, and Alorria shared. The innkeeper knocked.

"Yes?" a woman's voice called. Sarai had not entirely adjusted to her new hearing, so much more sensitive to high-pitched sounds, so at first she didn't recognize it.

"There's a woman here to see your husband," the innkeeper called.

Sarai heard footsteps, and then the door opened; Alorria leaned out. "Tobas isn't here," she said. She spotted Sarai, and said, "Oh, it's you, La . . . it's you, Sarai. Is there anything I can do?"

"I hope so," Sarai said. "May I come in?"

"Oh. All right, come in." She swung the door wide.

Sarai stepped in, and Alorria closed it gently in the innkeeper's face.

"Thank you," she called to him as the door shut.

Then, for a moment, the two women stared at each other, Sarai unsure how to begin, Alorria unsure she had done the right thing admitting anyone when she was alone and so clumsy and helpless with her swollen belly.

But after all, Lady Sarai was a friend and a fellow noblewoman.

Sarai looked around the room, at the three beds, the table that held basin and pitcher, and the two large trunks, while Alorria studied her guest's face. "Why do you want to see Tobas?" the princess asked.

"Well, I probably don't need to," Sarai said. "I really just need to borrow some money. I'll pay it back as soon as things are back to normal."

Alorria blinked, slightly startled. "Why do you need to borrow money?" she asked.

"To buy an ox."

Alorria stared at Sarai. "Why do you want an ox?"

"To kill," Sarai explained. "As part of a spell."

Alorria frowned. "*You're* doing magic now? Isn't there enough of that already?"

Sarai shrugged. "I don't know," she said. "Is there?"

"Well, I certainly thought so," Alorria said, settling awkwardly onto the edge of the nearest bed. "That's where Tobas and Kara are—the Wizards' Guild is trying some horrible spell on Tabaea, with the help of the warlocks, and Karanissa and the other witches are all standing by to help, at the palace or the Guildhouse or places in between."

"What kind of a spell?" Sarai asked, seating herself on the next bed over. She berated herself for not realizing that the wizards would still be trying their spells on Tabaea, even without knowing the Black Dagger had been removed, and she suddenly wished that she had gone straight to the Guildhouse when she had first stolen the dagger. She didn't like it when things went on that she didn't know about, particularly anything as bizarre as wizards and warlocks working together.

And how could warlocks help with anything, when Tabaea was a warlock herself? Warlockry didn't work on warlocks.

"Oh, I don't know," Alorria said, flustered. "I leave all the magic up to Tobas and Kara, and I take care of the rest of it."

"Oh, but . . ." Sarai began.

Alorria interrupted, "It's called the Seething Death; Tobas

got it from that horrible old book of Derithon's, and nobody's used it in about five hundred years.''

Sarai's mouth twitched. ''I thought you didn't know anything about magic.''

''I don't,'' Alorria insisted, ''not really. But I do know about my husband.'' She smiled weakly.

Sarai smiled back, but it was not a terribly sincere smile. ''The Seething Death'' sounded dangerous, and she had never heard of it before. Maybe building up her strength with an ox could wait; watching this spell might be more important. And some high official of the overlord's government ought to be there when Tabaea died. The overlord himself had sailed off to Ethshar of the Spices with Lord Tollern and Sarai's own father and the rest, and Lord Torrut was in hiding; Sarai knew she was probably the highest-ranking official available.

That assumed that the spell would work on Tabaea, but with the Black Dagger gone Sarai thought that was a reasonable assumption. And if it *didn't* kill her, Sarai wanted to see that, too, to see how Tabaea defended herself without the knife.

''The Seething Death,'' the spell was called. Where had it come from, anyway?

''Who's Derithon?'' she asked.

''Derithon the Mage,'' Alorria said. ''Karanissa's first husband—or lover, anyway. He's been dead for centuries. She had his book of spells when she first met Tobas, and she couldn't use it, since she's a witch instead of a wizard, so she gave it to Tobas, and that's where he got most of his magic.''

''Centuries?'' There was obviously even more of a story to this threesome than she had realized.

''Derithon put a youth spell on her. How much does an ox cost, anyway?''

''About three rounds of silver, I think. So Tobas is working this Seething Death spell?''

''Oh, no!'' Alorria said. ''He thinks it's much too dangerous, that it's really stupid. Telurinon did it before Tobas could stop him.''

The last remnants of Sarai's smile vanished. She stood up.

''I think I better go,'' she said. ''Forget about the ox; I need to see what's going on at the palace.''

Alorria smiled up at her. ''Be careful,'' she said.

Sarai didn't answer; she was already on her way out the door. Tobas was a sensible person, despite his peculiar domestic arrangements, but Telurinon—Telurinon was an overeducated idiot who wanted to prove to the Inner Circle how powerful he was. What's more, he was an overeducated idiot who still thought Tabaea had the Black Dagger protecting her.

Whatever this spell was, Telurinon expected it to overpower the Black Dagger. Sarai was sure of that; Tobas or Heremon or Algarin might have found some way around the dagger's magic, but Telurinon would have just thrown more and more magic back at it. Unchecked wizardry could do an amazing amount of damage, and there was no Black Dagger in the palace to blunt this Seething Death.

Sarai had to force herself not to draw attention by running as she headed for the palace.

CHAPTER 36

*E*veryone knew that there were things in life that stayed interesting, and things that got dull fairly quickly; this was no revelation to the Empress Tabaea, who considered herself to be an intelligent person, and who thought she had a pretty good idea of how the World worked.

All the same, she was rather surprised to find that ruling a city was one of the things that got dull quickly.

In fact, by the end of her first sixnight as empress, she was bored with the whole business and had begun trying to find ways to make it more enjoyable.

An obvious one would be to appoint someone else to handle the tedious parts of the job, but that would require finding someone she trusted to do it properly, and as yet she hadn't found such a person. Sometimes it seemed as if there wasn't anyone in her entire court with the wit of a spriggan.

There were times she wasn't sure she was much better than the others, at that.

And then there was the loneliness. She had never exactly been popular company, but at least she had usually had friends to talk to, just about everyday matters. She could discuss the fine points of housebreaking with other burglars, gripe about the city guard to anyone in the Wall Street Field—but all her old friends were scared of her now. Not only was she the empress, but she was a magician, with her superhuman strength and all the rest of her abilities. And she *had* beaten Jandin and thrown that stupid old woman around.

So everyone was frightened of her.

She could still talk to them, of course, but it wasn't the same; they wouldn't dare say anything she didn't want to hear, or, rather, anything they thought that she might possibly not want to hear.

The remaining palace servants were actually better company now; they were accustomed to dealing with powerful people, and they weren't anywhere near as frightened of her as most of the others—but on the other hand, they didn't seem to have much to say. They were mostly concerned with clothes and meals and furniture, with how to keep the rugs clean, and what tunic went well with which skirt.

And they were all women. Tabaea didn't understand that. Surely, the overlord had had male servants; where had they all gone?

Wherever they were, she didn't see them. Perhaps they were still there, working down in the depths of the palace kitchens, or the stables, or any of the other places that the empress didn't go, but they certainly weren't bringing her her meals or waiting on her in her apartments.

They might be mixed in with the crowds in the corridors, of course.

And that was another source of her displeasure, she thought as she left her apartments and headed for the throne room. Here she had done everything she could to be an enlightened and benevolent ruler, and nobody seemed to appreciate it. She had freed all the slaves, had emptied the overlord's dungeons, had pardoned any number of criminals, had invited the entire population of the Wall Street Field to live in the palace, had in fact thrown the palace open to anyone who cared to enter—by her order, all the doors were kept open in good weather, and were always unlocked in *any* weather—and what had it gotten her? Had those people been grateful to her? Had they taken advantage of this chance to improve themselves? Had any of them tried to repay her by helping out, even such little things as cleaning up after themselves, as she had asked?

No. Of course not. All she had to do was glance about to see that. The palace corridors were littered with cast-off rags, with fruit rinds and chicken bones and other remnants of stolen meals, and they stank of urine and worse. Dead bodies were left unattended until they began to stink, if she or one of the servants didn't happen on them; out in the Wall Street Field someone would have informed the city guard and the body would have been removed, but here no one seemed to know who should be told.

What was worse, not all the deaths were from disease or age; not counting the assassination attempts, there had definitely been at least two murders in the palace since her ascension, both apparently the result of fights over unattended goods. There were reports of other fights that had not ended quite so badly, and stories of rapes and molestations.

It was just as bad as the Wall Street Field had been. Didn't these people appreciate the fact that they had a roof over their heads now, that they weren't outcasts anymore?

Obviously not. About the only comfort was that the population of the palace seemed to be declining; there were clearly fewer people in the corridors now. They might just be moving into the rooms and chambers, or down into the deeper areas where she didn't see them, but Tabaea liked to think that they were finding places for themselves outside, in the houses her people were taking back from the old overlord's tax collectors, or with their families, or *somewhere*.

She frowned. There had been that rumor that some were moving back to the Wall Street Field. She didn't like that.

And then there were all the complaints from the other people, the outsiders, the merchants and nobles and even sailors and craftsmen and the like, worried about the absence of the city guard, complaining about the loss of their slaves, claiming they had been robbed and the thieves had taken shelter in the palace, and any number of other things . . .

The pleasures of ruling, Tabaea thought as she neared the steps that would lead her up to the start of her working day, were overrated, and it didn't help at all that she had gone and limited what pleasures there were, in her idealistic drive to improve the lot of her subjects. She could think of interesting ways to pass the time with a handsome slave, now that she could afford one, could have had one for the asking—but she had abolished slavery.

She sighed, straightened her skirt, and proceeded up the steps toward the throne room.

At least she had finally had the sense to give up on those silly gowns and gewgaws. She didn't need to look like some jewel-encrusted queen out of an old story to convince people that she was the empress; all she needed was to be herself, Tabaea the First.

As always, there was a crowd waiting for her; as always, she ignored them and marched straight toward the dais, expecting them to get out of her way.

Then, abruptly, she stopped. Something was wrong. She sniffed the air.

Someone in the crowd was terrified—not just nervous, but really scared, and at the same time she scented aggression. And it wasn't from someone lurking in a back corner, it was someone nearby. She saw movement, a hand raising.

Another assassination attempt, obviously.

Well, this time she didn't intend to be killed. Even if she always recovered almost instantly, it still hurt; in fact, it was downright agonizing, for a few seconds. It used up precious magic energy, and besides, it made a mess, getting blood all over everything.

This time she sensed warlockry, just a trace of it, a tiny bit of magic. That had happened before; warlocks had tried to stop her heart, had tried to throw knives at her, had tried to strangle her from afar, and every time, she had blocked the attempt easily. Warlockry didn't work on warlocks, and she, thanks to that silly Inza, was a warlock.

Usually, though, the warlock attacks had come when she was alone, not here in the throne room.

Well, those attacks hadn't worked, so a change in strategy was sensible enough. She wondered just what was intended this time.

All this ran through her mind almost instantly; she was reacting far faster than any ordinary human could, faster than any ordinary warlock.

The frightened warlock in the crowd was holding something in his upraised hand, something small and golden, and then he was releasing it, sending it flying toward her at incredible speed, supported and propelled by magic.

An ordinary woman probably wouldn't have seen it in time to react. An ordinary warlock probably couldn't have gathered the will to respond before the gold thimble reached her.

Tabaea had no trouble at all knocking the thing aside while it was still three or four feet away; the thimble dropped to the floor, rattling on the stone, and the single drop it held spattered out.

Immediately, a white vapor arose, hissing.

Tabaca didn't concern herself with that; she had an assassin to stop. She leaped over the smoking thimble, reaching the warlock in a single bound; she grabbed the front of his tunic with her left hand, and her right snatched her dagger from its sheath.

Then she stopped.

People were screaming and backing away, the white vapor was spreading, and Tabaea could smell it, a horrible, burning stench like nothing she had ever smelled before; the assassin, more frightened than ever, was struggling helplessly in her grip, trying to get free. Tabaea ignored all that.

The knife in her hand felt wrong.

It was a fairly subtle thing, and she couldn't have described exactly what the difference was, but the instant her hand closed on the hilt, she knew, beyond any doubt, that this knife was not the Black Dagger. A person gets to know a tool when it's handled with any frequency, gets to know its feel, its shape. Without question, Tabaea knew the Black Dagger.

And without question, the knife in her hand was not the Black Dagger.

Furious, she rammed the blade into her would-be assassin's belly, partly to be certain that this was not just some inexplicable transformation that had left the magic intact, and partly because after all, even if she couldn't steal his life, this man had tried to kill her, and was therefore a traitor who deserved to die.

She felt no surge of energy, no tingle of magic, as the man screamed and clutched at her hand.

There was no magic. The Black Dagger was gone.

She threw the assassin aside, unconcerned whether he was dead or alive, and turned to face the stairway she had just ascended.

Where could the Black Dagger have gone?

She had some vague idea of retracing her steps, but when she turned, she found herself face-to-face with that stinking smoke. It was still rising, still spreading. She looked down.

The contents of the thimble had spread, and now completely covered an area the width of her hand, perfectly circular in shape—and Tabaea knew that that perfect a circle was unnatural. The stuff should have sprayed unevenly across the stone in a fan shape.

What was more, within that circle the floor was completely invisible, hidden by a layer of . . . of *something*. Tabaea had no name for it, either for the substance or even for its color. It wasn't exactly green, wasn't exactly gray or brown or yellow, but it was closer to those colors than to anything else. It was liquid, but she couldn't say what kind; it was shiny and looked somehow slimy, but it wasn't quite like anything she had ever seen before.

And it wasn't still; it roiled and rippled and bubbled and steamed, though Tabaea could feel no heat from it. It moved almost as if it were somehow alive.

She had assumed at first that the drop was some sort of concentrated acid, or virulent poison, but this stuff was obviously magic.

What's more, it was spreading.

And, she realized with a twinge of horror, it wasn't spreading *on top* of the marble floor; it was eating *into* the stone.

And someone had wanted to put that stuff *on her*, and she didn't even have the Black Dagger to protect her; it would have eaten away at her, just as it was eating at the floor. She shuddered.

Who was responsible for this? She looked up and around at the throne room. Most of the crowd had fled, but some were still there, staying well away from her and from the little pool of whatever-it-was. No one was smiling; no one seemed to stand out as reacting oddly, unless she counted the assassin, who was still breathing, still alive.

Had the assassin known that her dagger was gone, that she was no longer protected against wizardry? Had he taken the dagger himself?

She strode over to him and used one toe to roll him over onto his back. He lay there, gasping and bleeding. The knife on his belt was obviously not the Black Dagger; Tabaea could see that at a glance.

"Who sent you?" she demanded.

He made a strangled choking noise. He clearly was in no condition to answer, even if he had wanted to. Tabaea frowned.

She reached out, warlock-fashion, and tried to sense the damage her knife blow had done.

The wound was pretty bad, but she thought it could be healed if someone, a powerful witch or a warlock who had been trained properly, got to it before the man finished bleeding to death, or if a theurgist managed to get the right prayer through in time. Unfortunately, Tabaea could not do it herself; she had never learned to heal, with either warlockry or witchcraft.

She turned and spotted Arl, standing by the dais. "You, Arl," she said. "Find a witch or a priest or someone; I want this man healed, so he can tell me who sent him. And be careful, he's a warlock."

"Uh . . ."

"Hurry! And I won't be holding court today, so the rest of you can all . . . no, wait a minute. You, and you—find something to cover over that stuff, I don't want anyone stepping in it. It looks nasty. And then get out of here, all of you. Get going, Arl."

"Yes, Your Majesty."

A moment later the throne room was empty, save for Tabaea and the wounded assassin. The empress glanced around and noticed that even here, in the imperial audience chamber, trash had piled up in the corners.

And over by the stair, the little pool of magical gunk was still bubbling and smoking. Tabaea didn't worry about it; she was far more concerned just now with the whereabouts of the Black Dagger.

After all, whatever that stuff was, it would surely dry up and die soon enough.

CHAPTER 37

A farmer's wagon was sitting by the palace door in plain sight in the morning sun, Sarai noticed. It looked incongruous; when the overlord was in power, deliveries had been made as quickly and unobtrusively as possible, over at the southeast entrance.

People were milling about, some in rags, some in commonplace attire, some in finery—though most of the last seemed uncomfortable in their obviously stolen clothes, and sometimes combined their finery with familiar rags. Those who were just emerging from the dim interior of the palace blinked in the bright sunlight; hands shading eyes were common. No one seemed to be paying any attention to the wagon or its driver.

The mix of clothing was familiar to Sarai from her stay in Tabaea's palace, but she had never noticed wagons at the northeast entry before. She took a good look at it as she approached—and then stopped dead in her tracks.

The wagon's driver was Tobas, the wizard. He was dressed in rough brown wool instead of his usual wizard's robe, but it was unmistakably him. He was leaning down from his seat talking to someone, and Sarai recognized the young woman in the black dress as Teneria, the witch.

Sarai took a second to gather her wits, then hurried forward again; a moment later she hailed Tobas. She had to shout twice before he looked up, startled. Even then, he didn't answer at first; he stared blankly at Lady Sarai until Teneria said, "Oh, it's Sarai!"

Two or three passersby looked up at that and glanced curiously at Sarai. Sarai hurried up to the wagon, not at all pleased by this attention; she didn't want to be recognized, and with her disguise gone, it was entirely possible that someone would know her face.

Well, it was her own fault for calling out.

"Pharea," Sarai said. "I'm called Pharea. What's happening?"

"Well, right at the moment, there's a warlock in the throne room, waiting for Tabaea to make her entrance, and when she does, he's going to try a spell of Telurinon's on her," Tobas explained. "Karanissa is in there, too, keeping an eye on everything."

"That's the Seething Death?" Sarai asked.

"Now, how . . ." Tobas began.

Teneria said, "She talked to Alorria. Excuse me, Sar . . . Pharea, but Tabaea's coming up the steps right now, she's at the top."

"So you know about this?" Tobas asked.

Sarai nodded.

"And you know about the Black Dagger."

"Yes," Sarai said.

Tobas sighed uneasily and said, "Well, in a moment we should find out if the Black Dagger can stop the Seething Death. And if . . ."

"No," Sarai interrupted. "We aren't going to find out anything about the Black Dagger."

"We aren't?" Tobas stared down at her. "Why not?"

Sarai hesitated, and before she could say anything, Teneria cried out, "Oh, no!"

Tobas whirled back to the witch. "What happened?" he demanded.

"She spilled it! She knocked it aside and spilled it on the floor, and now she's grabbed Thurin and . . ." Teneria winced. ". . . and she's stabbed him, and it hurts really bad . . ." She closed her eyes and leaned against the wagon.

Sarai bit her lip and watched as the witch tried to continue. She had worried that something might go wrong, ever since she had used the Black Dagger herself and discovered how Tabaea saw the World—or rather, how she sensed it. She could *smell* danger. She could move inhumanly fast. The slightest movement could alert her. She could hear a whisper from across a room. None of the magicians would realize that—at least, Sarai didn't see how they could. The witches might have sensed something, but would even they have really appreciated just how fast and how sensitive Tabaea was?

Well, either they hadn't, or they hadn't been consulted in setting this up.

"Now what?" Sarai asked.

"Now she's trying to get Thurin to talk, but he can't; he's dying, he's bleeding to death, and she doesn't know how to heal him. She's sent her chancellor for a healer, and Karanissa wants to know whether we should send a volunteer—she'll try it herself, if you want, but she isn't sure she can heal a wound that bad; a warlock would be better—Tobas, warlocks have trouble at healing, they don't have the subtlety of touch, but if *I* did it, with a warlock helping, I know how to draw on a warlock's strength . . ." She looked up.

"Who's the Council got nearby?" Tobas asked.

"Vengar is in the antechamber . . ."

"All right, then, you go find Vengar, and the two of you help

Thurin, but you be *careful* around Tabaea! And send Karanissa out here, so we can stay in touch!''

Teneria nodded, then turned and ran into the palace.

As she did, the first of those who had fled the throne room in panic began to emerge, shoving the young witch aside as they hurried out into the sun. She fought her way past and in.

Tobas sighed as he watched her go.

''It all went wrong, didn't it?'' Sarai said.

Tobas nodded.

''So how was it *supposed* to go?'' she asked. ''How does the Seething Death work?''

Tobas sighed. He climbed down off the wagon, patted the ox, and turned to stare at the door to the palace.

''The Seething Death,'' he said, ''creates a drop of . . . well, it's more or less liquid chaos. It's the raw stuff that wizardry is made of, I think; the descriptions aren't very clear. But whatever it is, once it's activated, it spreads. It expands, and as it expands, it consumes everything it touches. Anything that comes into contact with it dissolves away—the book says that first it loses solidity, and then all the different elements that make it up blend together into a sort of boiling slime, and then it all becomes more of the Death itself, more pure chaos.''

He was interrupted by the screams of three women who came running out the door just then. When they had passed, Sarai remarked, ''Sounds nasty.''

''It is,'' Tobas agreed. ''It hasn't been used in centuries because it's too dangerous, but Telurinon was desperate to find something that could get at Tabaea despite the Black Dagger, so he tried it.''

''Someone was supposed to get it on Tabaea and dissolve her?''

''That was the idea,'' Tobas agreed. ''A warlock named Thurin of Northbeach volunteered—but he missed, I guess, and Tabaea caught him and stabbed him. I don't know why he's still alive; I thought the Black Dagger stole the souls of anyone it cut.''

Sarai started to say something, to explain that Tabaea didn't have the Black Dagger anymore and that that wasn't how it worked anyway, but then she stopped. There would be plenty of time for that later. ''So the spell didn't work?'' she asked.

''Well, it didn't work on *Tabaea*,'' Tobas said. ''If the stuff landed on the floor, then right now it's dissolving away the floor of your throne room, and there's no way to stop it.''

Sarai had been watching the people emerging from the palace; now, startled, she turned back to Tobas.

"No way to stop it?" she asked.

He shook his head. "No way we know of," he said. "If it had been confined to Tabaea's body, we could have transported her to a place where magic doesn't work—that's what's in the wagon here, a magic tapestry that would send her there. But I don't see how we can send an entire floor through the tapestry."

"There isn't any countercharm?"

Tobas shook his head.

"So how much is it going to dissolve, then?" Sarai asked. "I mean, it won't ruin the whole palace, will it?"

Tobas sighed. "Lady Sarai," he said, "For all I know, in time it will dissolve the whole *World*."

She stared at him. "That's ridiculous," she said.

He turned up an empty palm. "Nonetheless," he said, "that's what may happen. It's what the old books *say* will happen; every text that mentions the Seething Death agrees that unchecked, it will indeed spread until it has reduced all the World to primordial chaos."

"But that's absurd!"

"I wish it were," Tobas replied, and Sarai realized for the first time that despite his calm answers, the wizard was seriously frightened. He was almost trembling.

"But there *must* be a countercharm," she said. "If the spell was written down, then someone must have performed it, right?"

Tobas nodded. "I can't see any other way it could have been," he agreed.

"Well, the World's still here," Sarai pointed out. "*Something* must have stopped the spell, mustn't it?"

"Yes," Tobas admitted, "something must have. Someone must have tried the spell at least once, at least four hundred years ago, so it must have been stopped, or it would have dissolved the World by now. But we don't know *how* it was stopped."

"Well, find out!" Sarai snapped. "Isn't that one of the things magic is good at?"

"Sometimes," Tobas said, "but not always. Spying on wizards, even dead ones, isn't easy, Lady Sarai; we tend to use

warding spells, since we don't *like* being spied on; we're a secretive bunch. And even if we don't use warding spells, learning
a spell by watching a vision of it being performed is not always
reliable.''

"Well, has anyone *tried* to find the countercharm for this
Seething Death?''

Tobas laughed hollowly. "Oh, yes, Lady Sarai,'' he said. "Of
course they have. A spell that destructive has been a temptation
for generations of wizards. But no one's ever found that lost
counterspell.''

Sarai sputtered. "Then how could Telurinon . . . Why
didn't . . . What kind of *idiot* ever wrote the spell down in
the first place without including the countercharm?''

Tobas turned up an empty palm. "Who knows?'' he said.
"Lady Sarai, we wizards do a good many things that don't make
much sense; it's been our policy for a thousand years to record
everything, but to keep it all secret, and that means we have
situations like this one. It doesn't surprise me at all, I'm sorry
to say.''

Sarai was too worried and angry to correct him for calling her
by her right name; she turned and stared at the palace.

"What's happening in there?'' she asked.

Tobas shrugged again. "How would I know? I'm not a seer,
and Teneria isn't here.''

"I'm going in to see.''

"I don't . . . well, be careful, Sar . . . Pharea. Don't go near
the Seething Death. And Tabaea's still in there, you know, still
the empress.''

"I know, I know,'' Sarai said. She waved a distracted good-
bye to Tobas, then marched on into the palace.

CHAPTER 38

*T*abaea stepped back as the witch knelt by the assassin's side,
giving her room to work. She glanced quickly at the wooden

bowl that someone had placed upside down atop the puddle of magical gunk; it still looked secure enough, but the nasty odor of the stuff lingered, making it unpleasant for someone with the empress' superhuman sense of smell to breathe.

Whatever that fluid was, Tabaea was very glad she hadn't touched it, or gotten any on her. She had tried moving it by warlockry and had found that as far as a warlock's or witch's special senses and abilities were concerned, it didn't exist; she couldn't affect it in any way, with any of the limited magic at her command.

What's more, everything she had dropped or poked into it had dissolved. Wood, cloth, metal—anything at all, it didn't matter, whatever touched the stuff would dissolve like ice shards dropped in boiling water.

At least the goo didn't splash.

She wished the spell would hurry up and burn out; it was beginning to worry her. Maybe there was more to it than she had thought at first.

She would have to ask the assassin, if he lived. She turned back to him and to the witch tending to him. Tabaea could feel the witch's energy gathering in her hands, then transferring out through her fingers into the assassin's belly, knitting together the ruined tissues . . .

And she could feel something else, too; something was strange about the flow of power. It wasn't witchcraft; something else was at work, as well. The witch was drawing power from somewhere else.

Tabaea had heard that witches could share energy; was there another witch nearby, then, who was helping this Teneria? If so, why didn't the other witch step forward and help openly?

The empress turned and nervously looked over the people in sight. Arl was there, of course; it was he who had brought the witch. There were half a dozen others on the stairs behind him, watching from what they presumably thought was a safe distance. As Tabaea watched, another woman came up and peered into the room.

There was something familiar about this new arrival; not her face, which Tabaea was fairly sure she hadn't seen before, but something. Perhaps her scent was one that Tabaea had smelled somewhere.

Whatever it was, she couldn't place the woman immediately. She wasn't a witch, though, Tabaea could sense that, and it was magicians who worried the empress just now. With the Black Dagger gone she was not at all sure of her ability to fend off hostile magic.

One of the other women, the tall dark one with the long hair, was a witch, but she wasn't sending Teneria any power. She was doing *something*, but it wasn't helping Teneria.

Then the tall woman noticed Tabaea's interest and instantly stopped whatever she had been doing. That was annoying of her. Tabaea wished she hadn't been so careless in her investigation; that witch was on her guard, now.

But that wasn't where the power was coming from, anyway; Tabaea tried her best to see where this not-quite-witchcraft was coming from, and suddenly something dropped into place.

It wasn't witchcraft; it was warlockry. It was coming from a man on the stair. Teneria was taking the warlock energy and using it for witchcraft.

That was interesting and a little frightening; Tabaea had not known that that was possible. She had discovered for herself that the two varieties of magic were surprisingly similar, but she hadn't realized that anyone else knew it, since no one else was both a witch *and* a warlock, and it had never even occurred to her that anyone might have learned how to use the two in combination.

Magicians, it seemed, were just full of unpleasant surprises today—a warlock had used wizardry against her, and now a witch was using another warlock's power to heal the attacker.

They were joining forces.

They were joining forces against *her*.

And the Black Dagger was gone.

Just then something hissed; everyone but Teneria and the unconscious assassin turned at the sound, to see the cloud of noxious grayish smoke that rose from the pool of whatever-it-was as the bowl sank down into it, dissolving away as it went.

"By the gods," someone muttered.

Tabaea, shaken, stared at the puddle. It was almost a foot across now, still a perfect circle.

How large would it get? It had only been there perhaps half an hour, starting from a single drop.

She turned back to Teneria and demanded, "Hurry up! I need him conscious!"

"I'm hurrying," Teneria said quietly, in an odd, distracted tone; an ordinary woman wouldn't have heard her, but Tabaea,

Empress of Ethshar, did. She heard everything, saw everything, smelled everything; she had the strength of a dozen men and the speed of a cat. She was a witch and a warlock both.

But she wasn't a wizard anymore, with the Black Dagger gone, and her enemies were working together.

And this Teneria was one of them, wasn't she? She was working with a warlock, and the warlocks had sent the assassin. When the man was healed, what was to keep him and the other warlock and the two witches from turning all their power on her, their common foe?

Tabaea could counter a warlock and fight off a witch, but she wasn't sure about the combination, and two of each; the dagger had always helped her, had blocked part of *any* magic. And witches were subtle.

She took a step backward, away from Teneria, and then caught a whiff of the fumes from the wizard-stuff. Without thinking, she took a sniff and almost choked; the stuff was unbelievably foul. It covered other scents, as well—but not completely; Tabaea realized that she could still smell the blood from the assassin's wound, the nervous sweat on Teneria's skin, the distinct odors of the people on the stairs, some familiar, some strange.

There was another odor there as well, a very faint trace, that somehow seemed important. The fumes were making her dizzy, and she had too much to think about, with the assassin and all the magicians working together; if she still had the Black Dagger . . .

When had it disappeared, anyway? How had they taken it? Magic wouldn't work on it, so it couldn't have been taken magically; someone must have slipped it away while Tabaea was asleep—but she had always kept the knife close at hand, even when she slept, she only took it off to bathe.

It must have been one of the servants. It was not Lethe or Ista. She could trust them; she knew by the smell. And they had still been here when she came down to the throne room.

Pharea.

That woman who had only been there once, who had helped her clean off the blood, then disappeared. She must have taken it.

And that's who that was on the stairs, Tabaea realized, the woman with the familiar scent. That smell was the peculiar odor the woman had had that Tabaea had thought was just some odd sort of perfume—but it was too faint for perfume, an ordinary human probably couldn't smell it at all.

Her face was different, but that must have just been a disguise of some sort, probably magical. There was no mistaking the scent. That was Pharea, and she was in it, too—in the plot against Tabaea, against the empress.

Tabaea whirled and stared at the group on the stairs. "Arl," she said, "bring those people in here."

Arl blinked; he had been staring at that horrible puddle. "What people, Your Majesty?" he asked.

"Those people on the stairs. You, all of you—come closer." Tabaea beckoned. With varying degrees of reluctance and much glancing at one another, the little group stepped up into the throne room. Arl stepped in behind them, herding them forward.

"Line up," Tabaea ordered. Something drew her attention; she turned to see Teneria looking up. "Go on healing him!" Tabaea snapped.

"Yes, Your Majesty," the witch said, turning back to her work.

The people formed a ragged line, and Tabaea looked them over. "You," she said, pointing at the tall witch, "get over there." She gestured toward the dais.

The woman glanced at the others, then obeyed.

"You, too," Tabaea ordered the warlock. He hesitated, then went.

"And you, Pharea."

"I don't think so," the woman replied; her hand dropped to the hilt of the knife she carried on her belt, concealed by a fold of her skirt. She never questioned how Tabaea had recognized her, never tried to deny her identity; the empress thought she knew what *that* meant. "The rest of you, get out of here," Pharea said. She waved at the others still in the line.

The three of them looked at Tabaea.

"She's right," the empress said. "Get out of here. Now."

"Your Majesty . . ." Arl began.

"Shut up," Tabaea commanded. She was watching Pharea's hand closely, the hand that was on the hilt of a knife.

Tabaea knew that knife well. She had carried it herself for four years. Witchcraft couldn't sense it; warlockry couldn't touch it; although she had no spells to test it with, Tabaea knew that wizardry would not work on the person who held it.

That meant that it would have dispelled a magical disguise, didn't it? So this was Pharea's real face, and the other had been an illusion.

The bystanders departed, and now the sides were clear, the stage set, Tabaea thought; she and Arl on one side, Pharea and the four magicians on the other. When the footsteps had reached the bottom of the stairs, and her enhanced senses assured the empress that there were no other intruders around, Tabaea demanded, "Do you know what you've got there, Pharea?"

"I think so," Pharea said warily; something about the way she stood, the way her eyes moved, told Tabaea that she had already used the Black Dagger herself, had killed at least one cat, and perhaps other animals.

A movement on the dais attracted Tabaea's attention for an instant; the older witch had moved, had taken a step toward Pharea, and was staring at her.

"I don't think your friends know," Tabaea said. "You are working with the magicians, aren't you? They're all working together, now."

Pharea smiled crookedly. "We haven't always been as coordinated as we might be," she said. "But yes, we're all on the same side."

Behind Pharea, Arl was moving up slowly and quietly, clearly planning to grab her from behind; the tall witch was about to say something, and Tabaea did not want Pharea warned. She turned to the witch and demanded, "And who are you, anyway? I can see that you're a witch, but you didn't volunteer to help heal this killer you people sent. Who are you?"

Startled, the woman answered, "My name is Karanissa of the Mountains," she said.

"And you aren't helping Teneria; why not?"

"Because she doesn't need help," Karanissa said. "I would if she wanted me to; I was going to try it myself, but Teneria thought . . ."

She was interrupted by Arl's lunge—and his falling headlong on the marble floor, as Pharea dodged neatly and drew the Black Dagger. Before anyone else could react, the false servant grabbed Arl by the hair and stood over him with the knife to his throat.

"It's not that easy," Pharea said to Tabaea. "I've got the dagger, and I'm keeping it. *And* I'll use it to defend myself if I need to."

Tabaea frowned. "You think you can handle *all* my followers so easily?"

Pharea smiled grimly. "Why not?" she asked. "*You* handled the city guard. And they're on our side, too, by the way—Lord Torrut is still in command, and only a few dozen men deserted or went over to you."

Tabaea stared at Pharea, trying to decide if that was a bluff. Hadn't Lord Torrut fled with the others, sailed off to wherever they all went? "Who are you, anyway?" she demanded, stalling for time to think. "You're no magician, so far as I can see, and you don't look like a soldier."

The woman Tabaea called Pharea smiled an unpleasant smile. "I'm Lady Sarai," she said. "Minister of Investigation and Acting Minister of Justice to Ederd the Fourth, overlord of Ethshar."

"Ederd's not the overlord anymore," Tabaea replied angrily. "I'm *empress!*" She tried to hide how much she was shaken by the discovery that she was facing Lord Kalthon's daughter; for all her life until the last few sixnights, Tabaea had lived in terror of the Minister of Justice, and for the last few months of that time Lady Sarai had been feared, as well. Tabaea had tried to dismiss her as a harmless girl, but here was that harmless girl, in her own throne room, holding the Black Dagger.

"You're Tabaea the Thief," Sarai said. "Four years ago you stole a spell from Serem the Wise, but it came out wrong and made this dagger I'm holding. For a long time you didn't do anything with it—maybe you didn't know what it did—but then you killed Inza the Apprentice, and Serem the Wise, and Kelder of Quarter Street, and others. And when the guards came to arrest you for those murders, you declared yourself empress, and used the knife's magic to occupy the palace."

"I *am* the empress!" Tabaea insisted. "I rule the city—the old guards don't dare show their faces, and the overlord and his family all fled before me!"

"But that," Sarai said, holding up the dagger, "was when you had *this.*"

"And I'll have it again! Give it back to me!"

Outrageously, mockingly, Sarai laughed. She dared to *laugh* at the empress of Ethshar!

Moving faster than humanly possible, Tabaea lunged for Sarai, intending to snatch the knife away from her.

Moving faster than humanly possible, Sarai dodged, flinging

Arl aside, and spun to face Tabaea again, with the enchanted knife raised and ready.

"Think a minute, Tabaea," the noblewoman said. "We both have stolen lives and stolen talents—but I have the dagger. If you stab me, I lose a life—but if I stab you, you not only lose a life, I gain one. And *maybe*, you know, maybe *this* dagger will take more than one at a time. Maybe I only have to kill you once."

Tabaea, hearing this, started to turn, then stopped herself. No ordinary enemy would have seen the tiny little twitch, but Sarai saw it.

"And yes, you're right; I'm not a witch nor a warlock," the overlord's Minister of Investigation said. Then she pointed with the dagger to her companions, and added, "But *they* are, over there, and they're on my side."

Tabaea glanced at Arl—but there was no need for Sarai to say a word about the rat-faced little chancellor; he was crawling away from both women, heading for the stairs, obviously wanting only to be out of sight.

But Sarai hadn't cut his throat when she had the chance, when Tabaea had attacked; Lord Kalthon's daughter was apparently not as bloodthirsty as her father was said to be.

"Are you planning to kill me?" Tabaea demanded.

Sarai blinked, catlike and quick. "I suppose we ought to," she said. Tabaea thought she sounded almost startled, not at the question, but at her own reply. "After all, you're a murderer. But there were some exceptional circumstances here, and I think my father and I, acting in the overlord's behalf, would accept a plea for mercy and commute the sentence to exile from the city—if you surrender *now* and don't force us to do any more damage to depose you."

"You *think*," Tabaea said. "And what if I *don't* surrender, then? I've seen you move—you're fast, all right, and yes, you have the dagger, but I think I'm still faster and stronger. Your magicians and I cancel each other out. Are you ready to take me on and try to kill me, here and now?"

"Oh, no," Sarai said, smiling again. "I don't have to. All I have to do is get us all out of here alive, and I think I can manage that much. And after that, we'll let the wizards and the demon-ologists try out their spells on you—now that you don't have the Black Dagger. Or maybe we'll just wait."

"Wait for *what*?" Tabaea demanded, shaken by the woman's

confidence and the threat of demons and wizardry. She could still counter witchcraft, since she had the talent and more raw vitality than any three normal witches; she could still counter warlockry because of the inherent limits on every warlock; but without the dagger she had no defense against other magicks.

"For the Seething Death to get you," Sarai replied, pointing to the pool of wizard-stuff. "True, it didn't get you immediately, but it will keep spreading until it *does*—unless we use the countercharm to stop it."

Disconcerted, Tabaea turned to stare at the puddle—and the instant she did, the two witches and the unhurt warlock dashed for the stairs. The assassin, still unconscious, sailed along behind them, unsupported through the air—his fellow warlock was doing that, Tabaea sensed.

She let them go. This was between Sarai and herself, now.

Sarai seemed very sure of herself—but was she really? The sight of the fleeing witches reminded Tabaea of her own witchcraft—she had so many choices now, so many things she could do, that there were times when she forgot some of them.

"That stuff is going to go on spreading?" she asked.

"That's right," Sarai said—but Tabaea, witch-senses alert, knew that was a half truth. Sarai was hiding something.

"Until it kills me? It's after me, specifically?"

"That's right," Sarai said—but this time it was a lie, Tabaea knew.

"Unless you use the countercharm?"

"A wizard working for us," Sarai said, "not me."

And that was a lie, too.

It was all lies and tricks.

Except, perhaps, the part about using wizardry to kill her.

Tabaea was between Sarai and the nearest staircase; the other exits were far across the throne room. Sarai was fast, but Tabaea thought she was faster. Sarai had the Black Dagger—and Tabaea *needed* it. Only the dagger could guard her against wizards.

She had killed a Guildmaster; even if Lord Kalthon gave her mercy, the Wizards' Guild never would. She knew that. They hadn't killed her yet—but Tabaea remembered when Sarai had first shown the dagger. The other magicians had been surprised. The Wizards' Guild must not have known about the theft, either.

And only the fact that they didn't know Lady Sarai had gotten the Black Dagger away from her had kept Tabaea alive *this* long, she was suddenly certain.

She might lose a fight with Lady Sarai, but at least she'd have a chance; if she didn't get the dagger back, she was as good as dead.

She lunged.

CHAPTER 39

*S*arai had watched from the stairs as Teneria worked at her healing and had watched as the Seething Death dissolved the bowl Tabaea had used to cover it, had seen and smelled that Tabaea was on the ragged edge of panic, and had realized that the situation was critical.

Tabaea had to be removed, and the Seething Death had to be stopped.

The wizards could handle Tabaea now, once they knew the dagger was gone; all Sarai had to do was to tell Tobas, or even just Karanissa or Teneria, that she had stolen the Black Dagger.

Stopping the Seething Death wouldn't be so easy.

Or would it? The Black Dagger negated most wizardry; would it be able to stop the Seething Death?

That was something to think about, maybe something to try if Tabaea ever left the room—but at that thought, something occurred to Sarai that she should, she told herself, have considered sooner: Bringing the Black Dagger so close to Tabaea might have been a foolish risk to take. If the self-proclaimed empress were to realize that the knife was there . . .

Just then, Tabaea demanded, "Arl, bring those people in here."

The funny little man who was acting as Tabaea's majordomo looked up. "What people, Your Majesty?" he asked.

"Those people on the stairs." Tabaea waved for them to come forward, and said, "You, all of you—come closer."

Sarai cursed herself for getting into this dangerous a position. She should have slipped away while she had the chance, gone to the Guildhouse, and told them everything.

"Line up," Tabaea ordered. Then she turned and shouted at Teneria, "Go on healing him!"

"Yes, Your Majesty." Teneria replied.

Tabaea pointed at Karanissa. "You," she said, "get over there." She ordered Vengar to the dais, as well.

And then she turned back and pointed directly at Sarai and said, "And you, Pharea."

For an instant, Sarai froze; how had Tabaea recognized her? "Pharea" had had a different face.

But then she realized what had given it away, what *must* have given it away: her scent.

She should have known; after all, she could now recognize the odor of anyone she had been near herself, and Tabaea had killed not just one dog, but several.

The method didn't really matter, though; all that mattered was that Sarai had been spotted.

But of course, Tabaea didn't know everything; she didn't know who "Pharea" was, didn't know everything that was going on. She couldn't. She had magic, she had superhuman senses, but she wasn't omniscient. If Sarai let Tabaea control events now, that might ruin everything. Tabaea might take the dagger back, she might kill Thurin and Teneria and Karanissa and Vengar, and she might let the Seething Death spread unchecked; Sarai hoped that if it was dealt with while it was still small the spell could be stopped.

She didn't dare let Tabaea tell her what to do—but what choice did she have?

She had to bluff. She had had four years of practice in talking information out of people; maybe she could talk Tabaea into giving herself up.

And what choice did she have?

"I don't think so," Sarai said, as confidently as she could. She let her hand fall to the hilt of the Black Dagger.

It seemed to go well at first; she dodged Tabaea's first attack, removing whatever threat Arl might pose. A moment later, the distracted would-be empress let the four magicians escape.

And it all seemed to be working, right up until Tabaea dove at her.

Sarai just barely dodged; she had not been ready for it this time, as she had before. And the little empress looked so small and harmless—it was hard to remember that she had torn men apart with her bare hands.

Tabaea whirled and struck again, and again Sarai dodged.

She couldn't keep this up, though, and she didn't dare actually fight; Tabaea was much faster, vastly more powerful, and had her magic, as well. Sarai had to escape, to get away—and even that would be difficult. She remembered the assassins Tabaea had run down and butchered. She had to do something they hadn't, something unexpected—but what?

Lord Torrut had mentioned a trick once, when he and Captain Tikri had been joking with each other; Tabaea came at Sarai again, and she tried it, putting her hands on Tabaea's shoulders and vaulting over her head.

If the throne room had had a normal ceiling, it would never have worked, but there under the great dome, with cat-reflexes and her augmented strength, the move sent Sarai sailing a dozen feet through the air. She landed, catlike, on her feet, and immediately sprinted for the stairs most nearly straight ahead, which happened to be the right-hand set as seen from the dais.

Tabaea needed a second or two to whirl on one toe and set out in pursuit, but she closed much faster than Sarai liked. At the very brink, Sarai dodged sideways and ran along the throne-room wall toward the rear stairs.

Tabaea was unable to stop until she was four or five steps down; Sarai had gained at least a second this time.

As she ran along the side of the throne room, Sarai's feet stirred through the trash that had accumulated during Tabaea's reign; she took a fraction of a second from her narrow lead to stoop and scoop up a handful of garbage. She flung it over her shoulder, in Tabaea's face. The empress screamed with anger as a chicken bone hit her in the eye, but she hardly slowed at all.

As she neared the corner, wondering why Tabaea had not cut diagonally across the room to head her off, Sarai scooped up more debris; this time she tossed it, not at Tabaea, but at the Seething Death.

Trash rattled and skittered across the stone floor—and then some of it skidded into the Death, and dissolved with a loud hiss and a billow of stinking white vapor.

Startled, Tabaea turned, and stumbled, then caught herself—but by then Sarai was on the stairs, descending in four-step leaps, constantly on the verge of tumbling headlong.

At the foot of the stairs she turned left, ignoring the broad straightaway directly ahead; she wanted to get back to Tobas and his wagon, in hopes that he would be able to help. Besides, there were fewer people in the way by this route; that long south-east corridor had several dozen of Tabaea's "guests" scattered along it, sprawled on the floor or seated against the wall, and any one of them might decide to trip her or try to grab her. Furthermore, Tabaea might not expect her to turn.

But that last hope was dashed almost instantly; she heard Tabaea's steps on the stairs and knew that the empress had seen her make the turn. Running with all her might, not daring to look back, Sarai ran on, leaping over the one startled, rag-clad figure in her path.

Tabaea had stolen more strength and more speed, Sarai reminded herself, but her legs were still shorter, and her skirt longer; there was still a chance.

She cut toward the inner side of the curving passageway at first, then back toward the outside as she neared the next turn. She skidded around the corner so fast, making her right turn, that she almost collided with the left-hand wall of the passageway and with a frightened old woman who crouched on a ragged blanket there.

Tabaea made the turn more neatly—Sarai could tell by the sound. Her own breath was beginning to come hard, while Tabaea still seemed fresh.

Fifty yards ahead she could see the rectangle of sunlight that was the open door; she charged for it full tilt, trying to think of somewhere she could dodge aside, or some ruse she could use.

Nothing came, and Tabaea was gaining, inch by inch, step by step—but Sarai judged she would reach the door first, and maybe if she dove aside . . .

And then, when she was less than a dozen yards away, the sunlight vanished; a drapery of some kind had fallen across the door.

Sarai's heart sank, but she had no choice. She could only hope that Tabaea would become entangled in whatever the obstruction was. She dove forward, hoping to hit it low and crawl underneath.

As she crossed the last few feet, as her eyes adjusted, catlike, to the dimness, she could see that it was a tapestry, one that showed a very odd design, an amazingly realistic depiction of an empty room. Who would want something like that on his wall?

And then she dove, and her hand touched the tapestry, but there was nothing there—she felt no fabric at all, nothing that would slow her headlong plunge onto the pavement of the plaza. Magic, obviously, she thought, an illusion of some kind. She closed her eyes, anticipating the impact.

And sure enough, she struck hard stone—but not the warm, sun-drenched pavement of the plaza; instead, she sprawled on a sloping floor of cold smooth stone in chilly darkness.

She still managed to scrape one cheek raw and give herself several bumps and bruises, as well as banging her head. Dazed, she scrambled up on all fours, eyes open again, and started forward, down the slope, sure that Tabaea was right behind her.

Then she stopped and stared.

Tabaea was nowhere to be seen. In fact, there was *nothing* to be seen; she was in near-total darkness, a deeper and more complete darkness than any moonless midnight she had ever seen. The only place Sarai had ever before encountered anything so dark as this was in the deeper dungeons of the palace.

It was not *perfect* darkness, however; she could make out very faint differentiations around her, places that were tinged with the darkest of grays, rather than utter blackness.

But her eyes were unable to adjust. Even a cat, she decided, couldn't see here.

She listened for Tabaea, but there was no sound of pursuit; in fact, there was no sound *at all*, of any description. Sarai had never before experienced such absolute silence, not even in the dungeons.

And she couldn't smell anything.

That wasn't right; at the very least, with her canine senses she should have smelled her own clothes, her own sweat, and the stone of the floor she had landed on. But she couldn't.

Was she dead, then? Was this darkness part of an afterlife of some sort?

What sort of afterlife was built on a slant?

But no, she could still *feel* perfectly well; she could see, however faintly, and she could hear the sound of her own hand slapping on the stone. She wasn't dead, she had just lost her sense of smell.

Or rather, she had lost the sense of smell she had stolen; she realized that she *could* still detect odors, very slightly. She lifted her skirt and sniffed at the hem, and the familiar scent of wool was there, faint and muffled.

Maybe a cat *could* see here, after all, and she had lost that, as well.

Where *was* she, then? And why hadn't Tabaea come after her, wherever it was? She crawled down the slope, feeling her way in the darkness.

She came to a wall, and followed it along for several feet, still sloping downward.

And then she heard footsteps behind her—not approaching, just suddenly *there*, out of nowhere. She judged they were no more than a few feet away from where she had first fallen when she came through the magical tapestry.

Sarai raised the Black Dagger, ready to defend herself.

Then the newcomer said, "Sarai? Are you there? Damn it all, I forgot we'd need a light."

The voice was not Tabaea's; it was a woman's voice, and it sounded familiar, but Sarai couldn't place it. She turned over into a sitting position, the knife still in her hand.

"Are you in the passage? Did you find it?" the newcomer called, a bit louder. "Sarai, it's me, Karanissa!"

"I'm here," Sarai said, lowering the knife; the voice *was* Karanissa's.

A faint orange witch-light appeared—but at first even that dim illumination seemed almost blinding in such deep gloom. By its glow, Sarai could see that she was in a stone corridor, just around a corner from a fair-sized room or chamber. The glow, and the voice, came from the room.

She backed up far enough to see into the chamber and found Karanissa standing in the center of an utterly bare stone room, a simple rectangular box with straight sides and square corners—but the entire place was on a slant. The witch's upraised hand was glowing, casting an eerie light on her arm and face, as well as the stone walls.

"Karanissa," Sarai asked, "where *are* we?"

CHAPTER 40

Tabaea saw the sunlight vanish ahead, plunging the corridor into gray dimness, and she slowed slightly; was this some new trick? Had Lady Sarai and her magician friends set a trap of some kind?

And then Sarai dove toward the cloth and vanished, and Tabaea threw herself to the ground, rolling, to stop her forward motion.

Wizardry! That had to be wizardry!

It *was* a trap!

Furious, growling, she got to her feet and stared at the fabric that blocked the door.

It was a tapestry, one of fine workmanship—she could hardly see the stitches, and the depiction of the empty room was flawless. It was extraordinarily ugly, however; it showed only bare stone, in black and shades of gray, with no bright color, no graceful curves, nothing of any interest to it at all.

A tapestry, a magical tapestry—she almost reached out to touch it, and then stopped herself.

A *Transporting* Tapestry! That was what it must be! Shuddering, she drew back. She had spied on wizards as they spoke of such things. A Transporting Tapestry—and one that, by the look of it, would deliver her directly into a prison cell somewhere. The room in the picture had no doors, no windows; in one of the rear corners was an opening that might have been a passageway, or might just have been a niche, perhaps where a cot or privy might be.

They had wanted her to plunge right into it, after Lady Sarai—and she almost had!

If she had, of course, they would have had some way to get Lady Sarai out, leaving Tabaea trapped there forever as her punishment for killing their Guildmaster Serem. That would be their revenge—not merely death, but perpetual imprisonment. Perhaps they had other plans for her, as well.

Well, she wasn't going to fall for their tricks. She turned and marched away, back up the corridor.

And then, as she remembered that Lady Sarai still had the Black Dagger, and that Lady Sarai had just dived headlong into a wizard's tapestry and was therefore back in contact with the Wizards' Guild, and that the Wizards' Guild surely wanted to kill her for what she had done, she began to run.

"I abdicate!" she called as she ran, hoping that someone was listening. "I abdicate! I give up!"

Maybe, she thought, just maybe, if she escaped quickly enough by another door, she could still hide, could find somewhere even wizards couldn't get her.

But she doubted it.

"I think they're coming this way," Karanissa shouted. "They're still on the stairs, but Sarai *wants* to come here. And Tabaea's gaining on her, she's *much* faster. Quick, Tobas, do something!"

"Do *what*?" the wizard asked. "I didn't bring anything but the tapestry!" He looked around helplessly. Teneria and the warlocks were off to one side; Teneria and Vengar were once again working at repairing Thurin's wound, but the situation was no longer desperate, and Thurin was conscious and watching.

None of them were making any suggestions.

"Well, then do something with the tapestry!" Karanissa called. "Set it up somewhere Tabaea will run into it!"

Tobas hesitated, then said, "All right, give me a hand with it, will you?" He hurried to the wagon.

A moment later, carefully holding the tapestry by the supporting bar and not allowing themselves to touch any part of the fabric, Tobas and Karanissa had the hanging unrolled, and up against the wall beside the door.

Passersby were staring, but no one interfered. This was clearly either the work of magicians or Tabaea's followers, and no one wanted trouble with either group.

"How do we get her into it?" Tobas asked.

"Put it across the door," Teneria called. "Then she'll run right into it."

"But Sarai will run into it first," Karanissa objected.

Teneria pointed out, "Well, at least she'll get away, then—and with the dagger."

Karanissa looked at Tobas, who shrugged.

"All right," the witch said, "let's do it." She swung her end around, and a few seconds later they draped the tapestry across the open doorway.

Vengar, using warlockry, helped them to raise it until it hung perfectly smooth and unwrinkled—the spell might not work if the fabric wasn't smooth.

"Now what?" Tobas said. "Do you think we could lift it while Sarai dives underneath, and then drop it back before Tabaea could stop?"

"I don't . . ." Karanissa began. Then, as the sound of desperately running footsteps suddenly became audible, drew near, and vanished, all in a few seconds, she said, "No."

"What happened?" Tobas asked.

"Sarai hit the tapestry. She's gone."

"What about Tabaea?"

"Stopped in time."

"Then should we put it down?"

"No!" Teneria called. "If we do, she might come out here and attack *us*!"

Karanissa nodded confirmation, and for a long moment she and Tobas stood absolutely still, holding the tapestry up against the palace door.

Then, at last, they heard retreating footsteps; cautiously, Tobas began to lower the rod, just in time to let them all hear Tabaea shrieking, "I abdicate! I abdicate! I give up! Just leave me alone!"

Karanissa lowered her end, too. "Now what?" she asked.

"Well, if she's serious, we just forget about her for now," Tobas said. "We have to deal with the Seething Death."

"What about Lady Sarai?"

"Oh, damn." Tobas frowned. "That's right, she doesn't know where she is. She's probably terrified. Someone had better go after her and bring her home."

"I'll go," Karanissa said. "After all, I know the way."

Reluctantly, Tobas nodded. "You're right. You go." He beckoned for Vengar to come hold the other side of the tapestry while Karanissa stepped into it.

Wizard and warlock supported the hanging, one on either side, while the witch stepped up and put her hand on it.

Nothing happened.

"She must still be in the room," Karanissa said. "It won't work while she's in the part that's in the picture."

"That's it, of course," Tobas agreed. "I guess we'll just have to wait until she finds the passage, or wanders into one of the back corners."

He and Vengar stood patiently for a moment, while Karanissa kept her hand on the fabric. "I'm getting tired of holding this," Tobas said. "Maybe we should put it aside for now and see if we can do something about the Seething Death, and then try again later."

Karanissa, her hand still on the tapestry, started to say something—and just then, she vanished.

Karanissa found herself standing in complete darkness, and the silence was startling after the constant hum of the city. She stepped forward and peered into the gloom, trying to make out whether Sarai was anywhere nearby. "Sarai?" she called. "Are you there? Damn it all, I forgot we'd need a light."

No one answered; Karanissa frowned. Maybe Sarai had already found the corridor out to the rest of the castle.

"Are you in the passage?" the witch called. "Did you find it? Sarai, it's me, Karanissa!"

"I'm here," Sarai's voice replied. Karanissa still couldn't tell where it was coming from, though.

Well, she was a witch; she could do something about that. She raised her hand and concentrated.

The hand began to glow, a weak orange witch-light. At first, Karanissa saw only the bare stone walls of the arrival chamber, but then Lady Sarai, crawling on hands and knees, backed into the room from the passageway out, and turned to look up at her.

"Karanissa," the Ethsharitic noblewoman asked plaintively, "where *are* we?"

"In the mountains between Aigoa and Dwomor," Karanissa answered. "In a secret room in a castle that Tobas and I own."

"What!?" Sarai shrieked, as she turned to a sitting position. "We're in the *Small Kingdoms*? A hundred leagues away?"

"Not much more than eighty, by my best estimate," Karanissa corrected her. "But yes, we're in the Small Kingdoms. I came after you to show you the way back. Now, can we get out of here, please? This light's very tiring, and there isn't much to eat around here."

"Yes! Where? Where's the door?" She was almost pathetically eager—but then, Karanissa could understand that.

"That way," she said. "Down the passage to the end, and out through the door."

Sarai stood and proceeded down the corridor, never more than a few feet ahead of Karanissa for fear of losing the light, until at last the two of them emerged into daylight in a room lit by a single high window.

Sarai stopped and stared. The room was lined with bookshelves, but most were empty, many broken or rotted; a table had been shoved to one side. And like the dark room and the connecting corridor, everything was at a slant. It was as if the entire building, whatever it was, had tipped.

She remembered what Karanissa had said; the words hadn't really registered, as she had been more concerned with getting out of that horrible darkness. "A castle?" Sarai asked. "You two really have a castle?"

"We have a couple of them, actually," Karanissa said. "Both of them were built by Derithon the Mage, hundreds of years ago. This one used to fly, until it ran into a place where wizardry doesn't work."

"Oh," Sarai said. Understanding slowly dawned. "*Oh*. A place where wizardry doesn't work? You wanted to send Tabaea here. That's why I lost . . . why I'm back to just myself. And she would have been, too."

Karanissa nodded. "She dodged the tapestry, though; she wouldn't touch it."

Sarai held out the Black Dagger, which she had not yet sheathed. "So this thing is useless, now? The spell on it is broken?"

Karanissa frowned. "No," she said, "it doesn't work that way. As long as we're in the no-wizardry area, that's just an ordinary knife; but once we're back out, it'll be magical again. We've brought a magical tapestry and an enchanted mirror through this place, and neither one worked here, but they both worked just fine elsewhere."

"Oh." Sarai looked at the dagger. "Maybe we should leave it here, then, where it can't harm anyone."

"Not without a guard," Karanissa said. "We tried that with the mirror. For one thing, there are spriggans around here, a lot of them, and they just love playing with magical things." She hesitated, then added, "Besides, we might need it."

"Against Tabaea?"

"Or against the Seething Death; I don't know if that thing will do any good against the Death, but it certainly stopped every other spell Tobas and Telurinon sent against Tabaea."

Sarai looked at the knife, then nodded and tucked it into the sheath on her belt.

"All right," she said, "how do we get out of here, and back to Ethshar?"

Karanissa considered that. "Well, we have to walk to the edge of the dead area, of course," she said. "Usually, we have a flying carpet to take us from there, but I'm afraid we don't have it with us—after shuffling the tapestries about I'm not sure whether it's in Dwomor or Ethshar or somewhere else entirely, but it's not here." She sighed. "So unless Tobas or one of the other wizards has arranged something special, I think we'll have to walk the entire distance to Dwomor Keep."

"Not all the way to Ethshar of the Sands?"

"Oh, no!" Karanissa replied, startled. "Of course not! We have another tapestry down in Dwomor, even if the carpet isn't there. Once we get to Dwomor Keep, we can be back in Ethshar in no more than a day, probably no more than an hour."

"Oh, good," Sarai said, relieved. "And how far is it to Dwomor Keep?"

"Three days," Karanissa said. "Two, if we really hurry."

"Three days," Sarai repeated, thinking of Tabaea roaming freely about the city, of the Seething Death spreading in the throne-room floor. She wondered what the Wizards' Guild would do with those three days. Would anyone tell the exiled nobility that the Black Dagger was gone and Tabaea's power lessened? Would Tabaea cling to her title of empress right up until someone killed her, or would she flee?

What would Ethshar be like when she got back to it?

Well, there was no use in wondering; she would see for herself soon enough.

"Let's get going, then," she said.

CHAPTER 41

*T*obas *watched intently as the dozen volunteer warlocks went* about their work, cutting deep grooves in the marble floor in a circle around the Seething Death. The lamps set on every side did not burn well, but smoked and flared—Teneria thought the fumes from the pool were responsible. Whatever the reason, the magicians worked in a dim and smoky light, surrounded by gigantic shadows, adding to the strangeness of the task at hand.

Telurinon was still trying counterspells; he had brought three cartloads of raw materials from the Guildhouse and set up shop in the meeting room directly below, where a roiling bubble of the Seething Death now hung from the ceiling, hissing and smoking and dripping corrosive slime on the floor beneath—but *not* spilling through. The stuff remained a perfect hemisphere, demonstrating irrefutably that despite appearances, it was not a liquid in any normal sense of the word.

It wasn't a solid or a gas, either; it was magic.

And it was, Tobas thought, damnably powerful and stubborn magic. It had already dissolved a bottomless bag when Mereth had attempted to scoop the goo into it, on the theory that Hallin's Bottomless Bag could hold *anything*. It had been utterly unaffected by Thrindle's Combustion, Javan's Restorative, the Greater Spell of Temporal Stasis, Tranai's Stasis Spell, the Spell of Intolerable Heat, the Spell of Intense Cold, Fendel's Accelerated Corruption, and Javan's Contraction. It had expanded unhindered through Verlian's Spell of Protection, Fendel's Invisible Cage, Cauthen's Protective Cantrip, Fendel's Elementary Protection, and the Rune of Holding. If Tobas had interpreted Telurinon's latest efforts correctly, the Guildmaster was currently attempting the Spell of Reversal, but Tobas did not expect that to work, either—and even if it did, it would only shrink the Seething Death back to where it had been perhaps an hour before. The prospect of wizards endlessly working the Spell of Reversal to keep the Seething Death contained for the rest of time was not appealing.

There were still more spells to be attempted, and Tobas expected Telurinon to attempt them—if his own scheme didn't work.

Marble dust sprayed up as the warlocks used their mysterious powers to slice through the stone of the floor, cutting out the chunk that held the Seething Death. It was perhaps twenty hours since that one fateful drop had been spilled, and the bubbling, boiling, smoking pool was more than a yard across, the outer edge expanding fast enough that if a person watched for a moment he could see the surrounding stone melting away.

Tobas felt he had to work fast if his plan was to have any chance at all. Once the Seething Death was wider than the tapestry, it might not *fit*.

He had hoped that the warlocks would be able to simply scoop the stuff up, out of its hole, but they reported that there wasn't anything there that warlockry could touch. Whatever the stuff was, though, the *floor* could hold it, and the warlocks could touch the floor, so they were cutting a chunk free, intending to lift it up to the Transporting Tapestry. It meant doing serious and permanent damage to the overlord's Great Hall, but the Seething Death would do that anyway—had *already* done that.

The rest of the mess Tabaea had made could be cleaned up fairly easily, Tobas thought, but this might be difficult. He supposed a good stonemason could handle it, somehow.

At the thought of Tabaea he glanced around nervously. The would-be empress had vanished without a trace that morning, after announcing her abdication—which meant she was still around someplace, and could spring out at them at any time, complicating matters.

Once the Seething Death was dealt with, the Guild really would have to track down Tabaea and kill her. Maybe they should go ahead and throw a death-spell after her right now—but Tobas didn't want to take the time and was reluctant to act on his own in any case. The Guild might want to use something especially horrible.

"We almost have it, wizard," one of the warlocks said—a tall, black-clad man whose name Tobas did not know.

"Good," Tobas said. He bent down and picked up the tapestry that lay at his feet.

He hoped that Sarai and Karanissa were well clear; in theory the stuff would be completely harmless the instant it passed into the dead area around the fallen castle, but Tobas had his doubts about just how fast it would lose its virulence. The Seething Death was not just another spell.

Teneria helped him unroll the tapestry, lift it, and smooth it.

"It's free," another warlock announced.

"All right, then," the black-clad man said. "Lift!"

The marble circle, four feet in diameter, shuddered, and then began to rise, up out of the surrounding floor.

Unfortunately, the Seething Death did not rise with it; instead, Tobas stared in horror as the steady hiss of dissolving marble suddenly became a roar, and dust and smoke boiled up from the circular hole in the center of the ascending marble cylinder.

A warlock coughed; then another.

"Stop! Stop!" Telurinon shrieked from below.

The steady ascent slowed; the stone cylinder wobbled, and still more smoke and powder spilled out of the central hole.

"You might as well keep going," Tobas said. "It's too late now."

A warlock doubled over, coughing, as more of the reeking cloud of smoke rolled over the magicians.

The marble cylinder, four feet across and fifteen inches high, was clear of the floor now—and clear of the Seething Death. Still following the original plan, the warlocks started to move it toward the tapestry.

"No!" Tobas shouted, suddenly realizing what they were doing. If they sent the chunk of stone through the tapestry, the tapestry would no longer function—not until somebody hiked out to the fallen castle, in the mountains between Dwomor and Aigoa, and removed the cylinder from that hidden chamber.

The warlocks paid no attention, and in desperation Tobas simply dropped his end of the tapestry's hanging rod; Teneria, not entirely sure why but following the wizard's lead, dropped hers as well. A moment later the marble cylinder hung suspended in the air, touching nothing, above the tapestry.

"Put it down somewhere," Tobas called. "Somewhere out of the way. It didn't work."

The cylinder wobbled, then glided to the side and settled to the floor.

Tobas stared at it for a second, then turned his attention to the Seething Death. It was hard to see clearly through the swirling vapor, but at last Tobas convinced himself that he was not imagining it.

The Death was hanging there, totally unsupported, exactly where it had been before, in the center of a ring of empty air. It was a perfect half sphere, flat side up.

Not that the flat side was truly flat; it bubbled and, just as the name said, seethed.

"It's dripping all *over* now!" Telurinon wailed from below.

"You people aren't holding it, are you?" Tobas asked the nearest warlock.

"No," the woman assured him, smothering a cough. "We couldn't if we wanted to."

"I was afraid of that." Tobas stared at the Death.

This was not a possibility he had considered. This meant that his back-up plan, of having relays of warlocks transport the entire thing to Aigoa, was totally impossible, not just incredibly difficult and impractical. The only way to get it to the dead area would be through the tapestry.

Well, if he couldn't move the Seething Death to the tapestry, he would just have to bring the tapestry to the Seething Death.

"All right," he said, "time to try it another way."

It took another half hour to cut away more of the floor, so that the tapestry could be suspended flat beside the expanding hemisphere; the first faint light of dawn was beginning to show in the dome's skylights, high overhead, as Tobas and Teneria maneuvered the hanging into position. In the interim, Telurinon had established that Kandir's Impregnable Sphere did not live up to its name; the Seething Death had burst it, popping it like a soap bubble.

And afterward, the Seething Death had still touched nothing but air.

The circle had grown at least an inch in diameter, though; Tobas was certain of that. He and Teneria had to approach it much more closely than he liked; he moved with exaggerated caution, dreading the possibility that he might lean out too far and touch that stuff, or worse, lose his balance and fall into it.

Finally, though, the tapestry was in position, hung through the floor, its lower edge dangling into the meeting room below, its supporting bar in Tobas's and Teneria's hands. Several of the warlocks had left to escape the fumes; those who remained, though no longer involved now that they had cleared away the chunks of marble flooring, watched from the sidelines with interest.

"Now what?" the young witch asked.

Tobas had maneuvered the tapestry as close as he dared, without touching the stuff; whatever was to be transported had to come to the tapestry, not the other way around, to be certain the spell would work.

"Now we wait," he said. "When it expands far enough, it'll touch the cloth, and then poof! It's gone!" He smiled; then the smile vanished, and he added, "If we're lucky."

They waited, seated cross-legged on either side of the hole, the tapestry between them.

At last, after a quarter-hour of growing nervousness and worsening sore throats from breathing the foul air, the Death touched the tapestry—and did not vanish. Instead, stinking white smoke billowed up from the point of contact.

Teneria looked up and stared across at Tobas, looking for some sign as to what she should do.

Tobas stared in horror.

"My tapestry," he said weakly. He could see the fabric dissolving, the threads unraveling, where the Seething Death had touched it.

"What should . . ." Teneria began.

"Pull it out!" Tobas shouted, before she could finish her sentence, but he knew it was already too late.

They pulled the tapestry back, away from the Death, then lifted it out and spread it out on the floor; Tobas studied the semicircular hole, six inches across, and the blackened, frayed edges around it.

"It's ruined," he said. "A four-hundred-year-old Transporting Tapestry, ruined."

"You're sure?" Teneria asked. "It won't still work? It can't be repaired?"

"I'm sure," Tobas said. "The tapestry has to be perfect, or the spell is broken, and you can't put it back without reweaving the entire thing." He looked up from the hanging and glared angrily at the Seething Death.

"There must be *some* way to stop that thing!" he growled.

"Maybe the dagger Tabaea had," Teneria said. "It stopped all the *other* wizardry."

"Maybe," Tobas agreed, "but that's in Dwomor with Lady Sarai right now."

"Tobas," Teneria asked, "what *about* Sarai and Karanissa? How will they get back, without the tapestry?"

Startled, Tobas looked at her. "Oh, they couldn't come back through that anyway," he said. "The tapestries are only one-way. They'll have to walk to Dwomor Keep, and then they can come through the other castle and the new tapestry the Guild-masters gave me to replace this one. They should be back here in a couple of days."

"Is it safe?"

Tobas shrugged. "Pretty safe. Karanissa's walked that route a few times before; she knows the way." He glowered at the Seething Death again. "I suppose we might as well keep trying things until they get here, though. And what we're going to do if the Black Dagger *doesn't* work . . ."

He never finished his sentence.

CHAPTER 42

*W*hoever occupied the house on the corner of Grand Street and Wizard Street now was more careful than old Serem had ever been; Tabaea had found every door locked, front, back, or side-alley, with warding spells protecting them. The Black Dagger could have cut through the wards as if they weren't there, but the Black Dagger was gone.

Whoever the wizard was who had placed the wards had been more careful than Serem, but he hadn't been ridiculous about it. He hadn't put wards on the roof. The idea that somebody might climb up on the roof and pry the tiles up with her bare fingers, one by one so they wouldn't clatter, in the middle of the night so she wouldn't be seen—well, no one had worried about anything as unlikely as that.

Even with a cat's eyesight and the strength of a dozen men, the job took hours. The sky was pale pink in the east by the time Tabaea lowered herself, slowly and carefully, through the hole into the attic.

She didn't know who lived here, or what the house had become, but she had seen the magicians going in and out, the messengers hurrying to and from the front door, and she knew that this place was somehow important. She guessed that her enemies had made it their headquarters.

Why they weren't operating out of the palace, now that she was gone, she wasn't quite sure. Maybe they were waiting until the overlord came back—one of the messengers had said his ship was on the way; Tabaea had heard it quite clearly from her place on the rooftop.

The city guard was back, even if the overlord wasn't; from atop the house Tabaea could see the uniforms in Grandgate Market, the formations of men marching back and forth as they resumed their duties and "restored order." Much as she hated to admit it, the sight was somehow comforting.

Less comforting was the knowledge that the guard was clearing out the palace, room by room and corridor by corridor, but oddly, even the processions of the homeless finding their way back to the Wall Street Field were almost reassuring; Tabaea was relieved that her people weren't being sent to the dungeons, or slaughtered. Everything was to be returned to what it had been before, it seemed.

Everything, that is, except herself. There was no way they could turn her back to the harmless little thief she had once been. They would have to kill her—if they could.

And it seemed to her that the best chance of making sure that they couldn't would be to find out just what the wizards had planned. And since the wizards seemed to hold their meetings here, in Serem's house . . .

Well, that was why she was standing on the bare, dusty planks of the attic floor, peering through the dimness, looking for the trapdoor that would let her down into the house itself.

She found it at last, over in a corner, and lifted it with excruciating slowness, in case anyone was in the room below. The trap was larger than she had expected, and when raised it revealed not a ladder, or an empty space where a ladder might be placed, but a steep, narrow staircase with a closed door at the bottom.

She crept down, and slipped through, and she was in the wizards' house, able to spy on all that went on.

Except that nothing was going on; everyone in the place—and there were several people there—was asleep, or nearly so;

from the central hallway of the second floor Tabaea could look down the stairs and see that one woman sat by the front door, presumably standing watch, but even this guard in fact dozed off and on.

None of the people were witches, which was a relief; a witch, or possibly even a warlock, might have been able to detect her presence, no matter how quiet she was. Wizards, though, needed their spells to do anything like that.

Of course, even a witch wouldn't spot her when the witch was asleep, and everybody here was asleep.

This was hardly surprising, with the sun not yet above the horizon; after some thought, Tabaea crept back to the attic, closed the door carefully, then curled up on the plank floor for a catnap.

She awoke suddenly, as cats do, aware that she had slept longer than she had intended to; quickly and quietly, she slipped back downstairs.

A meeting was going on in the front parlor; she crept down the hall and stood by the door, out of sight, listening.

". . . at least sixty feet across now," a man's voice said. "It's taken out a section of the back wall and rear stairway, while mostly maintaining its hemispherical shape. It seems to send appendages up the walls, breaking off chunks and pulling them down into the main mass. On the stairs, the upper edge sags somewhat, rounding itself off, now that it's above the level of the step it's dissolving. It's penetrated the floor of the meeting room below the Great Hall and worked deep into the storeroom below; in a few hours, at most, it should pierce *that* floor, as well, and begin dripping into the dungeons. The Greater Spell of Transmutation, generally considered to be a tenth-order spell, has had no effect, any more than any of the earlier attempts at finding a countercharm. The Spell of Cleansing, third-order but requiring extensive preparation, should be complete soon. Llarimuir's Vaporization is in progress, but requires twenty-four hours of ritual, so we won't know the results until late tonight."

A dismayed silence followed this report; Tabaea tried to figure out what it was all about. A meeting room below a great hall? That sounded like the palace. Something was dissolving things in the palace?

Then she blinked, astonished. They were discussing the Seething Death! ". . . earlier attempts at finding a countercharm . . ." They didn't know how to stop their own spell!

And Lady Sarai had laughed at *her*!

As if prompted by her thought, someone asked, "Is there any word from Lady Sarai?"

"Not yet," a man replied, "but she and Karanissa should reach Dwomor Keep late this evening or early tomorrow, if all goes well, and they can be here within an hour after that. The tapestry we gave Tobas comes out in an unused room in one of the Grandgate towers; we have a guard posted there, ready to escort them here the moment they appear."

"That assumes, of course," someone said, with heavy sarcasm, "that they're coming back at all, that it isn't raining or snowing, that they haven't been waylaid by bandits or eaten by a dragon, that they haven't gotten lost in the mountains, that Lady Sarai didn't panic and kill Karanissa the moment she appeared, that someone at Dwomor Keep hasn't inadvertently ruined the tapestry there . . ." Tabaea recognized the speaker as the one who had reported on the Seething Death.

"Oh, shut up, Heremon," a different voice said, speaking with weary annoyance. "Karanissa is fine; she spun a coin the day we arrived in Ethshar, and it's still spinning, without the slightest slowing or wobbling. I checked less than an hour ago."

"That doesn't prove she isn't holed up somewhere waiting out a blizzard, or warding off wolves," Heremon argued.

"There are no wolves in Dwomor," the tired voice said. "And for that matter, even in the mountains, it doesn't snow in Harvest."

"Still . . ."

"Yes, they might be delayed," the tired voice agreed. "We just have to hope that they aren't." He sighed. "The overlord's ship is due tomorrow afternoon, I understand. It would be nice if we could present him with a palace, even a damaged one, that's safe to enter and not in danger of being reduced to bubbling slime."

Someone answered that, but Tabaea was no longer listening; she was thinking.

Lady Sarai would be returning soon, to one of the towers in Grandgate—and she would have the Black Dagger with her, surely; that was why all these wizards were so eager for her return. Tabaea had figured it out; the Black Dagger was the countercharm for the Seething Death! And when Sarai had carried it off to wherever that magic tapestry went, apparently some place called Dwomor, that had left them unable to stop the Death from spreading.

If Tabaea could get to Sarai before the magicians did, she could take back the Black Dagger. Then she could stop the Seething Death, renounce her abdication, and resume her rule. Old Ederd was coming back, too—she could catch him and kill him and put an end to attempts to restore him to the throne. Stopping the Death would make her a hero; even those who had fought her would see that.

And she would do better this time; she wouldn't make the same mistakes. Letting everyone live in the palace—well, there would have to be rules. And the city guard was useful; if she couldn't make the old one obey her, she would organize her own.

She would do it *right* this time.

First, though, she had to retrieve the Black Dagger, and that meant finding Lady Sarai when she came back, before she was surrounded by guards and wizards.

She would be coming through an unused room in the Grandgate towers, the man had said. There were eight towers in the Grandgate complex: the two gigantic barracks towers, and then the six lesser towers, three on either side of the entry road. Each of them contained dozens of rooms, Tabaea was sure, and many of those were unused; she would have to search them all until she found the right one.

But how would she know which was the right one?

She smiled. The wizards had told her that. When she found someone guarding an empty, unused room, she had found what she was after.

And she had until that evening, at the very least. She scampered for the stairs, her eagerness making her so careless that in the parlor Tobas looked up, thinking he had heard something in the hall.

But of course, that was ridiculous. No one could possibly be in the Guildhouse but the wizards, who were all gathered in the parlor—unless a spriggan had managed to hide somewhere.

That was probably it, he decided; a spriggan must be running about somewhere. That was nothing to worry about, then; annoying as they were, spriggans were relatively harmless.

"Has anyone tried Lirrim's Rectification?" he asked. "I've never used it myself, but it's in the books . . ."

* * *

Dwomor Keep was not a particularly attractive or well-designed structure, but Lady Sarai thought she had never seen anything so beautiful. However ugly and decayed it might be, it was a *building*, and after two days in the wilderness, anything that could possibly be considered urban was an absolute delight. That this ramshackle fortress was also the gateway back to her beloved Ethshar of the Sands only added to its appeal.

The walk down through the mountains had not been enjoyable at all. Karanissa had taken it all in stride, but Sarai, accustomed to city streets and flat terrain, had been constantly tripping over stones and stumbling on the steep slopes. She had kept hoping, also, that her enhanced senses would return once they were free of the dead area, but that had never happened. With Karanissa's witchcraft to help she had managed to catch and kill a rabbit with the Black Dagger, which provided both dinner and proof that the Black Dagger's spell still worked, but the better hearing, tiny added strength, and slightly improved vision and sense of smell didn't amount to much.

The little animal had been good eating, though, she had to admit.

Half a rabbit, however, and a few apples stolen from a farmer's orchard were not much food for an entire two days, which made Dwomor Keep, where Karanissa assured her they could expect to be fed, very attractive.

The guard at the gate greeted Karanissa familiarly in a language Lady Sarai had never heard before; the two women were then escorted inside, where Sarai got to stand idly by, studying the architecture and interior design, while Karanissa carried on several conversations with assorted people dressed in varying degrees of barbaric splendor. Some of the people she spoke to seemed concerned, others inquisitive, still others casually friendly; most of them, judging by gestures, inquired about Lady Sarai at one point or another, and each time Karanissa answered without bothering to explain to Sarai what was being said. In fact, throughout her stay in Dwomor Keep, including a bath, a change into fresh clothing, and a generous supper, Sarai had no idea at all what was going on around her. As far as she could tell, nobody present spoke a word of Ethsharitic.

At last, however, Karanissa waved a farewell to three people and led Sarai down a passageway into a lush bedchamber, where she drew aside a drapery to reveal a truly bizarre tapestry.

The image was absolutely perfect and incredibly detailed; it showed a path leading from a stone mound across a narrow rope bridge to a castle out of someone's nightmares, a fortress of gray and black stone encrusted with turrets and gargoyles, much of it covered with carven faces—most of them leering monstrosities, while the few that appeared human were screaming in terror. Even the front wall of the nearest section was a face, the entryway a yawning, fanged mouth, two windows above serving as eyes.

This structure stood against a blank background of red and purple shading into one another in vague, cloudlike patterns, and the reddish highlights on the castle made it plain that these colors were part of the picture, intended to represent a sky unlike anything in the World.

"You better hold my hand," Karanissa said.

"Oh, you don't . . . We aren't *going* there . . ." Sarai said, trying to back away.

The witch grabbed her by the hand and yanked, pulling them both forward into the tapestry. Lady Sarai screamed and fell to her knees.

She landed on the rough stone of that pathway; on either side was empty, bottomless void, purple shot through with crimson.

"Welcome to my home," Karanissa said, smiling. Then she led the way across the little bit of bare stone, over the rope bridge, through the fanged entryway and the open door within, into the castle.

Lady Sarai followed wordlessly, staring at her strange surroundings, as Karanissa explained, "Derry—that's Derithon the Mage—made this place, hundreds of years ago, and brought me here. Then he got himself killed when his other castle, out in the World, crashed, and I was stranded until Tobas found the tapestry and came in here and found the way out, through the tapestry that took us to the fallen castle. Except Telurinon traded with him, to get the tapestry to the dead area—he wanted to send Tabaea there, or else the Seething Death after it killed her. So now we've got another tapestry, one that will bring us out in one of the towers in Grandgate." She paused for breath.

Sarai didn't say anything; she was too busy looking around at the forbidding, torch-lit corridor, with its gargoyles peering down from the ceiling corners.

Karanissa led the way up a broad spiral staircase, saying, "I suppose we'll have to move now, take the other tapestry out of Dwomor to Ethshar—it's just not practical, having our front door and our back door so far apart. The walk down the mountains was bad enough, even with the flying carpet; having to cross a hundred leagues of ocean is just impossible.''

They emerged in an arched passageway; Karanissa lifted a torch from a nearby bracket and led the way down a side passage.

"I don't know if Alorria is going to like that much," Karanissa said, as they turned a corner. "And I'm pretty such that her father, King Derneth, isn't going to like it at all. He likes having Tobas as his court wizard, and he likes having his daughter nearby. Alorria's never lived anywhere but Dwomor Keep—well, and here, of course." She waved at the castle walls.

Sarai shivered slightly; this place made her very nervous. There was something utterly unnatural about it. They had entered from bright sunlight, but most of the castle was dark except for Karanissa's torch, and where light *did* get in through windows, the light was an eerie reddish purple.

It didn't seem to bother the witch at all; she prattled on cheerfully as she led the way through a maze of chambers and passages until at last they arrived at a door, several stories up from the entrance. "We need to go through together," she warned Sarai, as she opened the door.

Cautiously, Sarai stepped into the room beyond, and looked around. Karanissa stepped in behind her and reached up to set her torch in an empty bracket.

The room was small and simple—no gargoyles or black iron here, just plain gray walls, on one of which hung a tapestry. There were no other furnishings.

"Maybe we should move this downstairs, nearer the entrance," Karanissa said, considering the tapestry carefully. "That would save time when we're just passing through like this."

Sarai gazed at the hanging, too, but with relief, rather than consideration. The room it depicted was so utterly normal and ordinary! A simple room, with off-white walls, an iron-bound wooden door, and one of the standard-issue wooden tables the Ethsharitic city guard used. "Come on," she said. This time, *she* was the one who grabbed and pulled, and an instant later she and Karanissa stepped out in Ethshar.

The light was brighter here and the color of normal daylight, rather than the orange of a torch or that weird reddish purple; Lady Sarai blinked and looked around.

The tapestry was gone; from this side it simply wasn't there. Instead she saw the other half of a nondescript and unused little room, with a single narrow window providing illumination.

"North light," Karanissa remarked. "It's steadier, doesn't change much over time, so it doesn't matter where the sun is, or whether it's cloudy." She frowned. "I'll wager the tapestry doesn't work at night, though; I hadn't thought of that before, and that could be inconvenient." She stared for a moment, then turned back to the door. "Oh, well," she said, "there isn't much we can do about it now." She lifted the latch and opened the door.

Before she could get a glimpse of what lay beyond, Lady Sarai heard the thump of a chair's front legs hitting the stone floor and a soldier getting hurriedly to his feet, kilt rustling and sword belt rattling. She followed Karanissa through the door into a wide hall, where various military equipment was strewn about or leaning against walls and pillars. Hazy sunlight poured in through skylights; voices and footsteps were audible in the distance. Close at hand stood a soldier and a chair; the soldier saluted, hand on his chest, and announced, "I'm Deran Wuller's son, ladies; if you'd come with me, please, Captain Tikri wishes to see you."

"Tikri?" Sarai was astonished and delighted; she hadn't seen Tikri since the day Tabaea first marched on the palace, when he had gone off to defend the overlord. She had feared he was dead, or at best driven into exile, yet here he was, apparently back at work.

"Yes, my lady," Deran answered. "This way."

Sarai and Karanissa followed him across the room, toward a stairway leading down. "Where are we?" Sarai asked.

"Officers' training area, my lady," Deran answered. "Top floor of the North Barracks, in Grandgate."

"So the city guard is back here? Everything's back to normal?"

Deran kept walking, but hesitated before answering, "Not *everything*, my lady. The guard's back, all right—Lord Torrut saw to that as soon as he heard that Tabaea had given up her claim to be empress—but I wouldn't say everything's back to normal. The overlord is still aboard his ship down in Seagate—there's something wrong with the palace, something to do with the Wizards' Guild. Nobody goes in there without the Guild's permission. And Lord Kalthon . . ." He broke off.

"What *about* my father?" Sarai demanded.

"They say he's dying, my lady," Deran reluctantly admitted. "The sea journey was bad for him; they say he has a sixnight at most, even with that witch Theas tending him. But the overlord won't appoint a replacement, and we *need* a Minister of Justice right now, to sort out the mess. Lord Torrut's doing what he can, but . . . well, I wouldn't say everything's normal." He stopped in front of a door and knocked.

The door opened, and Captain Tikri glared out angrily. When he saw Sarai, though, the anger evaporated; he smiled.

"Lady Sarai!" he said. "You're back!" Belatedly, he added, "and you, Karanissa!"

The two women smiled and made polite noises, but then Tikri held up a hand. "We don't have any time to waste," he said. "We need to get you to the palace immediately; the wizards have been very emphatic about that. We can talk on the way; just let me get my sword."

A few minutes later, a party of four—Deran, Tikri, Sarai, and Karanissa—emerged from the barracks into the inner bailey of Grandgate, walking briskly; they passed through the immense inner gate into Grandgate Market, headed for the palace.

And atop the south inner tower Tabaea leaned over the battlement, glaring furiously. She could not see faces clearly from that distance, could not be sure of the scents, but two women in aristocratic garb, accompanied by two soldiers—that had to be Sarai! She had missed them! After all this time spent searching through the absurd complexities of Grandgate's many towers, she had missed them!

She ran for the stairs, berating herself for being overcautious. She had searched all six of the gate towers, and most of the South Barracks, but had left the North Barracks, with its hundreds of soldiers, for last.

But of *course* it would be the North Barracks—that was where everything important was. She should have checked there *first*, despite the soldiers.

Furious, she plunged down the stairs, in hot pursuit of the Black Dagger.

CHAPTER 43

Lady Sarai stared in shock and dismay through the stinking, unnatural white mist at the bubbling, steaming, swirling mass of greenish slime before her. It blocked the entire corridor, wall to wall and floor to ceiling, at an oblique angle.

"It's slightly over a hundred feet in diameter now," Tobas told her. "It's down into the lower dungeons, and as you can see, it's consumed the rear half of the throne room, including the entire rear staircase and the corridor below. It's also eaten its way through into the passageway above, there, but hasn't reached the overlord's apartments yet."

"And you expect the Black Dagger to stop *that*?" Sarai demanded, turning to face the party of magicians and soldiers jamming the corridor behind her, and holding up the knife so that everyone could see just how small and harmless the enchanted weapon looked when compared with that gigantic mass of corrosive, all-consuming wizardry.

For a moment, no one answered; Sarai could see them judging, comparing, contrasting, considering.

Then one of the warlocks giggled nervously.

The giggle caught and spread, and in seconds several magicians—witches, warlocks, and even a wizard or two—were laughing hysterically. The soldiers were grinning, but not openly laughing.

Angrily, Telurinon shushed them all; after a few moments, with the soldiers' assistance, order was restored. Then the Guildmaster turned angrily on Lady Sarai.

"What do *you* know about wizardry?" he shouted. "Size is irrelevant! What matters is the strength and nature of the enchantment, nothing else!"

"And you think a dagger enchanted *by accident*, by a girl who knew almost nothing of wizardry, is going to stop a spell you say can destroy the *entire World*, Guildmaster?'' Sarai shouted back.

''It might!'' Telurinon answered, not as certainly as he would have liked.

''*I* don't think so,'' Sarai replied. ''I think that stuff will dissolve the dagger, just as it dissolved Tobas's tapestry and everything else, magical or mundane, that it's touched.''

''And what would *you* suggest, then?'' Telurinon sarcastically demanded. ''Do you have some clever little counterspell that's somehow eluded the attention of the Wizards' Guild? We've tried everything we know; the warlocks, the witches, the sorcerers, they've all tried. The theurgists couldn't even find anything to try; the demonologists marched a score of demons and monsters in there, and it consumed them all. Nothing stops it.''

''And the Black Dagger won't, either,'' Sarai retorted. ''*Look* at it!''

''The dagger cuts all *other* wizardry,'' Telurinon insisted. ''We've never found anything else that stops wizardry so completely.''

Startled, Sarai glanced at Tobas and Karanissa, then announced, ''That's not true, Guildmaster, and you know it.''

Telurinon gaped. The rest of the party, soldiers and magicians alike, was suddenly absolutely silent, and Sarai could feel them all staring at her, giving her their full attention. Accusing a Guildmaster of lying, before such an audience as this . . .

''I saw it myself,'' Sarai insisted. ''There's a place in the Small Kingdoms somewhere where wizardry doesn't work; it brought down a *flying castle*, by the gods! *That* could stop the Seething Death!''

Telurinon recovered quickly. ''Oh, *that*,'' he said. ''Well, yes, there is such a place. We had hoped to transport the Seething Death there, in fact, but it turned out to be impossible.''

''It dissolved the Transporting Tapestry,'' Tobas confirmed.

''It ate away the chunk of floor we tried to move,'' a warlock added.

''It can't be moved,'' Vengar agreed.

Sarai looked from face to face, trying to think. ''You can't move the Seething Death,'' she said.

Several voices muttered affirmation.

''Can you move the dead area?'' she asked. ''As the saying has it, if the dragon won't come to the hunter, then the hunter must go to the dragon.''

For a moment, silence descended, broken only by the hissing of the Death, as everyone considered this.

"I don't see how," Tobas said at last. "It's not a thing, it's a *place*. Certainly wizardry couldn't move it, since wizardry doesn't work there."

"Witchcraft does," Sarai pointed out. Karanissa had demonstrated as much.

"Yes, but Lady Sarai, it's a *place*," Tobas insisted. "Even if, say, moving that entire mountain would be enough to move it, how could you bring it eighty leagues to Ethshar? Witches couldn't do it, not unless you had thousands upon thousands of them, probably more witches than there are in the World. Warlocks could, perhaps—if they were all willing to accept the Calling. Sorcery, demons—I don't think so."

"Not sorcery," Kelder of Tazmor agreed.

"Nor demonology," Kallia confirmed.

"Then can you create a *new* one?" Sarai demanded. "A new dead area, here in the palace?"

Tobas hesitated and looked at Telurinon.

"No," the Guildmaster said, quite emphatically.

"The spell is lost," Tobas agreed.

Intending to make a point, Sarai turned to look at the Seething Death and involuntarily found herself backing away—the wall of seething ooze had drawn visibly nearer while she argued. Shaken, and after having moved several feet farther down the corridor, she turned back to Tobas and demanded, "You're sure of that?"

He nodded. "The only Book of Spells that ever held it was burned, over four hundred years ago—in 4763, I think it was." He added helpfully, "They hanged the wizard who used it."

"But it was done by wizardry in the first place?" Sarai asked.

Telurinon glared at Tobas.

"Yes," Tobas said.

"And the spell was written down?" Sarai asked.

"By Ellran the Unfortunate, in 4680," Tobas said. "That was when he discovered it." He smiled wryly. "By accident. Just the way Tabaea made the Black Dagger by accident. Ellran never used the spell again, but his apprentice did, and got hanged for it. And the book was burned."

"You seem to know a lot about it," Sarai remarked.

"It's a sort of specialty of mine, if you'll recall—I told you that," Tobas said. "It's why I was brought here in the first place. As you know, I have a personal interest—or at least, I used to."

"If you know that much about this spell," Vengar asked, "can't you recover it somehow?"

"If you know the true name of the apprentice, and when the spell was used," Mereth volunteered, "the Spell of Omniscient Vision ought to let me see the page it was written on. We never knew enough about the countercharm for the Seething Death, but this one . . ."

"No!" shouted Telurinon. "Mereth, I forbid it! Stop and think what you're proposing! The *overlord's palace*, dead to wizardry? The Guild could no longer . . ."

He stopped, abruptly, looking about wildly, as if realizing that he was about to say far too much in front of far too many people. Then he shouted, "No! We'll try the Black Dagger, and if that doesn't work we can evacuate the city . . ."

Lady Sarai, moving as quickly as she could without her cat abilities—rabbits were quick, but not as fast in their reactions as cats—stepped up and, with her left hand, grabbed the front of Telurinon's robe. The Black Dagger, in her right hand, pressed against his chest.

"Listen to me, Guildmaster," she said. "You and your stupid spells are *destroying* the overlord's palace—and maybe the rest of the city, maybe the rest of the *World*—and you're worrying about saving your Guild's secrets, your Guild's power? You're worried that maybe you won't be able to eavesdrop any more, won't be able to threaten the overlord with your spells and curses? That you might have to *really* give up meddling in politics? Well, I've got a *real* worry for you, Telurinon—this dagger. I don't intend to try it on the Seething Death, Telurinon—I intend to use it on *you*. It'll eat your soul, you know—it sucks the essence right out of you, doesn't even leave a ghost."

She didn't know whether this was truth or lie—but right now, she didn't care. She pressed the point harder against the old wizard's chest, piercing the fabric of his robe.

Telurinon gaped at her. "You can't do this!" he said. "The Guild . . ."

"The Seething Death is going to kill us all anyway if we stay here," Sarai told him. "And besides, I don't think your Guild is on your side in this one. Has anyone tried to stop me?"

Telurinon turned and looked.

Tobas and Mereth and Heremon were standing there, unmoving; Heremon at least had the grace to look somewhat abashed, and Algarin had turned away rather than watch. Further back, the other magicians were watching, but showed no signs of helping the Guildmaster. The soldiers were obviously ready to cheer Lady Sarai on.

"I don't know what spells you people are talking about," a soldier called, "but I've about had my fill of the Wizards' Guild here. If anyone harms Lady Sarai, he'll answer to me!"

Several growls of agreement, not all from soldiers, were enough to convince Telurinon.

"Very well," he said, "very well. We'll try the Spell of Omniscient Vision, as Mereth said, and if we can find Ellran's forbidden spell we'll try *that*. But if it doesn't work, Lady Sarai, *then* we'll try the Black Dagger!"

"Agreed," Sarai said, stepping back and releasing the Guildmaster's robe.

"I need my scrying stone for the Spell of Omniscient Vision," Mereth said, "and I left the stone at home. Besides, I need a totally dark room, and I don't know of any in the palace."

"Then go home and do it there," Sarai said.

"I'll come with you," Tobas offered, "to write down Ellran's spell. Besides, I want to see this."

Telurinon started to say something, but before he could speak, Sarai said, "And I think it would be best if Guildmaster Telurinon returned to the Guildhouse, wouldn't it, to see how things stand there?"

He glared at her, then looked over the crowd of magicians and decided not to argue.

Sarai knew she had made an enemy for life of Telurinon, but just now she really didn't care. As Mereth and Tobas headed down one corridor, circling around toward the northwest gate, while Telurinon and Heremon headed out toward the northeast and the others scattered in various directions, she just wanted to find somewhere to rest. She wondered whether her old room was safe; the Seething Death was nowhere near the southeast wing yet, where her family's apartments were, but it seemed to be spreading quickly.

Someplace nearer a door would be better. She stopped into one of the little waiting rooms along the northeast corridor, where petitioners could prepare for their audience before the overlord.

The place was a mess; she stared around in dismay, unable to decide whether someone had lived here during Tabaea's brief reign, or whether it had been used as a garbage dump.

Karanissa appeared behind her. "What are you doing, Lady Sarai?" she asked.

"I wanted to . . . oh, just *look* at this place, Karanissa!" She waved a hand at the disaster. The two little silk-upholstered benches had lost their legs and become crude beds; the pink silk itself was slashed and stained several places. The gilded tea table was on its side. Three rotting blankets were heaped on the floor, amid orange peels, eggshells, chicken bones, and other detritus.

Karanissa looked and found nothing to say.

Sarai picked up one of the blankets, holding it between two fingers, then used it to sweep a pile of trash out into the corridor.

"You shouldn't bother with that, Sarai," Karanissa said. "For one thing, the Seething Death may eat this room before we stop it."

"Before the *wizards* stop it," Sarai snapped, flinging the blanket aside. "Those idiots who *started* it in the *first* place! Wizards who showed Tabaea how to make the Black Dagger, wizards who started the Seething Death, wizards who *wouldn't* help my father . . ."

"Wizards like my husband," Karanissa replied gently. "And your friend Mereth."

"Oh, I know," Sarai said, peevishly. "Most of the wizards I've known have been good people, really. But sometimes they don't know what they're *doing*, and it can be so dangerous! And they talk about these stupid rules about not meddling in politics, and then that old fool Telurinon practically admitted they spy on the overlord . . ." She sat down abruptly, on the floor of the passage.

Karanissa settled down beside her, and for a time the two women simply sat, side by side. In the distance Sarai could hear footsteps and voices—and the hissing of the Seething Death. She looked down at the Black Dagger, which was still in her hand, and noticed a tiny drop of Telurinon's blood on the point. She shuddered.

"I think I really would have killed him," she said.

"Probably," Karanissa said. "Something we all knew during the Great War was that *anybody* can kill, under the right circumstances. *Anybody* can be dangerous."

"Even a harmless little nobody like Tabaea the Thief," Sarai said. "With this knife in her hand, she was empress of Eth-shar." She shuddered. "Maybe I *should* have tried it on the Seething Death—at least then we'd be rid of it."

"Why didn't you?" Karanissa asked.

"Oh, I don't know," Sarai replied. "It just seemed like such a waste. You have no idea what it's like, Karanissa—being able to smell *everything*, to practically *see* with your nose. And seeing in the dark, like a cat, or hearing all those sounds we can't hear; being strong and fast . . ."

"Are you going to do it again, then? Kill more animals?"

Sarai hesitated.

"No," she said at last. "I don't *need* to, with Tabaea gone, and I don't like killing anything. I don't *want* to like killing."

"Then what will you do with it?"

"I don't know," Sarai replied slowly. "I'll have to think about it." She stared at the dagger for a moment longer, then looked up at Karanissa and asked, "What's it like, being a witch?"

Karanissa tried to explain, without much success; from there, the conversation turned to what it was like to be married to a wizard, then what it was like to share a husband, and how she had come to marry Tobas, and how Alorria had come to marry him, as well. Some of this Sarai already knew, of course; the two women had talked during the long walk down the mountains, but only now did Sarai feel able to ask the questions that *really* interested her.

At last, though, the conversation ran down. The daylight was starting to fade, and the hissing of the Seething Death seemed significantly closer.

"I'm hungry, and you look tired," Karanissa said. "Would you like to come back to the inn with me for dinner and then borrow a bed?"

"That would be wonderful," Sarai admitted gratefully. She got to her feet; the Black Dagger tumbled from her lap to the floor, and she picked it up.

She did not sheathe it immediately, but carried it loose—not for any particular reason, but on a whim. The hilt felt curiously reassuring in her hand.

Together, the two women strolled down the northeast corridor and out onto the plaza.

CHAPTER 44

Tabaea had been waiting. She had not caught up to Lady Sarai and her escort on Gate Street, Harbor Street had been crowded, and Quarter Street had soldiers patrolling it; Tabaea had not dared to jump Lady Sarai anywhere on the way. She had not dared to enter the palace, either, with all those guards and magicians about, not without the Black Dagger in her hand. Sooner or later, though, Lady Sarai would come out again; surely she wouldn't sleep in the palace with the Seething Death still there. She would go out to Serem's house, or to the barracks in Grandgate, or somewhere. Sooner or later she would be careless, would travel with a small enough escort that Tabaea would have her chance.

There was an abandoned wagon on the plaza, and Tabaea had seized her opportunity; she had lain down in the wagon, out of sight, and watched the door through a crack in the side.

Soon, soldiers and magicians came pouring out the door and marched or ambled away without seeing her; Lady Sarai was not among them, however.

At last, though, as evening approached, Tabaea's patience was rewarded—out the door, all by themselves, came Lady Sarai and that tall black-haired witch.

And Lady Sarai was holding the Black Dagger in her hand.

Using all her speed, all her agility, Tabaea leaped from the wagon and threw herself at Lady Sarai's arm.

Sarai didn't even see her coming; she was still blinking, letting her eyes adjust to the fading sunlight, when something smashed into her arm, spinning her around, knocking the Black Dagger from her hand. She staggered and fell as pain shot through her hand.

"Tabaea!" Karanissa shouted.

The self-proclaimed empress was already past them, and in-

303

side the palace, running down the corridor with the Black Dagger in her hand.

"I think I sprained my wrist," Sarai said, sitting dazed on the pavement. "What happened?"

"It's Tabaea!" Karanissa told her, reaching down to help her up. "She took the dagger!"

Sarai blinked, then got to her feet as quickly as she could. "I thought you said she was gone," she said.

"She's back," Karanissa answered.

"Why haven't the wizards killed her?" Sarai asked, still slightly dazed. "They were so hot for vengeance . . ."

"They hadn't got around to it yet," Karanissa answered. "They were too busy worrying about the Seething Death. And what difference does it make why? They *didn't* kill her, and she's back. Come on!" As Sarai moved uncertainly toward the palace door, Karanissa cupped her hands around her mouth and called to a pair of guards nearby, "Tabaea! Tabaea's back! Get help! Bring torches!"

Then she and Sarai stepped cautiously into the palace.

Tabaea ran into the dark corridors, dagger held out before her, hurrying toward the throne room. Had Sarai already stopped the Seething Death? That would ruin her plan to become the city's savior—but on the other hand, she could still resume her role as empress, now that she had the dagger back.

She wondered how big the Seething Death was now—had it kept spreading? Was it still sixty feet across, as Heremon had reported, or had it grown even larger?

Then she heard the hissing and came skidding to a stop.

Full night had fallen outside; the passageway ahead was utterly dark, even to Tabaea's enhanced vision, but she could hear the Death hissing and bubbling, and she could smell its foul reek.

She needed light; guided by smell, she groped on the floor and found a fragment of greasy cotton rag. She wrapped it around a broken table leg and knotted it; then she held this makeshift torch up over her head and felt for the whisper that gave a warlock power.

She knew how to use warlockry to light fires, but she was too nervous to concentrate properly; she had no more than warmed her makeshift torch when a golden light sprang up behind her. She whirled and saw the tall witch holding up a glowing hand— witch-light, Tabaea realized. Lady Sarai was at the witch's side.

"Stay back!" Tabaea shrieked, brandishing the dagger and backing a few steps down a side-passage.

The other two followed her. "What are you doing in here?" Sarai called. "I thought you had abdicated!"

"That was conditional!" Tabaea shouted back. "That was if you people stopped the Seething Death, but you didn't! *I* will, and then I'll resume my rightful throne!"

Sarai and Karanissa looked at each other.

"You can't," Sarai said.

"*Yes I can!*" Tabaea screamed. "I have the Black Dagger back, and it can cut *any* wizardry!"

"Not *that* it can't," Sarai said. "Just *look* at it, Your Majesty!"

Karanissa added, "If you just wait, we have a way to stop it—my husband should be here soon, with the spell."

"*No!*" Tabaea shouted. "*I'll* stop it! Not you! *I* will!" She looked past the two women at the sound of approaching steps, heavy boots on marble—soldiers, not magicians.

That was all right; she wanted witnesses, wanted all the soldiers to side with *her* this time. Torchlight gleamed from stone walls. She waited.

A moment later, a band of torch-bearing guards trotted around the corner and stopped, startled, at the sight of their former empress, clad in black rags, holding off Lady Sarai with a knife.

"Don't get too close," Karanissa warned, as she extinguished her witch-light. "She's got her magic dagger back."

"That's right," Tabaea said, "I have my dagger back, the one I made with a piece of my own soul, and I'm going to use it to save the city from the evil magic *these* two, and their magician helpers, loosed on us."

"All right, then," Sarai said, "if you're going to do it, do it."

"I will," Tabaea retorted. She turned and marched toward the center of the palace, toward the Great Hall, toward the Seething Death. Behind her came Lady Sarai, Karanissa, and half a dozen soldiers, Captain Tikri commanding, Deran Wuller's son among them.

Then Sarai stumbled and tugged at Deran's sleeve; he stepped aside to steady her, while the others moved on past. Quickly, she stood on her toes and whispered in his ear, "Go find Tobas of Telven, the wizard; if he can work his spell while Tabaea's still in the palace, she'll lose all her magic, just be an ordinary girl with an ordinary dagger. Tell Tobas to *hurry*." She spoke in as low a tone as she could manage; she well remembered, from her own experience, that dogs and cats would hear best in the higher registers. She would have preferred to have sent Captain Tikri, whom she knew better, but his absence would have been too noticeable; she at least knew Deran as a familiar face, and hoped he was up to the task.

Tabaea whirled at the sound of whispering, but over the growling and hissing ahead she couldn't make out the words. She saw Lady Sarai hanging back, though, and called, "Come on, Pharea, or Sarai, whichever it really is—come on and see why I deserve to rule Ethshar!"

Sarai came, trotting to catch up—and Deran, moving as silently and quickly as he could, trotted in the other direction, to start a search for Tobas.

A moment later the party reached the point where the Seething Death blocked the way, a wall of greenish boiling ooze across the corridor. At the sight of it Tabaea hesitated, but then she stepped resolutely closer.

"Watch!" she called. She stepped up and slashed at the stuff with the Black Dagger.

The Seething Death erupted in a gout of white steam and a roaring, boiling hiss, and for a moment the watchers were deafened, the vapor blocking their view.

When they could see again, they saw the Seething Death still blocking the passage, unmarked by the dagger's cut. Tabaea stood before it, holding up the Black Dagger's hilt.

The blade was gone, dissolved away down to an inch or so from the crossguard.

Tabaea screamed, and Sarai remembered what she had said about putting a part of her soul into the knife. Sarai started forward to help, Karanissa beside her.

"*No!*" Tabaea shrieked. "Stay back!" She whirled and waved the ruined stump of the Black Dagger at them, and Sarai and Karanissa stopped short. Then the empress of Ethshar turned back to the Seething Death and cried, "It *must* work," and thrust her hand at it, stabbing into the ooze.

Her hand went in clear to the wrist.

She screamed again and drew back the stump of her arm, blood spraying. Clutching at it with her left hand, she staggered and toppled . . .

Into the Seething Death.

Her scream was abruptly cut short, but again, a roar of magical dissolution and a gout of stinking vapor erupted; the two women and the five soldiers backed away.

When the scene quieted, all that remained of Tabaea the Thief was one bloody, severed bare foot, lying on the marble floor of the corridor, inches from the Seething Death.

"Gods," Captain Tikri muttered under his breath. For a long moment, they all simply stared.

And then, abruptly, the hissing of the Death faded away, and the wall of magical chaos puffed outward and vanished like mist that blows in a doorway. The close confines of the corridor were suddenly at the edge of a great open space, a vast bowl-shaped hole in the palace, beneath the soaring central dome.

The Seething Death was gone. Not so much as a single drop of corrosive slime remained; the cut edges of walls and floors shone clean and sharp. Sarai and her companions could see the fragment of wall that had once been one end of the throne room, could see into rooms and passageways on six levels, from the lower dungeons to the overlord's private apartments. Sarai imagined that the Arena might look like that, if all the seats and floors were removed.

And standing in the open end of the corridor directly opposite their own was Tobas, holding a knife and a handful of brass shards. He waved.

For several minutes no one did much of anything; they were all shocked into inactivity by the suddenness of it all.

Then Deran came trotting up from behind. "I didn't find him, but I saw that the Seething Death was gone," he called. "Was it in time? Where's Tabaea? Where's the dagger?"

Sarai looked down at the hideous fragment that was all that remained of Tabaea the First, Empress of Ethshar.

"Nowhere," she said. "Nowhere at all."

CHAPTER 45

"*What did you say the spell was called?*" the overlord asked, leaning heavily on Lord Torrut and staring at the hollowed-out ruin of his home. "The one that stopped it?"

"Ellran's Dissipation," Tobas answered. "The Wizards' Guild outlawed it over four hundred years ago, but this was a special case."

"Telurinon didn't like it," Lady Sarai remarked.

"I suspect the higher-ups in the Guild aren't very happy about it, either," Tobas said. "In fact, they'll probably be very annoyed with Telurinon for making it necessary by using the Seething Death."

"*Are* there higher-ups in the Wizards' Guild?" Lord Torrut asked, startled.

"Oh, yes," Tobas said. "But I don't know much about them—and I shouldn't even say as much as I have." He smiled crookedly. "Fortunately, they can't see or hear me here."

The overlord nodded thoughtfully. "That's going to make rebuilding difficult," he said. "This place was all built by magic originally, you know—my ancestor Anaran managed to get the largest share of the wizards when the war ended and the army disbanded, and the Guild was a good bit less troublesome about these things back then." He sighed. "Of course, Azrad lured most of them away later."

"I'm sure that there are good stonemasons around," Lord Torrut said.

"Besides," Tobas pointed out, "it's only wizardry that won't work here; you could have warlocks, or witches, or even demonologists do the repair work, if you wanted to."

"I might just leave most of it open," the overlord said, looking up into the dome. "As a sort of memorial." Then he turned to Lady Sarai and said, "It's going to make your job as Minister of Justice more difficult, too."

"My father usually relied on theurgy, my lord," Sarai replied. "That won't have changed." She thought, but did not mention, that just now she wasn't particularly inclined to *trust* wizards—or any other magicians, really.

Ederd nodded. "I suppose," he said. "And if I haven't said so before, let me say now that I share your loss; your father was a good man and a faithful servant. I truly regret that my own health would not permit me to attend the funeral." He coughed, as if to demonstrate that he was not yet fully recovered from the indisposition that had kept him in seclusion for a sixnight after Tabaea's death. Then he turned to Tobas. "You know, I used to have protective spells around this place," he said. "Wards and alarms and so forth. Not that they did much good against that poor girl and her magic dagger. Do you think you could put them back? They were on the outside of the building, I believe."

"No, my lord," Tobas said. "While I kept it as confined as I could, even to the point of risking failure, the dead area extends over the entire palace and the surrounding plaza and out onto Circle Street to the northwest—I wasn't at the center of the building when I performed the spell, of course, since the Seething Death was in the way. I'm afraid that the wards can never be restored."

"All the way to Circle Street? That will make the parades at Festival a bit difficult."

"It might be, my lord," Lord Torrut ventured, not looking at Ederd, "that we have, perhaps, used more wizardry around here than is entirely good for us."

Ederd snorted. "We often haven't used as much as I would *like*," he said. "The Wizards' Guild hasn't always been very cooperative. And they always seem to know what's going on—when I want something done, they'll insist I yield on some other point."

"That should change," Lady Sarai pointed out. "They can't see what happens in the palace anymore."

"Which might mean that they'll assume the worst," Ederd said. Then he shrugged. "Well, there's nothing to be done about it now." He turned away, forcing Lord Torrut to turn, as well.

"At least they can maintain their reputation for implacable vengeance," Lady Sarai pointed out. "It was Telurinon's spell that killed Tabaea."

"And don't doubt for a minute that they'll take every advantage of that," Lord Torrut said. "They'll boast of having saved Ethshar."

"But on the other hand," Tobas replied, addressing himself to Ederd, "it's going to be hard to hide the fact that we made some very bad mistakes, especially if your lordship *does* leave the interior of the palace open, as you suggested. I doubt that even the Guild will be able to stop the rumors of how Tabaea came by her abilities, or to hide how badly we bungled the use of the Seething Death."

"And that will probably turn most of them foul-tempered and reluctant to serve me," Ederd pointed out. "It's been my experience that most wizards are not so reasonable as yourself, Tobas."

Tobas acknowledged this praise with a nod of his head.

"It may be, my lord," Lady Sarai said, "that there will be gains elsewhere, to offset any loss of cooperation from the Wizards' Guild."

The overlord glanced at her as he started down the corridor. "Oh?" he said.

Sarai nodded. She looked quickly at Tobas, the only magician present, and decided that he could be trusted. Besides, it could hardly stay secret for long. "It would seem," she said, "that the Council of Warlocks is interested in leasing space here in the palace that would be used for their meetings and, perhaps, other activities. I was approached on the matter this morning."

Ederd looked at her thoughtfully. "Go on," he said.

"Well, naturally, I said that I would need to consult with you about it, but that I thought it might be done—and that perhaps arrangements could be made to pay part of the rent in services, rather than gold." She smiled. "Of course, we all know that they want to be sure their meetings can't be observed by wizards; despite their cooperation against Tabaea, they do see the Wizards' Guild as a rival."

"You think allowing these warlocks in the palace would be wise?"

"I think that if they meet here, wizards won't be able to observe them, but *we* will. And I think that having the Council of Warlocks in your debt can't hurt."

Ederd nodded.

Sarai cleared her throat, and added, "If you wish, my lord, I could send messages to the two witches' organizations, the Sisterhood and the Brotherhood . . ."

"It bears thinking about," the overlord agreed. He glanced at Sarai again. "It interests me, Lady Sarai, that the warlocks came to *you*."

"Well, my lord," Sarai said, "I've dealt with them before, in my duties as your investigator."

"My investigator," Ederd echoed. "And my Minister of Justice, at least until your brother is old enough, and well enough, for the job—if he ever is. And it seems that your recent actions have made you my liaison to every magician in Ethshar, as well. You'll be a very busy young woman."

"In your service, my lord." She bowed.

"While we were in port, the rumors among the sailors aboard my ship mentioned you, you know," the overlord said.

"Really, my lord?"

He nodded. "They scarcely mentioned the Wizards' Guild. It seems they credit *you*, Lady Sarai, with forcing Tabaea back into the palace and trapping her with the Seething Death while this counterspell of young Tobas's was performed. That you offered Tabaea her life, but without magic, and that she chose to perish instead. The tone of the accounts was frankly admiring." He smiled. "It's a good beginning for a Minister of Justice to have such a reputation."

"It isn't . . ."

The overlord held up a hand, silencing her. "The truth of the matter really isn't as important, you know, as what people believe."

"But . . ."

"There are also stories," Ederd continued, "about the meetings you held before Tabaea's identity was known. They say you have sorcerers who would do anything to please you, that a cult of assassins fears you. And it's said you can vanish and reappear at will, that you're a master of disguise."

Sarai was too astonished to protest further.

"You will understand, I am sure," the overlord said, "that at my age, I am no longer looked upon with awe or fear; that my son, while a good man, has utterly failed to distinguish himself in a lifetime of being my heir and nothing else, and furthermore managed to do nothing but flee when Tabaea threatened his inheritance; and that it's therefore very useful for me to have someone in my service who *is* looked upon as a hero, who is believed to have performed superhuman deeds in the interest of keeping me on my throne, or restoring me to it—and who had a chance to take that throne herself, as you are presumed to have had when Tabaea was dead and I not returned, yet who turned that chance down. The existence of such a hero will, I am sure, discourage attempts to emulate poor little Tabaea. I therefore *order* you, Lady Sarai, as your overlord, not to deny any rumors about your abilities, or about secret knowledge you may possess, no matter how absurd.''

Sarai's mouth opened, then closed. She stared at Ederd, then finally managed, ''Yes, my lord.''

''Good. Then I believe we part here; I'm using Lord Torrut's quarters until my own apartments are repaired.'' He turned, supported by the guard commander, and hobbled down a side corridor.

For a moment, Lady Sarai watched him go. Then she walked on, not toward her own apartments, but toward an exit from the palace. She wanted to walk in sunlight and fresh air, to think. She did not feel ready to talk to her brother and his nurse.

Besides, she had not yet decided which quarters were hers; should she return to her own old room, or take her father's?

It was a trivial matter, really, but right now, after sixnights of worrying about usurpers and murderers, World-shaking magic and matters of life and death, she preferred to think about trivia.

She emerged onto the plaza and looked out at the city of Ethshar of the Sands, the streets and houses stretching away in all directions. Directly ahead of her a wisp of smoke from a kitchen fire was spiraling slowly upward.

It reminded her of the smoke from her father's pyre. He was really gone, now—his soul was free, risen to the gods on that smoke.

She wondered whether Tabaea's soul had been freed when her body was destroyed, or whether the Seething Death had consumed that, as well. And what of the various people killed by the Black Dagger? No necromancer, of any school, had ever been able to find any trace of their ghosts, either in the World or elsewhere.

She supposed she would never know. There were a great many things she supposed she would never know.

But that would never stop her from learning what she could.

GODS
BOTH KNOWN
AND UNKNOWN,
SEEN AND UNSEEN...

...THE
LORDS OF DÛS

by Lawrence Watt-Evans

Come experience magic, wizardry, and the supernatural
mixed with strong adventure in the exploits of Garth
the overman—an unusually determined hero.